Bet

(Little Basement) Garden

TVJPWWKPZD

Betty's

(LIttle Basement) Garden

By Laurel Dewey

THE
STORY PLANT

The Story Plant
The Aronica-Miller Publishing Project, LLC
P.O. Box 4331
Stamford, CT 06907

Print ISBN-13: 978-1-61188-038-0
E-book ISBN-13: 978-1-61188-039-7

Visit our website at www.thestoryplant.com
Like Laurel Dewey on Facebook at https://www.facebook.
com/pages/Laurel-Dewey-Author/200115782067

For information, address The Story Plant.

First Story Plant Printing: June 2012

Printed in The United States of America

"When all your desires are distilled you will cast just two votes — to love more and to be happy."
— Hafiz (Sufi Mystic)

"The fact that an opinion has been widely held is no evidence whatsoever that it is not utterly absurd; indeed in view of the silliness of the majority of mankind, a widespread belief is more likely to be foolish than sensible."
— Bertrand Russell

After great pain, a formal feeling comes –
The Nerves sit ceremonious, like Tombs –
The stiff Heart questions was it He, that bore,
And Yesterday, or Centuries before?

The Feet, mechanical, go round –
Of Ground, or Air, or Ought –
A Wooden way
Regardless grown,
A Quartz contentment, like a stone

This is the Hour of Lead –
Remembered, if outlived,
As Freezing persons, recollect the Snow –
First – Chill – then Stupor – then the letting go
– Emily Dickinson

Acknowledgements

This book would never have been possible without the dedicated support and assistance of numerous medical cannabis growers, caregivers, patients, dispensary workers and owners I met during the research process. Their openness and willingness to give me access to their grow operations, as well as the numerous kitchen table discussions, were invaluable in the writing of this novel.

I also want to acknowledge the many authors, bloggers, medical cannabis breeders and activists whose work was instrumental in gaining a greater understanding of this "budding" industry. These include Rick Simpson, Dr. Mark Sircus, Jorge Cervantes, Michael Pollan, Steve DeAngelo, Ed Rosenthal, Old Hippie, Trish Regan, author Joan Bello, the generous members of the greenpassion.org forum, Jaime from Resin Seeds and Farfel Couscous.

Finally, thanks to Peter Miller and a huge thank you to Lou Aronica for his patience and steadfast support.

Dedication

I dedicate this book to my husband, David, who tirelessly went above and beyond in his support of this book. I could not have done it without you, babe.
I love you with all my heart.

And to my late father, George Marshall Dewey, whose conservative suit belied his more open-minded beliefs.

It was Saturday, May 1st, 2010 and everything was exactly the way it had always been...

Chapter 1

People only see what they are shown
and believe the tale they are sold.

Everything was perfect.

Well, okay, as close to perfect as Betty Craven could conceive. And *that* was always above and beyond what the average person ever achieved. But as Betty so often lectured herself, perfection was an elusive bitch; just when she thought she'd manipulated all the pieces into place, some goddamned force of nature with a chaotic agenda took control, vanquishing her precise plans. Perfection wasn't easy, but it was what kept Betty motivated. Sure, it also kept her jaw unusually tight and even popping at times from the extreme tension. And that neck pain that often paralyzed her range of motion? Yes, that was also a health casualty in her quest for excellence. Oh, and the syncopated flutter that occasionally rose up in her right inner ear that not a single doctor could diagnose, except for citing "stress" as a factor? Yes, that too was just another consequence of what it took to *be* Betty Craven.

But no one saw the struggle under the polished veneer. People only see what they are shown and believe the tale they are sold. Her dearest, closest friends admired her strength and willpower. She was solid and dependable, but she was also beautiful. A former beauty queen with classic features, Betty's curvaceous, five-foot-ten-inch frame was envied by other women, who suffered silently as they stood within her stunning orbit. Her hips, sculpted by gourmet cuisine and decadent desserts, were in suitable proportion to her voluptuous breasts that she reined in with custom brassieres. To Betty, exercise was not about cavorting on gym equipment;

rather, exercise was a rousing few hours of weeding and digging in her prize-winning garden.

At the age of fifty-eight, she carried herself well. Her
blond hair – touched up every twenty-eight days like clock-
work – was the same shade as on the day she stood on the
stage in the middle of the football field and was crowned
Homecoming Queen of Spring Woods High School in
Houston, Texas. The same, suitable coif adorned her smiling face on that perfect June day in 1974 when she married
Frank Craven, her military beau, at the age of twenty-three
in Colorado Springs, Colorado. And nary a hair was out of
place in the photos six years later, as she held Frank Jr. in
her arms and gazed at the camera in an appropriate manner.

And now, at this moment, her wavy, blond locks were
still flawless as they skimmed just below her porcelain ears
with their pearl stud earrings. Except for the infuriating fifteen pounds she couldn't lose around her waist and stomach,
Betty Craven still had that indefinable "it" factor. To anyone
who knew her longer than five minutes, Betty was the personification of perfection. She was the woman every other
woman wanted to be.

And if she could just hold it together for three more
hours – *just three more goddamn hours* – another day would finally expire and she could retreat into the claws of regret
and her beleaguered memories. *Simmering discontent* best described Betty Craven lately. The undercurrent of grief had
never abated since the day he died. After a few strong drinks
at night, she'd often see him in her dreams. But then she
wondered if they were really dreams, or if he was stuck between the worlds and destined to spend eternity navigating
the tortuous maze of purgatory. From the moment he passed
from this world, her body felt weighted by lead. Betty could
keep up a good front, because she'd done it for so damn long.
She'd trained her body to move and react with such precision that nobody would ever know the acute disconnect beneath the facade. "*The Feet, mechanical, go round,*" wrote Emily
Dickinson, a favorite of Betty's. "*Of Ground, or Air, or Ought,
a wooden way, regardless grown, a quartz contentment, like a stone.*

This is the Hour of Lead." Yes, that was an ode to Betty Craven. She closed her eyes and took another anxious breath.

The doorbell rang. Smoothing her freshly ironed, creamy yellow dress across her hips, she re-adjusted the elbow-length sleeves. If Betty ran the world, no one over the age of forty would be caught dead in a sleeveless dress or shirt. There are things you do and there are things you *never* do, and dammit, sleeveless numbers are *verboten*. Betty quickly swept the living room with her steely blue eyes, programmed to root out any un-fluffed pillow, a chocolate candy or delicate cucumber sandwich askew on the hand painted platters, or an errant carpet fiber that had resisted the domination of the vacuum. She adjusted one of the large featured flowers in the vase she'd grown from heirloom seeds in her immaculate garden. It was a magnificent bloom with bold orange and crimson striations. But was it *too* bold? Betty's jaw clenched. Did it overpower the presentation?

The doorbell rang again, this time with more urgency. They'd all arrived nearly simultaneously, parking their cars in her circular driveway and issuing a penetrating, humming natter outside her spotless cherry-red front door with the spring wreath on it. A wave of apprehension overwhelmed her. Would their expectations be met? Would the food be as impressive as the last get-together she hosted? But far worse, would she fail? Failure wasn't an unknown visitor in Betty Craven's house. In fact, failure was sitting thirty-five feet outside the kitchen door, down a short, brick path and slowly decaying in the empty, 600-square-foot, sunny space above her garage.

And there was always Frankie, her greatest failure.

Enough! She shook off the chatter in her head, let out a deep, authoritative breath and cheerfully opened the door.

Chapter 2

"Everything's fine. No worries at all.
Have you tried the chocolates?"

"Welcome!" Betty exclaimed, beaming that trademark pageant smile she still knew how to skillfully manufacture on cue.

A stream of well-dressed women entered, loudly talking amongst themselves and greeting Betty with effervescence and accolades.

"Your house looks *beautiful!*"

"Oh, *look* at the table!"

"What smells so *divine?!*"

Betty counted heads, instantly vexed that she hadn't made enough food. There were twenty-five women, three more than expected. Her gut compressed. *Quick. Think.* She still had a large pineapple in the refrigerator. Yes, she could cut that up if necessary. *Goddamnit,* she fumed, *why do people show up uninvited and not have the decency to give her advance warning?* Spontaneity was fine, as long as it was well-planned in advance.

But Betty kept smiling like a pro. Judi Hancock, a wiry, fifty-two-year-old high school art teacher, and one of Betty's three closest friends, strode closer, air-kissing Betty's cheek. As always, her red, polka-dot-rimmed eyeglasses, strung with a decorative necklace, hung around her neck. "Oh, Betty! You didn't have to go all out for us. *What a spread!*"

"It's nothing," Betty assured.

"Nothing to *you,* maybe. You always make everything look so easy!" Judi exclaimed.

Renée Holder brushed against Betty's back. "A few extra gals asked to come to the meeting," Renée stated, her tanned, fifty-five-year-old face still rosy from a game of tennis on that May Day afternoon. "It's such an important issue, and we need to get more people involved, so I *knew* you'd be on board."

"Of course!" Betty replied with an agreeable tilt of her head. "We've got to get the word out, don't we?" *Guacamole.* That was always filling. She could whip up a bowl of guacamole during the break and serve it with the bag of corn chips she'd stuffed in the back of the pantry. *Wait, what was the expiration date on those damn chips?* Betty suddenly looked around the room. "Where's Helen?"

"Bringing up the rear!" Judi said, pointing to the last few women entering the front door.

Helen Wheeler steadily made her way into the living room, carefully closing the door behind her. At sixty-nine and widowed for fifteen years, she was the oldest member of Betty's tribe and the one she could always count on to be the most pessimistic. She moved slowly and ate slowly and listened more than she spoke, but Helen was like an old couch in Betty's eyes – usually comfortable to be around but always with the possibility of a rusty spring erupting suddenly and catching her off guard. If that rusty spring did poke through Helen's demeanor though, any rancor was usually subdued. Anger took energy away from Helen's preoccupation with everything that can, and does, go wrong. Helen didn't the see the glass half empty. No, it was full all right; full to overflowing with whatever poison could kill you.

Helen, Judi and Renée may have occasionally gotten on Betty's nerves, but they were there for her when Frank learned he needed a liver transplant four years ago. They were still there while Betty and Frank waited for the call that never came. And finally, they were an impenetrable force field that stood by her when Frank died thirteen agonizing months after his first diagnosis. Helen, Judi and Renée were three rocks in Betty's life and cornerstones of her faith in the power of unwavering friendship.

"Where's Ronald?" Judi enquired as she secured a seat on the exquisite, rose-colored love seat with the fleur-de-lis pattern.

"Upstairs on the master bed watching television," Betty replied, directing a quartet of chattering women to the seats.

"*Animal Planet*, no doubt!" Judi exclaimed.

Betty smiled. She would never force her fourteen-year-old, black and white cat to watch *Animal Planet*. It was too predictable. Ronald was upstairs at that moment enjoying *The Discovery Channel*, while classical sonatas played softly in the background.

Renée nervously waved to Betty from across the room and motioned her to corral the women.

"Everyone! Please take your seat," Betty announced in her trained hostess tenor. "I promise you, there will be plenty of time for conversation and food at the break!" She adjusted the sleeves on her yellow dress once again and patted the back of her blond locks as she moved in front of the crowd. "Before I begin, I want to apologize for the mess at the corner of the house. I've got a gentleman working piecemeal on roof repair, and I know it's unsightly." The group regarded Betty with uncertainty.

Judi piped up, "I didn't see a thing, but I'll make a point to look later."

Betty was flummoxed. It was an eyesore. At least it was to her, putting another damper on her bid for perfection. "Well," she continued, "moving along. I want to thank you all for giving up a few hours on this beautiful, early-spring Saturday to listen to this timely presentation. I'm cheered to see so many people who care about our community." She took a deep breath, hoping to tamp down any hint of her Texas lilt that tended to surface whenever she spoke in a front of a crowd. "I know as members of the *Paradox Republican Women's Group*, we all share a growing concern – no pun intended, of course – regarding the upsurge of medical marijuana dispensaries and grow operations in our tightly knit neighborhood. Like you, I am..." she searched for the proper word, "disheartened whenever I see another one of these *medical*," Betty rolled her eyes, "establishments taking over an empty storefront that used to house a favorite gift shop or coffee house. We are all concerned as to where this undeterred expansion of drug dens, albeit *legal* according to our liberal state constitution, could lead –"

"Legal *schmegal*!" Renée interrupted from her perch near the front of the attentive group. "None of *us* voted for this insanity!"

The group softly chuckled.

"And with that deft interjection," Betty continued, "I would like to introduce Renée Holder, who will help us navigate through these uncharted waters, and hopefully propose a few gems of action we can use to regain our comfortable foothold in this conventional, but oh-so-charming, enclave we call home." With that, Betty motioned for Renée to take the helm.

Like an impatient tigress, Renée leapt forward, and arranging her stack of notes with a nervous edge, she spoke. "Well, as always, Betty, you are blessed with a poetic command of the English language. While I might lean toward the prosaic, I more than make up for it with the real life, 'been there and done that' reality."

Betty quietly took a seat on the last available chair, a French provincial with a stunning, polished-pecan frame. Renée was right, when she admitted to not being poetic. While they were coming up with names for their Republican women's group, Renée seriously wanted to call the group the *Colorado Republican Association Political Society*. Not only was the name long-winded and difficult to fit on the stationary, but Betty noted that the acronym spelled CRAPS. It was tough enough to hold your head high as a dyed-in-the-wool Republican in their modest but upscale city just thirty-five minutes south of Denver. If they were known as CRAPS, Betty knew the liberals would have a field day. Thus, Betty's simple but effective proposal of the *Paradox Republican Women's Group* moniker was chosen. As hard as the liberals tried, they couldn't make any word out of PRWG, except possibly the word *prig*. But since Webster's defined a *prig* as someone who took pride in behaving in a correct and proper way, and who felt morally superior to people with more relaxed standards, the aberration of their group's name by some liberal malcontent didn't concern Betty. Even three years after their inception, she still wasn't sure if Renée held the name change against her.

"For all the newcomers here today," Renée continued, "I think it's important to mention a little bit about my personal background and what I bring to this discussion."

Betty's tight jaw clamped down. *Good God*, she thought, Renée was about to voluntarily dig up her personal dirt once again. How many times would she have to hear about the Twelve-Step Program? It was becoming tedious.

"As a recovering alcoholic and drug addict," Renée zealously announced, "I *know* the lifestyle better than most of you. I started down *my* rocky road of addiction *with marijuana* and I can tell you, as I approach my thirty second year of sobriety, that pot...marijuana...dope...grass...weed...doobie...ganja...a big fat blunt...whatever you want to call it, *is* a gateway drug."

Betty felt herself disconnecting. That familiar sensation always happened when the emotional pain started churning in her gut. She pressed her hand against the dip in the arm of her chair, finding momentary solace in the tactile connection.

"*That* is the opening of my letter to the editor of the *Paradox Press*. It's a letter I'm reading to all of you in the hopes you will sign your name to it, so we can create a lot of attention and buzz in our community."

Judi chuckled. "Buzz? Isn't the point to *stop* the buzz?"

"You know what I mean!" Renée replied, looking down at her notes and getting back on message. "The Democrats choose to ignore it, the Libertarians opt to dismiss it and even some in our own Grand Old Party choose to believe marijuana is not harmful. Some of them even refer to this green menace as '*medicine*.' Really? *Medicine*. I find that word insulting when it's connected to a Federally confirmed Schedule I drug that has torn apart and destroyed so many families in our nation. Penicillin, morphine, cortisone, insulin, digitalis – *those* are medicines and serve a purpose in society. *Those drugs* save lives and aid in relieving discomfort, whereas marijuana does not. Marijuana, as I can sadly attest, creates a lack of initiative in people. A sense of *what's the use?* And when that occurs, motivation ceases to exist. The need for a stronger, more potent high is sought out, and with that, the increased need for hardcore drugs begins." Renée hesitated before continuing. "And as some of us have personally experienced," she cleared her throat, "the graduation to cocaine and heroin often ends in death, and those left behind are consumed with grief."

Judi glanced toward Betty but quickly turned away. Betty swallowed hard. She wasn't prepared for the reaction, especially not in front of strangers. Remaining stoic was a gift and a necessity. One didn't allow others to chafe that well-honed surface. Betty took a shallow breath. Her right inner ear began that damn syncopated flutter that came from nowhere and ended when it felt like it.

"Have you seen the fine citizens who run and operate these medical marijuana dispensaries?" Renée continued with derision. "Sources tell me that a criminal element – i.e., former street drug dealers – might own and operate many of these dens of iniquity. And possibly over seventy percent of the people working in these drug establishments are more than familiar with the long arm of the law. Are they not laughing at us right now? Have the liberal laws of our venerable state finally gone too far? *Yes!* A resounding YES!" Renée looked at the audience. "I put that in caps for effect." She resumed reading her letter. "With this information, ask yourself: Are these the types of people you want in *your* neighborhood? And don't get us started on the whole caregiver and patient fiasco! Since when is an unemployed twenty-year-old high school drop-out with a green thumb and an empty basement considered worthy of being given the moniker of a healthcare professional *with patients under his care?!* Don't insult our intelligence! These stoners are not 'caregivers,' because the plant they are pushing is *not medicine!*" She let out a meaningful breath. "Marijuana equals death. Death to our communities. Death to our collective integrity. Death to our way of life. Death to the family. Death to the children." She paused for dramatic effect. "Death to the country." Renée waited. "That's it. That's the end of the letter."

"Well done," Helen said. "I'll be happy to add my name to your letter."

Considering that she rationed her words so carefully, this was high praise coming from Helen.

"Well, thank you, Helen," Renée replied. "That means a lot to me. I bet you could give us insight into what your generation would tell these young people and others who use, grow or dispense this drug."

Helen pursed her lips. "That's simple. First we'd tell them to 'smarten up.' Then we'd tell them to toughen up, if they don't want to end up being a leech on society. Weakness. That's what it is. Plain and simple."

Good Lord, Betty mused, Helen was on a roll. *Weakness*, she stated. Where had she heard that gem before?

"Would anyone else like to share their thoughts?" Renée asked the group.

Judi raised her hand and leaned her lithe body forward. "Hi, everyone. I'm an art teacher over at Paradox High School. This one student of mine is nineteen. He had to make up a grade, so he's the 'wise sage' who puts the *fun* in our dysfunctional motley crew. He's really popular because he got his dope card..." she feigned embarrassment, "uh, excuse me...*medical marijuana card*, because of a bad back. Seriously, I never knew until recently there were so many nineteen-year-old kids with bad backs." Judi used air quotes with her fingers to stress *bad backs*. The women chuckled softly. "So, numb nuts has his pot card, and he brazenly goes to the marijuana dispensary, located exactly one thousand and one feet away from the school – so it's, you know, in *legal* state limits – to get his 'medicine.' *Then* he meets his buddies, all around sixteen years old, and doles out the treats to them in his beater car. I saw it with my own eyes! Oh, and they don't call it 'getting high' anymore. They call it *medicating*. I mean, *please*. This whole *medical* classification is, excuse my language ladies, *pure bullshit*! I am married to a doctor. I *know* what real medicine is. Medicine is for people who need to manage their physical problems. Marijuana is for brain-dead losers who move their lips when they read or watch television."

The conversation continued for another hour. Betty excused herself before the break and slipped quietly down the hallway to the bathroom. Closing the door behind her, she stood motionless at the sink, relieved to be away from the zealous exchanges continuing in the living room. The thump-thump in her right ear had thankfully ceased, only to be replaced by an intruding stiffness in her neck. For a moment, Betty let her guard down, allowing a long, tired breath to escape her lips. It shouldn't be like this. After all, it was spring, when life is renewed and possibilities are endless. Already a cascade of eye-candy color and sweet scents swept across her front yard, as the oversized tulips, narcissus and daffodils displayed their vibrant faces. Even during the worst times, that sight alone ordinarily buoyed Betty's spirits.

However, it wasn't working anymore. Betty could spend hours digging and transplanting in the garden – it was still a meditative draw, that allowed her mind to temporarily quiet. But it was getting harder to get up in the morning and easier to feel discouragement settling in like an unwelcome houseguest. She heard the gaggle of women stir, a sign that the much anticipated food break beckoned. *Two hours tops.* That's what she told herself. Two more hours and they'd be gone, and she could sink into the silence with a stiff bourbon to escape. With every bit of reserve she had left, Betty stood straight and faced the mirror. Dabbing on a quick touch-up of lipstick, she smoothed her dress, chided herself silently about her minor paunch, sucked in her gut and flashed her pageant smile. She adjusted the unused guest towels with the large embroidered "C" so that they lay identically. As she turned to leave, she realized the missing ornate mirror on the rear wall had left an obvious outline on the wallpaper, where it had hung for so long.

What if someone noticed it? How would she explain it? Her mind ran laps of anxiety until the cackle outside the door grew louder. She had to reappear and reclaim her host-ess mantle. Hunting in the vanity drawer, she found a lonely nail. Removing her shoe, she pounded the nail twice into the wall and cleverly hung a spray of dried lavender she'd deco-ratively placed on the side of the vanity. Slipping her shoe back on, she centered herself, opened the door and walked into the hallway.

Rows of framed photographs lined the wall. Each photo was a close-up of another triumphant entry from Betty's garden. She stopped momentarily at one that meant more than all the others. It wasn't a photo, but rather an antique watercolor of stunning white violets amidst a spring garden, framed in faux gold. Betty felt her heart sink as she stared at the picture, losing herself in the moment. She touched the edge of the frame, a wave of sadness unexpectedly over-whelming her.

"Compassionate Care Centers!" Renée derisively de-clared. "That's what they like to call some of these marijuana dispensaries. How disingenuous can you be? That's like try-ing to make prostitution a noble venture, by just throwing the word *compassion* in there. 'Come visit our *compassionate* call girls.' Can't you just see the ad? As if the guy is going there to discuss his issues. No. He's paying her to screw him. Just like people are paying for marijuana, not because they need compassion, but because they need to get loaded."

"Betty?" Judi called down the hallway.

Betty turned, still faraway. "Coming!" She shook off the memory, and by the time she joined Renée and Judi, the "hostess with the mostest" was back on track.

"Everything all right?" Judi asked.

Oh, God. What did she see? "Everything's fine. No worries at all. Have you tried the chocolates?"

"Not yet!" Judi said. "Gotta start with the delectable sandwiches first and then move up the food chain to the *pièce de résistance*."

Helen joined the women. "I signed your letter," she stat-ed to Renée. "Now let's hope it makes an impact. So many times these things fall flat."

Yes, there was the inimitable Helen in action, Betty thought. Always seeing a silver lining of plutonium around those clouds.

"I better get in the kitchen and whip up a little guacamole, just in case we need it," Betty stated, starting to make an exit.

"We'll help you," Judi insisted, pointing to Renée. "But I wanted to ask you, where's that divine antique chair with the needlepoint seat that always sits by the front door?"

Betty's stomach lurched. "Out for repair. Ronald had an impetuous moment and clawed it underneath."

"Ech, cats," Helen moaned. "Did you know a form of AIDS exists in cats?"

Betty gently patted Helen on the shoulder, smiled and headed quickly to the kitchen. Like little superfluous lemmings, Renée and Judi followed. Betty reached into the vegetable compartment of the refrigerator and brought out several avocados, an heirloom tomato from the local farmers' market, a few stems of cilantro and a lime. As she stood up, she felt a twinge in her neck and slightly winced.

"You okay, Betty?" Renée asked, leaning against the kitchen sink.

"Of course," Betty said, waving it off. "Just been battling a bit of muscle tension lately."

"That ear thing going on still?" Judi stressed.

"Now and then." Betty wanted to concentrate on the avocados and this damn chatter wasn't helping.

"Would you go see Roger already?" Judi stressed.

Roger was Judi's husband, a General Practitioner who never met a pharmaceutical drug he didn't love to prescribe to his patients. Doctor Hancock was the personification of "Dr. Feel Good." Thanks to his devotion to Big Pharma and the perks that go along with it, Judi and Roger enjoyed outstanding vacations in Mexico and Hawaii, all paid for by the drug companies, in exchange for good ol' Doc Hancock's support. Betty knew it was only a matter of time before she'd end up in his office. The almost incestuous, entangled connections with her friends made it difficult to guard her privacy.

"Yes," Betty said. "I'll do it." She needed to change the subject. "Love your pants. Are they new?"

Judi seemed a bit taken back. "Yeah. Linen. I love them. I bought several pairs."

"Well, you'll have to tell me where you got them," Betty smiled, mashing the avocados with purpose.

"Oh, I think they're all sold out," she replied. "They were on sale." Judi cut the lime and squeezed the juice into a bowl. "Hey, not to be maudlin, but have you stopped by lately to see Peggy?"

Betty's jaw tightened. She could lie and say she'd visited regularly, but the deception would be revealed eventually. "No...I just...I really *should* –"

"She's not doing well, Betty," Renée interjected, chopping up the tomato in her typical manic manner. "I dropped by her house last week, on the way home from one of my meetings." Even after thirty-two years of sobriety, Renée still felt a need to attend both AA and Narcotics Anonymous meetings. "God, it was awful. The pain from the cancer is off the charts. Moaning, screaming, vomiting," she shook her head. "Peggy stopped the chemo, did you know?"

"No," Betty replied, trying desperately to focus on the avocado and tune out the discourse. "Why?"

"Her doctor told her there was no point," Judi declared. "She was told she has fewer than two months. So they've got hospice at her house, and her family takes shifts."

Betty stopped mashing the avocado and looked at the women. "Jesus, I had no idea. I...keep meaning to go see her...I just..."

Judi put a comforting hand on Betty's shoulder. "I get it. You've had your fill of sterile hospitals. But she's home now, so it's not like what you experienced with Frank."

But Judi didn't really "get it." It wasn't the hospital. Betty had no problem showing up at a hospital, with flowers in one hand and candy in the other, and sitting by someone's bedside, if the person she visited was expected to leave the hospital *alive*. It wasn't the damn hospital she feared; it was death. Between 2005 and 2007, she'd held the cremated remains of her husband and her only child. One urn was buried in a military cemetery and the other ashes, secured in a plain brown box, were sheltered on a shelf in her closet. Given the choice, she'd run from any tint of death. Asking her to voluntarily show up at Peggy's bedside while she "moaned, screamed and vomited," was asking too much.

Renée piped up. "Why don't you bring her a big box of your chocolates? You *know* how much Peggy is addicted to your chocolates."

It was a classic comment for Renée to make, Betty thought. She stepped foot in Betty's former chocolate shop only once, and that was for the grand opening celebration. Instead of enjoying the event and indulging in a cornucopia of decadent cacao confections, she spent the evening frantically zipping from one guest to another, droning on about the perils of addiction. It was like inviting an Amish elder to a keg party.

"It's the high altitude honey," Judi exclaimed, carefully mincing the cilantro. "I *swear* that's your secret ingredient! Given the choice, my Roger would grind up all his pills and melt them into one of your incredible chocolates. I tell you, Betty, the day you closed *The White Violet*, Roger nearly wept. I kid you not! You were the like the local crack house, where he'd always stop on Fridays to get his weekly cacao fix."

Betty managed a weak smile. Talking about her failed entrepreneurial gourmet chocolate shop, that lasted fewer than eighteen months and chewed through every cent of Frank's life insurance policy, was not fodder for friendly banter across a kitchen counter. "I just wish there'd been a few hundred more die-hard people like Roger out there. I'd still have the shop if that were the case."

"You haven't been able to sell any of the commercial equipment you bought?" Renée asked.

"No," Betty quickly replied, adding the lime juice, cilantro and diced tomatoes to the avocado. "I really should do that soon. So much to do!" She tried to sound cheerful as she sprinkled a pinch of salt and spices into the guacamole.

Judi leaned forward in a faux clandestine manner. "Hey, Betty, I know we've mentioned this before, but it's been three years since Frank Sr. died. It's time for you to get out there and...you know...mingle."

Betty regarded Judi and then Renée with suspicious eyes. "Mingle?"

Judi hesitated before launching into her animated spiel. "We have found the *perfect* man for you!"

"*What?*" Betty's anxiety level shot up. "I don't want a man!"

Renée raised an eyebrow. "Don't tell me you want a woman."

Betty's ire rose. "Good God *no!* I'm saying I don't need a man in my life, *thank you very much!*"

"I told you, Judi," Renée stressed. "The wound of grief with Frank Sr. is still too fresh. She still hasn't processed the experience."

Betty stood there, towering over both of these women and wondered why in the hell she felt cowed by them. *Process the experience*, she thought to herself. *Jesus*, Renée was talking more and more like an overly *therapatized* veteran. There was nothing to process. She was married to Colonel Craven, the only man she'd ever known in the biblical sense, for nearly thirty-two years. Thirty-two long, painful, suffocatingly tense years, where she'd perfected the art of walking on eggshells, quickly assessing the level of stress in others so she'd know what emotion *she* should feel, feigning interest in matters that bored her, parroting others' words and observations, and doing it all with a plastic smile on her face. Between the day Frank got the diagnosis that he needed a liver transplant and the death knell that followed a little over one year later, Betty continued to play the loyal, supportive wife. But thick fibers of contempt wove through each marathon bedside vigil and depressing update from the doctors. And yet, no one ever knew. By the time the great Colonel Craven was laid to rest in a "balls to the wall" military send off, Betty had to force herself to focus on the event and not on the fifteen-pound roast she had slow-cooking in the oven back at the house.

"His name is Tom Reed," Judi slyly offered. "And he's your type."

Betty turned to Judi with an incredulous eye. "Type? I have a type?"

"Well, yeah," Judi gently said. "He's six years older than you, quite comfortable, President of Rotary, divorced for five years. Um, let's see. He's stable, owned his own insurance company, obviously a Republican, well admired in the community...Oh Betty, come on, just meet him for drinks and see what you think."

Betty was of the opinion that men were way over marketed to single women over fifty. The last offering foisted on her was an arrogant specimen by the name of Harold. Betty was forced to sit next to him at Judi's yearly summer soirée last August. His silly comb-over was the least offensive part of his social strategy. In anticipation of meeting Betty, he prepared a bright-yellow postcard onto which he wrote everything he felt she might want to know about him. Betty realized she was in trouble when she noted his favorite leisure activity was "power napping." Somehow, Harold failed to include his other leisure activity – compiling inane statistics about himself and writing them on yellow postcards.

The phone rang. She checked the Caller ID and quickly lowered the volume on the voicemail. "Damned salespeople!" Her head spun as she spooned the guacamole into a green dish, shaped like an avocado. "I can't make any promises regarding Mr. Reed."

"Would you at least promise us you'll think about it?" Judi asked.

Betty felt cornered, a feeling she'd grown accustomed to over the last thirty plus years. She'd learned that placating was the best approach. "Yes. Fine. I'll think about it." She headed toward the kitchen door, ready to present the guacamole to her guests. "Now, if you don't mind, girls, the gazpacho is getting warm."

The spare but elegantly appointed luncheon went over well with all the women. But the elicitations of delight were broadcast the loudest when the group indulged in Betty's sensuous chocolate medallions. Simple yet divine, the darkest cacao embraced the finest cocoa butter from Bali, sweetened with the smoothest ambrosia honey. With subtle yet defining undertones of cinnamon, fresh ginger and superior Madagascar vanilla beans the chocolates melted on the tongue. Looking at the group while they indulged in one chocolate after another, Betty felt as if she were witnessing an orgy of edible delights. She had single-handedly made a roomful of women forget their individual dramas, if only for a few minutes. Something about that always warmed her heart. It was difficult to fall back into the "battleground" mentality after that kind of gourmet indulgence, so the rest of the meeting was brief. Renée's letter was passed around the room and signed by everyone. Betty, always one to be formal, signed the letter "Elizabeth Craven" in her finest penmanship.

As the women left, Betty made a point to thank each of them personally. Manners were such a thing of the past, but in Betty's world, they still reigned supreme. She heard Renée's strident voice ring out across the driveway. "Fight the good fight, ladies! Never fear! We can and *will* win on this issue!"

Judi was the last to leave. She hugged Betty tightly and held her hand. "You *are* making an appointment with Roger, right?"

Betty smiled but the weariness was setting in quickly. "Yes. I will."

"In the meantime," Judi stated, jotting down some words on a piece of scrap paper she pulled from her purse, "there's this incredible salve that was recommended to me by one of the other teachers. It's called 'Mama's Muscle Mojo.'" She rolled her eyes. "I know it sounds sketchy but it really works. It will help until you can get in to see Roger, and he can give you something to really relax the muscles. It's only available at one health food store." She jotted down the info and handed the note to Betty.

Betty read the name of the store. "The Hippie Dippie Health Food Store?"

"Hey, I didn't name the place. But it's a very cool store. They have this awesome juice bar and make the most outrageous organic soups."

Betty folded the scrap of paper and placed it on the entry table. She wasn't interested in drinking juices from juice bars, and if she wanted "outrageous" soups, she'd make one. But she thanked Judi nonetheless and wished her a happy weekend, before closing the door and falling into the silence.

~~~

It took Betty another hour to clean up and put away the few plates of leftover food. She collected two-dozen of the chocolate medallions she'd set aside in the kitchen, wrapped them in diaphanous gold tissue paper and placed them into one of her trademark crimson and gold boxes, left over from her shop. Circling the box with a matching elegant crimson bow, she placed the box to the side. The blinking light on the voicemail caught her attention. She turned up the volume and played the message.

"Hello, Mrs. Craven. It's Lily from Classical Consignments. I wanted you to know your antique chair with the needlepoint seat just sold. Talk to you soon!"

One more gone, Betty mused. She felt the same brief pull of regret and sadness that always followed, when another material possession evaporated from her existence. *It'll be all right.* She had to keep telling herself that, even though the sense of loneliness and fear tugged relentlessly at her heart. She finished the few remaining cucumber sandwiches and scooped up the remnants of guacamole. A cup of gazpacho soup cleansed her palate as she looked at the time. Six o'clock. Yes, it wasn't too early to start imbibing. She poured herself a stiff glass of bourbon from the Waterford decanter sitting on the credenza in the living room. It used to hold the expensive brand, but now it cradled Old Crow, an amber liquid good enough to satisfy the likes of Mark Twain and Ulysses S. Grant. Heading upstairs to her bedroom, she passed the door that led to the attic. Betty hovered by the door, taking a sip of bourbon and falling carelessly into a memory. Tears welled up in her eyes, and she knew it was time to retreat into the safety of her bedroom.

Three hours later, she was still awake and lying in bed, floating on the fumes of her fourth drink. Ronald continued to snooze happily at the foot of the bed as Betty pulled the comforter toward her chest. Surfing the TV channels, she came across the early local news. Reverend Bobby Lynch, a grey-haired, controversial fixture in Colorado Springs, was being asked for his opinion on the plethora of medical marijuana dispensaries cropping up around his mega-church. Utilizing the most fervent Saturday afternoon modulation of his Sunday pulpit voice, Reverend Lynch condemned what he called "the slow slide into Hell." He stressed that this issue was about "morality," and that "the moral fabric" was being ripped to shreds by "the abomination of these drug havens." He then added that he "wept for the children." When the interviewer asked him what "children" had to do with the topic, Reverend Lynch replied with his standard "children are our future" line and then randomly added, "Jesus never needed to smoke a joint."

This odd conversation was sharply contrasted against a sound bite from a marijuana activist, who went by the unusual name of "Doobie Douggie." With his long, unruly mane of grey hair and multiple tattoos, Doobie Douggie was a longtime expert grower of "the herb." At the age of seventy, and wheelchair bound from taking a shot to the back in Vietnam, he wore a t-shirt with the statement "Legalize the Weed" emblazoned on the front. Douggie believed that cannabis was given to mankind by God, and due to its varied usefulness as both fiber and medicine, anyone who wanted to could and should grow the plant in their backyard based on their God-given, inalienable rights. Even though Douggie qualified for a cannabis "red card" under Colorado law, he refused to play by the system's rules and openly grew close to fifty varieties of medical marijuana inside and outside his rural home, forty-five miles south of Paradox. For this, Douggie had been caught "green handed" and arrested countless times. He was commonly seen wheeling himself out of the courthouse after each arrest, wrapped in the American Flag and screaming, "Give cannabis a chance!" and "Marijuana doesn't kill people! Government kills the people!" To the growing marijuana activists, Doobie Douggie was their patron saint of pot. He was edgy, fearless and angry as hell. Just as Reverend Lynch talked about the moral fabric, Douggie stressed the usefulness of hemp fiber and the fact that Jefferson drafted the Declaration of Independence on hemp paper. He explained that *can*vas hailed from *cann*abis, also noting that ships' sails were made from the hemp plant, as well as the rope onboard those vessels. After a one-minute rant that was intelligently stated, but filled with rage and a few bleeped expletives, the interviewer had to cut Douggie off and wrap up the segment.

Betty clicked off the TV and fell into the silence. It wasn't even 9:30 but she could feel the suffocation of the night. She used to be a night owl, but now it was the avowed enemy. She felt like a hostage, held in a fist of darkness. The shadows and thumps woke her from shallow sleep and tormented her racing mind. The numbness of the bourbon didn't help either. Instead of reducing the anxiety, it seemed to incite both paranoia and ghostly images.

Through the glaze of booze and angst, she heard a defined thud and checked to see if Ronald heard it too. But the ol' boy was sound asleep. Creeping from the bed, Betty lay an unsteady, bare foot on the carpet and slid open the drawer on the side table. Removing her small-but-effective Beretta Tomcat handgun, she slinked to the bedroom door and peered into the upstairs hallway. She heard the same *thud* again and located the origin. Turning back into her bedroom and looking outside her window, she noted an errant branch on the large canopy elm that hugged the corner of the backyard. Her favored, stately tree needed to have its dead branches pruned, but it was another expense she couldn't afford.

Betty sat on the edge of the bed, turned on the bedside lamp, and gently concealed the Tomcat in the drawer. The room suddenly felt heavy around her, as she sensed *his* presence bleed through the darkness and sit behind her on the edge of the bed. The fourth Bourbon always fueled these discarnate visions. She didn't want to turn around, because she hated the way he looked. The sunken cheeks, vacant eyes and the weeping sores that festered on his arms and neck reminded her too much of the last time she saw him on that cold slab five years ago.

"Mom?" she heard him whisper.

"Yes, Frankie? I'm here."

"I can feel your fear."

Betty nodded. "I know. You always could."

Chapter 3

"Fun" had a cost and it was steep and unrepentant.

Betty opened her eyes and watched the early morning light creep into her bedroom and vanquish another restless night. She was still alive. *Dammit.*

The "hour of lead" Dickinson wrote about had arrived again. Hell, Dickinson should have titled it "the twenty-four hours of lead," because the weight of anxiety never seemed to lift off Betty's shoulders. But the sun was out and the pulse of a new, albeit uncertain, day beat outside her window. She could finally exhale, at least until the next sucker punch hit her. Even her closest friends never saw the meek Betty; the one who hovered a little longer each morning under the covers, girding her loins and gestating the nerve to get up and face the unknown. She had been given much, but much had always been expected of her. And now, the pageant queen with the radiant blond hair and buxom figure had fallen hard from her gilded perch.

The deconstruction of Betty Craven began five years ago. Up until that point, she had been able to keep up appearances and strategically live her life so the dust never settled and the shine never dimmed. But a raw, ruthless vulnerability engulfed her when Frankie died and hijacked any chance of living a normal life again. She was still buried in tacit grief when one year later, Frank Sr. was diagnosed with a failing liver. The booze, cigarettes and military lifestyle finally caught up with him. When he died in 2007, Betty felt pinpricks of rebellion, but she had no vessel in which to pour her mutiny. She was like a chained tiger, bent on tasting life for the first time on *her* terms but ignorant of how to accomplish it. The volatile fuel of bitterness is often ignited when a woman has willingly allowed herself to be held down at the hands of another for years. The explosion that follows is typically erratic and shockingly unpredictable.

But as Betty liked to say, "I never fail to plan and I *never* plan to fail." The birth of the idea was quick and made perfect sense to her. Yes, yes, *yes*, she would invest in *Betty*. After years of feeling the yoke of domination around her inquisitive neck, she decided to visit France, a country she saw as refined and in touch with fine culinary pursuits. Betty withdrew thirty-five thousand dollars from her savings account – which nearly emptied it – and enrolled in a six-week cooking, baking and gourmet chocolate course, conducted at a prestigious school in Paris. After packing on an extra twenty pounds around her middle, she decided that as long as she was in the vicinity she'd hop over to Switzerland to see what type of scrumptious sweets they had to offer. That last minute sojourn left a three-digit balance in her savings account, but she didn't care. The bonfire of resentment she'd felt for so long was burning red hot.

When she returned home, the flames were as intense as ever. Another swift decision was made. Buoyed and inspired by the skills she'd learned overseas, Betty formulated the perfect small business. Since she was already known as "the connoisseur's connoisseur," she decided to put her expertise to use. After researching the upscale marketplace in Paradox, she realized a gourmet chocolate shop would be a spectacular standout. She'd been dabbling in homemade chocolates for years, giving them as gifts for Christmas and birthdays, and receiving gushes of effusive response. Best to focus on one thing, Betty mused, and do it better than anyone else, in order to ensure the success she knew was heading her way. And with her confidence in creating cacao creations that left her classmates back in Paris orgasmic, her conviction was stronger than ever.

How would she pay for this bold endeavor? Simple. She would take out an equity loan for one hundred thousand dollars on the value of her home, which in 2007, was over *eight hundred* thousand dollars. The interest was eight percent. No big deal. Betty was confident in her abilities, and with her hard work ethic, success was assured. After securing a one-year lease for a charmingly chic, seven-hundred-square-foot retail space, in one of the most desirable locations in downtown Paradox – and paying the pricey two thousand dollar rent six months in advance as a sign of "good faith" – she set about purchasing the necessary top-grade commercial equipment she'd learned to use during the culinary arts course, which was vital to creating a myriad of chocolates en masse. From the high end, German-made melting and tempering unit, to the tables, confectionary cabin, refrigeration units and silicone moulds, she was quickly writing checks exceeding forty thousand dollars. That was *before* the cost of the hundreds of pounds of imported cacao powder, cacao butter, luxurious flavorings, Madagascar vanilla beans, and gallons of high altitude honey from the Flat Tops Wilderness area in Colorado. By the time she was done, nearly sixty thousand dollars was invested. But that was all right, she counseled herself. Even though in 2007, parts of the country were feeling the economic downturn, Colorado was still flourishing financially. And while cautious optimism had always been Betty's trademark, she couldn't help but feel great pride and accomplishment in what she was doing. In her mind, legions of connoisseurs, who demanded the pinnacle of perfection, would travel to her little store and word-of-mouth would spread across the country, generating a healthy mail order business. Magazine articles would surely soon follow, launching her into the rarified realm of epicurean superstardom.

She would name the store, *The White Violet*. None of that ridiculous, cheap, trailer park nomenclature for Betty Craven. She wouldn't be caught dead in a store called the "The Chocolate Hut," or "The Chocolate Cave." Huts and caves were not places Betty occupied. *The White Violet* had an elegant sound to it, and it spoke to her supreme passion of gardening. Did she grow white violets? Yes. Were they her favorite? Well, no. But in the darkened hallway just outside the bathroom, hung the antique, faux-gold-framed, watercolor print of white violets she held so close to her heart. It meant such a great deal to her, and naming her store – her future – after those flowers in that watercolor was her way of paying homage to the person who gave it to her.

And thus, right before Thanksgiving in 2007, Betty enthusiastically opened the doors of *The White Violet* and threw the shackles of monotonous servitude from her fifty-six year old shoulders. She convinced herself that the emptiness and utter uselessness dogging her since her beloved son's death would magically disappear, once she became independently successful. Success, after all, was its own reward. That was the plan, and everyone supported her, because after all, she was Betty Craven – a formidable woman with stamina, intelligence, creativity and a belief that whatever you set out to do, you do it well.

As all this excitement was churning, she looked at herself in the mirror, and since Betty was so identified with her pageant smile, she decided to invest in a set of porcelain veneers that would both brighten and improve that outward expression. Growing up in the well-bred circles of Texas, it was terribly important for her to present herself in the most stately and attractive manner. She was brought up by her parents to believe that how she looked and presented herself was far more important than anything she could possibly say. And besides, she counseled herself, it simply wouldn't do to present a pricey chocolate to a customer and then smile, exposing yellowed, imperfect teeth that screamed, "sugar rot." The price for this "investment in Betty," as she called it, was a cool twenty-five grand. She'd never spent that kind of money on herself before, but damn, she was worth it.

In the fevered midst of all this internal revolution, Betty looked at her home – her nest for twenty years – and decided to give it a new shine. After all, a successful woman needed a home that reflected her achievement. Frank had been reluctant to put much into the homestead except for a few coats of fresh paint every decade. Since the kitchen was Betty's favorite room, she started there. She hired a top designer, who she felt mirrored her impeccable taste and precision, and they went to work. It had to be perfect, with marble counter tops, a built-in stainless steel refrigerator, a separate high-end freezer, wood flooring, and all new cabinets. And light. *Lots and lots* of light. The damn kitchen had always been too dark. She and the designer agreed to purchase three extraordinary windows with handcrafted etching on the sides, so when the sunlight hit the motif, the room was infused with a rainbow of colors. *Stunning.* Yes, this is what Betty envisioned everyone telling her when they saw the kaleidoscope across the pale peach walls.

Unfortunately, her old house wasn't as dedicated to keeping up its end of the deal. Not a day went by when she didn't get a call from either her designer or one of the workers at the house, telling her in graphic detail about some sort of "issue" that had arisen. One day it was the discovery that the house wasn't up to code with the electric, and it needed to be addressed. *Cha-Ching!* The next day, a worker cut into a supporting beam by accident and now that had to be rectified with a specialty crew and overtime. *Cha-Ching!* Then an entire wall of mold was found behind the old insulation when the construction workers were about to set one of Betty's stunning etched windows. Progress stopped immediately because a mold remediation team had to be brought in to remove the toxic debris and check for *more* mold. And they found it...one rotting beam after another. A month later, they were still debating about whether the area was safe for human habitation, let alone food preparation. *Cha-Ching, cha-ching, cha-ching!* The hundred thousand dollars had quickly run out, and Betty's kitchen looked like it'd been hit by a surface-to-air missile. With nothing left in her savings, the only liquid asset she had was the one hundred and fifty thousand dollars from Frank's life insurance. That was supposed to be her "cushion," but now it had to be tapped. Yet, she kept her head up, flashed her shiny veneers and told herself it was just a temporary hiccup, and things would be better soon.

But things didn't get better. One year later, by the Fall of 2008, she had her dream kitchen, but she'd also eaten through one hundred thousand dollars of the life insurance policy. By the time she was "up to code," she'd said good-bye to the pricey designer and worked as hard as she could to personally button up that never-ending nightmare. She essentially had a one hundred and twenty thousand dollar kitchen surrounded by a dilapidated and outdated house. A hideous, sobering reality set in. Betty could lean against the marble countertop and stare out one of the three large, handcrafted, etched windows and wonder what in the hell she was thinking a year prior when she came up with this terrible idea. There was nothing to smile about now. No reason to flash her twenty-five thousand dollar grin. She had less than thirty grand left from Frank's insurance policy. Her large cushion had turned into a small pillow, and she would have to dip into the fund again in order to keep *The White Violet* afloat.

By the late spring of 2009, it became patently clear that the economic downturn had finally skulked into Colorado. Gourmet chocolate was not at the top of people's "must have" list when holding onto their home was the key priority. It didn't help matters that sixty percent of the businesses around *The White Violet* shut down, leaving the once fashionable locale looking like a boomtown gone bust. Empty storefronts and poorly maintained landscaping around the area didn't exactly attract out of town visitors or locals.

Thus, *The White Violet* doled out its last elegant chocolate confection in May of 2009. With fewer than ten thousand dollars left of Betty's "cushion," she retreated to her home, shoved the chocolate equipment in the workspace above the garage and wondered what in God's name she was supposed to do with the rest of her life. A year later, she was still asking herself the same question. However, now the ache of failure and confusion permeated her bones. She still had to pay back the equity loan, and the monthly interest payment of $666 – a number with obviously sinister connections – was barely covered by Frank's death benefit. His pension of Full Colonel, Rank O-6, gave Betty fifty-five hundred dollars each month. Nothing to complain about, she reasoned. But between property taxes in her upscale neighborhood, utilities, food, and sundry expenses, she was left with around three thousand dollars. Again, not something that was forcing her into Tent City. But it seemed every month, something monumental occurred to the house that needed drastic and immediate attention.

It was as if the kitchen remodel had triggered a cascading march of house repairs. Tug at one thing in nature and you affect something else; knock a wall down in the kitchen and suddenly it weakens a shaky foundation and the chimney falls over. That damaged the roof, leaving a hole in the attic. Then an old, imposing sycamore fell down in the driveway, seriously uprooting the cement. The plumbing was the next to blow. Bit by bit, the extra three grand quickly evaporated every month.

The only area of the house that didn't seem to be affected was the basement. But that didn't surprise Betty. Frank's sacred domain was built like a bunker. There, amidst his medals, uniforms and enormous gun collection, Frank whiled away his retirement years drinking, smoking and reliving his beloved, brutal moments during his thirty year military career. Betty rarely spent much time down there, except to do the laundry or remove another gun from Frank's collection to sell to a gun dealer across town. Those sales had helped supplement her income, but all the guns were gone now, save for the Beretta Tomcat she kept for home defense.

She was caught between that familiar rock and a very hard place. In order to sell the house in the quickly deteriorating economy, she needed to put at least fifty thousand into it. And even that would be inadequate to attract a buyer in such a competitive market. However, the house was now worth *half* of the eight hundred thousand appraisal when she got the home equity loan. She didn't have fifty grand, so she was stuck, and mortified she'd allowed herself to reach this point of helplessness. All the derisive lectures she had to listen to from her husband, telling her she lived in a bubble or had no sense of "the real world" haunted her. Even her parents, rest their judgmental souls, never raised her to be this liberal with her resources. She'd had some fun and now she suffered for it. But she always knew that would happen because "having fun" was not in the game plan. Not under her parents' roof or in Frank's grip. "Fun" had a cost and it was steep and unrepentant.

But there was always something else tugging at her heart. Even if she could sell the house, the emotional toll would be tremendous. It wasn't that the old, broken down domicile held beautiful memories. If anything, the walls still shuddered from her husband's alcoholic rages, the deafening silence of regret and the thunder of pain Betty suppressed her entire marriage. No, it wasn't the house. It was what surrounded the house. It was the show-stopping front yard, ablaze with botanical colors from April through October. And it was the large backyard with the swinging bench hanging on the large canopy elm with those words her son carved into its trunk the last time she saw him alive. When life became too difficult, Betty could always sit on that swinging bench and pretend Frankie was sitting beside her, sharing a story and hurriedly eating whatever she could whip up before his father got home and found him. Their visits had to be clandestine and so brief after Frank kicked his namesake out of the house when he was eighteen. She begged Frank to pay for rehab for their son but his chiseled pride would have none of it. "I don't invest in failures!" Frank would shout. "He got himself into this fucking mess, he can get himself out!

It killed Betty to watch Frankie's decline. Each time he'd show up for another stolen moment, the roadmap of pain was carved onto his face. It wasn't just the slaughter of hardcore addiction; it was his ache of feeling cast out and left to flounder in a world that had always been too harsh for a boy that sensitive, reflective and gentle. As macho and arrogant as Frank Sr. was, Frankie was the polar opposite.

He was different almost from the beginning. As a youngster, Frankie spent hours alone, playing with imaginary friends only he could see. Betty would observe him in the backyard and sense he was straddling between two distinct worlds. At times, Frankie appeared to have a deeper connection with things unseen than with the three dimensional world. His clear, hazel eyes held wisdom far beyond his years but that didn't garner popularity with his peers, especially when he would imprudently make what some of his friend's mothers called "a bizarre comment" about some event that was going to happen in their future. The odd thing was that many incidents young Frankie foresaw came true in one form or another. That just made him a freak in the eyes of his friends and his father, so he learned to keep his mouth shut. He was the epitome of that line from the song, "Vincent" – "And how you suffered for your sanity. And how you tried to set them free..." He was too tender for this world, and Frank Sr. never let an opportunity go by to remind his son of it. Even as the drugs began tearing at his soul, Frankie never became violent. If anything, he became more internalized, grasping daily for the meaning of life.

Frankie had been dead for five years, but his imprint remained in the house and always under the large canopy elm. No one ever knew it, but after his death and during the time Frank was sick and waiting for his liver transplant, Betty would wait until her husband was asleep and then creep out into the backyard. There, she would lie in the grass under the elm with the fragrant flowers around her and absorb the serenity. It was like a botanical IV that shot her full of just enough energy to get up and face another dreadful day. That tree, the grass, the flowers and the manicured bushes were her truest and most loyal companions. She couldn't express all that pent up anger and resentment to her friends, but the elm tree knew. The grass and the flowers never judged her. And those manicured bushes even relaxed enough to listen to her when she talked to Frankie and cried for all the reasons she failed him. Betty's connection with nature defied her upbringing and appearance. Looking at her, you'd never know that without her plants, she would be a shell of a person. They embraced her when nobody else did, and for that she would never forsake them.

So as she lay a little longer under the covers on this spring morning, Betty steeled herself against the dogged fears biting at her heels, and she slowly threw back the covers. Sleeping in, Betty still believed, was for people who hadn't planned their day correctly. She had to keep busy. God, that was imperative. Keep moving. Keep *doing*. "It is in the doing," her father used to tell her as a child, "that progress begins." And Betty had been praying at the altar of progress her entire existence.

As she moved around the bedroom, stretching and getting her bones to stop creaking, she planned her day to the minute. She would shower and select the appropriate outfit for the day. After breakfast and just one cup of coffee, she'd hoist the American flag outside her front door and set off in her fifteen-year-old green Ford Taurus, praying it would continue to run for just one more day. Her first stop would be the consignment store two towns south of her. Nobody knew her there, and that was vital in order to maintain a semblance of anonymity as she sold her cherished antiques to total strangers. Little by little, the house was losing a few more items, but she was able to cover it up by rearranging furniture and filling in the empty spaces with large vases of flowers from the yard. The lie she sold to Judi at the get together the day before about her needlepoint chair being fixed was unplanned, and she realized she'd have to come up with a better story if she was confronted with the same situation again. Like a boy scout, Betty would be prepared. None of this fly by the seat of her tailored dress crap for her.

After the consignment store, she'd drive back to town and visit Peggy. The chocolates she'd set aside for her dying friend were already wrapped in a *White Violet* gift box. She just hoped to God that Peggy wasn't moaning or throwing up when she arrived. That would be too much for Betty to handle. Her inexorable fear of death had become so persistent that it dominated her life now. It was strange in many ways, since for the past year, she really wasn't that invested in living. Death, in some ways, would be welcome, if anything just to break the daily boredom.

She was just about to lay out her outfit for the day when that familiar syncopated flutter began again in her right ear.

It was enough to drive her crazy. She pressed her hand tightly against the ear and felt her jaw tighten and then *click*. That was followed by an uncomfortable *pop* in her jaw. Good God, this day was getting off to a helluva start. She dressed in a cheerful salmon colored dress and donned her favorite, off-white, springtime sweater with its jaunty embroidered collar. She'd parted with many of her cherished designer sweaters and coats over the past year when she found out they could fetch a decent price. But she couldn't part with this one and found herself wearing it more than ever before. Selecting the ideal brooch to doll up the outfit, she came upon Frank's gold wedding band in her jewelry box. Squinting, she read the inscription inside the ring: THIS WE'LL DEFEND. It was the motto of the U.S. Army. Ever the combatant, Frank somehow thought it was the most romantic thing to carve into his wedding ring. But to Betty, the dictum made her feel like she was a territory that needed to be secured and conquered. As she re-read those three words, the familiar tightness in her neck began to creep up. Setting the golden band in her palm, she assessed the possible weight of the metal. Last time she checked, gold was going for nearly twelve hundred dollars an ounce. She debated what to do. But then she could almost hear Frank's coarse voice telling her to put the goddamned ring back in the jewelry box. He wasn't even there, but he still had his thumb wedged on her spirit. She obliged his phantom order and slammed the gold band back into the drawer.

An hour later she headed out the door. She advised Ronald she would return shortly and to "keep watch." His failing, fourteen-year-old eyes could hardly find his dish let alone an intruder, but he played along. Outside the front door, she raised the American Flag into its secure slot and gently unfurled its colors. Walking past the white wooden garden sign that simply stated, BETTY'S GARDEN, she heard footsteps coming from on top of her roof. Spinning around, she was shocked to see Buddy, her portly maintenance man securing a piece of insulation.

"Buddy! I wasn't aware you were working today. You realize it's Sunday?"

"Yes, ma'am," Buddy replied, heaving his work belt lower on his overhanging gut. For a guy who wasn't even thirty-five, he moved like someone twice his age. "But my regular job has me doin' overtime and I just figured you needed to get this done before the end of summer."

Betty regarded him with uncertainty. "Is that a joke, Buddy?"

He scratched his scraggly brown beard that still had specks of the morning's donut in it, complete with sprinkles. "Well, yes and no, ma'am. I always have to allow for my low back goin' out and gettin' me stove up."

She furrowed her brow. "Stove up? What in the world is that?"

His jaw slacked and then came to attention. "Stove up," Buddy countered, as if it was perfectly clear. "Stiff, sore, can't move. Stove up."

"Well, of course," Betty said with a slight Texas inflection. The poor man needed to lose the fifty pound barrel around his gut. That would certainly do wonders to lessen the strain on his back, but Betty sure as hell wasn't going to be the one to tell him that. "Listen, I have to go out and run errands. So, I might not be here at lunchtime to make you something to eat."

"That's okay, Mrs. Craven. I'll figure it out."

Betty observed Buddy's demeanor. He seemed saddened by the news. At least, that's what she believed. He could have just had gas. She started toward her car and then turned back, "Oh, Buddy, I'm running a bit tight this month. So, if you could –"

"Don't worry about it, Mrs. Craven. I know you'll pay up when you got it."

Betty smiled, trying to hold her head high, but she was both appreciative and appalled by Buddy's seemingly lack of concern as to when his work would be compensated. His trust in her was something she took quite seriously, and even though she tended to speak to him in a tenor set aside for workmen and bathroom attendants, she was fond of the big, slack-jawed scalawag. She tried valiantly to introduce him to culture, once playing Tchaikovsky's "Nutcracker" while he worked. When he asked her what the "song" was called, she told him. He laughed so hard mucus ran from his nostrils, and from then on he called it "that ball-buster music." Sadly, Betty surmised, the only culture some people experience is the mold growing on cheese in their refrigerator.

With Peggy's box of chocolates secured safely in a cooling bag – one of the many accessories left over from *The White Violet* – Betty locked the car doors and put on her seatbelt, making sure not to create any unsightly wrinkles in her dress. Then she did what she always did before starting the car. She prayed. If she were Catholic, she'd pray to St. Christopher, the Patron Saint of travelers. But since she was a Methodist, she silently bowed her head and prayed to God to make the car start and continue to run until she reached her destination. As the turned the key, God answered her prayer.

Chapter 4

"That gentleman over there is checking out your Biedermeier."

The Gilded Rose was not exactly bustling when Betty arrived. There was only one man perusing the furniture section and a young girl waiting at the empty counter. Sure, it was Sunday but where were all the customers she was told adored this high-end antique store? As she moved closer to the counter, a wave of patchouli assaulted her senses. It appeared to emanate from the young girl now leaning on the counter and playing with the business card holder next to the cash register. Betty regarded the girl, who looked to be in her early twenties, with silent disparagement. Her fingers were painted in coal black polish, making it look to Betty as if she'd dipped her nails into Satan's burnt caldron. Hoop earrings adorned her right eyebrow and left nostril. Betty never understood this accessory, always picturing a leash attached to the hoops so the unrefined colt could be led around the paddock. To add another dose of chaos to this unfortunate young woman's appearance, a black streak of hair coloring extended down the middle of her bleached blond hair. The image of a cheap skunk materialized.

Betty erected a steel wall between herself and the girl, making a point to turn away and pretend to take an interest in a red velvet Victorian couch that looked like it belonged in the lobby of a brothel.

"Hi!" the girl said sweetly.

Betty turned to her. Even though she was appalled by the girl's appearance, her upbringing dictated that she posture politeness. "Hello."

"I think Lily's in the back room. She'll probably be out any second."

"All right."

"Hey, um, can you crack a Benji?"

"A Benji?"

She held up a one hundred dollar bill. "Benjamin Franklin? I just came over to get some change. I work a couple doors down, and all we're getting is hundies."

"No. I don't have change for your Benji." Betty turned away but couldn't help but be curious as to what business had a problem of bringing in too many hundred dollar bills. "Where do you work?"

"At *The Green Wellness* dispensary. We've been slammed this weekend."

A cold shudder iced Betty's spine. Well, that explained the appearance, she thought. What a waste of a good life. With marijuana dispensaries outnumbering Starbucks in Colorado, it was hard to believe they all were rolling in "Benjamins." But the Colorado green rush was obviously a profitable endeavor. However, Betty told herself, so was being a high priced escort. The strain now between these two was thick. Well, it was thick for Betty anyway; the girl seemed completely oblivious and laid-back. Thankfully, Lily strode out from the back, and upon seeing the girl and Betty together, tensed up considerably. "Yarrow?" Lily said, her eyes jetting nervously to Betty. "This is not a great time to visit."

Yarrow, Betty thought. Who in the hell names their kid Yarrow? Hyssop was probably too hard to spell.

"I just need some change," Yarrow said off-handedly.

"I don't have any. It's too early."

"Bummer. Okay, I'll come back later. See ya!" She nearly skipped out of the store, clearly immune to the strain at the counter.

"She works —"

"At the dispensary," Betty quickly said. "Yes, she told me. Do you have to deal with that type of intrusion a lot now?"

Lily looked ill at ease. "She's in here once or twice a day."

"You don't have to put up with that. You should say something to her. She could attract the wrong clientele to your business." Betty leaned forward, speaking in a confidential tone. "Criminals, if you get my drift."

"Oh, I don't...most of the people over there are..." Lily smiled, clearly uncomfortable. "Anyway, you got my message about your chair." Betty nodded. "I've got your check right here." Lily opened the cash register and handed Betty the check.

Betty swallowed hard. "A hundred and fifty-two? I don't understand —"

"I had to mark it down. That's in our contract. After sixty days if it's not sold, I have the right to do that."

Betty's head reeled, but she maintained her composure. "Well, somebody is sitting on a really good deal right now."

"Betty, it's nothing against you or your beautiful items. Blame it on Ed."

"Who's Ed?"

"Economic Downturn. Hey, you've still got plenty of incredible things here that haven't passed their expiration. In fact," she furtively stole a glance behind Betty's back, "that gentleman over there is checking out your Biedermeier."

Betty turned. The man she half-noticed when she walked in was indeed eyeing her historic, German walnut writing table, circa 1825. However, he certainly didn't appear to be someone who would ever own such a refined piece. He was probably in his early fifties, possibly younger, and wore a pair of black jeans and a well-worn leather motorcycle jacket. His reddish brown hair was pulled back into a neat ponytail that hung five inches down his back. A smartly trimmed goatee framed his healthy-looking face, which was tanned by the Colorado sun. No, this was not someone who would ever plunk a cent down for her cherished desk. Besides, Betty factored his height to be at least six foot three inches tall, which was certainly not a figure that would comfortably fit under that writing table. Still, he was spending a great deal of time examining the piece and reading the price tag. A sale was a sale, dammit, so she stepped forward to see if she could shrewdly close the deal.

Betty tried to appear as nonchalant as possible as she sashayed in the vicinity of the desk. Moving closer, she noticed a metal sign propped onto the piece with the quote:

ALL A GIRL REALLY WANTS IS FOR ONE GUY TO PROVE TO HER THAT THEY ARE NOT ALL THE SAME. It was apparently a direct quote from the pouting lips of Marilyn Monroe but it was certainly not something Betty Craven would ever dream of placing anywhere near her beloved Biedermeier. Like a fine hostess changing a place card in order to facilitate a better seating arrangement, she craftily removed the metal sign, placed it face down on another item and feigned great interest in the writing desk

"Oh my, *a Biedermeier!*" she gushed in a low-key tone, brushing her palm against the wood. "You certainly don't see these every day."

The man looked at her with his intensely blue eyes. A soft smile followed. "Really?"

"Oh, I mean it. It's quite a find! I don't remember the last time I saw a Biedermeier like this."

He leaned over and checked the price tag. "I'd say the last time you saw it was shortly before April 11th."

Betty's mouth went dry. "Excuse me?" She could feel that plastic smile forming on her face.

"The tag?" he noted, with a mischievous grin. "Lily always shorthands the name of the person who brought it in along with the date, right above the price. See? It says here: 'B. Craven, 4/11.'"

Betty wasn't about to let some guy with a quick mind outfox her. "Yes, but, why on earth would you think that –"

"Betty, I've heard you speak at the town council meetings. You always sit on the right side of the aisle and I'm always on the left. Kind of like our politics." He smiled again and extended his hand. "My name's Jeff Carroll. I'm glad to finally meet you."

She stood there, momentarily speechless. But her manners quickly resurfaced. "Pleased to meet you too," she replied, hoping her disingenuous tone wasn't too obvious. His handshake was firm, not like so many men who are afraid to demonstrate their spirit. On closer examination, Betty surmised that Jeff looked something like a healthier, more muscular version of General George Custer and a sexier, thinner, and far younger version of Colonel Sanders. With a ponytail. And a biker jacket.

"What part of Texas are you from?" he asked.

Betty wasn't aware she was letting her Texas inflection give her away. He was rather forward, Betty judged. But if a few moments of harmless banter sold her Biedermeier, she was willing to drop her guard just a bit. She'd pretend she was back on the pageant stage with her big bouffant, answering asinine questions about which world leader she most admired. "Houston. But we moved to Paradox in 1980, so I'm working toward becoming a semi-native."

"We?" Jeff leaned against an oak chifferobe wardrobe in a relaxed posture.

"Uh, yes." She realized she was rusty on the pageant *shtick*. "Well, my husband. But he's since passed away."

"I'm sorry," he said. But to Betty, it didn't appear he was sorry at all.

There was an uncomfortable pause before Betty turned to the desk. "You know, I bought this piece –"

"I live outside of Paradox, in the unincorporated part." He chuckled. "*Paradox*. Sure is an odd name for a town, isn't it?"

Betty wasn't sure where in the hell this conversation was headed. "I'm sorry, but I don't follow you."

"It means irony or contradiction."

"Yes, I'm aware of the definition of the word, but I'm not clear on –"

"I think it just seems like a paradox in itself that somebody would give a town that name. 'I live in Paradox.' It's like saying, 'I live in an illogical place.'"

Betty actually pondered this concept. "I never really thought of it that way."

"Really? I thought of it the first time I heard the name. That's why I chose to live outside the city line. I prefer to live outside the irony."

Betty looked at Jeff, not sure what to make of him. He seemed to be someone who took time to actually *think*. But he also appeared to spend time thinking of the most peculiar things. "Yes. Well, right." She turned to the desk, but was pretty sure any possible sale was dead in the water. "I'm running late to see a sick friend."

Jeff smiled. "Sure. A sick friend."

She realized her reply sounded like a worn out excuse used to hasten a quick exit. "No, really. I am going to see a sick friend. A *very* sick friend." Her right ear began to flutter once again as her neck joined in the spasm.

"You okay?"

She was bewildered. She didn't think she'd made any wincing facial movements or drawn attention to her annoying issue. "Yes, of course, I'm fine."

Jeff cocked his head to the side. "You sure?"

Good Lord, this guy was persistent. "Yes," she replied, as her ear played "Babaloo."

He walked out with her and said goodbye before straddling his black Harley and zooming off into the distance. Damned noisy modes of transport, she said to herself, which seemed so inadequate for comfortable travel. But it did seem to start right up quite well without the need of a prayer. One could call that a bit of a paradox.

~~~

Peggy's hospice nurse answered the door and solemnly ushered Betty inside. She was a black woman with a tidy bun of braids bundled in the crook of her neck. Betty lingered a tad too long in the front entrance, clutching the cooler that held the box of chocolates. The house smelled toxic, like dirty metal burning.

"How's she doing today?" Betty managed to say as her stomach churned.

"Not good, I'm afraid," the nurse replied with the hint of a Caribbean accent. "She's got company right now but she's in a lot of pain."

This was already too much for Betty. She removed the elegantly wrapped box of chocolates from the protective cooler. "Perhaps, I can leave these chocolates with you and I'll come back another time —"

"Another time?"

Betty looked at the woman, not sure what to say. Her reply suggested that time was of the essence if one wanted to see Peggy outside of a casket. With reluctance shading each step, Betty walked down the dim hallway and around the corner. The foul aroma grew more penetrating the closer she got to Peggy's bedroom. Betty knew it all too well; Frank Sr. reeked of the same odor just days before he died. Reaching the doorway, she stopped in her tracks. There was an older gentleman around eighty years old on one side of Peggy's bed. But the young man with his back to Betty, holding Peggy's hand looked like...Betty clutched at her heart, fixated. Peggy was clearly out of it, tossing her head to the side and mumbling incoherencies. But Betty couldn't take her eyes off the young man.

He gently rested Peggy's hand against the comforter and turned. Betty stared at him. He was about five feet eight inches tall, with a chaotic swath of dark brown hair that hadn't seen a comb in quite some time. His loose fitting t-shirt sported three large letters in black: G.Y.O. His jeans hung dangerously low on his slender frame, giving her concern that the slightest tug would force them down around his ankles.

The young man quietly moved away from Peggy's bed and stood next to Betty. Once there, she noted a peculiar scent that seemed to be attached to his clothing. It wasn't awful but it wouldn't fetch much at the cologne counter.

"Do I know you?" he asked.

Betty realized she must have stared far too long. "No. You just look like..." She peered down at her sweater. The cuff had obviously gotten caught on something and was beginning to unravel. This particular embarrassment had never happened before, and Betty blamed the regular wear and tear on this dreadful mishap. She quickly folded the cuff so as to conceal the unsightly damage.

He leaned forward and looked at her more intently. "Like what?"

Betty turned away. Yes, there was an eerie similarity but on closer inspection, his eyes were different and his lips were thinner. "Nothing. Never mind."

"I'm Peyton."

He waited but Betty remained silent, staring straight ahead but avoiding Peggy with every ounce she could muster.

"And you're....who?" he asked with an unusually purposeful manner.

"Betty," she said in a hushed tone, never looking at him.

He checked out her dress. "Did you just come from church?"

"Church?" Now she turned. "No."

"Oh. It's just that you're dressed kinda formal."

Somehow she relaxed a bit. "Formal? This is not formal. I simply believe that it's important to present oneself in a proper manner when one is visiting a sick friend."

Peyton eyed her closer as if he were reading tea leaves. "Well, you may not dress formal but you sure do talk formal." His voice was nowhere near as low-key as Betty's. "And, to be dead honest, it doesn't matter what you're wearing. Aunt Peggy won't know who you are, let alone what you got on. Seriously, dude, I'm not kidding."

Any imagined sense of kinship she might have felt for this boy was lost at that moment. "*Dude*? Do I look a dude to you?"

Peyton looked confused. "No. I think you, like, misunderstood me. It's just, like, a word. You know, like...'hey.'"

"Can't you throw another 'like' in that sentence. I don't think you've exhausted the word enough."

"Are you, like, a school teacher?"

This was growing tedious. "No, dude, like I'm not."

Peyton caught the sarcasm and let out a stifled laugh. He looked at the elaborately wrapped box in Betty's hand. "What's that?"

"A box of chocolates."

"Oh, yeah? Where from?"

Betty let out a tired breath. "Behind the preposition."

Peyton cogitated briefly. "Huh?"

"Never mind. I made them."

"No shit? Are they any good?"

"What?" She turned to him, irritated and appalled. "Who in the hell raised you?"

"She did." He pointed to Peggy. "My mother – her sister – wasn't really invested in my emotional, physical or spiritual development."

Betty colored with embarrassment. "Sorry. I didn't know you were Peggy's nephew."

Peyton visibly pondered that statement. "So, it would make a difference if what I just told you wasn't so?"

"Excuse me?"

"Well, are you sorry because there's suddenly a family connection here and I'm not just some ass-wipe hangin' out, or are you sorry because you think that's the 'proper' thing to say?"

She turned to Peyton, unable to fathom how the exchange degenerated to this level. "I can't have this conversation with you right now."

"Oh, dude, hang on! I know who you are! Yeah, my aunt talks about you a lot. You had that whoopty-whoop chocolate store that went belly up, right? And you got the big, fancy garden with all the prize winning shit in it."

"All the prize winning *shit*? They're called flowers, dear."

"Dude, I didn't mean any offense. 'Shit' is just an all-encompassing word that means a group of stuff. It's like the word, dude. You can be a dude. I can be a dude. The dog can be a dude. It's just a word."

"Thank you for the clarification."

Peyton leaned a little closer to Betty. "Hey, you wanna know something? I'm a gardener too, just like you."

Betty smoothed the fabric on her dress and checked to see that the hem on the sleeve of her sweater was still turned under. "Oh, I seriously doubt that."

"That I'm a gardener or that I'm as good as you?"

"Yes."

He waited, watching Betty observe his aunt who was still fighting to get comfortable. "So, are you gonna go sit with her or just stare at her from this doorjamb?" Peyton waited but Betty remained reticent. He regarded her with more intensity. "Hey, I'm sorry. This is really hard for you, isn't it? I can see that."

"Oh, please, don't be ridiculous. I just don't want to... she looks preoccupied. I'd hoped the chocolates would lift her spirits."

"As much as she loves your chocolates, she won't eat them. She can't hold anything down. Fuckin' chemo." Betty turned to him with admonishment. "Hey, it *is* fuckin' chemo. It's fuckin' poison, too. You know, you don't die of the cancer anymore. You die of their 'cure.' She can't even connect to anybody. All she can do is just lay there and moan until it's time for another happy dose of morphine. And then she's out until she wakes up and the nightmare starts all over again." He traced the lines in the carpet with his foot, obviously distressed. "It's tough, you know? All I want to do is to be able to look into her eyes and have her recognize me, even for just a second, before she dies."

Betty softened. "I understand. Truly I do." She called up a phrase she'd used many times in the past few years. "Remember, Peyton, this too shall pass."

He shook his head. "God, I hate that saying. Want to know why? I hear that from a lot of people who play the victim game. And when they whine, 'this too shall pass,' what I really hear is 'this too shall pass so the next miserable event can move in to take its place."

Betty felt indignation worm closer. "*I* didn't mean it that way. I simply meant that this will pass."

"And so will my Aunt Peggy. Sooner rather than later. I can handle her death, but I can't handle her suffering. Hell, I offered to bring a vaporizer over here but Nurse Ratched isn't cool with it."

"A vaporizer? To help her breathe?"

"No. A vaporizer. To inhale some medical grade cannabis. It's a million times cleaner than smoking a blunt."

Betty's soft stance and gentility ceased. She stiffened, moving a few inches away from Peyton. "Get away from me."

"Huh?"

"This conversation is over." Her tone was succinct and unforgiving.

Peyton stared at Betty, trying to rationalize what just occurred. The doorbell rang, affording Peyton an opportunity to make a reasonable exit. He answered the door, and Betty heard Renée's strident inflection.

"Betty?"

Betty edged closer to the doorjamb. "Hello, Renée."

"How's she doing?" Renée asked with her characteristically vociferous voice.

"Not well." Betty clutched at the chocolates, feeling terribly awkward.

Renée checked behind her and then turned back. "God, did you see that nephew of hers? *Peyton?* He absolutely reeks of pot!"

So that was the peculiar odor Betty noted on the boy. "Really?"

"Oh, honey, trust me. The smell of Mary Jane is burned into *my* brain cells! Peggy must be devastated by how he turned out!"

"Apparently, Peggy's not devastated by much of anything right now. She's not really all there."

"Let the morphine kick in and she'll be fine."

Betty watched Peggy continue to struggle. "Yes. Right. She'll be wonderful." She handed the box of chocolates to Renée. "Would you leave these for her on the side table?"

Renée took the box. "Oh, Betty. It's too soon for you, isn't it? Frank Sr.'s demise is still too fresh. I can see it in your eyes. You can't deny it."

Betty had no clue what Renée was seeing in her eyes, but it sure as hell had nothing remotely to do with Frank. "Yes," Betty replied with fabricated sadness. "Still too fresh." She patted Renée on the shoulder and started down the hallway when a thought crossed her mind. "Do you have any idea why they named our town Paradox?"

Renée furrowed her brow. "What are you talking about?"

"I don't know. When you think about it, it's an odd name for a town, isn't it?"

Renée looked at Betty with slight concern. "What's so odd about it?" she sighed. "Oh, Betty, Betty, Betty. This whole thing with Peggy is really doing a number on you."

Betty wasn't sure what one thing had to do with another but she ignored it. It was time to get home and see if Buddy was still there. He'd be hungry and she couldn't bear the thought of him forced to eat some fast food tripe. There were plenty of leftovers from the get together the day before. She'd previously introduced him to gazpacho soup, and now she could invite him to enjoy a cucumber sandwich with a hearty dollop of homemade guacamole on the side. Buddy was like her own little outreach program.

The car started up a little throaty, but it ran quite well for about five miles before it started sputtering whenever she slowed at a red light. Her jaw clenched. She needed to put off this expense as long as possible, since she knew the aging vehicle would need a massive overhaul. Pulling into a parking spot on the side of the street, she turned off the engine. Glancing at the name of the store two doors down, she smiled. It was the "Hippie Dippie Health Food Store" Judi had raved about exclusively stocking "Mama's Muscle Mojo" salve. While Betty didn't usually enter establishments with the word "Hippie" or "Dippie" on their signage, she figured she had to give the Taurus at least twenty minutes to cool down. Maybe a fresh orange juice from the juice bar would lift her blood sugar just enough to get her through until lunch.

The store was not what she expected. It was actually *quite* lovely. The clean, pine panels and high ceilings gave it a light, airy feel. The place smelled inviting with a cheerful citrus bouquet. A large skylight in the center of the store held eleven crystals that twirled and swayed with the breeze, creating an intoxicating, prismatic ballet of color. In the back of the store was the juice and food bar Judi had raved about. A banner shouted, "WE PUT THE LIFE BACK IN YOUR JUICE!" On a large blackboard, the menu included clever names for the blends, including "The Triple-B Blaster," "Hiker's Help-er" and "Calcium Kicker."

The aisles were wide and neatly filled with locally pro-duced products as well as established national brands. In the background, soothing classical music played. There was no dust or grime or the sense that one was visiting a question-able establishment. Surely, Betty surmised, the owner could have come up with a more fitting name than the "Hippie Dippie Health Food Store." You know, something more el-egant that reflected the ambiance Betty was truly enjoying. Just as that thought crossed her mind, she heard a familiar voice behind her.

"Are you following me?"

Chapter 5

"So, who's the pain in your neck?"

Betty turned around. There was Jeff. The man who was checking out her Biedermeier at *The Gilded Rose*.

"Following you?" she said with slight irritation. "Of course, not! Perhaps, you're following me."

He flashed that engaging smile she was sure he used to his advantage many times throughout his life. "Nope. I own this joint."

Betty was momentarily stunned. Glancing around the place, it had such a lovely vibrance and *je ne sais quoi* that was so lingeringly inviting. Looking at Jeff with his neat little ponytail and sans his biker jacket, he didn't seem to Betty to be someone who could create such an appealing enterprise. The book didn't match the cover, so to speak. Besides, he didn't smell at all like celery. That's the scent she'd always associated with people who worked in health food stores. Celery and body odor – such an unpleasant combination to unite with healthy living.

"How's that sick friend of yours?" he asked.

"Not well at all. She's...dying, actually."

"I'm sorry." He really meant it. "How about if I make her up a good, healing juice, and you can take it to her. It's on me, of course."

What a curious man, Betty thought. He didn't really know her, and he certainly had no connection to Peggy, but he seemed to genuinely want to help. "That's quite kind of you, but she can't hold anything down. I brought her some of my chocolates, but I'm sure the family and her nurse will end up eating them."

"You make your own chocolates?"

"Yes," Betty said with a bright tone. "With honey. You'd approve of that, I'm sure."

"Why does it matter if I approve of it or not?"

"Excuse me?"

"If that's the way you want to make them, that's your business."

"Well, I just...I mean..." Betty floundered and tried to regain her composure. "You own a health food store. So, I just figured...*health...honey* –"

"I think it's too soon for you to call me 'honey,'" he dead-panned. "Let's stick with Jeff for now."

Betty regarded him with stunned silence. She gauged he was at least seven years her junior and clearly not someone she'd be remotely linked to on a social level, let alone romantic basis. "You misunderstood. I didn't mean –"

"I'm joking, Betty."

Betty let out a breath. "Oh, right. Yes. Of course you are."

"Dodged a bullet there, didn't we?" Jeff grinned just like a fourteen-year-old who knew how to charm and get away with mischief. He eyed her closer. "Damn, you're wound pretty tight."

"What are you talking about?"

He pointed to the right side of her face. "Your clenched jaw. Lots of tension going on there."

She wasn't comfortable having a near-stranger be this bold with her. "Yes, well, my friend, Judi, told me about some sort of salve you have that's good for –"

"Mama's Muscle Mojo," he said without a missing a beat. Turning, he moved about five feet down the aisle and snagged a jar from the shelf. "Made locally by this cute little gal who grows all the herbs organically in her garden." He handed the jar to Betty. "It's not going to cure that tension, but it'll sure relieve it."

She tried to discreetly check the price on the bottom of the jar. "Well, thank you."

"I've got a few one ounce giveaways in the back if you want to sample it before committing."

"I don't need any giveaways," she quickly replied with pride.

His blue eyes pierced through her. "Okay."

The tension began to creep around her neck. A stiff bourbon would help, but it was nowhere near five-thirty. She worked her two fingers down the muscle spasm in an attempt to halt its forward progress.

"If you don't mind me asking," Jeff said, leaning against the shelf, "who's the pain in your neck?"

"Who?"

"Yeah. Most problems start with our emotions or in our mind. Someone can break your heart, somebody else can give you a headache, another can be a pain in the ass and then there's the one who's the pain in your neck. So, who's the pain in your neck?"

Betty wanted to dismiss him but she couldn't. He was so relaxed when he mentioned it all. No judgment; just a matter-of-fact comment that had depth and merit. "I'm not sure. I think it's more likely the four 'D's.'"

"What's that?"

"Take a look around. It's everywhere. Disappointment, despair, disharmony...death."

"Really? Maybe you've got to start hanging out in better places."

"Oh, please. Look what's happening in this world! How can you possibly be blind to all that?"

"I'm not blind to it. I know it's out there. But if that's all you're focused on, that's all that's going to get fed back to you. Look in another direction. Up, down –"

"Up? You mean like in God?"

"No, I'm not going religious on you. God's not just up there anyway. He's everywhere. Even in your 'four D's.' Your disarray, dysfunction –"

"Disappointment, despair, disharmony and death," she reiterated with precision.

He laughed. "Yeah, you've got that welded into your psyche, don't you? You really do buy into it."

This was getting too personal for Betty. "I have to –"

"You're a gardener. You know what I'm talking about."

"How did you know I liked to garden?"

"I'm psychic," he said with a straight face and a long pause for effect. Finally, he smiled. "Actually, I saw the dirt under your fingernails. Either you like to garden or you're filthy. And by the way you dress and carry yourself and speak, I know you're not the latter."

She glanced at her fingernails, silently chiding herself for not noticing the packed mud beneath her nails. "Yes. Right. I'm a gardener."

"So, you know what I'm saying. When you're one with the soil and the plants, and that silent ballet between the two of you occurs, there is only delicious, delectable, dizzying...uh, I've run out of positive words that start with 'D,' but you get the point. I'm not a wordy person like you."

"Wordy? I wouldn't call myself that –"

"You think you have to explain yourself a lot. Somebody must have spent a lot of years driving that into you."

"I believe that being precise is important."

He looked at her. *Really* looked at her. "Why?"

She wasn't about to back down, even though she had no clue what she was about to say. "It clarifies one's approach. It allows one to be understood. It avoids chaos."

"It keeps you in your head and not your heart. And when you spend all that energy in your head, that damned tension builds up. And then your neck starts to spasm, and your jaw clenches and then you show up here looking for a salve, thinking that's going to fix it. All that's going to do is address the symptoms."

Betty felt lost. "Symptoms...well, that's all we can hope for, right." A familiar sadness crept up. "Never address the heart of the problem."

Jeff's eyes softened. "You okay, Betty?"

She swallowed hard. Think, think, *think*, she counseled herself. Think about what to fix Buddy for lunch. Think about the marigolds that need to be re-potted. Think about all those damn weeds that have to be pulled. *Think*. "I'll just go purchase this now. Thank you for your help." She started down the aisle, gathering her resilience with each step. "We must fight the good fight and carry on!"

"No, actually," Jeff countered. "It's the fighting that got you to this point. It's the letting go that matters."

Betty stopped as a familiar image surfaced. Her head spun with apprehension. The raw emotion began to churn in her gut and she knew she had to get out of there as soon as possible. She paid for the salve and hurriedly left the store. But she could feel his knowing eyes on her, even as she drove away.

~~~

She tried to swallow the grief as she drove home – to think of anything else but her only child. But lately, all attempts at pushing it away were met with resistance.

Death, she'd come to discover, is a frigid woman – isolating and unable to be penetrated. The glory of the afterlife is left to faith, but to those left behind it can be a shrouded specter. For a moment, you can believe you feel the presence of your loved one but then the distance of death surfaces and you realize faith can only carry you so far. Letting go and allowing is the only way to traverse the distance and the loss of someone whom you once held. But how in the hell do you let go when you can't forget?

Her body felt the ache of Frankie's death long before her mind was willing to accept his permanent absence. He'd been in and out of touch for six years, going as long as three months without contact. He had an uncanny ability to know exactly when his father was away from the house, because Betty would hear a tap-tap on the back door and see him standing there with that innocent smile and beguiling hazel eyes. He could charm mostly anyone, but Betty was like clay in his hands. She'd fix him something hearty to eat and make a pot of tea, and then they'd sit beneath the old canopy elm in the backyard with its heavy branches and fluttering leaves. He was her joy, and she never gave up hope that he would get help and be made new again. But his visits were always rushed and anxiety framed, because Betty never knew when

Frank Sr. would return. He'd made it patently clear that his son was never allowed back into their home and that Betty was to have no contact with their son until he was clean and sober. So, their visits usually lasted less than an hour. She'd give Frankie food to take with him and a few hundred dollars, kiss him on the cheek and then hug him tightly, imprinting that moment into her heart so she could hold onto it when he was absent.

He was the best thing she ever created. In her eyes, he was almost perfect. Lost but nearing perfection. He was the reason she got up in the morning when he was a boy. She fixed him wonderful breakfasts, buoyed his spirits when he felt depressed and cheered with him when he accomplished his goals. Her love was unending and unconditional. She understood his pain because she felt that same pain for so long herself. But she was a master at cover-up, whereas her son was unable to mask his angst except through the temporary stony solace of drugs. She hated his lifestyle and would never have welcomed any of his fair-weather drug friends into her backyard, let alone her home. But with Frankie, she threw all her judgments to the wind, because she knew what he could have been if he'd had a different father. And even when Frank Sr. ordered him out of the house at eighteen, Betty always felt that connection with him. Her son might be a thousand miles away, but she still knew he was part of her world, even when his addictions removed him from her home.

But when Frankie overdosed on that final pill that cut the cord with this earth and all the weight that came with it, Betty was unable to fully comprehend the loss. Sure, she'd seen his body at the morgue to identify it. That helped seal the reality. But for whatever reason, his death was like a dream. And like a dream, she lost connections she'd taken for granted. The sense of taste was the first to go, followed quickly by the sense of touch. Hearing went next. Music lost its timbre; voices spoke with no sound. There were days that held only staggering silence. There were hours that passed without notice. Gaps of time lost forever, numbed by grief and shots of bourbon. Her friends recalled events that took place during those days of lead but it was as if they were sharing memories that didn't belong to her. There weren't even glimpses or remembrances of what they talked about. But she never let on. She pretended so well and they never knew better. She called that time her "misplaced" period, when part of her soul departed and would never be recovered.

But when Betty's mind caught up with the heartache her body had embedded, it was like a center punch to her chest. The pain was unbearable and there seemed to be no escape from it. Relentless, it shared her bed, sat across from her at the table and rode next to her in the car. The only time the pain stepped aside was when Betty immersed herself in her garden. There amongst the living things that thrived and flourished, Betty found the solace she'd forgotten existed. It was her church and her salvation. And through that garden, she slowly regained awareness of her surroundings and was able to gradually feel and taste and listen. But still, there was that part of her that was as dead as Frankie. Recovering that missing piece and feeling it integrate back inside of her seemed impossible. It was the part of her that recalled what happiness was, even though happiness was not something she'd ever allowed herself. And somewhere within that missing piece of her soul, was her smile. Not that fake, pageant smile, but a smile that grew effortlessly and warmed her from within.

She turned into her driveway, cheered to see that Buddy was still there. Jerry, her neighbor across the street, enthusiastically waved and barked his appreciation for her "stellar front yard." Yes, everything was back to the way she was accustomed. None of this unpredictable, time-chewing introspection that ambushed her daily routine. She vowed to spend the rest of the day fixing Buddy a plateful of lunch, occupying herself with yard work and tidying up from the gathering the day before. "It is in the doing that progress begins," she reminded herself.

But it was the physical *undoing* that occurred just as she handed Buddy his epicurean meal and turned to head back into the house. Without warning, Betty's neck seized up. She couldn't turn her head right or left, up or down without excruciating muscular pain. Buddy held the phone book as Betty dialed Dr. Hancock's emergency office line.

Chapter 6

"It's more like anxiety wrapped in a crêpe of depression."

"Roger will be right with you, Betty," the nurse advised, handing her the latest *People* magazine. Betty carefully sat down, avoiding any unnecessary neck movement. Thankfully, she'd nabbed one of Dr. Hancock's first appointments that Monday morning. It was one of the perks, she supposed, of counting Judi as a best friend. Tossing the *People* magazine to the side, she brought out the jar of "Mama's Muscle Mojo" from her bag and rubbed another dollop on her neck. As Jeff told her, it was only helping the symptoms, but that was good enough for now. And if Dr. Hancock asked her what that bright, wintergreen smell was, she'd just tell him his own wife suggested the salve.

Eyeing the Monday morning edition of the *Paradox Press*, she flipped through the pages until she landed on the "Letters to the Editor" section. There at the top was Renée's searing diatribe against medical marijuana and the dispensaries creeping into Paradox. Thanks to the digital age, one could write a letter on Saturday, email it and see it published on Monday. And given Renée's penchant for using high-strung volatility to get what she needed – not to mention having a friend who worked at the paper – it was no wonder the letter was given a bolded banner headline: LOCAL WOMEN'S GROUP SAYS 'JUST SAY NO' TO POT IN PARADOX! Betty scanned the letter counting how many times Renée overused exclamation points, and saw that the first name on the list at the end of the letter was "Elizabeth *Cragen*."

"For Lord's sake," Betty muttered to herself. Good proofreaders were becoming as rare as a bucktoothed rooster.

There was a soft knock on the door and Dr. Hancock appeared. "Hi, Betty."

"Hello, doctor," she said, forcing a weak smile.

"Christ, Betty. It's Roger."

Yes, of course it was Roger, Betty silently agreed. But that was fine for backyard soirées and Christmas parties. Formality was formality and the man hadn't diligently toiled to reach his position to be called anything but "Doctor" in her eyes.

He peered down at the newspaper in Betty's hands. "Ah, you saw Renée's letter!"

"I signed it, but the idiots spelled my last name wrong. Turned a 'v' into a 'g.'"

"They were probably stoned, huh? So, what's happening with the neck?"

Betty momentarily bristled at his terminology. "The neck" sounded like it wasn't even attached to her body. She precisely explained what she was feeling, down to the finest twitch. She was about to delve into further detail when he moved forward and began pushing his fingers and thumb into her neck. Betty let out a contained exclamation of pain.

"Sorry about that. How long has this been going on?"

"How long? Well, let's see, we moved from Houston in 1980..." She pondered a bit more. "It was definitely happening prior to that –"

"No. I mean recently. It hasn't been *this* bad for over thirty years has it?"

She wanted to answer the question correctly so as not to make herself appear too sickly or weak. "Well, no, not *this* bad. But I guess I'd have to say that I've had issues with my neck and tension since I was a child."

"Okay." He continued to push his thumb into her neck, not really interested in what she revealed. "It could be serious."

"Really?"

"I could run some tests. On the mild side, it could just be a spasm and on the other end, it could be structural and you might need surgery, given the length of time you've had the problem."

"*Surgery*? No, no, no. You know, there might be a connection somehow to the flutter I sometimes get in my right ear."

"Flutter?"

Oh, God, now she *was* starting to sound like she was falling apart. "A beating rhythm, like a –"

"Let's take a look," he interrupted, probing Betty's ear with an otoscope. "It appears that one of your ossicles is prominent. You could have had it since you were a child. Have you ever fallen on that ear or been hit on that side of the head?"

"No. No, thankfully that's one thing I have not experienced."

He stood back. "Uh-huh. Well, fixing that ossicle *will* require surgery."

This was getting to be far too much for her to absorb. "It comes and goes," she feebly offered, not wanting to sound like she was completely deteriorating. "But when it does come, it can keep me awake. Just like my neck spasms do –"

"How is your sleeping in general?"

"Oh, I sleep just like a baby. I wake up every two hours screaming," she deadpanned.

He regarded her with a confused expression. "Screaming, huh? Nightmares?"

It was a joke but come to think of it, yes, there were nightmares. The trivial ones had something to do with putting on a large party and running out of butter. But the worst nightmares were the ones she couldn't remember – the ones that left her cold and terrified and desperately alone.

"How long ago did Frank Sr. pass away?" he enquired.

The question came out of left field. "Just over three years ago, but –"

"Well, that's got to be a big part of your tension, right?" He leaned back on the examination table, clipboard in hand. "Anxiety? Depression?"

Betty wasn't ready for all this. "Yes."

"Both of them?"

"Hard to pin that down. It's more like anxiety wrapped in a crêpe of depression."

"Crêpe of depression? Never heard that one."

It was so much easier to see her mental issues personified in food. "Yes, well it's far more akin to a crêpe than a pancake. Does that make sense?"

"No. Not really."

"I can't really choose whether it's anxiety or depression. Why does it matter?"

"It matters because it will determine what medication I prescribe for it."

"But I'm not here for anxiety or depression. I came in for my neck –"

"I know. But it's important to cover all the bases." He brought out his prescription pad. "I'm going to start you on a generic anxiety drug. Perfectly safe. Just make sure you read through the insert regarding the side effects –"

"What about my neck?"

"I'm getting to that. I'm also prescribing a muscle relaxant. Same deal. Read the insert. You may experience dizziness, confusion, blurry vision, headaches, and insomnia. But all in all, it shouldn't be too bad."

"Insomnia? Wait, the neck spasms *cause* insomnia. This drug for the spasms might *give* me insomnia?"

Roger scratched another note on his prescription tablet. "We'll throw some Valium in the basket. Just don't overdo it. And check the –"

"Insert," Betty added. "Right." She wondered how many trip points to Maui Roger would earn from the pharmaceutical company thanks to her visit. "Mother's little helper," she said, trying her best to sound cheerful.

"What's that?"

"Valium. That's what they called it back in the day."

"I see. Okay, you can start the muscle relaxant right away. Take three a day and one before bedtime." He continued to rattle off how and when to take the Valium and anxiety drug. The pharmacy was located three stories down from his office so, as Roger said, Betty could "get on the program pronto."

Betty dutifully filled the prescriptions and popped the first muscle relaxant. She wasn't ready to commit to either the anxiety drug or the Valium. Within twenty minutes, she felt a slight lessening of her neck pain but an uneasy sense of detachment also set in. She pulled into one of the many burgeoning farmers' markets that filled the now empty mall parking lots outside of Paradox and figured a walk might help clear the disconnection. A half-hour later, with her plastic basket in hand filled with bags of organic lettuce, beets, cilantro and arugula, she felt somewhat better. She heard a discordant voice over a loudspeaker, abrasively insisting that people "wake the hell up" and "practice tolerance." Moving closer, Betty noted the banner above a folding table and chairs under a white umbrella. It read, COLORADO ACTIVISTS 4 NATIONAL TOLERANCE, whoever the hell they were. Betty bristled as she walked by the group, realizing what had once been a pleasantly provincial gathering of Colorado farmers, had now been ingloriously usurped by a liberal fringe element wearing homemade moccasins and tattered tank tops. "*Activists*," she murmured to herself. It was a label she deplored and seemed to unite those who had a bug up their ass with those who enjoyed too much free time.

Just as Betty returned her plastic basket to the stack and was quickly hastening her departure, her cell phone rang. She checked the Caller ID and saw it was Peggy's home phone number.

"Hello?" she said, a hint of apprehension in her voice.

"Hey, Betty?"

She didn't recognize the voice. "Who's this?"

"It's me. Peyton. We met yesterday?"

This was far too forward for Betty. "How did you get my cell number?"

"I called the number on the back of the box of chocolates from *The White Violet*, and it was forwarded to this number."

"Oh. Right. Yes. Why are you calling?"

"I'm sitting here with my aunt, and she'd like you to come over." A shrill bleat from one of the *Colorado Activists 4 National Tolerance* punctured the air. "What in the hell was that?" Peyton asked. "Where are you?"

"I'm attempting to escape a gaggle of misinformed liberals."

"Dude, that sounds totally treacherous. So, can you motor over here ASAP?"

Betty arrived on Peggy's doorstep fifteen minutes later. The muscle relaxant appeared to be in full swing as the nurse led Betty down the hallway toward Peggy's bedroom. Seated on one side of Peggy's bed was Peyton, while the elderly gentleman Betty noted the day before sat on her other side. The aura in the whole room felt completely different than it had just twenty-four hours prior. Peggy was softly talking to her nephew and even smiling. Gone was the struggle and moaning.

"Hey, hi there," Peyton softly said, motioning Betty closer.

She held back, a knee-jerk reaction she'd acquired over recent years.

Peggy slowly turned her head, and when she saw Betty standing helplessly in the doorway, smiled warmly. "You came over," she said, somewhat floating above the words but focused on Betty. "Thanks, sweetie."

Peyton stood up and waved Betty to his spot on the bed. "It's okay."

Betty sat on the bed. Her box of chocolates was covered. "Had a chocolate?"

"I did," Peggy sweetly replied, taking Betty's hand in hers. "They were spectacular as always."

"It's the honey," Betty said, feeling terribly ill-equipped for this impromptu visit. Peggy stared at her, a caring smile lingering on her face. A ball of emotion welled up in Betty's throat, which she valiantly tried to swallow. "I'm so happy to see you feeling better, darling." She turned to Peyton. Tears rolled freely down his young face. Looking at the elderly man, Betty introduced herself. But he kept his focus on Peggy.

Peyton leaned closer to Betty. "That's my grandpa," he whispered. "He doesn't talk much.

Peggy stroked Betty's hand. "It's so beautiful, Betty."

"What's beautiful?"

"Everything...it's all connected. It all makes sense now."

Betty cocked her head. "What makes sense, darling?"

"Life. Death. It's just a circle, isn't it? I understand it now. I just can't explain it with words. I don't think words are invented that can describe it. But it's there. And I feel like...like if I could dive into this moment and into the still-ness, it would all make sense. There's absolutely nothing to be afraid of. *Nothing.*"

Betty looked into Peggy's eyes. In all the years they'd known each other, she'd never seen her so at ease and filled with true contentment. "I think you've reached a turning point, darling. It's all up from here!" Betty felt that damned ball again in her throat.

Peggy chuckled and then broke into a soft laugh. "Yeah, you betcha. All up from here!" She stared off into the distance, a smile forming. "I'll be dancing tonight, Betty. I'm going to be free." A tear fell down her face, but it didn't come from sadness.

Betty leaned forward and kissed Peggy's cheek. "Fight the good fight, dear," she whispered.

"No. No more fighting," Peggy gently whispered back to her. "Just love."

Betty stood up, feeling a little unsteady. She wasn't sure if it was the muscle relaxant or the emotional toll she felt at that moment. "I love you, Peggy."

She made it into her car just before the floodgates opened. She sobbed uncontrollably for fifteen minutes. But somewhere within the grief, she knew her tears fell for the pain she'd held at bay far too long. Deep within that well of emotion, she wept for the weighty regret that boiled in her gut. Was life just a series of broken promises and neglected dreams, put to rest by a deathbed enlightenment of what living was really all about? Was this the way she would wind up her time on earth?

Betty was still contemplating this terrifying prospect later that evening, after her third muscle relaxant and clutching her first bourbon. In a slight haze, she was just about to pour her second drink of the night when the doorbell rang.

Chapter 7

"Didn't you read the insert?"

Betty opened the front door and was startled to see Peyton standing there. "What are you doing here?" The ice in her glass of bourbon clinked on cue.

"Aunt Peggy died two hours ago."

Betty felt her heart sink. She held onto the doorknob for support. "Oh, dear God..."

"You okay?" Peyton took a step closer.

"Yes...yes, of course, I'm fine..."she mumbled. Everything seemed foggy and discombobulated. She turned from the door and wandered into the living room, taking a seat at the dining room table.

Peyton walked in, gently closing the door behind him. He looked around the room, briefly fixating on several objects before returning his focus to Betty.

"Wait a minute," Betty said, still not all there. "How did you know where I lived?"

"I found your address on my aunt's Christmas card list. Did a MapQuest locator and motored over." He sat down across from her. "Seriously, dude. Are you okay?"

"God, why does everybody keep asking me that?"

"I don't know. You might want to explore that. How much have you had to drink tonight?"

"Oh, please. This is only the start of my second."

Peyton furrowed his brow and took a quick gander around the room. He spotted the white "Rx" prescription bag and the single orange tube lying next to it. Getting up, he checked the label. "Hey, Betty, how many of these did you take?"

"Two...no, wait...three."

"Didn't you read the insert? You're not supposed to drink when you take these. That's actually kinda dangerous." He quickly walked back to the table and grabbed the glass of bourbon from her hand.

"What in the hell are you doing?"

Peyton was already in the kitchen. Betty followed, gaining a modicum of mental precision but still faltering.

"I don't need to watch two people die today," Peyton casually said as he tossed the bourbon into the sink and set the glass on the counter.

"Hey, kid. You have a lot of nerve!" Betty noted that she was slurring her words. "You don't just come into someone's home and..." Her stomach heaved. "And..."

Peyton saw it coming before Betty had any clue. He pushed her toward the sink just in time. Without missing a beat, he rubbed Betty's back and grabbed a paper towel, handing it to her when she was done emptying her stomach into the polished sink.

Betty dabbed at her mouth, embarrassment plainly evident. "Oh, Lord sake," she whispered. She swished her mouth with water and spit it back into the sink.

"Nice kitchen," he commented.

Betty was still bent over the sink. "Thank you very much. Would you like to buy the house? I'll make you one helluva deal."

Peyton smiled, holding his hand protectively on Betty's back. "No. I'm good. I live with my grandfather. How you doin' there?"

Betty slowly stood up as her head spun. "You can cut off a dog's tail, but you can't sew it back," she mumbled.

"Huh? You sound delirious."

She leaned on the sink. "It's an old Texas saying I grew up with. It means think first before you make a bad mistake that can't be corrected."

"Hey, your doctor made the bad mistake of giving you those pills. You just didn't read the insert. The side effects are ridiculous! This might sound random, but by any chance is your doctor Canadian?"

Betty managed to lift her head to look at Peyton. "Canadian? I...I don't think so. Why?"

"I've had some bad luck with Canadians in my short life. I'm not really sure what it is. They just don't feel fully committed to their own existence, and they seem to project that onto others."

Betty considered his observation and smiled. "Is that right?"

"That's been my experience. Let's go in the living room and sit down." He led her back to the dining room table and helped her into a chair. "If you don't mind me asking, what happened to your teeth?"

Betty looked at him, confused. "Nothing happened to my teeth."

"You got veneers on them. Were you in an accident where your teeth got bashed in?"

"No! It was something I had done to improve my smile."

"Shit. You did that on *purpose*? Dude, how bad was it before?"

"You really are quite the charming fellow, aren't you? You don't have to stay with me. I'm fine."

"No worries. I'll hang for a bit." He scanned the living room again.

Betty gathered her thoughts. "Did...did Peggy suffer at all at the end?"

Peyton smiled and shook his head. "No, not at all. It was beautiful. I came here to tell you that *you* helped make that happen."

"Me?" Betty's head started to throb as a headache worked its way into her orbit.

"Aunt Peggy and I had always been tight, but the cancer made her pretty mean toward the end. And the pain...well, it was awful. She couldn't talk or focus enough to tell us what she needed. She'd been there for me when nobody else was, and I promised I'd be there for her, no matter what. She always accepted me for who I was even though I thought different."

"*Ly*," Betty corrected, holding her head in pain.

"Dude, you really *should* have read that drug insert. Confusion is another one of the many side effects." He leaned forward and touched her hand. "My name's Peyton, not *Lee*."

Betty peered at him through orbs that now pounded. "I know your name's Peyton! You said, 'different.' It's 'different-*ly*!'" Betty believed the only people who should be allowed to bastardize the English language were those who actually knew how to speak it. Everyone else shouldn't flaunt his or her ignorance. "You don't want to sound like a cretin, do you?"

"Depends if the cretin is worth knowin', I guess."

Betty was functioning on fumes. "Peyton, it's late. Is there something else I can do for you before I bid you goodnight?"

He paused, gathering his thoughts. "Your box of chocolates was the perfect delivery system. Aunt Peggy loved your candies, so I knew she'd eat one."

"What do you mean, 'delivery system?'"

"I melted one of your chocolates and added two good teaspoons of my cannabutter to it. After I hardened it up in the freezer I gave it to her, and she was none the wiser."

Betty wasn't sure if it was her pounding head or the lingering effects of the damned muscle relaxant tablet, but she wasn't following anything Peyton said. "You melted one of my chocolates and added canna...what?"

"Cannabutter. It's butter that's been steeped and cooked with cannabis buds. You know? Marijuana?"

Betty's jaw dropped. For a moment, she sat speechless. Then the realization of what he had done hit her like a square punch to the gut. "*How dare you!*" she yelled, and then quickly grabbed her head in pain. Gathering her scattered thoughts, she spoke with more modulation but rife with anger. "You defiled my chocolates with a *drug*?"

"It's a plant, Betty. And I take exception to the word, 'defile.' I *enhanced* them."

"It's an illegal drug!"

"It's not illegal for me. I got a medical marijuana card. And I got five patients I grow for. My paperwork is up to date and I'd be happy to show it to you −"

"Oh my God!" She gingerly got up from the table and made it to the credenza before she had to stop, due to the room spinning.

"Listen, this is a beautiful thing, Betty. Because of your chocolates and my cannabis addition, Aunt Peggy and I were finally able to connect for the last nine hours of her life. I'm eternally grateful to you for giving me that gift."

A horrifying thought crept up. "How do you know it wasn't the marijuana that killed her? Do you have any idea the kind of trouble you could put me in?"

"Are you serious, dude? You're, like, channeling a crazed character from *Reefer Madness*." He stood up, moving closer to her. "Betty, Google is your friend. Please use it and get educated. You're repeating gossip and hysteria and belief systems that are false. I've read the stats. Nearly eight thousand people die every year from aspirin. One hundred die from peanut allergies. Nobody has *ever* died from cannabis, which makes cannabis safer than peanuts. Ha! Put that on a bumper sticker!"

"Listen, kid, I don't need to hear your propaganda about how marijuana is legal and safe −"

"First off, the word *marijuana* should not be used. It's a Mexican slang term given to the cannabis plant by the U.S. government in the early 1920's to marginalize it. And if you want to talk about propaganda, it's not coming from me! The propaganda is coming from our own government, that − and here's some bold irony − currently holds at least one patent for the Cannabinoids in the cannabis plant which work as antioxidants and actually generate new brain cells. Makes you kinda wonder why they tell the public it's dangerous, addictive and has zero medical value on one side and then they tell their god, Big Pharma, that it's potentially life saving. Gee, follow the money trail and let's see where it leads!"

She held her head in pain. "I can't effectively argue with you at this moment −"

"Good! Because there's nothin' to argue about. I can't make up this shit, Betty. You gotta wake up and see where the propaganda is really coming from, hear the lies and taste the truth. Oh, and Colorado has an amendment to our state constitution that allows for legal use of medical grade cannabis. And yeah, cannabis *is* safe when you use the right strain at the right dose. It's a whole lot safer than that little cocktail of pills and booze that are still percolating through your bloodstream right now!"

Betty felt as if she were hanging on by her teeth. "Those pills and that bottle of bourbon are legal."

"Geez, Betty, are you not hearing me? So is the *medical* cannabis! It's just not culturally accepted by some individuals, so there's that damn stigma. But once people start researching it and stop buying into the bullshit lies, eventually it will be accepted. And, heads up, just because the almighty Feds have deemed pills and booze legal, doesn't make them safe! It just makes them available *to anyone* because the government says so and they can make a shitpot of profit from them."

"I'm not listening to this!" She attempted to move a few steps but her legs felt like rubber.

"But you *have* to listen!" He moved around to face her. "Don't you want to know the truth? I've memorized lots of stats for occasions just like this. Like more people died in 2008 from prescription painkillers than all the deaths that year from heroin and cocaine combined. And check this out, twelve *million* people admit to taking those painkillers *just* for the high." He paused momentarily to gather his thoughts. "Betty, you saw Aunt Peggy today. She was riding the wave when you visited with her. Did that look terrible to you? Or did that look peaceful and introspective?"

Another surge of realization sunk in. "Good God! You tainted my gourmet chocolates, and then you lured me there so I could sit with your aunt while she was stoned on them? Is this really happening? Wake me up from this nightmare!"

"Betty, Betty, Betty. Save the drama for the important stuff." He looked quizzical. "I don't get it. I'm pretty good at reading people. When I was watching you with Aunt Peggy, I didn't see the person I'm seeing right now. I saw your..." He stopped.

"Saw my what?"

"Your true essence. You know? In here?" He pointed to his heart. "And I'm tellin' you, it was not this hysterical, uptight woman I'm seeing right now."

"You obviously made a mistake in your assessment."

He looked at her for what seemed like an eternity. "No. My heart never lies to me. Maybe this essence I'm seeing is buried so deeply in you that –"

"For God's sake, Peyton. You're just making this up as you go along –"

He moved closer to her. "Why are you fighting your true nature? Why does it scare you so much? You've got a lot of power, Betty. Why are you suffocating it?"

Her head swam. That familiar tension began building in her neck. "I have no clue what you're talking about." The minute she said those words, they sounded like a lie. "You're trying to manipulate me, and it's not going to work."

He shook his head. "I'm not manipulating you. I'm speaking to you from my heart to yours. Open your mind to the possibility that cannabis is not the evil monster you've been told to be afraid of. Hey, how about this? Henry Ford saw the value in the hemp plant. He even built an entire car out of it."

"Is that so? When he put the key in the ignition, did he have a hard time firing it up due to the car's lack of motivation?"

"Yeah, yeah. Again, you're just parroting what you've heard. Look, an *Indica* strain will mellow you out, but a buzzy *Sativa* will get you so motivated you'll clean the house, mow the lawn and do five loads of laundry before sundown."

Betty looked at him aghast. "I cannot believe I am participating in this conversation right now."

Peyton walked over to the "Rx" bag and dumped the orange prescription bottles on the dining room table.

"What in the hell are you doing?"

"Let's see, you got your muscle relaxant....oh, a little anti-anxiety drug...and Valium. Guess what? Certain strains of cannabis are antispasmodic, reduce anxiety and help you sleep. One strain can fit all three of these!" He held up the bottles. "And if you use it in the right way at the right time, it won't fuck you up like you are right now."

Betty's back went up. "And you know this how?"

"Because I've been using cannabis for almost nine years, every single day. I wake and vape, Betty. I am one with the THC and CBD and they are one with me."

"Oh, Christ. You're high right now?"

"'High' is such a subjective word. It's in my system at this moment, yeah. But I'm able to function. I'm not into getting toasted. And I'm not out there ripping off car stereos. Don't be harshin' my mellow and call me a stoner, Betty. They exist, but I ain't one of them and I never will be. There's a huge difference between the typical stoner dude and the person who's using this herb strictly for medical reasons. A stoner dude blazes as much weed as he can until he hits the Sky Box, totally blotto, goonin', bent and stuck on stupid. But a medical cannabis dude takes the smallest amount possible to kill his pain and still be able to function. Can you tell which of those dudes I am?" He moved closer to her. "And here's another pet peeve. I actually hate it when medical cannabis patients call the herb 'medicine' or say they're gonna go 'medicate.' Cannabis is a plant. Terms like 'medicine' and 'medicating' makes it sound like it's just another Big Pharma drug. I prefer to say, 'I'm going to take my herb' because it reminds me that this *is* still a plant and not a pill." He put a reassuring hand on her arm. "Betty, cannabis can help a lot of people. *Really* help them. Pain, anxiety, insomnia, just to name three." He pulled out a dining room chair and sat down. "Here's what I'm thinking, Betty. Pay attention. I'll teach you how to grow the plant and how to add it to your chocolates. I can set you up with some patients – people I know that would love to have someone like you growing for them and making them quality edibles."

Betty's jaw dropped for the second time that night. "You really *are* stoned right now if you believe that's going to happen. Why in God's good name would you think I would *ever* be open to such an enterprise?"

"Simple. Out of the gate, you're a prize-winning gardener and an incredible cook. Right there, you have the talent needed in spades. But you've also got something else. You've got heart. You're a natural caregiver. I saw it when you were talking to my aunt today. You *really* care. There's no faking that. And I think helping people makes you feel..." He searched for the right word. "Useful."

Betty looked at him, stunned. How in the hell could some kid who used marijuana every day have this kind of insight into the way she operated?

"And when you don't feel useful," Peyton continued, "you lose your purpose in life. And that's a dangerous place for any of us to go."

Through the haze of the pills and bourbon, Betty found herself in agreement with Peyton. But the second she felt the concurrence, she stiffened. "No. This goes against everything I've ever —"

"You can also use a little extra cash," he quickly added.

Betty tossed him a snobbish glare. "I beg your pardon. Does this look like the home of someone who is in need?"

"Yes. Actually, it screams it. Over on that table where you're leaning —"

"It's not a table. It's a credenza."

"Whatever. I saw the outline of two candlestick holders that had probably been occupying that space for years. And over there," he pointed to where the antique chair used to sit, "you didn't vacuum out the grooves enough where that chair used to be."

"I moved the candlesticks, and the chair is out for repair."

He peered at her from his seat at the table. "Nah. I don't buy it. You're too defensive when you say it. Your garden out front is lush and your house feels thin. I can almost feel the dining room table trembling, wondering if it's the next to go on the auction block."

Betty wasn't about to give in. "You have a very potent imagination, young man."

"That sweater you wore yesterday? You kept messing with the cuff. You know, the one that was unraveling?"

She remained stoic. "So what?"

"It's just another piece of your puzzle that gives you away. You carry yourself with a lot of pride. Somebody like that would have a different sweater to go with every outfit, and they'd never have one that had a cuff unraveling. They'd throw that one out or keep it to wear around the house. But you wore it and you tried to hide the cuff. You don't want people to think you'd wear something that was unraveling... maybe 'cause you're unraveling?"

Betty stared at him, taken aback.

"You know what?" he continued, "under the surface, we're all unmade beds searching for the perfect comforter." He watched her intently. "I'm not trying to embarrass you, okay? I want to help you because you helped give me my aunt back, and nobody can ever take that away. She never would have eaten the cannabis, but *your* chocolates were the clincher." He dug into his jeans' pocket that still hung precariously low on his waist. "And I already know that others will feel the same." He handed her a wad of money.

"What in the hell is this?"

"I only had to give Aunt Peggy one of the chocolates. I took the rest and melted them down, added the right amount of cannabutter and ended up with forty-two pieces. I had 'em sold within hours to my patients. There's four hundred and twenty bucks there. I didn't take a cut. It's all yours."

Betty handed the money back to him. "I would never accept drug money."

He pushed the cash back to her. "It's not drug money, Betty. I have legal patients on record with the state of Colorado who bought these from me, and I'm just handing that cash over to you."

"Patients? So now you're a doctor?"

"I'm a caregiver. It's the name they've come up with for people like me who grow for five people who don't want to go to dispensaries because they want more control over how their medicine is grown. Hey, given an option, I'd call them my 'peeps,' or 'my dudes.' But as it stands now with the state, I'm the caregiver and they're my patients."

Betty stood there, clutching the cash and feeling adrift.

"You know, Betty, a lot of people think that what Colorado is doing with cannabis is a sign of the cultural apocalypse. But I respectfully disagree. I'd say it was more akin to an evolution of consciousness when you wake up and realize you've been misinformed about this magnificent plant. Hey, if you're so worked up about dangerous plants, you better get rid of the Belladonna and the Digitalis I saw in your front yard. Oh, and the Angel's Trumpet too. Pull that sucker out of the ground. That's a crazy-making plant. Back in 2003, this German dude drank some Angel's Trumpet tea and cut off his penis and his tongue with a pair of garden shears." Peyton crossed his legs. "As far as this whole deceptive campaign about cannabis is concerned, I look on it as an epic battle between the sacred and the profane. It's the sacredness of the herb and the profane disinformation foisted upon the people who believe whatever they hear."

Betty placed the wad of cash on the credenza and opened the center drawer. "It's not just what I hear, Peyton. It's what I've personally experienced." Rooting through the drawer, she removed a small, framed photo. "That's my son, Frankie. He died in 2005 of a massive drug overdose. And it all started for him with marijuana."

Peyton intently studied the photo. In it, nineteen-year-old Frankie stood by a Colorado stream, staring off into the distance. "The cannabis didn't kill him Betty."

"He never would have started harder drugs if it weren't for marijuana. It was the gateway." Her voice shook with emotion.

"Oh, come on, Betty. Give me a break. I hate that whole 'gateway' crap. He needed to escape from something.

Something awful. If it wasn't drugs, it would have been alcohol. My cannabis use has never made me want to build a meth lab or light up a crack pipe." Peyton continued to probe the photo. "He was a lost soul, reaching out for something that would make him feel a temporary sense of peace. Hey, did you notice the doobie he's got between his fingers in this photo?"

Betty rolled her eyes. "Yes."

"What's that red stuff over his hand?"

"The head of the eraser I used to try and buff out the marijuana joint."

Peyton focused his attention back to Betty. "Wow. Okay. So, that's why you keep this in the drawer? 'Cause you don't want your friends to see it? It's a nice photo. I'd find new friends and display the photo." He handed it back to Betty.

She carefully tucked it back into the drawer. "You know, Peyton, you're not stupid. You have a lot of potential. If you spent half your time doing something that was more acceptable...more conventional...there's no telling how far you'd go."

"Gosh, Betty. If I did that, how would I find the time to grow cannabis?"

Betty looked at him like a stern schoolmarm. "You know what I mean."

"Conventional, huh? That ain't me. I march to the beat of a different banjo."

"You mean 'drum.'"

"Nope. I mean banjo. If I did anything conventional, wouldn't I just keep perpetuating more of the same mind numbing, insipid crap that keeps us all in the same fuckin' loop? No thanks, Betty. Hey, is this the way you used to lecture Frankie?"

"You keep my son out of this."

Peyton stood up. "Why?"

"He's a very sensitive subject for me."

"All the more reason to talk about him. And put out his photo. No reason to keep him in the drawer...in the shadows. You're not ashamed of him, are you?"

Ire welled up. "Of course, not! He was a wonderful boy who had tremendous –"

"Potential," Peyton quickly added. "Yeah, I know. Some of us take that potential, and if we're allowed to, we create ideas and build things that challenge the status quo. If your idea of 'potential' is just barfing up the same bullshit, count me out. And my guess is that Frankie looked at life the same way."

Betty shot him a hard stare.

"Don't tell me that idea hasn't crossed your mind, Betty. If you're not allowed to do or be whatever you need to be in this life, you get self-destructive." He took another look around the room and then returned his attention to her. "You know exactly what I'm talking about. This place is your cell. And you're the prisoner. But you're also your own jailer, too. You have the keys to break out. You just forgot where you put them."

Betty turned away from him.

He pulled out a crumpled receipt from his pocket, flipped it over and jotted down his phone number and address. "That's my info if you want to talk."

Betty turned over the receipt. "The Flying Pig Dispensary?"

"Yeah, that's one of my two jobs outside of my grow op. You know how people said that cannabis would be legal when pigs could fly?"

"Ah, and the Flying Pig was born," she said, shaking her head.

"I also work at Grow Do It, a grow store. Growers call it 'Grow Doobie.' My boss is a tool but I get twenty percent off lights and shit, so I suck it up." He headed toward the front door. "Hey, you know what I'd do if I had a lot of money? I'd buy an airplane and skywrite 'Why not?' all day long. And I'd hope that somebody would look up, see it, understand it and then change their life for the better."

~~~

Later that night, curled in bed with Ronald snoozing at her feet, Betty still couldn't shake Peyton's visit. She determined that his well meaning, yet insane proposition, was a passing impulse, brought on by the shock of his aunt's death. He was a nice boy, she decided, but certainly not tuned into the practicalities of life. Then again, his acute, candid observations seemed quite perceptive and dreadfully accurate.

The pills still made her woozy and ill at ease. She flipped on the TV to PBS, and through foggy eyes, watched the last fifteen minutes of *Nature*. The show was about a female insect somewhere in the world that spent every waking moment struggling for survival for herself and her offspring. She had to fight other, more formidable insects for food to bring back to her young, who constantly cried out for more. Finally, after the struggle reached a crescendo, her offspring left the nest, and cued by her DNA, she promptly died. Betty wasn't sure if it was the loopiness of the pills still churning in her body, but she found this segment sad and perverse. She began to blubber and would have continued if the phone hadn't rung. It was 10:00 – far past the acceptable time to call someone unless it was an emergency.

In her stupor, she forgot to check the Caller ID before answering. "Hello?"

"Hiya! Is this Betty Craven?" The male voice on the other end was unfamiliar and superficially overconfident.

"Who is this?" It was all she could do to maintain mental equilibrium.

"*Tom!* Tom Reed! I got your number from Judi Hancock. She said she mentioned me to you at some powwow over the weekend at your house?"

Powwow? In her uncertain state, Betty flashed for a second on herself dressed in Native garb, smoking a peace pipe around a fire. "Uh, yes...right...Tom Reed, I'm –"

"She thinks you and I should get together for drinks. How's tomorrow look for you? Five o'clock at The Phoenix?"

"Well, Tom, I really am not –"

"Hang on a second. Let's make that five thirty. I've got a tennis game that might go a little late."

In any other state of being, Betty could have cobbled together a reasonable excuse for not accepting his invitation. But it was all she could do at that moment to sit upright and focus. "The Phoenix?"

"Yeah! It's a nice little retro, sixties joint over at Franklin and Fifth Street. They don't mind if people linger there."

It sounded as if Mr. Tom Reed was all too familiar with how The Phoenix rolled. "Tom, I appreciate —"

"One second. Gotta another call comin' in. See you at five-thirty tomorrow!"

And with that, he hung up. Betty was so out of it she kept holding the phone to her head for another minute, not quite sure what had just transpired. Finally, the sound of the elm branch scratching at the bedroom window brought her back into the moment. And while she couldn't be certain, she sensed Frankie's presence nearby and a swell of agitation engulfing him.

Chapter 8

*"One never gets a second chance
to make a good first impression."*

Morning came far too soon with a pounding headache for added misery. Betty's neck still felt stiff, but a long shower with the pulsating showerhead thankfully lessened the tension.

As she dressed for the day, she recalled the late night phone call from Tom Reed and half-wondered if she dreamed it. When she realized it actually happened, she checked the Caller ID to retrieve his phone number and figure out a way to wrangle out of the engagement. But all she found was a glaring "PRIVATE" instead of his number. She could call Judi and get his number, but she knew that Judi would harangue her into accepting Tom's invitation for drinks. That familiar sense of being cornered reared up again. But this time... *this time* a gurgling sense of resentment accompanied it. This was new, and Betty wasn't quite sure if it was appropriate. She sat on her bed and waited for the sensation to pass but it didn't. In fact, it grew wings and began to zip up and down her body like a hummingbird powered on jet fuel.

Her neck tightened, her jaw clenched and that damned flutter in her ear resumed. She looked at Ronald as he turned onto his back and yawned before embarking on another marathon napping session. Oh to be a cat like Ronald, and not have to deal with this crap, sounded deliriously divine at that moment. The sound of footsteps on the roof brought Betty out of her rancor. It was Buddy and it was Tuesday and this was totally unexpected.

"Buddy?" she called, after walking outside and seeing him perched on the roof above the kitchen.

"How's your neck, Mrs. Craven?"

"Better. I wasn't expecting you today. I thought you had your day job!"

"I do. But the code inspector showed up and everything came to a grinding halt. I had a couple hours to kill, so I thought I'd come over here and work a bit."

Betty was touched that the big buffoon would think of her, when he could have easily chewed up the time taking a nap in his truck or staring into space. She spied the wad of cash Peyton gave her, still sitting on the credenza where she'd left it. That could certainly be used to pay Buddy part of what she owed him. But no, that was still ill-gotten funds in Betty's eyes. She quickly hid the tainted cash in the center drawer of the credenza and flashed on the one hundred and fifty-two dollar consignment check for her beloved antique chair. It certainly wouldn't cover all of what she owed Buddy, but she felt it was only fair to pay him something for his commitment to her deteriorating roof. After writing him a check for one hundred and fifty dollars, she advised him that the funds would be available by the end of the day. Hoisting the flag outside, she returned inside to grab her purse and leave for the bank when the front doorbell rang.

She opened the door to find Peyton. He wore the same loose fitting jeans and a new t-shirt that sported the phrase, "Doobie Douggie says 'It's just a plant, man.'" This morning was quickly turning into one unpredictable parade of people.

"Hey, Betty," Peyton said, much more reserved than he was the previous night.

"Peyton. I'm just leaving –"

"I just wanted to come over and apologize if I overstepped my boundaries with you last night."

"Regarding the mari...uh, cannabis?"

Peyton furrowed his brow. "No. Not that. I mean about your son, Frankie. That's none of my business."

Betty regarded the boy and how thin he appeared. "Have you had breakfast?"

"Huh?"

"You look skinny. You want something to eat?"

He smiled and wagged his finger at her. "You see, Betty? This is what I was talkin' about last night. You are the poster girl of caregivers. I'm surprised you don't take in stray animals."

"I can't do that. Ronald is too old to handle either the stress or the rivalry," she replied with complete sincerity. "Breakfast?" She waved him inside.

He walked in, closing the door behind him. "I'll take a rain check." He peered out her front window. "Hey, your garden's even prettier in the daylight. You really *do* know what you're doing. Most of your flowers are two or three weeks ahead of everybody else's."

"Well, I have my little gardening secrets I've perfected over the years."

"See, that's the difference between regular gardening and my kind of gardening. Those of us who grow and enjoy the herb, freely share our organic brews and compost tea recipes. It's not about competition, you know? It's about spreading the knowledge. The more people involved, and the more creativity and innovation, just moves the entire grow process into a whole new realm of unity."

"You're high again, aren't you? Or you're a Communist. Proprietary secrets are there to protect one's creation."

"We're talking about how to make a flower bigger, not some patented surgical technology. If you keep all your little gardening secrets to yourself, who does that benefit? Wouldn't you rather drive down this street and see everybody's yard looking like yours, instead of the way it looks now? Like a nuclear horticultural holocaust hit your neighborhood and your house is the only one that survived?"

Betty couldn't argue with his assessment of her neighbor's perplexing lack of botanical acumen. "I really do need to get going, Peyton –"

He stood in front of the door. "I'll cut to the chase. There are a lot of smart, innovative people out there who grow cannabis. It's not all a bunch of burned out stoners and hippies. Some of these guys know more about botany and the complex structure of the cannabis plant than any

professor out there. There's a shit load to know about growing the herb. You don't just pop the seed in the ground and
walk away."

"You call it an 'herb?' You're not growing chives,
sweetheart."

"But it *is* an herb. And it *is* medicine. Hey, you can't grow
Valium or Prozac –"

Betty heard Buddy's footsteps walking across the roof
and descending the ladder. "You can't be talking about this
in front of Buddy."

Peyton smiled. "*Buddy?* Your roofer dude's name is Buddy? *Bud?* Don't you see? It's like a sign from God."

"Back in Houston, my next door neighbor was Mary
Jane Blunt. Was that a sign, too?"

Buddy rapped on the windowpane, pointing toward the
bathroom off the kitchen. Betty smiled nervously and waved
at him, motioning him to come around the back. She took
Peyton's arm and moved him further into the living room.

"I appreciate your wanting to help me, Peyton," she
whispered. "But this is not something I can do."

"Why are you whispering? Betty, you're acting like it's
some back alley deal. It's not. It'll all be above board. First,
you'll get your red card – your medical marijuana card – so
you can legally grow for yourself and five other people. You'll
designate yourself to be a caregiver –"

Betty backed into the credenza. "Peyton, for God's sake!
You don't know me. You don't know who I am and what I
believe."

"Actually, I think I *do* know you. I wouldn't have come
back here today if I didn't know that in my heart. The problem here is I don't think *you* know who you are. Maybe what
you believe is wrong? Maybe you're holding onto beliefs that
aren't even your own? Maybe you should do some research?"
He stopped, realizing he was overpowering Betty. "Hey, I
want to talk to that person inside of you – the one who's
stored away but maybe can still hear me. Cannabis is more
than just THC. It has this stuff called CBD in it. CBD is
non-psychoactive and *cannot* get you high. What it *can* do is

reduce anxiety, melt away pain, reduce nausea and seizures, and protect against nerve damage, especially in the brain. Some people even think it can stop cancerous tumors from spreading. There are growers out there right now who are cross breeding various strains of cannabis, in order to make the perfect CBD-rich strain with low THC. When that happens, it's going to revolutionize the way people look at cannabis. The proof will be too obvious, and they won't be able to marginalize the herb as 'just something stoners do.' This is groundbreaking stuff, Betty. We could work together and you could be part of something that could literally change the way people deal with their pain and anxiety." He turned and looked at the credenza. "You still got your son in the drawer?"

"Yes."

"You ever talk to him?"

Betty was nonplussed. "Excuse me?"

"Okay. I read that as a 'yes.' What do you think your kid would say if you asked him about this?"

"You must be joking. He was a drug addict. What do you think he'd say?"

"I don't know. Why don't you ask him?"

"This conversation is making no sense." She walked past him. "Please, Peyton. I really *do* need to go."

"Me too. Let me walk you out to my car."

After locking the front door, Betty cautiously followed Peyton to his silver Prius. Sitting in the front seat was a gentle, grey haired woman who appeared to be in her late seventies. He opened the passenger door and helped her out of her seat.

"Betty, this is Gladys. She's one of my patients."

Betty tried her best not to look shocked. Gladys was slightly stooped over, moved carefully and could be the archetype of anybody's grandmother, not the epitome of someone who used cannabis. Extending her hand, she remembered her manners. "Pleased to meet you, Gladys. Betty Craven."

"Nice to meet you too, Betty," Gladys replied with a soft voice, her cherubic face brightening. "We're on our way to the grocery store."

Peyton explained that he helped out his patients whenever they needed a drive to the doctor's office, market, etc. Betty listened, but was still trying to envisage this darling, elfin woman chomping down on a cannabis brownie. Something about that seemed quite bizarre, and yet there she was. Gladys seemed happy as a clam and quite in touch with her surroundings. Betty surreptitiously checked closer for any telltale glassiness in Gladys' aging eyes, but came up empty.

The conversation quickly veered onto "the herb." Gladys put her hand on Betty's arm. "My blood pressure has dropped to almost normal since I began medicating."

Betty needed to check herself. Here they were, standing in the bright sunlight, discussing how marijuana was such a hit. Weren't these discussions usually done in the shadows of night, on dirty streets between men with sketchy background checks?

"Have you tried his cannabis hand oil?" Gladys asked Betty.

"No, darling, I have not."

"Oh, it's the best around!" She held up her hands. "I rub it on my joints three times a day and now I can actually open a pickle jar." She leaned forward. "At first, I got a little buzzy on it. But now, I'm quite used to it."

Her neighbor across the street, Jerry, emerged from his house and called out to Betty. "Hey, Betty! I saw the letter to the editor in the paper yesterday! That's your group, right?"

Betty felt her stomach lurch. She waved her best royal wave toward Jerry, followed by a thumbs-up. "Yes," was all she could manage.

"Well, you got my support!" Jerry yelled across the street, as he pumped his fist into the air. "Gotta keep the riff-raff stoners out of Paradox!"

Gladys looked around the front yard. "Beautiful yard, dear. Where are you growing your herb?"

Betty felt faint. "I'm *not* growing!"

"Really?" Gladys asked innocently. "Why ever not? With a green thumb like yours, your buds would be bodacious!"

Was this really happening? Betty wondered. Had the world gone mad? Peyton quickly interjected that Betty was a "newbie" but he had high hopes for her. Helping Gladys back into the front seat, he casually walked with Betty to her car.

She maintained a plastic smile for Gladys' sake, even though they were out of her earshot, as she spoke quietly to Peyton. "I know what this is all about. You brought her over here to try to manipulate and trick me."

"Maybe a little manipulation but no tricks," he assured her. "And I admire your ability to remain gracious, even though I knew it would be outside your comfort zone."

"One never gets a second chance to make a good first impression."

"You see?" He said, smiling. "Talent, sensitivity and courteousness. You're like the whole package, Betty!" He gently patted her shoulder before turning back to his Prius. "Hey, what letter was that dude talking about?"

Betty looked at Gladys tucked into the front seat and then to Peyton with his easygoing smile. "It's nothing. Nothing at all."

Chapter 9

"If the world were your oyster, who would be your pearl?"

After depositing the consignment check in her bank account, Betty started back home when her cell rang. It was Judi. She could have ignored the call, but she was still quietly seething from the ad hoc matchmaking Judi conceived behind her back.

"Hi, Judi." Betty purposely modulated her voice to show affection caramelized with a sprinkling of irritation.

"Hey, Betty! I just wanted you to know how proud I am of you!"

"Proud? Why are you proud?"

"I heard through the grapevine that you and Tom Reed are hooking up for drinks tonight at The Phoenix! Good for you, honey."

Well, for Lord's sake, Betty fumed. She must have missed the breaking news of her tête-à-tête on the local morning broadcast. Privacy was of utmost importance to her and to have her evening plans summarily advertised like some low-rent garage sale was more than Betty could handle at the moment. "Yes, Judi, about that –"

"I know it's baby steps, but it's a start! And I've heard he's really a stand up guy! I bet you and Tom will be like two peas in a pod!"

"Hang on." She pulled the Taurus into a parking spot. "If you've only *heard* that he's a stand up guy, how on earth could you fathom that we'd be like two peas in a pod?"

"Honey, I'm talking about on *paper*, you know? He's got all the things you need on paper. Just like you and Frank, Sr. did!"

Betty's mouth went dry. Her jaw tightened and popped.

"Did I lose you?" Judi asked.

Betty tried to quell the blood that was boiling in her veins. "No. I'm right here. I'm in a bit of a dither, right now. Every time I stand up, my mind sits down."

"What?"

Betty realized she unexpectedly discharged an old Texas saying. "I can't think clearly at the moment," she translated.

"Don't you worry one bit, Betty. There's nothing to be nervous about! I know you and Tom are going to hit it off. Gotta run, sweetie! Call me tomorrow and let me know how it went!"

Judi hung up before Betty had a chance to utter a word. She suddenly felt like a croquet ball, being batted around at everyone's whim except her own. It seemed to Betty that Judi had her future planned to a tee. She was probably already arranging the nuptials between Betty and Tom, buying bathroom towels with "R" sewn into them and drooling over the open bar at their wedding reception.

Marriage. Like all of her high school girlfriends, she used to wonder whose gold band she would wear. She romanticized about her future and the life she would lead as someone's wife. She bought into the fables and fantasies but then reality struck hard, and she developed a dispiriting mindset. In Betty's mind, marriage followed a certain pattern. You start out as whole people with energy and determination and dreams. Then regret, lies, anger, resentment, and all the other pillars of destruction chip away at the relationship until at the ten year point, you look at each other to see what's left standing. If there's a modicum of love left, you continue the assault. If there's a child involved, you carry on and stick it out. But then the years melt into each other and one day, you realize you can't remember who you were in the beginning. It's as if that person who once existed belongs to another lifetime. You melted into your partner, and he's melted into you; you've lost your core, but you can't make a move because you're numb and dead inside. You stop caring because it takes too much effort. And so you drift together, bumping into each other like wayward ships with no captain.

Then one of you dies, and as the one left standing, you have holes inside so deep it would take another fifty years to find the beginning of them. You are demolished. You have more years behind you than in front. But you still get up and go about the day. You smile and play the game. The wish to get all those burned years back is too much. So you keep pushing those thoughts away, because you know if you keep focused on it, you'll realize you have no one to blame but yourself.

Her neck tightened almost on cue, and she searched through her purse to uncover "Mama's Muscle Mojo." It was only two days old and it was halfway gone. There weren't many jars of the stuff on the shelf at Jeff's store, and she didn't want to run out. That's what she kept telling herself anyway, as she turned the Taurus around and headed to the "Hippie Dippie Health Food Store."

The store was buzzing with shoppers when she arrived. That clean, citrus scent greeted her, along with the calming classical interludes playing softly in the background. For some reason, the place felt like an odd refuge for Betty. It wasn't an establishment she'd have frequented in the past. But everyone who worked there looked so happy, healthy and carefree. Perhaps all those fresh juices really were putting the life back into them. Or maybe it was a trickle-down effect from their boss.

With that thought, Betty took a gander around the store, but Jeff was nowhere to be seen. Walking up and down the aisles, she took her time checking out all the locally made products, amazed that so many people had the courage to put themselves out there with such boldness in this stale economy. She worked her way over to where "Mama's Muscle Mojo" was located and found a single jar left on the shelf. It was the most successful sensation she'd felt that entire morning. Securing it in her hands, she turned and nearly ran into Jeff.

"Oh, my goodness!" Betty exclaimed.

"You've run out of the first jar already?" he said with a playful smile.

Betty felt a strange tremor in her chest. It was some-where between a shiver and a hot poker plunging into her sternum. "Um, I, ah…"

"You okay, Betty?"

The quaking seemed to worsen. "Yes, of course…" She feared she was going to have a heart attack but felt no numbness down her left arm. It was more like a fuse inside her had just been lit, but she wasn't aware she had a fuse to ignite. "I should have eaten a more substantial breakfast this morning."

"Oh, come on. Don't 'should' all over yourself. Let me get you something," he said, heading toward the juice bar.

"Oh, no, no, no. I –" she countered, helplessly following him.

"It's on me, Betty. We'll concoct a nice kale, beet, apple and carrot blend that'll raise your blood sugar. I'll throw in some astragalus and chlorella to bolster your immune system."

Before Betty could refuse, she was seated at the juice bar, and Jeff was busy behind the counter loading a juicer with all the ingredients.

"How long have you been involved in…all this?"

"You mean natural health? Oh, most of my adult life. I've always been fascinated by how plants and herbs can bring back balance in the body. Before I opened my first little store back in California, my brother and I started an organic lawn and landscape business. We called it 'Rake-y Masters – Esoteric Lawn Care.' We didn't just mow your lawn, we healed it. Even after transitioning to the health and wellness business, I've still maintained a fairly large organic garden on my property."

Betty felt the need to tweet her credentials. "I grow flowers. I've won quite a few blue ribbons for them over the years. I've even had recognition for some of the more or-dinary plants that don't get the judge's attention. Like my asters. I've been told my asters are quite spectacular."

Jeff stifled a smile. "Yeah, I bet your asters are beautiful." A gentle twinkle danced in his eye. "I saw your letter to the editor," he turned on the juicer as a loud buzzing ensued. "They spelled your name wrong!" he yelled over the din.

She leaned forward, attempting to be discreet. "How'd you know that was me?"

"I'm not stupid, Betty. Why'd you write 'Elizabeth' and not 'Betty?'"

"Formality."

"Really? I usually save formality for legal documents, not letters to the editor. Unless I want to obscure my name so people might not know I signed the letter."

"Well, that wasn't my intention." The minute she said that, she began to wonder if it actually was her intention. "And anyway, I had no control over the fact that they hired a dyslexic proofreader."

"Aw, don't take the misspelling too seriously. When I opened up this store, they came and did an article on the place. Took a photo of me outside. When I read the caption, instead of Jeff Carroll, it read Jeff Carrot. I figured it was an interesting, symbiotic mistake, since we do have a juice bar. I just chalked it up to a subconscious error on the part of the caption writer." He turned off the juicer and handed her the glass of frothy goodness.

Betty felt the need to explain her informal group. "We're not an organized association or anything. More like a grass-roots gathering."

He leaned on the counter. "I wouldn't use the term 'grassroots' if you're trying to stop medical pot dispensaries."

Betty couldn't help but smile. She took a sip of the thick concoction. It was sweet and yet so pure and healthy tasting. "I've never drunk anything like this."

"That's feeding your bloodstream right now. Flushing out toxins and reinvigorating your senses." He was earnest without taking himself too seriously.

"Thank you very much." She suddenly felt like a kid at an old-fashioned ice cream counter, batting her eyelashes at the soda jerk.

"You're welcome very much, Elizabeth *Cragen*." He moved around the counter and perched on the stool next to her. His auburn ponytail drifted around his shoulder. "So, how's that sick friend of yours doing?"

"She...she died last night."

There was a thoughtful pause. "I'm sorry to hear that."

"It wasn't unexpected," she replied, her trained elocution evident.

"Yeah, but it still hurts, right?"

She admired Jeff's ability to be so forthcoming. It was both refreshing and disarming. "Death and I are not anonymous bedfellows, but given the opportunity, I'd kick Death off the mattress."

Jeff looked at her perplexed. "Well, that's a long way around the barn to say you're scared of death."

She took another soothing sip. "It's not so much my death that concerns me. It's the loss of others I have a hard time with."

"You can change that, Betty. You can embrace death just like you embrace life."

She raised a judgmental eyebrow. "I don't know about that one. How can I embrace death if I can't..." She caught herself.

"When you can't what?"

What in the hell was in this green concoction? Betty felt as if she was drunk, without the wooziness or detachment. Her mind spun and before she could censor herself, she finished her sentence. "When I can't embrace life."

He leaned forward and smiled. "Wow. You just had yourself a moment there. Very cool to see that. I think it's the beets talking." He rested his hand on her arm.

Suddenly, that damned tremor erupted again inside her. What was going on? She was never this forthcoming. *Never.* Perhaps those damned muscle relaxants were still affecting her judgment and loosening her lips. "I need to go," she stammered. "I'll just go pay for the, uh..."

"Salve?"

"Yes. Right. The salve. Good stuff, by the way. Give Mama my compliments when you see her next."

Still trembling, Betty made her way to the front cash register, and fumbling with her purse, checkbook and driver's license, paid the young girl, before quickly dashing from the store. She was so flustered, she even forgot to say a prayer to the automotive god, but her old Taurus started up like a pro.

Once safely home, she grounded herself in the garden. She even removed her gloves and plunged her hands into the warm dirt, covering them like a blanket and letting them linger there. Betty felt herself steadily calm down and her breathing return to normal. It was all the mounting anxiety about her situation, she told herself. Although, she'd never in her life felt such an overwhelming vibration overtake her body. With her hands still buried under the cool earth, a sudden memory flickered. It was so quick, she might have missed it had she not been quiet and anchored to the soil. Yes, she had felt this exact sensation a long time ago.

She was six years old and standing alone in the center of the merry-go-round during recess. Jeremy Lindholm, a second grader, jumped on and pronounced his love for her. He then told her he was about to kiss her one hundred times on the cheek. Fortunately, the boy hadn't yet learned to count past fifty so he lost track early on. But Betty was smitten by his bold move. And even after the horn-rimmed, stern schoolteacher snatched little Jeremy off the merry-go-round and dragged him to the principal's office, he still had the cheekiness to turn around and toss Betty a roguish wink. That's when the shudder first coursed through her body. It wasn't just that she liked him; it was that he was brave enough to roam outside the predictable expectations of both his fellow seven-year-old buddies and the school's ridiculously stringent rules.

He wasn't what she was told to admire. His father was an Interstate truck driver and his mother took in sewing to make ends meet. He wasn't a good reader and his spelling was filled with backward letters. But he seemed so genuine and free-spirited and Betty couldn't resist him. Even at six years old she knew she could help him be a better student, and if she could do that, she could possibly convince her parents he was a good boy and someone they would allow her to love.

But none of that ever happened. Fettered by the velvet shackles of expectation, Betty was sternly admonished to stay away from Jeremy and to present herself in such a way that would not entice "lowlife losers" who were hopelessly dim-witted. And so she did as she was told. But that didn't stop her from observing Jeremy across the schoolyard at lunch or peering around a corner as his mother picked him up from school in a battered truck. The tickle in her heart still ached.

It wasn't until long after she'd married Frank that she opened the *Houston Chronicle* and saw a feature article on Jeremy Lindholm, the famous documentary filmmaker. His movie about Vietnam War veterans and their buried emotional traumas was making the rounds in order to be eligible for an Academy Award nomination. Years before PTSD was recognized, Jeremy was in the forefront and courageous enough to buck the formidable, ultra-patriotic Texas mindset by presenting a topic that went against the war machine. He was a trailblazer, Betty decided back then. But she could never whisper a wisp of what she thought, since she was married to a full-time military man. But somewhere up in the attic, hidden in an old dusty box, was that yellowed newspaper article from the *Chronicle*.

Sitting in the garden now, with her hands still covered in the dirt, a strange illumination came over Betty. She flashed on Peyton's heartfelt observation that he recognized an "essence" buried deep within her that she'd forgotten existed. Was it possible she *was* actually wired differently than what she had been told? The pitter-patter she felt for Jeremy Lindholm wasn't repeated when she was forced on a date with Frank Craven. But Frank was "suitable" and "a great catch," she was advised by her parents, family and girlfriends. How could they all be wrong? And since he was six years older than Betty, Frank was "secure and stable." They had her best interests in mind, didn't they? She didn't want to let them down. She needed to do what was right and appropriate for a young woman of her social class. And yet, it seemed there was never a quiet moment set aside where anyone asked her a very simple question: What do *you* want, Betty? If the world was your oyster, who would be your pearl? What would you become if fear and failure were removed from the equation?

Betty dug her hands deeper into the soil. It was as if she'd connected to some profound magnetic beacon that infused her with the strangest, yet compelling insights. She allowed this bizarre cocktail of information to fill her thoughts, without questioning or attempting to rationalize what was happening. What if those closest to her back then saw the same essence that Peyton perceived – a quality that perhaps bubbled closer to the surface when she was younger? What if that untamed spirit terrified them? What if they purposely pushed her into charm schools, pageants and "proper" after-school activities, in order to steer her away from what they perceived as a young woman who was really a wild horse and a loose cannon? What if they intentionally manipulated her values and thoughts, because they believed controlling her was the only way to rescue her from a life *they* deemed unmanageable? What if there was an entirely different person all these years concealed inside this suffocating conformist? What if she'd been living someone else's life for nearly fifty-nine years?

Betty exhaled a huge blast of air and quickly withdrew her hands from the dirt, shaking from the thoughts that raced through her head. What did she love? *Really love?* She loved the dirt, even though she was always told to stay clean. She loved tending her plants, even though she was told there were gardeners who took care of that sort of thing. She loved Colorado, even though she was told that Texas was in her blood. She loved her son, even though she was told he was worthless and a waste of space. And that's when Betty realized that the true person inside of her, that was meant to embrace life instead of fear it, was screaming to be released. It was similar to what she felt after Frank Sr. died and she went about "investing in Betty." But that was all surface – from her hundred-thousand-dollar-plus kitchen to her

shiny veneers. That was the manufactured Betty, who operated from what she thought was important and necessary. It
wasn't the real one still hidden deep inside that wanted to
emerge and breathe in the life force that had been withheld
for so many decades.

My God...this was all so fresh and still developing in her
mind. And while the traditional Betty was still formally in
charge, she could feel a not-so-gentle push in her gut from
the *real* Betty. But not knowing who that was yet, it seemed
reasonable to tamp her down. Let her out of the can too
soon and no telling what could happen.

Betty walked inside and was shocked to see that several
hours had passed. She had to get ready to meet Tom Reed
at The Phoenix. *Dammit.* It was the last place she wanted
to be, especially coming on the heels of this still-churning
profundity. Somehow, she needed to stuff down this growing
awareness in order to get through the night. Even though
it wasn't five-thirty, she knocked back a glass of Old Crow.
And then another one. Then, like Emily Dickinson wrote,
her "feet, mechanical" went round, moving through the next
ninety minutes, until Betty parked in front of The Phoenix.

Walking inside, she headed toward the separate bar
area. It truly was a retro establishment, with red vinyl
booths, black and white diamond carpeting and dim lighting. Sinatra's "Just As Though You Were Here" played in the
background. Betty checked herself to make sure she hadn't
slipped into a time warp. Everything about this place, sans
the rising Phoenix painted with broad red brush strokes
on the ceiling, brought back memories of meeting up with
Frank when they first got acquainted. Scanning the crowded
room, she spotted a tall, good-looking man, seated alone in
a booth that matched the age range Judi described. She approached the table. "Tom?"

He stood up, quickly unbuttoning his sports jacket and
extending his large hand. "Betty! Right on time!"

Betty felt her back go up. Punctuality was important to
him. How romantic. She shook his hand and took a seat in
the booth.

"Nice handshake," he commented, "I like that."

Now she felt like a horse being examined by a prospective buyer. She observed him through the vapor of two bourbons. On the outside, he was what most women would consider "attractive," which only meant his facial features were symmetrical and appealing to the eye. His voice was confident and his mannerisms were "take charge." Yes, all seemingly fabulous.

"What'll you have?" he asked Betty.

She really didn't want anything but figured it wouldn't hurt to have a prop in her hand to fill in the dead space. "Bourbon on the rocks, please."

Tom hailed the waitress to the table, telling her what "the lady" would like.

Betty suddenly felt removed from the scene. It was as though she were allowing herself to see the surroundings as they were, unfiltered. Tipping her head, she was taken by the dramatic expanse of the crimson-winged Phoenix on the ceiling, emerging from a caldron of flames. She didn't even hear Tom's voice for a brief moment.

He leaned forward. "I said, Judi tells me you're from Texas!"

"Born and raised in Houston, but I've lived in Colorado for thirty years –"

"Oh! I've got you by ten years on that one! Moved here in '70 when you could buy a goddamned corner of the state for a nickel!"

Betty glanced to the diamond alumni ring Tom wore on his pinky. His fingernails were clean and filed neatly; his salt and pepper hair combed with precision, and still slightly damp from the shower after his late tennis game. As Judi said, "on paper" he was a catch.

"I should have probably bought up some land, but I plugged it all into my own insurance company."

"And I'm sure you were successful –"

"I was!" He vice-gripped his glass of Scotch on the rocks. "I was a big fish in a little pond back then and I grabbed every opportunity with gusto. Before long, I had eight different satellite offices from Fort Collins down to Alamosa."

"Impressive," Betty rejoined as her bourbon arrived. She took a liberal sip.

Tom cringed as he moved closer to Betty in the booth. "You all right?"

"Yeah, yeah. Just got a knee thing going on that tends to creep up after I hit the court too hard. But," he shook his finger at her, "I don't let it stop me!" He lifted an orange prescription bottle from his coat pocket and popped the cap. "Gotta keep moving!" Like a seasoned pro, he lobbed a pill into his mouth and downed it quickly with ice water. "So, Judi tells me that you're a...a great cook and you love to garden."

Betty sat back. The comment seemed random. She'd had a conversation like this before back in 1973 in a bar very much like this one, seated across from a guy with a military buzz haircut and a confident air. She fell rock hard for it back then.

"Actually, I *am* a great cook," Betty replied, taking another heady sip of bourbon. This wasn't Old Crow and it melted like honey on her tongue. "And an incredible gardener –"

"The most gardening I've done is mowing the lawn. But my ex got the house in my divorce so I lost the lawn too. No hardship there! Best thing I ever did – short of my divorce – was investing in my condo at the Aspen Grove. Everything's covered in my dues. Yard maintenance, membership in the club, twenty-four-hour security. Not that it's needed since we're gated. They also have a killer, private, five-star restaurant for residents. I'd love to show you the place."

Betty knocked back another gulp. Her head felt tingly and she could tell her censor mechanism was going off duty. "Really?" She leaned forward in a semi-seductive manner. "Why is that?"

Tom took her cue and leaned closer. "Because I think it's the kind of place you would absolutely love."

She smiled warmly, tracing a circle around the lip of her nearly empty glass. "And how would you know that, Tom?"

He started to speak but Betty abruptly cut him off. "All you know about me is what you've heard from Judi. That I'm a great cook and love to garden. Oh, and that I used to live in Texas thirty years ago. How does this token information tell you I would love your gated condo?"

He let out a hearty laugh. "Because you would!"

"I'd love it because you're *telling me* I'm going to love it?"

He shrugged his shoulders and let out another laugh, this time with a dismissive undertone to it. "Yes!"

Betty sat back. Yes, she'd heard that same laugh before with that same trivializing quality. It was as if a million puzzle pieces fell into place all at once. And as each piece clicked, the haze that had shrouded her life for so many years began to clear. "Tom, you have no goddamn clue what I love or don't love. You've known me fewer than five minutes −"

"Hey, give me a chance," he said, inching closer. "I bet you and I have a lot in common when you cut through all the crap."

She smiled. "Whose crap would that be, Tom? Mine or yours? Hundred bucks says you meant mine." Betty scooted away from him. "Your confidence far exceeds your ability to close the deal," she whispered.

He grinned, not sure what in the hell she meant. "Huh?"

"You're not all hat and no cattle. You've *got* the cattle. But you've also got the bullshit to go with it." She downed the last of her drink, knowing there wouldn't be another one scheduled that night. Her head spun as a delicious warmth engulfed her body. "I'm disheartened to think that Judi and Renée thought you would be 'perfect' for me. I've already danced this dance. I've already dated you. I married you. I had a son with you. And you died. I don't need to repeat the past anymore in order to see my future." She pulled away, shoving her glass across the table. "Allow me to offer you a little insight. You're the type of man women refer to as 'interesting' when they really mean 'tedious.'"

Tom regarded her with a confused smile. "I'm not following any of this."

"Perhaps it's because you mixed your pain killer with your scotch. That's never a good idea." She heard her Texas drawl issue forth but didn't feel the need to hide it. "You see, Tom, you're still playing tennis as we sit at this table. Difference is, you're not serving the ball to me so I can return it. I'm just the wall onto which you lob the ball again and again. But I'm here to tell you, Mr. Tom Reed, that I'm not a wall anymore." She slid out from the booth and stood up. "See that phoenix?" she pointed to the ceiling. "That's me, sweetheart. Rising from the ashes."

He stared at her, mouth agape, as she stood straight as an arrow and walked out.

Arriving home, Betty felt like a caged lioness. She couldn't sit or stand still. She grabbed a few bites of cheese and gulped down the last of the gazpacho with a hearty slice of bread. The carbs seemed to slightly steady her but then that boiling in the pit of her gut erupted again. A recklessness overwhelmed her. Yes, she remembered feeling this sensation a very long time ago. It was right after she and Frank first met. She snuck out of her bedroom window at her parents' house on that hot summer night and ran at breakneck speed through the neighborhood. She wanted to keep running and disappear from the world that held her captive in its well-meaning dictums. Back then, she didn't have the experience or the heartbreak etched into her bones. She still distrusted her inner voice, abdicating her own desires and adopting the dreams of others. But now...now she was fourteen months from turning sixty. *Sixty*, for God's sake. How in the hell did that happen? All that life wasted and usurped by others because she allowed it. "Fuck it," she said, slightly surprising herself.

She tore around the house with no direction. Up the stairs and down, she kept moving, her mind racing with thoughts that had no answers. Twenty minutes later, she found herself standing in the living room, leaning against the credenza. Opening the center drawer, she dug out Frankie's framed photo and stared at it. "What in the hell am I going to do, Frankie?" She spied the wad of cash still secured in the drawer and then the sales receipt on the credenza with Peyton's address and phone. The fire in her belly burned hot and impetuous. Just like that summer evening in Houston thirty-eight years ago, she ran back into the night again. But this time, she had a plan and when she returned home *this* time, nothing would ever be the same again.

Chapter 10

"I'm shaking like a virgin at a prison rodeo."

There was barely enough moonlight to navigate the well kept brick path to the front door, but Betty managed, her heart racing exponentially with each step. The fog of Bourbon and the arousal of resentment carried her this far, and she wasn't about to turn back. She knocked with purpose on the door. After what seemed like an eternity, the door opened. The elderly gentleman Betty saw with Peyton at Peggy's bedside stood there. He wore a plaid shirt and vest that had both seen better days. A pair of wool slacks and an odd camouflage ball cap completed the ensemble. In his hand, he held a stack of thick plastic bags. He regarded Betty with silence and confusion.

"Hello. My name is Betty Craven." She extended her hand but gramps didn't move an inch. "We met informally at Peggy's..." She was about to say "deathbed" but figured that wasn't tactful. "Is your grandson here?"

"Yeah," he stated, still not moving.

Betty's nerves were prickling. "Could I could please speak to him?"

"You his girlfriend?"

"Good God, no! I'm just a friend...well, an acquaintance...is he home?"

Gramps moved slowly to a door just off the living room and opened it. "Peyton! Some woman is here to see you. What do you want me to tell her?"

Betty took a short step into the house. "Betty. My name's *Betty!*"

A loud thump emanated from downstairs, followed by rushed footsteps up the stairs. Peyton emerged. In one hand, he held a pair of small, razor sharp scissors. A lamp adorned his forehead, shining a peculiar green glow from the light. "Betty!" he exclaimed, grinning from ear to ear. "Is it like really you or did the *Indica* just kick in?"

"Yes. *Like* it is. I need to speak to you." She glanced at his grandfather. "Privately?"

Peyton turned to his grandfather. "Hey, Pops, how's it goin' on the shrink wrapping?"

"Goin' good."

"Awesome!" Peyton patted him gently on his back. "Keep up the good work, dude!"

His grandfather moseyed back into the kitchen as Peyton approached the door. "Come on in, Betty."

"I'd rather speak outside, if you don't mind." A loud *whirr* erupted from the kitchen. "What in the hell is that?"

"I bought a vacuum sealer to suck the air out of bags of cannabis for my patients. He's fallen in love with it and even figured out ways to improve it. Pops can suck the air out of anything now."

"Really? My late husband had that same talent when he walked into a room."

Peyton stepped outside, pulling the front door ajar. "Pops was a world class inventor in his day. Real simple stuff but really useful. He's got like three patents. But he's worried about people stealing his ideas. That's why I bought him that camo ball cap. I told him if he wore it when he was coming up with ideas, nobody could see what he was thinking and steal his thoughts. It's taken his anxiety level way down!"

Betty couldn't believe how on some peculiar level that made sense. "I'm sure you're wondering why I'm here –"

He turned off his green headlamp. "You changed your mind. Dude, that's why you're here!"

Betty turned away, a wave of apprehension gripping her. "I don't know that I've changed my mind completely. I just... I just..." She let out a hard sigh. "I've had an illuminating day and a strange early evening and between the two, I'm standing here with you and making no sense."

He put a reassuring hand on her shoulder. "It's okay, Betty. We'll take it slow."

"Oh, dear. That sounds really odd, coming from you to me." She glanced down at his drooping jeans. "Pull up your pants, would you?"

"Huh?"

She tactfully pointed to his trousers. "Your *pants*? It's not a good look."

"That's the way they're supposed to fit."

She leaned forward, attempting to be discreet even though no one was in earshot. "It's not a professional way to present yourself to your patients. Trust me on this one."

Peyton shrugged his shoulders and obliged, hiking up his jeans and tightening the belt around his waist.

Betty took a gander around the area. "Look, before I change my mind and run screaming into the night, here's my proposal. I purchase from you some....material, shall we say. And I make a batch of chocolates using my own method, and we'll see how it goes. If I fail miserably, then no harm, no foul –"

"*Fail?* You're not gonna fail."

"That remains to be seen."

"No way. I can feel it. You were meant to do this. You're gonna help a whole lot of people, Betty."

An unexpected wave of sadness came over her. "I tried to help someone once I cared a great deal for. It didn't do any good. He still died."

"Just 'cause your son died, doesn't mean you failed."

"I didn't say it was my –"

"Oh, come on, Betty. It wasn't your next-door neighbor in Texas, Mary Jane Blunt." He leaned against the doorjamb. "Hell, we never know the impact we have on someone. Even the smallest influence can make a huge difference. Like the way your chocolates and my cannabis came together to help my aunt. She still died, but she died with dignity. You were part of that. Shit, we're all gonna die. That's the destination but life's the journey, dude. I'm like totally more into the journey."

Betty pressed the skin between her eyebrows. *"Please stop peppering your vocabulary with 'like.'"* She reached into her purse. "I have the cash you gave me, and I want to keep this above board and buy −"

"Betty, I'm tapped out, and I don't have another harvest for two months −"

She shot him a dismayed look. "How in the hell was I supposed to do any of this?"

"Well, like −" he caught himself and started again. "You grow your own and until you get your own harvest, I can hook you up with a guy who grows medical cannabis organically −"

"Hook me up? Oh, my God! What?! *What?!* Are you nuts?"

"Whoa, whoa, whoa! Betty, chill. Take a breath. Louie is totally cool."

"Louie? What's the rest of his name? The Exterminator?"

"No. Parodi. He owns the automotive shop over on Sheldon Street. You know? Louie's Lube 'n' Tube? The big neon wheel with the fat, goofy face in the center? That's Louie's place. You'll want an ounce of 'sweet leaf shake' and an ounce of 'popcorn' buds mainly from an *Indica* strain." He thought for a second. "Blueberry! That's the strain you need from him. There are different Blueberry strains, and Louie's got the Centennial Blueberry strain that was bred to grow great in the high altitude of the Rockies. Man, does it have dank little greasy nuggets."

"Hang on, what's 'sweet leaf shake' and 'popcorn?'"

"'Sweet leaf shake' is the sticky, sugary trim from right around the bud and 'popcorn' buds are what grows on the bottom of the plant. When you combine those two for edibles, you get a nice pain-killing effect. I'll give Louie a call and set the whole thing up for you." He brought out his cell phone and started to dial.

"Wait! Right now?"

"Wasn't your objective coming over here to leave with something?"

Betty felt her throat tightening. "Yes."

Peyton dialed the number. As it rung, he turned to Betty.
"I got a lot of my cannabis clones from Louie when I started
up. He knows his shit. He was one of first people in Colorado to get his medical cannabis card." Louie answered and
the arrangements were made. If Betty could drive over there
within the next twenty minutes, Louie would have the bags
waiting. And as a sign of wanting to help a future medical
cannabis caregiver, Louie agreed to give Betty the "family
price" which came to one hundred and fifty for the ounce
of Centennial Blueberry popcorn buds, and seventy for the
ounce of premium Centennial shake.

Betty arrived under the big neon wheel fifteen minutes
later. She'd been told to walk around the back of the business, down a short walkway and then knock on the steel
door with the gold wheel decal. Louie must have been standing right there waiting, because the door opened before Betty finished knocking.

"Hey! Come on in!" Louie said with a welcoming tenor.
He was still removing grease from his huge, fat hands with
a pink soap that smelled slightly toxic with a grapefruit top
note.

Betty walked in, closing the door behind her. The bourbons had worn off completely, and it was as if she'd awakened into a reality she wasn't prepared to occupy. Doubt
began to inch its way into her mind. She looked around the
modest but well-kept garage. The floors were swept clean
and all the tools were lined up neatly on brackets against
the walls. There was no sense of anything shady or corrupt
going on in this place. As for Louie, he didn't put off the
vibe to Betty of anyone who would be involved in growing
marijuana. He looked to be in his mid-thirties. His round,
cherubic face and mass of tousled black hair, along with the
half undone blue work shirt with his name embroidered in
red, made him look like your standard grease monkey. Louie
washed off the last of the pink soap and dried his hands.

"I..." Betty felt a catch in her throat. "I've never done
this before," she whispered.

He smiled. "There's nobody else here. You don't have to whisper." He turned. "I'll go grab your stuff."

Betty stood still, clutching her purse and doing everything to stand as straight as she could, so as to appear confident. Looking around the immediate area, she spotted a pegboard filled with photos featuring Louie and his wife and three children. There were photos of them skiing, hiking, and hanging out at home. A small TV played in the background on low volume. It was the early Denver news broadcast, and Betty heard the male anchor mention marijuana. Her ears perked up as she strained to hear the segment. There was a crowd of people standing outside the State Capitol with banners proclaiming "D.A.R.E. TO KEEP CHILDREN SAFE!" and "EVER WONDER WHY THEY CALL IT DOPE?" Front and center was the inimitable Reverend Bobby Lynch, who had driven up from Colorado Springs for the news event. Standing in front of a crowd of over two hundred, die-hard anti-marijuana supporters who waved handmade signs and chanted, "Don't let our town go to pot!," Lynch took center stage as he spoke to the crowd.

"I'm not going to mince words!" Lynch yelled into the microphone. "This is not about medicine! They tell us that it's part of our state constitution and that the people want it! Well, I'm here to tell you there are plenty of people in this great Rocky Mountain state who are outright offended by this mockery against *real* medicine! Medicine that has been approved and used for decades by our physicians and trained pharmacists! This is just a convenient ploy to make marijuana acceptable in our neighborhoods. And when that happens, my friends, the family-centered community we love and have nurtured as a safe place to raise our children suddenly transforms into a gang-infested, rotting hole of sewage. Colorado citizens send a negative message to the rest of this great country when they allow and support the drug dens, the grow operations and the manufacturing facilities that process and distribute this dangerous plant! Do not let your towns go to pot!" The crowd erupted in applause and loud chants of "Say no to pot!"

Louie returned with a paper bag and turned off the TV. "Fucking idiot," he mumbled under his breath. Then he quickly looked up at Betty. "Excuse my language."

"Not to worry."

"I get pissed off when people just parrot whatever they hear without researching the facts. I mean, pot's only been used as a medicine for thousands of years and aspirin is, what...one hundred and twenty years on record? Don't get me started. I wonder how many pharmaceutical drugs Lynch is on and how many of those have side effects that include stupidity." He handed Betty the bag.

Betty glanced toward the pegboard of photos. "Your children are beautiful"

"Thank you. My oldest one just turned eleven. She's got a school pageant tomorrow, and I've got to pick up her costume tonight. So I can't linger here too long."

Betty didn't move. Her heart raced and her mouth went dry. "Yes, of course. Listen, I mean no disrespect given the reason why I'm here, but is this transaction legal?"

"Peyton said you don't have your card yet, so technically, no," he said forthrightly. "And I'm only doing it because I know Peyton, and he said you really needed some help. I don't turn down people in need."

Betty observed him. His face might have been caricatured on a big neon wheel out front, but there was nothing but honesty and a genuineness issuing forth at that moment. "That's very kind of you."

"Here you go," he handed the brown bag to her.

She took it and handed him a folded stack of cash. "That's two hundred and twenty dollars. I appreciate the 'family price.' Please count it."

Louie stuffed the money in his greasy pants pocket. "I trust you."

Betty stood frozen. A surge of emotion overwhelmed her and she started to cry. Turning away, she did everything possible to halt the waterworks, but it was useless.

"What did I say?" Louie asked, concern etching his chubby face.

"It's not you. It's me," she whispered, desperately trying to get hold of herself. "I'm shaking like a virgin at a prison rodeo."

Louie grinned. "Hey, I haven't heard that one in a long time. You from Texas?"

His relaxed demeanor calmed Betty, allowing the tears to slow. "Yes. You?"

"My uncle lives in Dallas."

Betty turned back to the photos of his children. "How do you...how do you do this," she motioned to the paper bag, "with children around? Aren't you concerned?"

"I don't grow it in our house. They've never seen the plants."

"But they must see the...material...around the house."

He scratched his head. "Yeah. They do. And I know what you mean. I have a lot of conflict about it too. Then I think, well, I drink beer in front of them and think nothing of it. So, I don't know. Until pot becomes completely legal for everyone, and not just medical patients, you walk a jagged line when you've got kids in the house."

"Yes. I agree."

Louie became pensive. "You know, growing isn't easy. Everybody who's not involved in this thinks you just throw a seed or a clone in the ground and come back five months later to cut down your crop. It takes a lot of time and talent. The time you put into it is not usually going to equal what you might get out of it financially, especially when you're a caregiver. You have to love it or else you shouldn't do it. I do it 'cause I want to pick specific strains that are known for reducing pain, and also because I have total control over how I grow it without using toxic chemicals. And truthfully, I think it's kinda cool to grow your own medicine, you know? But in the end, yeah, it's a lot of hard work. Hell, I probably tack on another three hours a day just keeping my grow going."

Betty nodded. "Well, thank you for this and for sharing your thoughts." She turned.

"Have you ever worked with marijuana before?"

"What do you think?" she asked, with a half-smile.

"It's just my advice, take it or leave it, but make sure you vent the room really well and maybe even wear gloves when you're handling that much of it...especially the popcorn bud. The resins can absorb through your skin, and until you get really used to it, it can pack a punch if you're sensitive."

"Thank you, Louie. But I don't think I'm *that* sensitive."

He grinned a knowing grin. "Okay. Whatever you say."

~~~

Betty drove home with the paper bag tucked between the two front seats and covered with her sweater. The smell was quite stout, so she opened her windows to let the aroma waft out of the car. The closer she got to home, the more her anxiety grew. She had no medical card and here she was, driving around with two ounces of cannabis in a bag. Once she arrived on her street, her anxiety lessened. That is until she saw a large motorhome blocking access to her home, as it attempted to back into Jerry's driveway across the street. Jerry was outside the motorhome, drinking a beer and help-ing the driver navigate his approach. He motioned to Betty to hang on a second.

Once the driver skillfully backed in and got out of his monolith on wheels, Betty quickly pulled into her driveway. In the rear view mirror, she saw Jerry sauntering over to the car. She got out, standing with her back against the open window of the driver's door. Betty could smell his heavy scent of beer soaked sweat.

"Hey, Betty! You're out late. That's my older brother, Jack," he said, pointing across the street. "Hey, Jack!" he screamed, "Come over here a sec."

Betty seized up. "I really have to get in and feed Ronald."

Jack opened the passenger door on the RV and let out an enormous German Shepard on a lease. Together, they crossed the street. But as the dog moved closer, he began to bark loudly and become agitated.

"Shush, Arnold! Shush!" Jack demanded, jerking the dog's leash. But the dog kept barking and bolting closer to Betty's Taurus.

"Betty, meet Jack!" Jerry yelled above Arnold's persistent barking, now mixed with a few growls. "He's visiting me for a few days from Wyoming."

Jack reached over to shake Betty's hand but Arnold's lunging prevented it. "Sorry about the dog," Jack apologized, trying to pull him back from Betty's car.

Jerry swigged the last of his beer and turned to Betty. "Jack works for the DEA. Arnold's his sidekick and drug enforcement canine. *Aren't you Arnold?!*" The dog went wild, growling with specks of foam emitting from his bared teeth. "Jack named him after Arnold Schwarzenegger, the 'Terminator.'" Jerry did his best, worst Schwarzenegger impression through his beer-goggled miasma. Arnold was bordering on ballistic. "Hey, Jack. What's the 'move away' code word for Arnold?"

"Strudel!" Jack yelled.

Betty was still backed up against the open window, a forced smile plastered on her face. "Arnold! It's okay! Strudel!" she said with a nervous chuckle.

"*Strudel!*" Jack yelled again, yanking the dog's collar backward. Arnold slowly calmed down, as drool hung down his mouth like icicles on a Christmas tree. "Damn, I've never seen him so pumped up!"

The men shared a laugh and then thankfully started off across the street when Jerry turned around. "Hey, I scanned that letter to the editor and emailed it to about fifty people." He stumbled over a pebble in the street. "Keep up the fight, Betty!"

She waited, heart beating wildly, until they were safely out of view before retrieving her brown bag and heading into her house.

Betty closed every window and pulled each curtain and shade. She carried the bag to the dining room table and sat down. After observing the bag for almost half an hour in silence, she opened it and removed the two plastic baggies.

The contents of one looked like small, curled grass cuttings, and it was labeled "Cent. Blueberry shake." The other was filled with marble-sized nuggets and labeled "popcorn bud/ Cent. Blueberry." Opening the popcorn bud bag, she took a quick sniff and sat back, closing it up quickly. She stared at the cannabis in stunned disbelief. The full effect of the last few hours hit her hard as she slumped over the dining room table, burying her head in her hands. "What have I done?" she mumbled to herself. After a few minutes of fretfulness, Betty turned her head toward the credenza. Frankie's framed photo was lying on top in the same place she'd left it. Quickly, she got up and sequestered the photo back into the center drawer. She packed the two plastic baggies back into the paper sack and carried them upstairs to the bedroom. Pacing back and forth, she realized she had no idea what to do with this rough plant matter. Peyton mentioned about his cannabutter, but that was Greek to Betty. Dashing to her computer, she brought up the search engine and tentatively typed "making medical cannabis edibles in chocolate." She quickly got four hundred and forty-nine thousand links. Everyone from "Aunt Mary Jane" to "Doctor Dorothy" had either a blog or a YouTube video tutorial on "medical edibles."

After reading six different blogs about processing cannabis six different ways, Betty's mind spun from confusion. The only thing perfectly clear was that the THC in cannabis had to bond to a fat, because it wasn't water-soluble. She'd always learned better from watching demonstrations than from reading. Thus, she clicked on the YouTube links. The one from "Doctor Dorothy" looked intriguing, until she realized Dorothy was as much a "Doctor" as Dr. Pepper. Dorothy also appeared stoned off her trotter during her lengthy cooking demonstration. There were long pauses where Dorothy stared into the pot she was stirring and seemed spellbound by the surface bubbles. At one point, Doc Dorothy advised, "You can take this oil *subliminally*" instead of "sublingually." Aunt Mary Jane was no better. She was pushing seventy, spoke with a raspy gravel, and wore a turmeric, tie-dyed caftan with long sleeves that kept dancing awfully close to the gas burner on her stove. Aunt Mary Jane also employed a sidekick in the form of her forty-something "nephew" she kept referring to as either "Cousin Timmy" or "handsome." When she'd lean over and say, "Hey, handsome, hand me the spatula," and then wink naughtily, Betty got the feeling their relationship was complicated.

The videos continued for hours, the viewing broken only by Betty dashing to her kitchen to grab some dinner, feed Ronald and then return for another marathon session. She understood the basics pretty much: for every ounce of cannabis, add one pint of liquid butter, olive oil or coconut oil. THC, the main psychoactive molecule in cannabis, needs to metabolize with fat in order to be really effective. Pre-heating the plant material for twenty to thirty minutes in an oven at a strict 225 degrees Fahrenheit, *decarboxylates* – or the friendlier, *decarbs* – the THC into a more active form. After that, the resinous buds and sweet leaf are ground up to allow more surface exposure, and then simmered on low heat – preferably in a crock-pot – at no higher than 205 degrees Fahrenheit for up to six hours, stirring regularly. Adding four cups of water to the mixture, Betty learned, pulls the terpenes and chlorophyll away from the oil, producing a cleaner taste in the finished product, while letting the oil reduce more slowly so it can absorb more of the resins and the multitude of *cannabinoids* in the plant. Since water boils at a higher temperature than oil, the addition prevents the oil and plant matter from burning. Before finishing, some suggested lobbing in an ounce or more of grain alcohol to aid in the absorption of THC into the fat and letting that evaporate off for another hour or longer.

Once complete, the plant matter is strained through a muslin cloth and then tightly squeezed to get every last drop from the cannabis. This fat and water mix is poured into a bowl and placed in the freezer for at least two days and allowed to harden, so that one simply has to remove it from the bowl and easily break off the frozen water which separated from the fat as it hardened. From there, one could take the oil or butter concoction and add it in specific amounts to baked goods, chocolates and the like. Some skipped adding it to anything and simply ingested this potent green "butter" by itself or in gelatin capsules. Still others used the cannabis-infused oils topically to reduce arthritic pain and muscle soreness.

From what Betty discovered, there was a dizzying, seemingly never-ending array of methods to incorporate cannabis into one's body. Ironically, smoking it was the *least* effective mode to "medicate" since one was "burning up" and losing many of the healing *cannabinoids* that are responsible for the pain-relieving action. But while edibles were the best overall way to ingest cannabis, Aunt Mary Jane explained that the effect could take anywhere from one to three hours to feel. When it hit, though, as "Doctor Dorothy" counseled, "you'll be floatin' on the light fantastic" for up to eight hours.

Betty checked the time and was shocked to see it was approaching midnight. There was still a pulse of reluctance inside her as she stared at the paper bag, now secured on her bedspread, several feet from where Ronald was sleeping. She began to question herself again and her possibly rash response to the staggering illumination she'd experienced earlier that day. As she'd done occasionally in her life, she decided she needed a sign that all of this was all right. Of course, according to Peyton, the fact that she had a maintenance man named Buddy was enough. But she asked for one, nonetheless. And she sat there, waiting for her answer. Finally, as the clock hit 12:30, she heard the tap-tap of the large elm tree's branch outside her bedroom window as the wind softly blew through its leaves. She turned back to her computer and perused the long list of educational videos on cannabis, and then quite by accident, found a four-part documentary series on the history of the cannabis plant, its systematic corruption over time, and how cannabis could fit into the medical paradigm of our future. It even featured Doobie Douggie. Betty clicked on the documentary and started to watch it.

Within less than a minute, she had the sign she was looking for. The documentary was produced, directed, written and narrated by none other than Jeremy Lindholm, her erst-while first love.

It had been a long time since Betty had stayed up all night cooking. But this would be the first night she stayed up cooking her first batch of cannabis.

Chapter 11

"Don't worry. You won't remember any of this."

Betty double-checked every kitchen window to make sure they were tightly shut, and closed all available shades. The back door was the only exposed area but the chances of someone coming in the back gate and seeing her, especially at this hour, were few and far between. With her carefully written notes on the kitchen table and a soft adagio playing on *Colorado Public Radio*, Betty went to work.

Since her goal was incorporating the cannabis into her chocolates without changing their texture, she figured the best way would be to infuse the cannabis into cocoa butter. But if that didn't work, to be on the safe side, she decided to also make a batch using coconut oil. Thus, she separated out half the "shake" and half the popcorn buds using a spoon, and factoring the proper proportions of oil to plant material, set about making two batches. All the information she'd read and viewed, strongly advised using a grinder that was exclusively dedicated for the cannabis. Betty had an extra grinder she hardly ever used and it was green, so she figured it would be the perfect choice. She spooned the "shake" and popcorn buds into the grinder; some fell out and she hastily collected it. Even though the popcorn buds were bone dry, the resins on the plant were still very much alive and slightly sticky against her fingers. After grinding the first few tablespoons, it was apparent there was a good reason for dedicating a grinder. All those resins adhered to the blade and sides, leaving a green, tacky carpet. Not wanting to use a knife against the metal, Betty wedged her thumbnail into the grinder and scratched out the caked remains. The odor of the Centennial Blueberry strain was like a summer fruit compote, with subtle earthy undertones. After removing as much of the remnants as possible from the grinder, Betty noticed that a line of resin had adhered under her thumbnail. She tried washing it off, but it was stubborn and absorbing into her skin. Instinctively, she stuck her thumb in her mouth, attempting to dislodge the packed resin. Instantly noting the bitterness of the resin, Betty quickly withdrew her thumb and attempted to wash the taste from her mouth. Satisfied it was out of her system, she went about measuring the correct amount of cocoa butter in one crock-pot and coconut oil in the other. While that melted, she carefully laid out the freshly ground popcorn bud and "shake" on two separate cookie pans and *decarbed* them in the oven for exactly half an hour.

After ten minutes, the kitchen began to smell like twenty people had just lit up joints. She opened the stove and was nearly overcome with a fine vapor that tickled her nostrils and created a growing buzz in her head. She recalled Louie told her to ventilate the area and wear gloves until she got used to it, but there was no way Betty was going to risk anyone smelling the aromatic brew, and gloves...well gloves were for moving hot dishes from the oven and wearing to church on Easter Sunday. Still, while the cannabis *decarbed* and the cocoa butter and oil melted, Betty began to feel a little disoriented. She sat down at the table and waited for it to pass, but then a fit of giggles ensued. It came out of nowhere and it grew. The problem was that nothing was funny and everything was funny. Within minutes, she leaned over the counter, convulsing with laughter. The timer went off, alerting her that the cannabis was ready to move from the oven into the oil. She regained control of herself, but still had to stifle an eruption of giggles here and there, as she stirred the herb into the two crock-pots. She added the required amount of water to each brew and checked the time. It was just after 1:00 AM. Securing two candy thermometers into the crock-pots under each lid, Betty monitored the temperature as the brews bubbled and the cannabis danced across the surface of the oil. From all the information she'd learned in her short tutorials, she knew the process could take anywhere from a few hours to two days, depending upon which "canna expert" you listened to. Betty figured she'd cook the herb for six hours, so she grabbed a few old gourmet cuisine magazines to peruse in the pursuit of killing time.

Every fifteen minutes, she got up and stirred the green, oily infusions with a wooden spoon, checked the temperatures and gradually inhaled more of the vapors. At one point, Betty lifted the spoon from the coconut oil brew and allowed the emerald drops of cannabis to fall back, one by one, into the crock-pot. This seemingly rudimentary process became fascinating to her. She'd never really looked at a droplet of oil before, but now she was focused and consumed by the sight. Betty allowed the jade-colored drops to fall into her palm, but instead of returning them to the crock-pot, she rubbed the oil into her arm. Holding her palm close to her nose, she was both attracted and repulsed by the aroma. Without realizing it, she started to rub the residue across her face and noted how warm her skin felt. Another half hour passed and Betty dutifully stirred the two concoctions. Dipping a tablespoon into the cocoa butter infused cannabis, she held the spoon to the ceiling light to check the color. And then, instinctively and strictly from force of habit, she put the tablespoon into her mouth, removed the smooth substance with her lips, and swallowed. There was about a three second pause before Betty realized what she'd done. Frantically, she turned on the faucet and did everything she could to rinse out her mouth, even taking the sprayer and blasting it across her tongue. She turned off the faucet and waited, wondering what in the hell was going to happen to her. How could she be so stupid? It was a cook's knee-jerk reaction, she kept telling herself. But then, part of her wondered if that was true.

Ninety more minutes elapsed and her kitchen smelled like Woodstock at high noon in 1969. She'd read the same damn paragraph in her magazine on marinating shallots five times, and it didn't make any sense. The second she thought that, she couldn't remember what she just thought. And the more she tried to remember even the concept of what she'd been thinking, the more elusive the thought became. "Oh, dear," she whispered, realizing now that proper ventilation and gloves were probably mentioned for a good reason. But it was too late for that. Each time Betty got up to stir the pots and check the temperature, the five-foot jaunt across the kitchen floor took more time and planning. By 4:00 AM, the simple process of extricating herself from the chair required the kind of advance planning that goes into royal weddings and shuttle launches. Her body felt exceptionally relaxed but also as if lead weights encircled her feet. Everything around her slowed down. What seemed like half an hour, took place in five minutes.

At first, there was detachment and her vision briefly blurred. Then, it was if she saw herself as two distinct personalities. One of them was familiar and the other distant. As odd as it seemed, the familiar persona was the one she'd buried so long ago. The distant one was who she had become. This strange division scared the part of her that continued to move into the distance. But the free spirit that had been hidden seemed to relish the sensation. Fear didn't touch that sparkling part of her. Regret and pain didn't seem to affect it either. And as she allowed that part of her to become dominant, she settled into the moment and just *was*. The lights in the room seemed brighter. The classical music playing softly on the radio was louder and more precise. In fact, Betty could hear every instrument in the piece, as well as the thoughts the composer had when he was creating the composition. She had to check herself on that one. *The thoughts he had*, she mused. But in that pocket of time, sitting there at the kitchen table, she felt connected to the music and could feel the breath of the composer over her shoulder.

Another hour passed, and the indiscernible vapors in the room deepened. It felt as though her head was being pulled backward. Her mouth went dry and there were abrupt missing pieces of linear time. Then the strangest thing happened. Time, it seemed, caved in on itself and was bendable. Fluid, like mercury oozing against a silver spoon and flowing back into itself, gently coalescing and flowing freely. Every time Betty let fear enter the equation, she felt the free spirit move into her heart and calm her anxiety. And then, quite suddenly, there was only the *now*. The past was dead and the future wasn't manifest. But it was deeper than silence. It was all that ever was and all that ever would be. It was nothing and it was everything. In essence, it just *was*.

She laid her head on the kitchen table, using the magazines as an improvised pillow. A distant but distinct hum filled her ears, as the pressure became more intense around her forehead. She heard herself speak a short prayer and then she fell asleep. Lifting her head, she was sure she'd melted into a dream. She was still in the kitchen but it appeared electrified. Sparks of light twinkled above her in a syncopated rhythm. Betty pinched herself. Yes, it was a dream. Time felt suspended and her mind was empty. "How odd," she said to herself without speaking. This was a dream, she kept telling herself, but then she began to doubt it.

Out of the ether, she heard a voice she hadn't heard in years. "You were always such a good girl, Betty. We never had a whisper of trouble from you. And you always did what you were told. Dear Lord, what happened?"

Betty turned around and saw her mother standing there. She was wringing her hands with worry and wearing an apron Betty remembered from her childhood.

"Where did I go wrong Betty?" her mother asked her, without moving her lips.

"Good God, Betty!" another voice bellowed.

Betty turned around. Standing in the corner of the kitchen was her father.

"I'm glad I'm not alive to see this!" he growled. "My heart couldn't take it, and I'd have another stroke that'd take me out!"

A fist bore down on the kitchen table. Betty jumped and spun around. She stared into Frank Sr.'s angry eyes. "What in the hell are you doing?" he barked, leaning over the kitchen table. "Have you lost your goddamned mind?!" Frank tilted closer to Betty. "Get rid of that shit *now*! Christ Almighty, Betty! What's wrong with you?"

Their voices tangled together, each one loudly demanding she immediately stop what she was doing. As the cacophony grew, Betty closed her eyes and pressed her hands to her ears to subdue the mounting fury directed toward her. Finally, she couldn't take it any longer and screamed, "*Stop it! You have no right anymore!*"

And then there was silence. She opened her eyes and saw Frankie standing in front of her. He was gaunt and pale but he held his hand out toward her. She heard his voice within her heart.

"It's okay, mom," he whispered and smiled. "Remember the words on the tree?"

Betty's eyes filled with tears. She nodded. "But I can't do that." She stared into his sad eyes. "God, Frankie. You're so real."

"You won't remember any of this."

"But I will," Betty heard herself mutter in her head. She reached out to take her son's hand but the distant bleat of the cooking timer tore her away. She jerked awake and quickly sat upright in the kitchen chair. It was 7:00 AM and she hadn't forgotten a thing. Through the dizzying blur of cannabis vapors that now saturated every inch of the kitchen, she could still feel those ghosts hovering close by. Staggering to the crock-pots, Betty checked the temperatures and turned off the heat. She managed to make it back to the kitchen table and sat down. Her head felt weighted to a wall of bricks. She stared across to the sink and fixated on the faucet. It was so comforting and completely enticing she couldn't help but stare even deeper, until there was just the faucet and Betty occupying that moment. In fact, she was so engrossed, she didn't hear the back gate open or the footsteps approaching the back door. And she didn't see the figure standing at the back door even after the distant taps on the pane of glass.

"Betty?"

Chapter 12

"It's time, Betty."

Betty turned to the back door. Jeff stood there, peering in with a look of concern. She didn't move a muscle.

"Betty?" Jeff repeated. "Are you okay?"

Somehow, she lifted herself out of the chair and opened the door, letting him inside. The second Jeff walked into the kitchen he backed up.

"Oh, hell!" he exclaimed, covering his nose, almost overcome by the intense vapors. It took him another few seconds to figure it out. *"Pot?"*

Betty stood motionless and then turned toward the open door, realizing how refreshing the morning air felt on her face.

Jeff checked the two crock-pots, lifting the lids and stepped back again from the heady aromas. "Betty, we have to open some windows!" He opened the door into the living room along with every window in the kitchen. "How long have you been inhaling all this?"

Betty was still drinking in the sweet, morning air. "About six hours I think."

"Six hours?" He took the lid off one of the pots. "Did you try any of it?"

"Yes. Purely by mistake."

"Right. That and 'No, officer, the pot belongs to my friend' are two popular responses."

Her mouth was seriously dry. "Okay. I might admit to taking more than I should have judiciously ingested. And there was that lack of ventilation part as well..."

He finished cranking open the last window and turned to her. "Are you okay?"

She touched the top of her head. "I can feel the part in my hair."

"I bet you can." He moved toward Betty, taking her hand. "Come on, let's walk outside in the backyard. Nice kitchen, by the way."

She slowly made her way out the door with him. "Thank you very much. It cost more to remodel it than to buy a nice motorhome. But the kitchen doesn't have any wheels so you can't go anywhere when you're in it."

"Oh, brother, you really are stoned." He guided her to the bench, underneath the elm tree.

"I'm not stoned," she replied, a sense of umbrage rising.

He grinned. "Yeah. Right. You're not stoned and chickens have four wings."

She looked at him, a sense of alarm tracing her face. "Oh, God. I *am* stoned. Lord help me. When will the paranoia start?"

"It already began when you registered as a Republican," he said, his blue eyes twinkling.

"Oh, hell. I don't want to end up like one of those people who hoist their old couch up on the roof so they can lie down and get loaded while they watch the sunset."

"Wow. Memories. It was a lawn chair for me. Easier to hoist." He turned to her. "Take a lot of deep breaths."

Jeff guided her through a series of deep breathing exercises that seemed to clear a few of the cobwebs in her head. After half an hour, the sense of detachment started to subside.

"Hey," she said, "how in the hell did you know where I live?"

He held up her driver's license. "You left this at the store yesterday. I found it on the floor by the cash register."

"Oh, dear. What if I'd been pulled over and didn't have this?"

"I think the amount of pot you were carrying would have trumped the missing driver's license."

Betty put a weary hand to her now pounding head. "Oh my God...this is not me...this is not me..."

"Maybe it is you. Elizabeth *Cragen* signed that letter to the editor. Not Betty Craven. Maybe Betty Craven is really a wild, unchained pot head –"

"Stop it! That's not what this is at all!" It took her twenty minutes, but she explained her altruistic medical motives behind the cannabis brews. With each minute, the clarity increased. She told him about Peggy and Peyton and summed it up by explaining Peyton's offer to help her become a caregiver and set up her own grow operation.

He sat back and pondered her words carefully. "I don't think there are a lot of women who do this. Isn't growing pot a young man's game. You know, twenty-somethings who are already living in their parents' basement and need a job?"

"I imagine it is." She thought for a second and suddenly brightened. "But I could bring some class to it, not to mention outstanding gourmet chocolate creations."

Jeff chuckled. "Betty, I'm confused. What in the hell happened between the time you signed that letter to the editor and turning your kitchen into a vaporizing hut?"

As hard as she tried, she couldn't figure out how to describe it. "I guess the pan began simmering with Jeremy Lindholm, and it boiled over with Tom Reed."

He regarded her with a look of confusion. "Okay."

Betty played nervously with the edge of her sleeve. "Did you ever wake up and realize you couldn't continue living your life the way you had been? That if you spent another goddamned day doing the same crap, thinking the same thoughts, and recycling the same mistakes, you'd just as soon not live at all?"

Compassion colored his face. "Yeah. It's been about twenty years since I felt that, but yeah. I went through the usual growing pains in my twenties. Did drugs. Drank booze. Got married way too young and divorced seven years later. Hit the proverbial wall at twenty-nine. One day, I had a come-to-Jesus moment and quit the drugs, quit the booze, quit California, and taking a revised page out of John Denver's songbook, I was born in the summer of my thirtieth year, coming home to a place I'd never been before."

"That's it? You just moved to Colorado and that solved everything?"

"No. I found my passion," he replied succinctly. "Plants, herbs, growing organic food, alternative health. Maybe I just poured myself into another addiction, but it's been working for over twenty years, so if it ain't broke..."

Betty ruminated on some quick math. He found himself at thirty and it had been over twenty years. So, what did that make him? Fifty-two? And then she quickly wondered why she even cared. "You found your passion. I like that term." She ruminated some more. There was still a vaporous edge inside her head, but the cobwebs were slowly clearing. "Marijuana is still a drug though, isn't it?"

"I don't look at it like that anymore. I think it's like any other healing herb out there; it can used or it can be abused. I've done a bit of reading on medical marijuana, given the industry I work in, and I'm really impressed by the research. There was this alternative doctor on NPR the other day, talking about some studies the government buried since the Nixon administration, on how marijuana can slow down cancer growth. Did you hear it?"

"No. I don't like NPR. All the male reporters sound like pussy whipped, castrated adolescents, and all the female interviewers sound like strident, feminist bitches."

He laughed a hearty chuckle. "Yeah, yeah, I know what you mean. But it *was* an interesting interview. Every part of the plant is useful, including the root. Most people who give their opinions about pot are just going by what they've heard or maybe some bad experience they had with some crap weed that was sprayed with chemicals during the growing process. I don't think a lot of naysayers take the time to do the research, because if they did, they would see they've been totally brainwashed by the powers that be." He leaned forward. "All those who wander are not lost. All those who drink are not drunks. And all those who use pot are certainly not losers. There's too much hysteria and not enough information. I mean, they make these incredibly stupid comments, like, "People who smoke pot are violent." Give me a break. If you're really stoned, you might get agitated with someone, but after one minute you'll forget what you were pissed off about. People who use pot don't get in cars and speed or drive aggressively. Most people who use and drive go thirty in a sixty mile an hour zone, and like the old joke, sit at a stop sign, waiting for it to turn green."

"Yes, well, that's a good example of why I've always been of the opinion that a society without self-discipline cannot be trusted to self-medicate."

Jeff sat back and stared at her. "Really? That's truly your opinion? You sure that's not someone else's words you're just repeating?"

Betty stopped and considered his question. "Well, I think the statement has some merit."

"Okay, so we allow drugs, booze, caffeine and cigarettes only to those who have self-discipline. And the rest who don't have self-discipline, what do we do with them? Shoot 'em?"

"I have no idea." Betty began to see the glaring holes in her declaration.

"If we shoot all the people who suffer from a lack of self-discipline, we'll have about three hundred and fourteen left on this planet, and they're all going to be monks, hermits, a few Olympic athletes, anal retentives and people with obsessive compulsive disorder." He shifted in his seat. "I mean, isn't this really just about control? Isn't all the legislation just another way of attempting to regulate human behavior? I don't care what laws you pass or how many flashy ad campaigns you pay for, people will *always* seek out ways to escape and dull their pain. It's built into our psyche. There's no way a government or a society will *ever* be able to control that. I'm of the opinion we all have the equal right to either destroy ourselves or succeed beyond our wildest dreams. It's our choice, and I don't believe somebody who doesn't know me has the right to tell me which one is better for me."

Betty was amazed. "You don't use marijuana but you're still open to it?"

"Hell, Betty, I hate rap music but I'm not going to ban it. I happen to believe in personal freedom. I know that's a revolutionary stance these days, but you might want to look into it. Look, Betty, when you stop buying into all the manufactured hysteria about pot – and basically *all* of it is manufactured – you're going to come out the other side and realize there are good and bad people involved in the business, just like the health food industry."

She seriously considered his words. "Well, *if* I do this, understand it's purely for the medicinal aspects. Pain reduction. Nausea. Muscle cramps."

He looked at her with a soft smile. "It's okay if in the midst of pain relief, euphoria happens to creep in. I remember when I smoked pot, I've never laughed so hard in my life. Who's to say that laughing your ass off is not 'medicinal?' I happen to think a big part of healing is allowing yourself to actually enjoy life." He shrugged his shoulders. "But there I go again. Radical ideas."

Betty grinned. "So...you think I should do this?"

He tilted his head. "You're 'shoulding' all over yourself again. It's your gig or it isn't. You want me to tell you what to do and I won't. You're the one who's going to be taking care of the plants and being a caregiver. You have a good head on your shoulders. Use it. Make a decision. It doesn't matter what I think or what anyone else thinks."

What a shockingly, enlightened reply, she thought. "Thank you. I appreciate that. Nobody...nobody has ever said that to me before." And then that shudder started again; that electrified quivering in her stomach that made her feel quite sick and slightly disoriented. She stared straight ahead waiting for the jitters to stop, but they didn't.

"Are you okay, Betty?"

She was about to speak when she heard the next-door neighbor's young daughter walk outside and start tossing a ball against the fence. "I think we should go inside." She got up quickly and turned back to him. "You coming?" she said quietly.

"You afraid the kid's going to see me and...what?"

Betty felt embarrassed. "No, no, no, it's not that...uh... it's just..." She snuck a look next door. "People see me a certain way and –"

"Finding a biker guy with a ponytail sitting in your backyard at seven in the morning isn't the norm?" He grinned like a Cheshire cat.

"Something like that." Her tone was semi-formal.

He followed Betty back into the house and through the kitchen, which still smelled like Ganja Central. Jeff observed the living room while Betty went about opening more windows to air out the house. Ronald sauntered next to Jeff, brushing up against his jeans.

"Who's this?" he asked, gently lifting up Ronald and petting him.

"That's Ronald."

"Why Ronald?"

"He's named after Ronald Reagan. He's actually Ronald the third. Ronald the first and second are," she put her hand to her mouth in a clandestine manner, "buried in the backyard."

"I bet you think Ronald's a Republican too. He's not. He's an Independent. *All* cats are Independents. So why do you name every cat Ronald?"

"Consistency. They're all black and white too. Frank always said that consistency was important in life. Structure was essential. Chaos breeds confusion and unexpected consequences."

Jeff scratched Ronald's chin. "Sounds like ol' Frank was a bucket full of fun." He set Ronald down on the carpet and took a gander around the living room. "Maybe that explains the vibe in this room. It's like a Catholic Church without the frivolity. Or a tomb without the bad lighting."

Betty opened the last window and turned to him. "What are you talking about?"

"This place is holding its breath." He let out a few long breaths.

"What are you doing?"

"I'm trying to get the house to loosen up a bit so it can teach the occupant a few things. I'm surprised you don't have plastic runners to protect the aging carpet."

"I do," Betty replied quickly. "But they're at the cleaners," she said, joking.

"Ah, you see? Underneath all that conventional skin is a whole different person."

She stared at him, somewhat shaken by his comment. "I think I know that now," she softly said. Betty couldn't believe she was admitting this to someone she hardly knew. The realization was still so new and unformed in her mind. "But I'm not sure I know who that person is." She felt a lump forming in her throat. "And it's too late in life to realize this. To think I've wasted so much time pretending and going along with other's plans that I never felt...fit." She did everything possible to hold her emotions at bay. "I'm too old not to know who I really am."

Jeff shook his head. "Would you rather wait and be five minutes from death to figure this out? You're not bedridden, Betty. You're not feeble or mentally incompetent. You could have at least another twenty-five or thirty good years ahead of you if you wanted it. Stop worrying about what other people think. I've never let someone's expectations of who they thought I should be get in the way of who I really am."

"How did you know who you really are?"

"I always listen to my heart, never my head. The heart doesn't lie."

She considered the comment. "But how do you know if it's really your heart talking. Maybe it's your head talking and you think it's the heart. Or maybe it's all complete nonsense? Or maybe you're lying to yourself −"

"Spoken like someone who still thinks from her head." He checked the time. "I have to go open the store."

Betty stood across the dining room table from him, suddenly feeling a sense of loss. "Oh?" She pulled herself together. "Yes, yes. Of course, you do."

Jeff headed to the front door and then turned in a contemplative manner. "There was a old woman who lived on our street when I was nine. We called her Aunt Mimi. She had been confined to her bed as long as I'd ever known her. One day her husband decided to move her bed to the front living-room window so she could see outside. Each day as we walked to school in the morning and came back in the afternoon, we'd go by her front window and Aunt Mimi would wave to us. That went on for years, until I was probably thirteen. And then one afternoon, we walked by that window and she was gone. I figured the worst, so I went up to the front door and rang the bell and damned if Aunt Mimi didn't answer the door. She was standing upright, her hair in a little neat bun and dressed quite nicely. I was stunned. I said, 'Aunt Mimi, what happened? How come you finally got out of bed after all these years?' And she said, 'It was time.'" He smiled. "It's time, Betty."

Jeff left as Betty peered outside the front window. He got onto his motorcycle, and drove away. She wondered if anyone in the neighborhood was watching. But that other part of her hoped they were.

~~~

She took a two-hour nap – probably the deepest sleep Betty had in years – and was awakened when the phone rang. Checking the Caller ID, she saw it was Judi and answered the phone.

"What in hell happened last night?" Judi asked, her voice slightly edgy.

Betty felt her stomach drop. "What do you mean?"

"I got a call from Tom Reed. He said you were very... how should I say this...*rude*. That's not like you, Betty. Is everything all right?

God, she wanted to scream. She wanted to tell her everything. But how? How in the hell do you tell someone you're not the same anymore?

"Oh, hell, Betty. It's Peggy, isn't it? Of course, it is. Her memorial service is tomorrow, and I know how those things affect you."

This was the first time Betty heard that Peggy was even having a service. "I was under the impression from some comments she'd made a while ago that she didn't want a service –"

"People say a lot of things when they're sick. She *has* to have a service. It's the right thing to do. It's at 10:00 AM at the church on Fourth Street. I'll see you there and we will talk."

And that was that. The conversation was over. Betty sat there for several minutes as her blood slowly boiled. She tore into the kitchen, reheated her two cannabis oil concoctions to re-melt the oils, and then carefully strained them through a piece of cheesecloth into a large bowl. Once completed, she transferred them into her freezer to allow the water and oil to separate. She stood there, arms crossed, and stared at the closed door on the freezer for what seemed like an eternity. A furnace of indignation fired up her resolve, and she picked up the telephone, dialing Peyton's cell number.

He answered, and Betty heard the sound of reggae music playing loudly in the background. Apparently he was working the first shift at the grow store. "I'm doing this, Peyton," she declared.

"Awesome!"

Even though she was alone, she spoke confidentially into the phone. "I tried a tablespoon of the oil...quite by accident, of course."

"A *tablespoon?*" he softly chuckled. "Wow. Did you surrender to the stone?"

"Excuse me?"

"Did you allow it to take you where your body and mind needed to go?"

Betty reflected on his question. "I don't think I had much of a choice, to be honest. One does have to..." she hesitated, realizing what she was about to say, "let go...and not be afraid when it hits."

"I read once that cannabis can act as 'training wheels' for meditation. It helps you become more receptive."

She cogitated on his statement. "Training wheels…I like that."

"Dude, I'm proud of you. Four days ago, could you ever have imagined all of this would happen?"

"You have no idea, Peyton. I hope I can find the right patients with your help."

"No worries. It's like *Field of Dreams*. If you make the chocolates, they will come."

She swallowed hard, realizing she was about to walk into a strange new world. "I need to get my card. Do you know of a doctor I can go to?"

"Absolutely! Dr. Jan. She rocks."

Don't these people have last names anymore, she wondered? "Where is her office?"

"She works out of different locations. But primarily, she's got a van."

"*A van?* Dr. Jan has a van?"

"Yeah. We call it the Canna Van."

Betty took a hard breath. "She's a real doctor, right?"

"Oh, yeah. I saw her degree…in a frame."

"A frame? Well, that certainly makes it authentic."

"Hang on a sec. I have her schedule on a piece of paper in my wallet." He recovered the information and came back on the phone. "Dr. Jan's gonna be at Irving and Cooper all day today. If you want me to, I can give her a call and see about getting you in today. It helps to have a referral, you know?"

Betty agreed. Half an hour later, he called back and told her she scored an appointment at the odd time of 4:20.

"That's another excellent sign, Betty!" he raved. "This is all meant to be! I'm tellin' you Betty, you get your card and I'll help you get set up with everything you need. Between your chocolates and your green thumb, you're gonna be the toke of the town!"

Chapter 13

"I have a 4:20 appointment with Dr. Jan."

Betty parked two blocks from Irving and Cooper at 4:00 on the dot. There was no way she was going to park her Taurus too close to Dr. Jan's traveling van and risk being seen. She had a difficult time figuring out what to wear to her visit, as suitable attire for such an appointment wasn't established yet. So Betty donned a floral summer dress with sleeves of an appropriate length and carried her favorite sweater with the unraveling sleeve tucked under just in case the Colorado weather took a turn for the worse. Her formal taupe heels clicked brightly against the pavement as she walked the short distance.

It wasn't tough to locate Dr. Jan's van. It was clean, sparkling white and painted with a huge cannabis leaf, a green cross and an "Rx" on both sides. At first glance, it didn't look like any place where "medicine" would be practiced. In fact, cut a window in the side and replace the marijuana leaf with a popsicle and it could be an ice cream van. Outside the vehicle, a dark-haired woman in her early forties sat on a folding chair, organizing multiple manila folders on her lap. Between her teeth, she clenched a pen and muttered indecipherable words.

"Hello," Betty said, greeting the woman. "I'm Betty Craven. I have a 4:20 appointment with Dr. Jan."

The woman looked up and chuckled. "I bet you do. You come from church?"

"What?"

"A wedding?"

Betty glanced down at her dress. "No. This outfit is certainly not appropriate for church or a wedding."

The woman regarded Betty with some apprehension. "Look, if you're with the Feds, we've got our paperwork all in order. I don't want any hassles."

After several minutes, in which Betty explained in great detail who she was and why she was there, the woman interrupted her.

"Okay, okay! *I get it*! Pull up a chair." She motioned to a canvas, folding chair that leaned against the van. "I need your driver's license to get started."

Betty sat down. "Who exactly are you?"

"I'm Jan's nurse, slash assistant, slash notary, slash mediator. You can call me Pam." She proceeded to jot down Betty's information on a sheet of paper.

"I'm new to all this, Pam" Betty meekly offered.

"No shit?" she said with a sarcastic, droll tenor. Pam filled out part of the page and then handed it to Betty, along with her license. She instructed Betty to continue filling out the form and then gave her three more pages filled with every known disease and malady. "Check off every problem you have," she instructed her.

Betty began filling out the form. By page two, she'd already checked off sixteen boxes. Yes, there was even a box for ear problems. But she wanted to be precise, so she told Pam that it wasn't always "pain" but more of a "disagreeable flutter." Pam regarded her with a look that's usually reserved for baristas dealing with difficult patrons, who order complex cappuccinos with a whisper of froth and soy milk at Starbucks.

"Check the box, Betty," Pam advised. "We're not splittin' the atom here, okay?"

Betty continued to fill out the form and then handed it to Pam. By that time, Pam had already finished all the important paperwork Betty would need when she sat down with Dr. Jan. She then began to explain the somewhat involved process of how she would notarize the official form, and that Betty could *only* use a blue ink pen on the form. When Betty asked why it had to be blue ink, Pam didn't have a clue but stressed that if it wasn't completed in blue ink, the form would be returned. The intricate process continued. Pam stressed, with great fervor, the importance of including a personal check, not a money order for the ninety dollar fee to the state. She also explained the need to mail the completed forms by "Certified Mail with Return Receipt Requested" as proof of delivery, as well as a few other vital steps to make sure the Colorado Department of Health didn't return the documents because of a failure to follow their complex protocol. It was obvious to Betty that Pam had repeated this process far too many times, as indicated by the singsong and somewhat irritated nature of her voice.

"Excuse me," Betty said, after closely listening to Pam, "but shouldn't we be discussing all this after I am approved for a card?"

Pam regarded Betty with that same tired look. "Honey, you're over fifty and you've checked more than thirty squares. You've got at least one of the qualifying medical conditions. The only thing barring you from getting a card is pissing off Dr. Jan." Pam glanced down to the first page. "Hey, right here where it says, 'Describe the intensity of your neck spasm pain,' you checked off 'mild.' Are you sure it's mild?"

"No. Sometimes it's quite debilitating and I can't move. It even froze up last −"

"Then why did you check 'mild'?"

Betty's back stiffened. "Because I don't want to appear like I'm an invalid. Plus, I don't think it's right to characterize something as 'severe' when it can be moderate."

Pam put down her files and stared at Betty. Just stared at her.

After a long thirty seconds, Betty spoke up. "Is there a problem?"

"You're not the typical patient who visits Dr. Jan. Let me be clear. Colorado requires certain wording accompany specific problems. When Dr. Jan asks you to describe your neck pain, you might want to tag it as sometimes *severe*. You hearin' me?"

Betty nodded. "Yes. Severe. Gotcha."

"Hey, you didn't fill out what you do for a living."

"Oh, I guess I'm retired."

"What did you do?"

She considered the question. "Well, I raised my son and...then...I gardened...and cooked...and, um –"

"Yeah, yeah, I get the picture."

Betty realized how vacuous she sounded. "I owned a gourmet chocolate store for a while. High-end cacao. Not pedestrian offerings. Specialties, you know?"

The look of bemusement on Pam's face was classic. "But you don't have that store anymore, do you?"

"No. The economic downturn took care of that."

"Wow. Imagine that. You'd think even with a depression where people are losing their homes and cars and jobs, they'd still want to fork out ten bucks for a dot-sized chocolate. We call that poor planning where I come from."

Betty slightly stiffened. "Well, now hang on. I thought I was contributing in my own little way and providing people with something beautiful they would appreciate, and they'd feel good about themselves when they ate my chocolates."

Pam sat back with a mystified expression. "Damn, honey. You really believe that, don't cha?"

"Yes. I do. What's wrong with giving someone something beautiful they can look forward to every day? For that short moment in time, they feel happy and special and everything's perfect. Just because we live in a chaotic world, doesn't mean you have to throw out all the beauty. For some people, those moments are what keep them going." Betty had never been so forthright with any stranger. She had no idea where this candor was coming from, but she didn't regret a word of it.

There was movement in Dr Jan's van as her 4:00 patient exited the sliding side door. Betty cautiously checked out the individual but didn't know them, thankfully. After another minute, it was her turn.

Dr. Jan greeted her with a warm handshake. She was in her mid-thirties, with short, curly, red hair and casually dressed in jeans and a neat shirt. Betty sat across from the doctor on a bench built into the van. After a few minutes of nervous, filler conversation on Betty's part, Dr. Jan looked over the many boxes that Betty checked on her form. When she was finished taking her blood pressure and pulse rate, she checked her eyes.

"How's your eyesight?"

"Oh, it's so good I'm seeing things that aren't even there."

Dr. Jan smiled. "I gotta remember that one." She brought out her otoscope and looked into Betty's ear. "You currently smoke pot?"

"Good God, no."

"So, why do you want a medical card?"

Betty considered the question carefully. She could give an answer that would sound good and legitimate, but the more she thought about it, the more she didn't want to just rattle off some pointless excuse. "I have a lot of pain," she said with a halting voice and then realized it was the very first time she had ever admitted that to anyone. "I know what it feels like to be stuck, physically and emotionally. Maybe...by being a caregiver, I can help people. And if I'm lucky, maybe I can also help myself."

Dr. Jan stopped what she was doing. "That's the best damn answer I've ever heard."

Fifteen minutes later, Betty walked out of Dr. Jan's "Canna Van" with her signed paperwork. After making copies and taking a short trip to the post office, Betty would be officially legal. It would take at least five months to get her Colorado license in the mail, but right now, she could walk into any dispensary and buy whatever she wanted, including three plants. Once she got another medical marijuana card-holder to sign up as her patient, she could acquire another three clones, until she reached her limit of five patients and eighteen plants in vegetative growth.

As she walked back to her car, a child-like giddiness enveloped her. All at once, she felt slightly devilish but also dutifully aware of what she needed to accomplish. Betty had a little secret folded in that envelope and she would keep it to herself. Well, okay, she'd show it to Peyton, of course. And if Jeff was still at the store, she'd covertly show it to him too on her way home. By the time she got to her car, the last vestiges of the old Betty Craven were beginning to fall away. And while she tried her best, she couldn't stop smiling the entire way home.

~~~

Sleep was an elusive bedfellow that night. It wasn't from anxiety; it was born from pure excitement as her mind reeled with all the things she would need to set up her grow operation. She'd used up every bit of the money Peyton had given her from selling her chocolates to his patients. Turning on the TV as background noise, Betty dug through her drawers and closet to find anything of great value she could sell quickly. Hearing a somewhat familiar gravel-toned voice, she turned to the TV. It was "Doobie Douggie, and he was rolling down the sidewalk in his wheelchair, draped in a scarf with marijuana leaves painted on it, ranting to a local Denver reporter about how "pot was the people's plant." Apparently, this pied piper of pot, arrested *again* for growing marijuana without a license, had held the courtroom captivated with an emotionally charged, yet compelling address to the judge. But then, feeling the need to give the other side of the story, the broadcast went live to the studio where the sharp-tongued, proselytizing voice of Reverend Bobby Lynch launched into a mini-tirade during an in-studio interview. Betty realized Lynch was quite a bit shorter than she'd thought. Strange how she'd never noticed it before. Also, unattractive beads of sweat formed above his lip as he spoke. When he started banging his bony fist on the arm of his chair, she turned the channel. Settling on another nature program, she continued to rummage through her bureau. She opened her jewelry box and brought out Frank's gold wedding band.

Sitting on the edge of her bed, she rolled the heavy ring back and forth in her palm, again factoring what it might weigh. She was aware of the coldness she felt and the palpable disconnect between that ring and her heart. In the background, the narrator's hypnotizing voice explained how various insects adopt the use of camouflage in order to blend in and adapt to their wild surroundings. Other insects had grown tougher shells over millennia as a response to weather conditions. The whole point, noted the rather dry narrator, was adapting to one's surroundings in order to survive. Adapting, he stressed, was what separated those who lived from those who perished. "Adapt or die," he stated in an offhanded manner. "Adapt or suffer."

The price of gold was currently twelve hundred dollars an ounce. And the irony of what that would buy sent Betty into fits of giggles for another ten minutes.

Chapter 14

"Well, I guess they can't un-ring this bell, can they?"

Betty awoke early the next morning and wasted no time lollygagging under the covers. The day was destined to be full of the most divergent activities. First, she'd visit a trusted jeweler she knew who was always in the market for gold rings. Then, there would be her required appearance at Peggy's memorial service. After that, Betty was determined to drive to Denver's "Broadsterdam" – a.k.a. Broadway with an Amsterdam twist. This street was known as *the* place to cruise the various medical marijuana dispensaries. One medical marijuana dispensary after another sat nestled between the well-loved antique stores that were the mainstay of the area. Betty figured if she could get a feel for the kind of edibles that were available to patients, she'd have a better idea of what her future patients might expect. None of these places seemed to be open prior to 11:00 in the morning, she discovered. She momentarily cast silent aspersions toward the people who ran these establishments and then quickly realized she would shortly be counted as one of them.

The phone rang and Betty checked the Caller ID. It was strange to see the words "HIPPIE DIPPIE HEALTH" on her phone, but she was quietly thrilled and picked up. After she enthusiastically announced she was now a "red card carrying" member and she was planning to dispensary hop that day, Jeff piped up.

"I don't think it's a great idea for you to go on Pot Row by yourself," he stressed. "That part of town can be kind of sketchy. Not all the dispensaries are bad, but some of them are owned and operated by the Bag Brothers."

"Who are the Bag Brothers?"

"Dirt, Scum and Flea. Hey, if you want me to, I can take a long lunch and meet you at your house and go with you."

At first Betty was impressed with his show of chivalry. Then she was quickly put off, considering that Jeff didn't think she could do this on her own. Seconds later, she was terrified of encountering a Bag Brother.

"Betty? It's okay if you say 'no.'" Jeff said, ending the silence.

Perhaps it was the fact he allowed her a choice, or maybe, she told herself, it was the fact she wanted to see him again. Either way, she agreed to his offer. But there was that little adjustment of where they'd meet. "I have to go to a memorial service for my friend who didn't want a memorial service. Why don't you meet me at 11:00 in that empty mall parking lot on south Fourth?"

"Why not at the church?"

Betty's gut clenched. "Well, they tow vehicles or motorcycles in their parking lot that are left unattended."

"Is that right?"

His tone was off-handed, but Betty sensed he unfortunately understood her not-so-delicate intention.

"Not a problem," Jeff stated and then added, "I'll be sure to rev my motorcycle engine very loudly as I pass the church on the way to the big empty parking lot."

~~~

The trip to the jeweler was surprisingly painless and expedient. After weighing Frank's hefty wedding band, he determined it was worth just over twelve hundred dollars. When he asked if she wanted cash or a check, Betty opted for cash and watched as twelve, crisp, one hundred dollar bills were laid out in front of her. She took one last look at the ring and waited to feel something, but nothing happened. Somewhere in the back of her head, Betty remembered hearing a grief counselor once advise that, "When you feel nothing, it's really over."

Betty arrived at Peggy's service right on time and was waved to the front row of seats where she greeted Judi, Renée and Helen.

Judi leaned closer to Betty and whispered, "You look different. Is that a new dress?"

Betty shook her head, as the nauseating organ music swelled to a crescendo. She briefly recalled how much Peggy hated organ music.

Judi leaned over to her again. "You and I need to talk. Tom has no idea what he did wrong, and he'd like to see you again."

He wanted to see her again, Betty questioned? Was this narcissist also a masochist? "I'm not interested, Judi," she whispered back, trying to end the subject.

"Honey, you've got to get back in the saddle, if you know what I mean."

Betty grimaced at the visual. "I don't like horses," she countered in a semi-whisper. "And I don't date a horse's ass like Tom Reed."

They were summarily *shussed* like disobedient schoolgirls by Helen who sat at the end of the pew. Betty had forgotten how much memorial services brought out an even more dour side to Helen. She figured Helen was taking mental notes and privately criticizing the choice of flower arrangements, while planning what she did and didn't want at *her* service.

The service began with random readings from the Bible and "reminiscences" read by a minister Betty was certain had never met Peggy. The whole thing started feeling terribly insincere. She casually took a gander at the crowd, but didn't see Peyton or his grandfather. About thirty minutes later, the door to the church opened rather loudly. Betty turned and saw Peyton standing there, his face red with anger and his fists clenched. He wore a white t-shirt with a picture of a light bulb growing out of a large, nondescript leaf. Underneath the picture, the words *Grow Do It!* were emblazoned in sparkly neon green. She sensed he was either about to start screaming or make a scene, so she grabbed her purse and quietly made her way to the back of the church. Once there, she discreetly motioned him to follow her out side.

By the time they reached the bottom of the marble steps, Peyton couldn't take it any longer. "This is bullshit, Betty!" he yelled, jabbing his index finger at the closed front door. "I just read about this fuckin' joke in the newspaper! Aunt Peggy didn't want any of this shit! Why don't people listen?"

She put a gentle hand on his arm to try to calm him. "Funerals and memorial services are not for the dead, Peyton. They're for the living."

He shot her a look of contempt. "Is that another tired old saw? Well, before you break out the other one about "when God closes a door He opens a window," save it! Maybe He opens a window so you can jump out! Ever considered that?"

Betty let out a long breath. "Point taken." She waited for him to stop fuming. "Pull your pants up, would you?"

"They *are* up!"

"I can see your underwear. Please pull them up."

Something in her tone convinced Peyton to acquiesce. After a hard minute of deep breathing, he relaxed. "I hate funerals. What about you?"

"I'd rather have a root canal without sedation."

"What was your son's funeral like?"

The question came out of nowhere and temporarily derailed Betty. "He didn't have one. His father felt it wouldn't be appropriate given the way he died. So he was cremated, and he's now in a plain box in my bedroom closet."

"Your husband sounds like he was a pain in the ass."

"Yes. And sometimes the pain migrates up to the neck." Betty was stunned she finally admitted that.

"You think Frankie committed suicide?"

The old Betty would have stopped the conversation at this point. But something within her wanted to keep talking. "I don't know," she said bowing her head. "I like to think the overdose was an accident. But then I think about the last time I saw Frankie and I wonder."

Peyton leaned on the metal railing. "What happened?"

"He showed up at the house like he always did, knocking on the back door with his battered backpack across his shoulders. His father was not there, of course, but I knew we only had about an hour before he'd return. Frankie looked awful. So thin and frail and his face had sores on it." The memory dredged up unforgiving pain again, but Betty continued. "I told him I'd fix him something to eat, but he said he needed to go up to the attic where his bedroom used to be and just sit there for a few minutes. So, that's what he did. And when he came downstairs, he walked out in the backyard; it was like he was saying goodbye to the place." The tears began to flow freely.

Peyton put a reassuring hand on her arm. "You don't have to keep going if you don't want."

"No," she countered, wiping away the tears, "it's okay. I actually want to." She gathered her thoughts. "He walked over to the big elm tree in the yard and started cutting into it with a knife. When he was done, he came back into the kitchen, put his arms around me and held me so tightly; he didn't let go for the longest time. He didn't say a word, but I realize now he was saying goodbye." Betty paused, pushing herself back to that moment and seeing everything again. "I gave him food and offered him some money, but he said he didn't need it. When it was time for him to go, he said the strangest thing. He told me he'd had one of his visions. At first, I chalked it up to all the drugs. But then I remembered all those uncanny incidents in his childhood when he predicted things that often came true. So I asked him what he saw. And he said that in the vision, he was in a field of white violets and he was told to come to our house and bring me a gift. That's when he brought out an antique watercolor of white violets he said he found in a dumpster. It was actually quite beautiful, and he made a point of saying I would understand what the gift meant one day if I paid attention. I asked him to explain, and he said I had to discover it for myself. Then he said the voice told him I needed to be brave and observant. 'Pay attention,' he kept saying over and over." Betty bowed her head in sadness. "And then he left. He was found dead on a bus stop bench, three days later in downtown Denver, wrapped in a hotel blanket. And our final goodbye was me holding him on a slab at the mortuary."

"Why didn't your husband identify him?"

"Because he was disgusted and didn't want to be associated with his son anymore. He was also very drunk that night and could hardly get out of his recliner."

Peyton regarded Betty with sincere compassion. "Jesus, Betty. And you seriously blamed cannabis for your son's problems? Dude, when it comes to addicts, don't blame the plant when you should blame the person or the event that pushed them into addiction. As far as your late husband, fuck him, Betty. I mean it. *Fuck him.*"

"I did exactly that this morning when I pawned his wedding band."

Peyton smiled. "Sweet!" He peered over her shoulder. "Hey, I think we got a peeper over there."

Betty turned around and saw Renée smoking a cigarette under the shade of a tree next to the church. She motioned Betty toward her. "I'll talk to you soon, Peyton."

"Hey!" he said quietly, reaching into his pocket. "I was gonna bring this over later." He covertly handed her a folded piece of paper. "It's a list of the most popular medical strains of cannabis. You can research them, pick and choose what you want, and then let me know. If I have any, they're yours. If I don't have them, I can source them for you."

Betty slipped the paper into her purse. "Thank you." He started to turn when Betty spoke up. "What kills the plants?"

"Knowing you hate them," he said with a straight face. "That gets 'em. Right here." He patted his heart and looked over her shoulder. "Incoming..." Spinning on his heels, he left.

Betty turned.

Renée was already halfway in her direction. "Betty, what's going on?" She nervously sucked another hard hit of nicotine. "You shouldn't be associating with him."

"What do you mean?"

"That boy is no damn good! Two people at my A.A. meetings mentioned in passing that he might be growing pot." She waited for a reaction. "*Marijuana?*"

"Oh, *marijuana?* My, my." She put on her most sincere face. "Are you sure?"

"No, I'm not sure. But it's fairly obvious when you look at him what kind of person he is."

Betty's back straightened. "Is that right?"

"You should hear what his mother says about him!" Renée inhaled deeply. "Useless, pointless, worthless and a waste of space. And those are the high points!"

Betty's lower lip trembled. "Really? Well then, Renée, I'll help him even more."

"*Help him?* What in the hell are you —"

"Yes, I think I'll mentor him. I've got nothing else to do, so why not?" She checked the time. "I have to go."

Renée stood there dumbstruck. "Where? We've got Peggy's memorial luncheon scheduled at the *Pirate Landing* seafood restaurant."

Betty shook her head. "Peggy detested pirates and she was allergic to seafood. Seems a tad ridiculous, don't you think?" She started toward her car.

"I'll save you a seat!" Renée yelled.

~~~

Betty arrived at the empty parking lot just as Jeff drove up on his Harley.

He opened her passenger door and leaned in. "All clear, Betty?"

"Oh, please. Just get in."

"I brought us lunch. I know you're into the whole gourmet *schtick,* so the bread is whole grain with fresh rosemary, the mustard is Dijon, the tomatoes are local and organic, the lettuce is from my garden and the sprouts are from the store. I made one with hormone-free roast beef and one with free-range chicken." He held out the wrapped sandwiches. "Which one trips your trigger?"

Betty was blown away but tried to hide it. "I'll take the roast beef."

He handed it to her and she unwrapped it, taking care to not drop anything on the car's fabric. This was certainly different. How strange for someone to take the time to make her a sandwich. She took a delicate bite and let the flavors mingle in her mouth.

"Well? What's the verdict?"

She didn't want to look a sandwich horse in the mouth but he *did* ask. "It's quite good. But..."

"What?"

"It could use some salt."

"I didn't salt it on purpose. I believe that's an individual choice that shouldn't be foisted upon another person, unless you know that person very well. So," Jeff pulled two small containers out of his jacket pockets. "I've got Himalayan Pink Salt and the ultimate, Fleur de Sel...from France, of course. Which one do you want?"

It wasn't polite to open one's mouth when it was full of food but Betty couldn't avoid it when her jaw dropped. She quickly recovered. "I've *always* wanted to try the Fleur de Sel."

"Well, there you go! One less thing on your bucket list."

She sprinkled the pricey salt on her sandwich and took another bite. Heaven. Pure heaven.

As they drove, Betty explained in precise detail what her objectives were that day at the dispensaries. Jeff listened patiently and then twenty minutes later, he finally interjected.

"I brought a book to read when you're inside. I'll sit in the front room since I can't go in without a card. Want to see the book?"

Betty nodded. He held up a copy of Jorge Cervantes' *Marijuana Horticulture: The Indoor/Outdoor Medical Grower's Bible*. It looked like the spine hadn't been cracked.

"Whatever are you doing with that?"

"I thought it might be interesting reading. I like plants. Pot's a plant. Besides, I think I'll look good sitting in the front rooms reading this book. Maybe I can pick up some hot dispensary chicks."

Betty shot him a look of disapproval.

"You know," he added, turning through the glossy pages of the book, "I've been doing a little research for you on this whole medical marijuana deal —"

"*Cannabis*," Betty corrected. "That's the proper name for the plant. The term 'marijuana' is a Mexican slang name that was adopted in the 1920's by the government to marginalize the herb."

Jeff smiled broadly. "*Okay*. I've been doing research into *cannabis* and found that while many in the state legislature might turn their nose up at it, they're also laughing all the way to the Treasury. Did you know they quietly transferred three million dollars out of the medical mari...excuse me, *cannabis* fund to pay off state debt? And apparently, from what I found out, if the budget shortfall continues, they may use three times that amount later this year to help with the debt."

"Well, I guess they can't un-ring this bell, can they? If the state is using fees from the registry to pay off their debt, they sure as hell aren't killing this fatted calf."

"No, they're not. Four things will always be popular during any economic recession or depression: cigarettes, booze, pot and prostitution...not necessarily in that order. But, Betty, there's still something to be said for staying low profile on this." His voice was serious for a change.

"I agree and I intend to do that."

"What kind of security do you have at your house?"

Betty turned briefly to him with a look of concern. "I have a gun and I know how to use it."

"Okay. But you might want to invest in carbon filters to vent the odor. You understand that these plants give off quite a sweet, pungent aroma, right?"

"Well, I do now." As long as the filters kept the odor from crossing the street into Jerry's nostrils, she was satisfied.

They arrived on Broadway and sourced the first of many dispensaries. The process was the same wherever she went.

Since she didn't have a card, Betty presented copies of her notarized and signed paperwork which served as a temporary medical card. Once she was entered into a dispensary's system, she was allowed through the locked door and into ganja heaven.

What struck Betty first about many of the dispensaries she visited was that most of them occupied old relics of buildings that weren't in the best shape. Unfortunately, about seventy percent of the establishments had a seedy quality that didn't generate a sense of class or safety. Posters of Bob Marley abounded, along with photos of Jimi Hendrix smoking a fat joint. Some of the businesses felt the need to blare heavy metal so loudly, Betty had to yell over the din in order to communicate. One dispensary's front door was plastered with random bumper stickers; everything from "FREE THE WEED" to "JESUS WAS A LIBERAL." covered the door. Some of the women who worked the front desk smelled quite skunky and took a little too much time entering her information in the computer. Another young girl had five face piercings and a large tattoo that wrapped around her neck in the design of a human barcode.

At a larger dispensary, a formidable Russian man in his mid-forties led Betty into a back room with a neon sign that read: "THIS IS NOT AN EXIT." After seeing what was in the room, she mused as to whether the neon sign was an existential statement or just a directional indicator. Draped in red and black satin, the small, windowless room held over twenty-five jars of cannabis, along with glass pipes, vaporizers and an assortment of tinctures, salves, oil capsules and the ever present medicinal brownie. The room felt like a faintly remodeled flophouse where women charge by the hour. There was also something unnerving about the way the heavyset Russian kept leering at her and pushing his offerings with his heavy accent.

"You come from church?" he asked her, observing her outfit.

Betty stood straight as an arrow, doing everything to hide her apprehension. "Yes. Actually, I did. It was a funeral.

The dearly departed was a dispensary owner, shot by a jealous competitor." The Russian regarded her with a stunned expression. She leaned forward, speaking in a fabricated covert manner. "Funny thing is, I'm actually friends with the jealous competitor."

That allowed Betty an uneventful exit. She continued her journey down Broadway. She discovered two quite-decent dispensaries that didn't make her feel like she was doing something dirty on her lunch hour. Both of these were clean, well-lit and staffed by neatly dressed employees. But in general, Betty was underwhelmed by what she found available in the edibles department. Even the dispensaries that touted "connoisseur" and "gourmet" edibles, failed to impress her. Betty found nothing original or enticing about a medicated Rice Krispy treat – the only selling point was the good lighting shining on it in the case. The added distraction of dispensary menus with horrible misspellings didn't exactly stir the cockles of her heart either.

"One usually has to travel to India and the slums of New Delhi to experience some of the establishments I've witnessed today," Betty summed it up to Jeff as they got back into her car.

"I told you it was sketchy."

Betty fell deep into thought.

"What is it?" Jeff asked.

"I can give my future patients something they've never eaten before. I could make cannabis medicine actually look and taste spectacular. Maybe even, transcendent." She turned to Jeff. "Does that sound silly to you?"

"No. I think it's absolutely beautiful." His eyes lingered a little too long on Betty.

She turned away as her gut started to quiver. "You need to get back to your store. I'm sure you have lots of work to do."

"Yeah. Lots of work to do."

She dropped him off in the parking lot, but he left the grow book on the seat, telling Betty she might want to "give it a gander."

"I can pay you for the book!" she insisted.

"Don't worry, Betty," he reassured her.

On her way back home, she spied another dispensary outside of Paradox that advertised clones on their signage. Betty parked her Taurus and checked the area, making sure she didn't know anyone. After submitting her paperwork, she was led into a brightly lit back room where temperature controlled glass cases were filled with dozens of cannabis strains, their delicate leaves gently fluttering from twelve small fans. Some plants were only five inches tall, while others reached upwards of over a foot. The "budtender" explained he grew a variety of pure *Sativas*, one of pure *Indicas* and crosses of both subspecies. Generally, one hundred percent *Sativas* had long narrow leaves and grew lanky and tall. Its effect on the body was very cerebral, often motivating and energizing, but could also promote paranoia, rapid thoughts and racing heartbeats, especially in people who were already hardwired to live in their heads or leaned toward obsession, fear or mania. On the other hand, *Indicas* grew squattier and had large, wide leaves. *Indicas* were used to relax the mind and create a "body high" or buzz that could be both comforting and calming. One hundred percent *Indicas* had the ability to put one "in da couch," so to speak and unable to lift one's arms off the armrest if the dose was overdone. In this budtender's opinion, most older medical patients with chronic issues were best off with a pure *Indica* for sleep and pain issues, as well as possibly specific strains that were either sixty/forty or eighty/twenty percent *Indica* to *Sativa*. As he put it, "the right sixty/forty, *Indica/Sativa* cross can be a real gem for some medical users who aren't bedridden, because the *Indica* relaxes their body and the *Sativa* keeps them awake and motivated."

He patiently explained about the specific uses for the different strains he grew. Some were perfect for migraines and nerve-related disorders, while others excelled at reducing muscle spasms and resolving insomnia. The gentleman, who Betty reasoned was quite educated and definitely sober, also mentioned that each available clone was a female, pointing out the delicate white hairs that protruded from the stems, indicating their sex. "That white hair shows you it's a female plant. Male plants literally have these little tight balls...kinda like a nut sack?"

Betty furrowed her brow. It had been awhile since she'd had the pleasure of seeing an actual nut sack, tight or otherwise. "Do you have a male plant I can see?"

"No ma'am," without cracking a smile. "We're not plant breeders here, and the male cannabis plants are only used for breeding purposes, not for medicine. If you grow from seed and you're not a breeder, you gotta kill the plants that turn male, or they'll pollinate your female plants, and then the ladies won't develop the sticky bud you're after."

Killing the males, Betty mused. A feminist's dream. She remembered the list Peyton gave her. Going over it quickly, she noted he put asterisks next to a few names. One of those was called Fucking Incredible. But Betty couldn't see herself asking for a Fucking Incredible plant, let alone telling her future patients that she had some great Fucking Incredible chocolates for them to enjoy. Thus, she shifted her focus to another starred strain, Centennial Blueberry. Since she'd been introduced into this new world with that strain, she figured it was fitting to make it her first purchase. She selected three of the larger, more developed Centennial Blueberry plants that looked vigorous and were well established in their two-gallon dirt containers. With tax, it came to just over two hundred dollars. She proudly pulled out the funds from the sale of Frank's wedding band and collected her emerald-leafed beauties. The budtender dropped a complimentary lighter in a bag that featured a smiling cannabis leaf. Betty almost returned it, but something about the lighter made her smile. She was still smiling when she secured her plants in the backseat of her car, and she couldn't keep the grin off her face the entire time she drove back home.

That is, until she saw the flashing lights in her rearview mirror and the black and white police car urging her to pull over.

Chapter 15

"You're trying to kill me, aren't you?"

Betty's heart raced, as she turned to her three plants secured in the back seat. A paper bag loosely covered them, but their scent was beginning to give them away. As the police officer got out of his patrol car, her mind raced. She could offer him her medical marijuana paperwork to explain everything, but what if word got out in the town about this?

"Hello, ma'am," he said dryly. "Can you please roll down your window all the way?"

Betty smiled brightly and complied. "Whatever is wrong, officer? I don't think I was speeding."

"May I see your license, registration and insurance?" Betty handed it to him. "Your brake lights are not working."

"Oh," she said, with a sigh of relief, "It's an old car. I'll have to get that fixed."

He screwed up his nose and sniffed.

"*Lovely day*, isn't it?" she quickly added.

He looked at her driver's license and then at Betty. Leaning forward, he scowled. "Well, we have a situation here, ma'am."

"Oh?"

"Yes. You're Colonel Craven's widow, aren't you?"

"Yes."

"Your husband trained my nephew down at Fort Carson and molded him into a first-class soldier we can all be proud of. I will always keep a place in my heart for your late husband."

"How special." Betty felt as if her face was about to break from her forced smile. "His legacy still continues to pay off in the most extraordinary ways."

Handing back her license and other cards, he bid her goodbye. By the time she got back home, she'd shaken off the adrenaline rush. She was surprised to see Buddy atop her roof. Again, it was an unscheduled visit. Betty carefully removed the covered plants from the backseat and walked with them toward the front of the house. Shielding her face from the searing sunshine, she called up to him, asking if he wanted any lunch. Buddy declined the offer, but she could see he was sweating like a stuck pig and struggling with his tool belt.

"Are you sure you're all right, Buddy?"

"Yeah. Just a little creaky in the back today."

Betty let out a sigh. The poor man desperately needed to lose at least fifty pounds and eat better food.

Inside the house, she quickly transferred the three Centennial Blueberry clones up to her bedroom and set them on the windowsill, where the sunlight streamed in consistently this time of year. Smiling, she stood back and admired them. The large, fat leaves were nearly the size of her palm and happily lifted their tips toward the light. She knew she would need better lighting, but that would take some research and a trip to the grow store where Peyton worked. But right now, she had two chunks of canna cocoa butter and canna coconut oil in her freezer that needed to be processed.

As Buddy's footsteps moved back and forth on the roof above her, Betty diligently removed the first bowl of canna cocoa butter from the freezer, and after loosening the sides under a stream of hot water, carefully slid the contents onto a cookie sheet. The water separated from the fat, and Betty was easily able to chip away the distinctive layer on top with a sharp knife. Once that was done, a beautiful two-inch-high, round chunk of cannabis-infused cocoa butter sat on a plate. Betty repeated the process with the coconut oil version, making sure to keep her activities limited to one section of the kitchen just in case Buddy showed up unexpectedly, and she needed to toss a few dishcloths over the evidence.

She really needed to figure out the location and design of her grow room, but she also wanted to see what tempting creations she could come up with using the green cocoa butter. So Betty quickly whipped up a chocolate base filled with local honey, cinnamon, a dash of nutmeg and a sprinkle of amaretto for added flavor. While that melted, she portioned off just enough of the canna cocoa butter from the chunk and factored that one good teaspoon per chocolate square was certainly sufficient. She recalled Peyton told her he added two good teaspoons to the chocolate he gave Peggy, but that was on the high end as far as Betty was concerned, since the tablespoon she took straight out of the bowl had put her into a semi stupor. By only putting in one teaspoon of the cannabis cocoa butter, it made sense that one could take a quarter of the chocolate square or even less, in order to get the desired pain-relieving or sleep-inducing effect. Thus, one bar could last a novice user like Betty four or more doses. Pouring the chocolate into the square moulds, Betty allowed enough space to add the extra teaspoon of medicine. Using a toothpick, she gently stirred the aromatic canna cocoa butter into each mould, making sure to spread it out evenly. From there, the moulds went into the freezer to harden.

Thirty minutes later, she heard Buddy's heavy footsteps cross the roof and head toward the front of the house as she removed the finished chocolates from the freezer. She popped them out one by one onto a plate; they looked like any other chocolate bar one might encounter, albeit this one was made from the finest ingredients and generously sweetened with honey. She was just about to decorate them with the silver and gold swirls she'd perfected at *The White Violet*, when she heard a horrible *thud* outside.

Covering up the chocolates with a towel, Betty raced into the living room to find Buddy tangled in the boxwood bush that framed the front window. "Oh, dear God!" she yelled, hurrying outside. "Don't move!" she frantically told him.

"Shit," he muttered, attempting to extricate himself from the foliage.

"Please, Buddy! Don't move! I'll call 9-1-1."

"It's my fault, Mrs. Craven. My back seized up." He worked his way out of the boxwood, but he was clearly in pain. "Don't call 9-1-1. I'll just drive myself to the ER."

Men could be so stubborn. "*I'll* drive you."

He tried to reach into his back pocket, but the pain was too much. "Hey, could you get my wallet out of my pocket? My insurance information's in there."

Betty obliged and slowly walked him to her car, helping him get in the passenger side. "I'll be right back. Gottta lock up the house and get my purse."

Racing back inside, Betty quickly shuttled the plates of chocolates back into the refrigerator and locked the doors. She wanted to be organized, so she quickly rummaged through Buddy's wallet for his driver's license and insurance card. That's when she saw it. Folded neatly behind his license was an eight inch by three and one-half inch, red and white certificate. Buddy was a certified patient on the Colorado Medical Marijuana Registry. And he had no caregiver noted. Without skipping a beat, Betty grabbed one of her newly-formed chocolate creations, and factoring in Buddy's large build, grabbed another one just to be sure.

Back in the car, she handed one to him. "Have a chocolate, Buddy!"

He ate it and didn't seem to notice the odd herby taste.

"When did you eat last?" she asked him, pulling out of her driveway.

"Probably five hours ago," he replied, wincing from pain in his lower back.

Empty stomach, she surmised. That would speed up the effects. Halfway to the ER, she didn't see Buddy pick up the remaining chocolate she'd set on the center console until he already had it in his mouth

"These are good, Mrs. Craven! You've outdone yourself."

Betty continued driving and remained silent. Since he obviously was already using medical marijuana, she hoped he was used to it, and his weighty frame could handle the hefty two-teaspoon dose he'd ingested. In the waiting room, it was evident there would be at least an hour wait before he could see a doctor. Betty sat next to him, filling out his paperwork and observing him every few minutes for any sign of the cannabis kicking in. An hour passed, and then ninety minutes.

They were told they could finally go into a room to wait for a doctor. She watched a nurse help Buddy into a wheelchair; it was obvious he was still in pain. Betty wasn't sure what to think as she followed the nurse who wheeled him into a curtained area in the ER. With Buddy placed on a gurney, Betty sat in an uncomfortable chair next to him and waited. And she waited. And waited a bit more.

She was just about to concede she had miscalculated how much cannabis cocoa butter to add to the chocolates when she looked over at Buddy again. He was staring at the ceiling, spellbound by a crack in the paint.

"Did you ever really look at a crack in a ceiling? I mean, *really* look at it?"

Betty observed him. "How's the pain, Buddy?"

He looked at her with a questionable expression. "It's there…but it's nothing like it was when we got here." He looked around the area. "Damn, these lights are bright!"

Betty moved her chair closer to the gurney and leaned in close to Buddy. "We need to talk."

~~~

By six o'clock that night, Betty was back home. And she had her very first patient on record. When she left Buddy at his apartment, he was still feeling the effects of the two chocolates he scarfed down, but after she prepared him a bowl of soup from a *can* — an act that rankled every fiber of Betty's body — and propping him up in his bed, Buddy told her he actually felt better than he had in awhile. Fortunately nothing was broken, but the docs advised him to take a few days off. He told her he'd have a friend come by and get his work truck out of her driveway.

Betty spent half an hour filling out the necessary paperwork for Buddy so she could become his caregiver. After a quick bite to eat, she checked on her three new additions to the family upstairs in her bedroom. They looked as cheerful as ever, and Betty would have sworn they'd already grown half an inch since she'd last seen them.

Settling in behind her computer, she began the arduous task of researching the intricacies of setting up a grow room in one's house. While some people converted a bedroom closet, she learned that having a dedicated room or area for the operation was the best idea. Basements were the most popular area, since they were separate from the main house and afforded the grower a better chance of being discreet.

The deeper she delved into the intricacies of cannabis growing, the more she recognized that the entire process was developed and perfected by a dedicated group of anal-retentives. She would need two separate rooms, each one having plenty of air circulation, and a way to continually feed clean air inside and dirty air outside.

The first room would be known as the "veg room." This is where the clones would live, until they reached two to three feet in height. Temperature control was vital in the veg room in order to keep the plants healthy and free of opportunistic diseases. In fact, one website stressed that a temp of seventy-two to seventy-eight was optimal and needed to be controlled with any means possible, either heaters to warm it up or fans to cool it down. At night, sixty-two degrees was the magic number when the plants needed to cool down. Anything below fifty-five degrees could shock the cannabis, causing stunted growth or death.

Special lighting was also required in the veg room. During the vegetative cycle, cannabis requires grow lights that put off a "spring" luminescence, which carries a slightly blue spectrum. Known as a "T5 light," twelve small plants or four moderately large ones could fit beneath one of these babies. The clones had to stay under this set of lights for at least eighteen hours a day, with six hours of total darkness. However, if one needed to speed up the growth of the clones, one could up the ante to twenty-two or twenty-four hours of continuous light, or as a cannabis website called it, "the summer Alaskan method."

Cost was around two hundred fifty dollars for one set of lights, not including the metal stand needed to support it. That cost another hundred and fifty. Throw in the carbon air filters and fans, and Betty realized this was not just a simple little basement garden. In fact, the more she researched, the more she realized growing cannabis was an industry unto itself. While none of the websites actually stated they were there to support your medical grow, they might as well have had cannabis leaves strung across their webpages. With nutrients called "Bodacious Bud" and "Resin Revolution," it was obvious one didn't purchase these items to grow imposing petunias.

The cost really accelerated when one needed to "flip" their vegetative plants into flower. *That* endeavor required an entirely different room, a grow light that put off a "bloom" radiance concentrated in the red/orange spectrum, more circulating air fans and an intake/outtake fan. For the lights, Betty could choose from four hundred up to one thousand watts. Based on what she read on a few cannabis forums, most growers obtained the best luck with the pricier-and-hotter thousand watt setups, since the bloom cycle of the plant's life was dictated and triggered by light. And that light cycle was regimented – twelve hours of light and twelve hours of complete darkness. According to one forum's "expert indoor grower," if you altered that 12/12 cycle, as it was called, even by one New York minute, or had any light leaks shining into your bloom room during the dark, twelve-hour period, you could "confuse" the plant and create any number of problems. These problems included irregular bud growth, reduced resin output in the mature bud, seeds in the bud and just plain old slow development of the bud.

The operative word here, as Betty quickly deduced, was *bud*. It was *all* about the bud. And the more she read, the more she realized a lot of people had spent a lot of time figuring out what type of light, nutrients, fertilizers and even music increased bud production. To say growing cannabis consumed people's lives was putting it mildly. A grower named "Bud Professor" – no one on the forums used their true names – wrote, "Cannabis is not addictive, but *growing it* is highly addictive. You're always trying to figure out the newest, best methods for growing exceptional herb." Betty could relate to that statement. She didn't cultivate a prize-winning garden and earn a wall full of plaques by following a predictable approach. Betty always sought out unique, organic enhancers to grow the biggest flowers possible. After reading a book years ago on farming in Colonial Jamestown, she experimented with burying a whole trout in each of several holes before transplanting a cluster of peonies. Of course, she did this using a flashlight at night to avoid being seen by the neighbors. When those peonies blossomed, they were enormous and almost looked fake. When Betty overheard one of the judges quip that, "something was fishy" about her entry, she smiled because she couldn't disagree.

After several hours combing the Web and taking copious notes, it was obvious to Betty that there was a thriving cottage industry of cannabis growers serving medical marijuana states. The industry had literally taken a lowly ditch weed and lifted it up into the echelon of a pampered diva. The more she read, the more she realized this extension of her gardening acumen could quickly take over her life.

It could also take over her wallet as well. A one-thousand watt, bloom-grow light set up was a cool six hundred dollars. That would only serve six to eight moderately sized plants. The state allowed Betty three plants in vegetative growth and three plants in bloom, per patient. If she were able to get five patients – her maximum stable of legal patients under Colorado law – and included herself on the list for a total of six, she would need thirty-six plants, eighteen in veg and eighteen in bloom. And that would require *a lot* of light, a lot of patience, a lot of ingenuity, a lot of money and a *whole* lot of time.

She sat back and felt an overwhelming wave of apprehension hit her squarely between the eyes. What had she gotten herself into, she wondered? Had she allowed herself to be taken down the cannabis path by Peyton, just as she allowed herself to be controlled by Frank all those years? This newfound venture certainly had the potential for colossal failure, not to mention the fact it had to be done surreptitiously, given her reputation and the way people viewed her.

After all, she'd signed her name to that damn letter to the editor in favor of banning all this. What in the hell *was* she doing?

She turned toward the window where her three new plants sat. The outside light was fading, and her mothering instinct kicked in. Gathering together several lamps and removing the shades, she circled them around the cannabis pots. It was then she noticed one of the leaves was drooping. Checking the soil, she was amazed how quickly it had dried. "Darling, you're thirsty, aren't you?" After giving them all a drink, she stood back and stroked the wide leaves. They didn't call it "weed" for nothing; they looked just like something she'd yank out of her flowerbed. And yet, there was something magnificent about them too. She couldn't put her finger on it. Perhaps it had something to do with what these plants would eventually transform into, laden with their sticky buds and exuding a provocative fragrance all their own. Right now, they were hiding their true potential, and all they needed was a patient, guiding hand that would allow them to become the majestic beauties that God intended. Yes, Betty realized, they needed her.

Returning to her computer, she did a search for more instructional videos on cultivating cannabis. One of the videos featured "Doobie Douggie," who apparently had his own Internet series that was more akin to several three-minute sermons. One was titled, "Did You Know?" and she clicked on it. There was Douggie sitting in his wheelchair, under the shade of an enormous outdoor cannabis plant in his backyard.

"Did you know we all have cannabinoid receptors in our brains?" he said, pointing his finger at the camera. "We do! And here's the thing: they can only be unlocked when the cannabinoids from the marijuana plant attach to them. So what does this tell us?" he asked, waving his hands in the air. He moved closer to the camera, almost distorting his face. "Is it possible we actually *need* the cannabinoids in marijuana to regulate our bodies, our moods and our sleep patterns?

Could people possibly be suffering from a deficiency of cannabis?"

"That's crazy," Betty mumbled.

"Sound crazy?" Douggie quickly added.

Betty checked herself. "Maybe."

"Well, it's not crazy!" Douggie yelled. "I've seen again and again how small amounts of this plant, taken on a daily basis, can regulate one's mood, appetite, energy and yeah, even the sex drive. And for all you greenies out there, I'm not talking about getting stoned! Far from it! Douggie is not about 'gettin' fucked up on the herb. Douggie is all about using this sacred plant responsibly and ethically, in the lowest dose possible." He picked up a bowl of green oil and held it up to the screen. Dipping the tip of his finger into the oil, he slid it into his mouth and swallowed. "That's all it takes, people! Just a few drops! It's not just a medicine, it's nectar from God's own green hand!" He jabbed his finger at the camera. "Signing off now! And remember what Douggie says. Legalize the weed...It's just a plant, man!"

The screen faded to black and Betty was left staring at her computer in slight disbelief. Checking the time, she realized it was way past the dinner hour so she headed downstairs. A crêpe sounded just about right, so she whipped up the flour, egg and milk base and spooned it into a hot pan. Adding cheese and some leftover chicken, she folded it into a lovely, half moon of delight. Sitting at the kitchen table, she thought about what Douggie said in his video. It seemed to go against everything she'd believed. Could someone really have a cannabis *deficiency* that might be alleviated by ingesting a little cannabis oil daily? Halfway through her delectable crêpe, she got up and pulled out the chunk of cannabis-infused coconut oil from her freezer. Carefully slicing off a three-inch piece, she plopped it into a dish and melted it over a low flame.

The phone rang. She checked the Caller ID. It read: PRIVATE. Betty hated it when callers did that and she almost didn't answer, but then she wondered if it was Peyton or someone else she wouldn't mind talking to.

"Hello?"

"Betty, it's me."

It was Judi, and she didn't sound like her usual, sparkling self. Betty returned to the stove to monitor the melting oil.

"Hello, honey," Betty replied.

"Listen, I'm just going to come out and say this, okay?"

Betty sensed something odd in Judi's voice. Her tone was more aggressive, and she was slurring her words.

"What's wrong, Judi?" Betty stirred the oil with the tip of a toothpick.

Judi let out a hard breath. "Something is different about you and we're worried."

"Who's worried? You and Roger?"

"No, not Roger! Renée and I...and Helen, of course."

"Of course. There's no need to be worried, Judi. I'm fine."

"You are acting different, honey," Judi argued.

Betty thought about it. "How?" She continued to stir the oil with the toothpick, making sure it didn't burn the dish. "What do you see that concerns you?"

Judi let out another tired breath. "I don't know. You're evasive with us. And you were rude to Tom Reed. That's not like you, Betty. You've always gone out of your way to get along and be nice."

Betty stopped stirring the mixture momentarily. "Yes. I have. You're quite right there." The oil started to sizzle and she reduced the heat further. "Regarding Mr. Reed, the poor bastard thinks the sun comes up every morning just to hear him crow. That's not someone I need in my life."

"Betty, he's perfect for you! This is someone who could be an asset to you."

"What? Financially speaking?"

There was sudden silence. "Well...yes...but companionship as well."

"Judi, how can I say this so you'll understand? I'd rather shoot myself in the foot and run a marathon before I ever laid eyes on Mr. Reed again."

"This is *exactly* the attitude I'm talking about, Betty."

"What? Because I'm not doing what you're asking me to do?"

"Well...it's not...*yes*. Yes, that's exactly it! You need guidance right now, honey. I can sense you're on a very slippery slope from all you've been through and as your friend, it's my right to say that."

Betty stared at the melted oil in the dish. Using a dessert spoon, she removed a small amount and blew across it to cool it down. "How many glasses of wine have you had tonight, Judi?"

"What?"

"You sound a bit tipsy, sweetie." She wanted to say 'drunk.'

"I'm fine."

"Okay." Betty dipped the tip of her pinky into the cooling oil and collected about five drops on her fingernail. Without hesitating, she licked it off. "I've got to get back to my dinner."

"Wait," Judi urged. "Have you seriously forgotten what tomorrow is?"

Betty stopped and thought. She was clueless. "No idea."

"*Betty?*" Judi chided in a sloppy tenor. "It's Helen's seventieth birthday!"

Betty swallowed hard. "Oh, dear. I don't have anything for her."

"She doesn't need a damn present. But she does need your *presence* at *La Bella Vita*. I have the day off tomorrow, and we're taking her to lunch there."

"I didn't know Helen liked *La Bella Vita*."

"Sure she does. She adores it. And besides, every Friday they offer a free glass of the house red wine with every featured item. Can I count you in?"

Betty surmised *La Bella Vita* was heaps better than the *Pirate Landing*. That post-memorial-service dining experience must have been a bust. Certainly poor Helen must have cringed when the scruffy server with a five o'clock shadow, a black patch over his eye and a plastic sword in his belt loop screamed "Ahoy Matey!" as he skimmed the greasy menus and peanuts across the table. She agreed to the lunch in Helen's honor.

"Oh, one more thing," Judi added, taking a sip. "I'm helping with the fundraiser at the hospital for Roger, and I need to borrow that brocade tablecloth of yours. Can you bring it tomorrow?"

Betty faltered. "It's in a box in the attic."

"Can you get to it?"

Now it was Betty's turn to sigh quietly. "Sure."

After finishing her crêpe, Betty returned the coconut cannabis oil to the freezer. She washed the dishes and put them away before heading upstairs. Standing at the door to the attic, she lingered too long before opening it. She flicked on the light switch and slowly ascended the narrow, dusty stairs. When she reached the top, she stood in the semi-darkness, holding her breath. Frankie's bed was still in the corner, as were his posters of the rushing Gunnison River and Mt. Evans in full, fall foliage. The place smelled dank and felt like a heavy heart still owned it. Finding the tall box, Betty quickly unpacked the brocade tablecloth.

While sorting through the box, she also found two exquisite hand sewn table runners. They'd been wedding gifts, and she'd used them only about a dozen times in her married life. She eyed them with an unemotional gaze, factoring what they might be worth. After removing them from the box and carefully wrapping them in a plastic, protective sheath, Betty sunk to the floor and stared across the tiny room. Why did Frankie want to be alone up here that day, five years before? He wasn't fond of the attic, but it was farther away from his father's unyielding presence. Betty rested her head against the side of the box and closed her eyes. "Frankie," she whispered. She felt herself sliding into peaceful slumber until she heard a *thud*.

Opening her eyes, she turned to the shadows where the ceiling slanted against the wall. Frank Sr. stood there, his fists balled and his face red with anger.

"You sold my wedding ring!" he growled. "My goddamned wedding ring! And now you're gonna sell those!"

He jerked his finger toward the table runners cradled in her arms. "You're trying to kill me, aren't you? *Aren't you?*"

Betty felt her heart race. She stood up, facing him. "You killed our son. And you killed me a thousand times. So I think it's only fair. Don't you?"

Frank started toward her as she jerked awake. The attic smelled acrid, as the rage still hung in the stifling air.

Chapter 16

*"Sometimes...the very thing we fight or protest against
is exactly the thing we actually need or lack."*

Betty waited at the empty counter of *The Gilded Rose*,
clutching the two table runners wrapped in plastic. Lily was
nowhere to be seen, and the place was conspicuously empty
of customers. She called out but got no response. Wandering over to check her various items for sale, she found the
Biedermeier still there and further reduced in price. Betty
sighed deeply at the prospect that it might never sell. Fur-
thermore, even though she'd made a point of moving that
damned metal sign with the quote from Marilyn Monroe:
ALL A GIRL REALLY WANTS IS FOR ONE GUY TO PROVE TO HER
THAT THEY ARE NOT ALL THE SAME, there it was again propped
up on her beloved antique. She started to move it when she
read the words again. And then again. It wasn't something
she'd normally be attracted to, with its rusty tin and faux,
antique edging. She set it down twice and then picked it
up again. She checked the price; it was twenty-five dollars.
Betty reasoned she had to save every cent from the sale of
Frank's wedding ring to support her grow operation, but
yet...the sign seemed to speak to her in the most unusual
manner.

She caught movement outside and saw Lily standing by
the front window having an animated conversation with Yarrow. After several more moments, Lily returned to the store
and spotted Betty, greeting her with a welcoming smile.

"We've had a few people admiring your Biedermeier,
Betty. I hoped reducing the price would spur a sale."

"Anything on the books?"

"No. Sorry. It's been slow."

Betty walked with Lily to the counter. She wondered how on earth Lily was able to keep this place going, given its size and the inventory that was still there. The last thing she needed was a call from Lily saying she was going out of business and needed to return all her items. With great flourish, Betty produced the table runners and gave a quick but thorough back-story on their history. Lily bit and agreed to sell them.

"Still having issues with that young girl who works at the dispensary? Yarrow?" Betty asked.

"No issues," she replied, placing tags on the table runners.

Betty looked outside and saw Yarrow lingering, smoking a cigarette. "She seems rather lost."

"Lost?"

"Yes. Is she all right?"

Lily was held back. "Yeah, I think so. She's going up to Canada for a week to see some family. Travel makes her nervous these days. It's so intrusive, you know?"

"Canadian, eh?"

Lily finished tagging the items and handed Betty a receipt. "I'm sorry there's nothing on the books for you today. But maybe with summer, things will improve?"

Betty smiled, handing Lily the metal sign. "Well, whoever owns this sign will have something on their books."

She had two hours to kill before her lunch date at *La Bella Vita*. And since every moment was critical, Betty headed to Grow Do It, the grow store where Peyton worked. Based on her research, she had a long list of equipment, organic nutrients and miscellaneous items she needed right away. Once at the store – located in a less-than-thriving, outdoor mall – she remained in her car for a few minutes, checking out the surrounding area for any sign of someone she might know. When she was certain it was clear, Betty entered the establishment.

The first thing she noticed was how clean the air smelled. Like fresh ozone in high-altitude. The second thing she noted was the enormous pallet of vigorously growing tomatoes, half of them still green and growing under a vegetative light setup and the other half full of crimson fruit, growing under a huge, bloom light. Two signs caught Betty's eye. The first one noted that the store was open on Sundays, but it closed at the odd time of 4:20. The second computer-printed sign was taped above the cash register and warned that: WE CAN-NOT DISCUSS ANYTHING THAT IS FEDERALLY ILLEGAL. THIS IN-CLUDES MARIJUANA CULTIVATION. PLEASE RESPECT THIS WHILE SHOPPING HERE. How odd, Betty thought. The store was obviously set up to cater to marijuana growers, just as the websites which featured products like "Bountiful Bud Brew" were obviously selling to the cannabis crowd. So it was a game, she reasoned. A wink-wink. A "let's pretend we're not doing what we're really doing" endeavor. Betty could play along.

"Who *is* this group, anyways?" a booming male voice in the back room asked.

Betty walked down a center aisle, passing rows of cloth pots, cloning machines and air purifiers.

"P.R.W.G.?" The man read. "Who in the fuck is that?"

Betty stopped in mid-step, realizing this individual was obviously reading Renée's stinging letter to the editor signed by the Paradox Republican Women's Group.

"Hey, I know!" the man said. "Pussy Republicans With Gonads!"

Betty stood there dumbstruck. She considered making an exit, when Peyton sauntered out from the back room. He was wearing his G.Y.O. t-shirt and sported an exceptionally-tousled head of hair.

"Hey, Betty!"

Betty relaxed when she saw him. "Hello, Peyton." Her voice was low-key. "I don't have lots of time, but I thought I'd come over and buy the first of the many accoutrements I'll need to grow the cannabis."

Cradling Betty by the shoulder, he ushered her to anoth-er corner of the store. "Okay, first off, ixnay on callin' them accoutrements and secondly, you don't mention the word cannabis, marijuana or any other slang term here. Got it?"

"But what if I have questions about growing canna – ?"

"You're growing tomatoes, Betty. We're *all* growing to-matoes. So far, the Feds don't have a problem with tomatoes. Got it?"

What a strange little world these people lived in. "Who is that in the back?"

"My tool of a boss, Justin. Ignore him. He's always jacked up about somethin'. He loves tellin' people how much ener-gy he has. I personally don't trust people who say they have tons of energy. It's not normal. The only people who should have tons of energy are kids under the age of fifteen. Any adult who claims that is either manic or on crack."

Betty explained she had just under a thousand dollars left from the sale of Frank's ring. She handed him her list.

"You've really been doin' your homework, Betty! Good for you!" Peyton enthusiastically chimed. "Why don't we hold off on the bloom light since it's a chunk of change, and you won't need it for another two months. There are a couple more important things you'll need right now," he stressed, mentioning the reflective silver wall coverings used to amplify the light against the plants, and liquid enzymes for bolstering the nutrients and reactivating the beneficial organisms in the soil. "You gotta put a lot of targeted nu-trients into the veg state," he said quietly, "in order to have the largest and healthiest plant when you flip it into bloom."

Peyton patiently went around the store explaining the various products and the pros and cons of each one. His grasp of the entire process impressed Betty, as well as his personal experience using the different nutrients. According to Peyton, a lot of the "stoner dudes" who had "secret gueril-la grows" were obsessed with toxic, chemical "nutes" – a.k.a. nutrients – because all they cared about was producing "fat, dank, gigantic bud." But, as he explained, those who grew with harsh chemicals ran the risk of those toxins seeping into the finished bud. "You know when people tell you they hurled their lunch and got a headache or stomach cramps after smoking cannabis?" he said to Betty. "My theory is that it's not the bud. It's the shit these idiots are spraying on their plants and watering them with." The stakes were high, Peyton declared, when you were a caregiver and responsible for growing cannabis for people whose health was often already compromised. "Patients have gotta *know their grow*. It's more expensive to grow organically," he revealed, "but it tastes better, and it won't make your brain twitch like chemically grown crap."

As they filled her basket, it became clear that the price of an organic product was often an indicator of its quality. A gallon of liquid enzymes was over one hundred dollars; a special seaweed and fish concentrate from Alaska cost nearly sixty bucks.

"Whatever happened to water and compost?" Betty asked.

"That won't cut it with the herb," Peyton whispered. "The whole point is to make it grow fast, hearty and healthy. Oh, one thing you've *got* to buy is over here." He walked to another aisle and pointed at three shelves of products. Everything from beneficial organisms that eat the mildew to bicarbonate of soda preparations filled those shelves. He turned to her with a look of seriousness, usually set aside for discussing political reform. "Next to spider mites, every grower's nightmare is powdery mildew. We call it 'PM' in the trade. And believe me, if you don't stop it, it'll wipe out your entire crop. PM is insidious and if you see it, you gotta get on it immediately."

He explained that the dreaded PM starts as a tiny, often imperceptible, white cloud of mildew on a lower leaf. It can be inherent to a specific cannabis strain, or it can be passed from one plant to another due to poor circulation and/or too much heat and moisture in the veg or bloom rooms. Once a plant has it, it has it forever. Anything you clone from an infected plant will have it locked in its DNA. Thus, many industrious people have sought to find the perfect solution for attacking this persistent problem.

Peyton pointed to a tub of yellow crystals. "If it gets really bad, you gotta sulfur the rooms. But there's a trick to it, and I'll need to walk you through that or you'll do major damage."

Suddenly, the entire growing process had taken on a rather dire prognosis. The thought of growing a room full of cannabis only to have it wiped out with PM sent a shudder down Betty's spine. She took Peyton's advice and purchased the product he trusted the most. She was just about to tell him her news about Buddy being her first patient when Justin strolled around the corner. He had the kind of purposeful walk that suggested a bloated over-confidence. His bulging, tanned muscles stretched uninvitingly against his "Grow Do It" T-shirt, while his soon-to-be bald head made him appear older than his late thirty-ish years.

"You finding what you need, ma'am?" he asked in a cocky manner.

"I am. Thank you." Betty replied, immediately not liking him.

"Hey," Justin said, addressing Peyton, "I can finish helping this lady. You left a pallet of perlite out in the sun. Get it inside, would ya?" Peyton nodded and turned to go. "And get with the program, poncho!" Justin barked.

Betty's blood pressure rose quickly. "Peyton, wait!"

Peyton stopped and turned back, somewhat perplexed.

Betty turned to Justin. "Peyton has gone out of his way to be more than helpful." Her voice was terse and abrupt. "I'd like him to continue to assist me today."

Justin let out a soft, dismissive chuckle. She'd heard the same trivializing response far too many times in the past.

"I'm sorry. Did I say something funny?" Betty asked, her face reddening.

"It's okay," Peyton said meekly.

Betty steadied herself against the clearance shelf. Her mouth went dry. "No, Peyton. It's not okay. Your boss apparently didn't get the memo that the customer is always right." Betty moved a step closer to Justin. Her imposing frame and stature nearly dwarfed him. "The only reason I'm spending all this money at your store is because of Peyton. He has a great deal of knowledge about growing tomatoes."

She inched closer to Justin. "Big tomatoes. Wonderful tomatoes. *Extraordinary* tomatoes. And *I* am a tomato grower."

Justin was cornered, but he maintained his pumped up
posture. "You don't look like someone who grows tomatoes."

"Well, you don't look like a business man, so there's the
irony." She heard her Texas lilt escape. "You walk with great
purpose in your step. Pity you have no idea where you're going." She turned to Peyton, who was now standing there frozen. "Peyton, I have more questions I'd like you to answer
for me." Brushing past Justin, she gently took Peyton by the
elbow and continued shopping.

Fifteen minutes later, Peyton loaded Betty's Taurus with
her bounty. She covered the large, T5 veg light in the backseat with an old blanket. She'd spent nine hundred fifty-four
dollars on lights, bags of organic soil, fans, carbon filters, gallons of nutrients, powdery mildew sprays, heat mats, timers,
rolls of heavy plastic, aerating watering cans, reflective wall
coverings and much more.

"I can't believe what you did in there," Peyton said, closing the trunk.

"I can't either. But I'm glad I did. He's a bully, Peyton.
Trust me. I know the breed. And like all bullies, he's terribly
insecure."

"Really?"

"Good God, yes! He absolutely reeks of insecurity!
Usually one only sees that level of insecurity when viewing
awkward boys forced to dance at cotillions." Betty issued
a meaningful pause. "Or men with...shortcomings." She
turned back to the store. "You need to stand up to him, Peyton. Don't let anyone ever treat you like that."

He shrugged his shoulders. "I need the job."

She looked at him. "No job or relationship is worth
your principles. Believe me, it'll wear you down after a few
decades."

Changing subjects, she quickly gave him the news about
Buddy and that she needed three more plants. They arranged to meet at his house later that day so she could see
his grow operation and choose from his available clones.

"I think I found you another patient," he said with a smile. "Her name's Dottie and she's cool. She got one of your chocolates from another patient of mine and she loves them."

"Peyton, I don't know if I feel comfortable having my canna chocolates shared willy-nilly, without having control over who tries them –"

"Betty, there's no way you can control whether somebody shares their edibles or even their bud with a friend or family member. Don't go all Stalin on me, okay? Look, Dottie got one of your chocolates, loved it and was thrilled to know you were looking for patients. I think you and her –"

"You and *she*," Betty corrected.

He sighed. "You and *she* would work well together. She's a little older than you, but she can still drive and work."

"Wow. Imagine that? That reminds me. I've got to pick up my walker from the repair store."

He smiled and gave her a gentle fist bump on her shoulder. "Okay, okay. Hey, one thing about Dottie is she's all about keepin' it on the down low, okay? Would Sunday work for you to meet her?"

"Sure. Give me her name tonight." She started to get into her car and then turned around again. "You need a haircut."

"No, I don't."

"Yes, you do. You want to put a clean face on the cannabis industry?"

"Yeah. Maybe."

"Get a haircut. It's like getting a fresh start for fewer than fifteen dollars."

~~~

Betty arrived at *La Bella Vita* with time to spare. Judi waved to her from an outdoor table on the brick patio. Renée was nowhere to be seen, but Helen was firmly ensconced in a seat, wearing dark glasses and attempting to dodge the piercing sun. After an effusive greeting from Judi and a hug from Helen, Betty took a seat.

"Happy birthday, darling," Betty said to Helen.

"Yeah. One more year of aches and pains. It's all down hill from here. You sure we can't get a table inside?" Helen asked Judi, hanging her head in a patch of shade.

"Honey, I told you, they're packed inside. Plus, a little sunshine won't kill you. Think of all the vitamin D you're absorbing right now."

"Tell that to my dermatologist," Helen mumbled.

"Where's Renée?" Betty asked, scooting in her wrought iron, padded chair and handing Judi the carefully wrapped brocade tablecloth she requested.

"Thanks, hon," she said, securing the tablecloth under her chair. "I'm not sure where Renée is. She called and said she'd be late and that she had a surprise for us."

Betty leaned over and checked out Judi's pants. They were the same linen ones she'd seen before but they looked a little different. "Hey, I thought you said they were sold out of those slacks."

Judi took a sip of red wine. "They are. These are the same ones."

"No," Betty noted, "those are slightly different with the tie at the waist."

Judi self-consciously looked down at her lithe waist. "Oh, right. I bought them at the same time. Just haven't worn them around you, I guess. Quite an eye for detail!"

"Yes," she picked up the menu, "I seem to be seeing a lot of things more acutely lately."

Judi noticed that Helen was about to take a pill from a tiny ceramic pillbox she'd brought out from her jacket pocket. "Oh, honey," Judi quickly said to Helen, "you already took your pill. Remember?"

"I took the pink one, right?" Helen asked, rooting through the rainbow of pills in the box. "I have to take the tan one now. Can you tell them apart? This sun is bleaching out all the colors."

Judi reached over, found the tan pill and handed it to Helen who downed it with water. The waiter popped over to announce the specials, none of which interested Helen, who wanted to know what dishes were not spicy, not salted and free of cheese. For someone who supposedly "adored" this place, she certainly seemed vexed. Before leaving, he laid out a warm basket of fresh bread and two side plates, one drizzled with olive oil and the other heaped with whipped butter.

He left and Betty piped up. "I think we need to change the name of our group." She helped herself to a center slice of bread and heaped on a large dollop of butter.

"Why?" Judi asked.

"P.R.W.G. could leave us open for some rather crude play on words."

Judi thought about it. "Like what?"

"I'd rather not say." Betty took a generous bite of bread and glanced at the menu.

"Oh, Betty, you can be so prim sometimes." Judi stole another sip of wine and leaned closer to Betty, speaking in a hushed tone. "Is that why you're afraid of getting to know Tom Reed?"

"I thought we were done with that conversation, dear," Betty replied, keeping her eyes on the menu and enjoying another butter-drenched bite of bread.

"God, honey, aren't you afraid of all that cholesterol?"

Betty savored the salty taste of butter against her tongue. "Not really. I'm famished. God, this tastes divine!" She lifted the basket toward Helen. "Helen darling, try some with the butter."

"No, thanks," Helen said with a scowl. "I don't want to have a stroke on my birthday."

Judi sat back. "How's your neck, Betty?"

Betty looked up and realized she hadn't had one problem with her neck, jaw or ear in days. "It's actually quite good," she said.

"So, Roger's pills worked! Great! I told you he could fix you up! Aren't muscle relaxants fun?"

"Every time I take them," Helen offered, "I can't feel my tongue."

"Are you kidding?" Judi insisted. "They're awesome! When you find something that works, it's like a good friend you can always rely on. Hey, when I was a young mom and had to take the boys for long, road trips in the car, I'd give them each a healthy dose of cherry-flavored cough syrup. Knocked their asses right out and presto chango, peace and quiet."

Betty stared at Judi. "Good God, Judi. You got them *drunk*?"

"It wasn't prescription! It was just extra-strength, jacked-up, cherry cough syrup." She took a sip of wine. "Too bad you can't buy that brand anymore. Something about too many lawsuits. God, people are too damn litigious these days."

"They stopped selling it, because it was cherry flavored booze for babies," Betty countered.

"Hey, I had four boys. *Four*. And they were eighteen months apart. Little stair steps, my mother-in-law used to call them." Judi swallowed another hearty sip of wine. "Riding in the car with those monsters was like recreating the Battle of Bunker Hill every damn time. So I gave 'em a little cherry flavored, somethin'-somethin'. So what? It worked. I'd drive in peace, they napped and they'd arrive at the destination a little groggy, a little detached, but *alive*. They might not have been alive if I'd have had to put up with their crap for six, steady hours."

Suddenly, it made perfect sense to Betty why three of Judi's four boys were alcoholics, and the fourth one owned a cherry orchard. "Mother's little helper," Betty added. "Valium for mommy and cherry-flavored cough syrup for the kids." She looked up from the menu. "It's all about escaping, isn't it?"

"What are you talking about?" Judi asked, her tone a tad terse.

"The pain? A need to temporarily disconnect. Why *do* so many feel the need *not* to feel? It's too bad all the things we can legally choose from don't really offer us any insight or introspection. They just knock us out or deepen the pain when they wear off."

Helen and Judi regarded Betty with confused glances.

"Well," Judi piped up, "that lightened the mood! Where in the hell is Renée?"

The waiter returned and Betty ordered a sparkling water with a lemon twist. Helen opted for room temperature water, no ice. She mumbled about not wanting to risk breaking a tooth on an ice cube. Judi ordered a second glass of red wine.

Betty closed the menu and stared at the ornate leather cover with the gold-embossed lettering. Tracing her fingertips across the words, she fell into thought.

"What is it?" Judi asked.

"*La Bella Vita,*" she said in a distant voice. "The Good Life. What makes it a good life?"

The waiter arrived with a fresh bottle of red as Judi drained her first glass and he refilled it. "I think the owners named it after some place in Italy they loved," Judi offered.

Betty turned to her. "No. I don't mean this restaurant, Judi. I'm talking about *life*. What makes us get up in the morning and embrace the day? How do we fill our days, so that as we lay our head on the pillow, we can drift off to sleep and know it was a good day?"

Judi stared at Betty perplexed. She reached over and placed a gentle hand on Betty's wrist. "Oh, shit. Have you got cancer?"

"Who's got cancer?" Helen asked, briefly joining the conversation before ducking back into the scrap of shade.

"*No*, I don't have cancer."

"Then why in the hell are you talking like this?" Judi questioned.

"Why is asking why we choose to do what we do every day, suspect?"

Judi took a hearty gulp of wine. "I don't know. It just seems unnecessary. If you stop to think about this kind of stuff too much, you just get morose."

Betty set down her menu. "I don't agree. I need to feel useful. I always have. What's the point of it all if you're not useful to yourself or anyone else? I mean really, is life just all about maintaining a prize winning garden from May to

October, decorating for the various holidays, giving and going to parties and get-togethers, lunching for hours, becoming addicted to mindless TV shows, and then feeling empty on Sunday because you don't know anything more about yourself than when you woke up last Monday?"

"Seriously?" Judi stressed, "you really don't have cancer?"

Betty shook her head. "I'm starting to understand how important it is to see what you don't want to look at. I think it's necessary to investigate various things in one's life and even question them. Sometimes...the very thing we fight or protest against is exactly the thing we actually need or lack." She was slightly amazed by her discovery. "Ha! How ironic!"

"Hey, ladies!" Renée's booming voice rang against the pavement as she quickly approached their table. In her usual manic fashion, Renée greeted each of the women, air kissing them and then erratically taking her seat as she placed her huge purse, phone and satchel on the ground next to her chair. She slapped her hands against the table. "*We* are here to celebrate, ladies!"

"Yes! Helen's birthday," Betty chimed in.

Renée temporarily lost her momentum. "Oh, right." She dug into her satchel and pulled out a small, hastily wrapped gift with no card. "Happy birthday, Helen."

Helen unwrapped the gift to find a bold, green and black, paisley sheer scarf. She stared at it, saying nothing. Betty recognized the scarf immediately. She'd given it to Renée several years ago. It was one thing to re-gift, but to re-gift in front of the initial giver took it to an entirely new level.

"*Now*," Renée stated, holding rank over them, "I have some incredible news to share with all of you. I don't just write letters to editors, I make things happen! As of nine o'clock this morning, there is one fewer marijuana dispensary in Paradox!" She clapped her hands together, in a somewhat, self-congratulatory manner.

Betty felt a ball form in her throat. "Which one?"

"That monstrosity over by the market," Renée said. "*Nature's Bud?* Surprise, surprise, the owner was selling weed to someone who didn't have a medical marijuana card *and* offered them psychedelic mushrooms as a back door purchase. *This* is exactly the kind of criminal activity we always knew existed in this pseudo-medical bullshit arena. So, a toast to us!" She raised her water glass.

Judi and Helen clinked their glasses against Renée's glass, while Betty simply lifted her glass a few inches.

"To criminals!" Helen barked.

"No, darling," Renée gently reprimanded, "we're not toasting to criminals. We're toasting to the abolishment of these dope dens that increase crime in our neighborhoods and give kids the perfect gateway drug to the hard stuff like China White, Horse, Hillbilly Crack, Roofies, Ludes, Dexies, Blotters and Disco Biscuits."

Well, Betty figured, that pretty much covered the hard drugs on the other side of the professed gate. "Who tipped off the cops?" Betty asked.

"You're lookin' at her, sweetheart!" Renée proudly exclaimed. "And we're not talking secondhand information here, ladies. I heard it straight from the lips of the dim-witted bitch who did the illegal deed."

"When?" Judi asked, taking another sip of wine.

"Yesterday, at my A.A. meeting. When they opened up the topic to the room, a certain woman confessed to us how she went in and scored some weed without a card and was offered magic mushrooms." Renée rolled her eyes. "What an idiot! I thought she was smarter than that! Needless to say, she had to turn in her six-month sobriety chip!" There was a deviousness to that last statement; a kind of "gotcha" mentality.

"Wait a second," Betty interjected. "Isn't the whole anonymous part of this group supposed to protect what people say in there? Isn't that rather sacrosanct?"

Renée guzzled her water again, spitting an ice cube back into the glass. "Hey, if someone mentioned they were diddling their kid, I'd report it too!" she replied in a case-closed tone. "Illegal activity is reported. Good God, this isn't a confession between a priest and one of his flock! This is a bunch of drunks and drug addicts sitting around spilling their guts about their private nightmares. I mean, the woman who committed this felony at the dispensary should have *known* better! She's constantly telling us in the meetings how street savvy she used to be. Good lord, her uncle was her pimp when she was twelve and her brother used to drive her to meet the johns!"

"*Renée!*" Betty admonished. "It's Alcoholics *Anonymous.* Not Alcoholics *Revealed!*"

"Oh, Alana could give a shit –"

"*Alana?*" Judi asked, wide-eyed. "Alana O'Donnell from Rotary?"

Renée nodded with a tap to her nose to stress the unspoken affirmative answer.

"Ladies! This is not acceptable!" Betty demanded, her Texas lilt issuing forth. "You can't be exposing people like this. Especially people who obviously have some deep-seated issues –"

"Yeah," Renée cattily chuckled, "like giving lap dances to returning Iraq War Veterans as a 'Welcome Home' gift?"

"Alana O'Donnell," Judi mused out loud. "Shit. She still has two folding chairs I loaned her for a mixer. God only knows what depravity took place on them."

Betty sat back, disgusted by the direction of the conversation. Renée continued to chirp about the dispensary and poor Alana O'Donnell, as a line of traffic backed up on the street. A convertible came to a stop in traffic with its radio blaring loudly. The sound of Reverend Bobby Lynch's voice could easily be heard. "A strong nation is not built on the shoulders of slackers and addicts who lack moral fiber!" he said. "I'm telling you that we're heading down a slippery slope when we identify marijuana as medicine!" Betty felt as if she were sandwiched between two strident, agenda-seeking lecturers who lacked both harmony and compassion.

"Who in the hell – ?" Renée barked, sternly turning to the sound of Lynch's voice.

"Reverend Lynch," Betty replied.

"I *hate* him!" Renée declared. "What a creepy pig! He's so...ugly! Everything is 'for Jesus' or 'the children.' Just add either of those onto any sentence of his. 'Collecting money, *for the children.*' 'Car wash, *for Jesus.*' 'Protecting the children, *for Jesus*'"

"Shutting down the dispensaries," Betty added, "*for Jesus* and the children."

"I know I've seen this scarf before," Helen suddenly said, staring at Renée's gift. "Or maybe I've just got sunstroke."

"Hey, Betty!" a voice rang out from the line of traffic.

Renée turned and frowned. "Oh, Christ."

Betty turned. There was Peyton stopped behind a car, his head and upper body poking out of the sunroof in his Prius. There was no way *not* to see his bold "G.Y.O." t-shirt, fluttering in the May breeze or his much shorter haircut.

He waved and smiled. "Check out the crown, Betty! Got a trim on my lunch hour! See ya tonight!" The traffic opened up and he slid back into the driver's seat.

Betty turned back to the table, expressionless.

"What's 'G.Y.O.?'" Helen asked, squinting.

"I believe it stands for God's Youth Organization," Betty said, thinking quickly.

Renée let out a hard sigh. "Oh, Christ, Betty! Try 'Grow Your Own.' As in grass? And I'm not talking about lawn care."

So that's what it stood for, Betty reckoned. "Really?"

"What in the hell was that all about?" Renée asked with a stinging edge.

"I told you outside of Peggy's service. I'm mentoring the boy. He's obviously a lost soul and I want to help him. As I said before you arrived, I want to be useful."

Judi took another sip of wine. It was clear to Betty she was already a little loose. "He looks terribly familiar, Betty. Almost a twin. Like a ghost from your past? Are you sure you want to drive down that road again?"

Betty regarded Judi's loaded statement with offense. Strange how none of her friends ever mentioned Frankie's name or referenced him in any way. And now, right then, it was done in a manner that suggested something shameful or pointless. She took a tense sip of her fizzy water with a lemon twist. "I don't want to just *drive* down that road, darling. I want to park on that road and put up a big tent with a sign that says, 'Come in Peyton. Lunch is waiting. Have a seat and stay awhile.'" Her piercing comment brought any hopes of a jovial follow up to a screeching halt. She could have taken it back, but Betty never considered that option. She could have also stayed and suffered through lunch, feeling sick to her stomach the entire time. Instead, she gently tapped her lips with the napkin and slid her chair from the table. "I think I need to go now," she said softly.

The women stared at her in stunned unison. Well, Judi was a little less stunned due to her gradual descent into tipsiness.

"*What?*" Judi questioned. "What did I say? *Betty?* Come on, *stay!*"

Betty turned to Helen. "Happy birthday, darling. And enjoy your scarf. Even though the color and bold design is infinitely more suited for Renée's skin tone than yours." She glanced knowingly at Renée who slunk slightly in her chair.

Betty didn't feel one bit remorseful for her comment. Not for one damn second. In fact, while people may not actually laugh all the way to the bank, Betty Craven actually smiled all the way home. She was able to unload the metal sign with the Monroe quote, the T5 light and everything else from the grow store without any suspicious eyes watching her. Once inside, she carried the metal sign and the light with the stand up to her bedroom. Betty determined that Marilyn's sign looked best propped up on the bureau that faced her bed. She then temporarily set up the light in her bedroom closet and placed the three Centennial Blueberry clones underneath it. The blazing radiance and heat that emanated was profound in that small area. Betty checked the plants thoroughly for any sign of the dreaded "PM" Peyton warned her about earlier. Seeing nothing to worry about, she watered her new beauties and told them how gorgeous they were. She wasn't sure, but it looked like of one them moved her leaf in appreciation.

Walking out of her closet, she glanced up to the top shelf. The plain brown box was a little dusty and the label from the mortuary was curling a bit. Reaching up, she smoothed the label until it lay flat against the box. Betty stared at the container and then gently brought it down. Pointing the box toward the three plants, she smiled. "Look what your mother's doing, sweetheart. Would you have ever guessed it?" She patted the box twice and reverently set it back up on the top shelf.

Wandering down to the kitchen, she passed the credenza in the living room. She stared at the center drawer and decisively opened it, removing Frankie's photo and resting it proudly on the table. "I would drive down that road for you again," she whispered. "Screw them all!" She strode down the hallway, removing the white violet print from the wall. Walking back into the living room, she searched for the perfect place to hang it. She glanced at Frankie's photo and set the framed print next to it, using several books to keep it propped up. "Much better," she quietly said with a smile.

She could have spent the next few hours in her garden weeding, but she had too much to learn. So the time was spent reading the "grow bible" Jeff gave her and watching more tutorials on the Internet. Later, she grabbed a quick bite and fed Ronald before heading off to Peyton's house. A giddy excitement filled her in anticipation of what his grow operation would look like, as well as meeting the next three plants that would soon join the ones in her closet. She decided they were her "girls." Yes, that's what she'd call them from now on. Her girls. Her little divas that only two people knew about.

She knocked on the front door and Peyton answered. Walking her to the basement door, he opened it, turned on the light and led her down the narrow steps. The heady aroma was instantly intoxicating. When she reached the final step, Betty was overwhelmed by what she saw.

"Welcome to the cannabis castle, Betty!"

Chapter 17

"It's six-thirty. Time for a little zither music."

It was like Willie Wonka's Cannabis Factory. The first thing Betty noticed was the loud humming and consistent breeze from the multitude of enormous fans positioned all around the periphery of the cement-floored basement. Four more fans on the floor cooled the eighteen, neatly-lined-up cannabis plants in their ten-gallon fabric containers. The plants, all in a vegetative stage, were between three to five feet tall. Most of them were squatty, with heavy, wide-leafed branches happily spreading out two feet. Three of them grew much more lanky, with narrow leaves. From what she'd learned, the taller, lankier plants were Cannabis *Sativa* dominant while the their fatter leafed, squattier sister were Cannabis *Indica* dominant.

When Betty commented on the rather blustery environment, Peyton shook his head. "Fans are your friends, Betty. You can't ever have enough fans. Keeps the PM at bay, keeps the ladies moving and strengthens their root stalks with all that swaying."

The plants stood on a thick, black-plastic bed liner, secured in a wooden frame in the center section of the roughly eight-hundred-square-foot room. Hanging about three feet above the plants were six, four-foot, T5 light panels suspended from chains attached to beams in the ceilings. The blazing light spread out well beyond the potted plants, illuminating the far reaches of the basement. Several tables lined the walls, neatly covered with soil, nutrients and books. Betty moved closer to the plants and noted a discreet but effective watering tube set-up that cleverly laced from one cloth pot to the other. Pinpoints of either a green or red light glowed on the tubes.

"That's one of Pop's inventions," Peyton said, pointing to the lights. "Green means the sensor is picking up enough water in the pot. Red means I need to add some. You don't want to over water them. Beginners always make that mistake. That and overfeeding the ladies. Too much water and their leaves will curl. Too much food and the leaf edges will get burned and turn yellow or brown."

Betty noticed four grey, six-inch round objects that freely whirred around the pots like a child's toy top. "What are those?"

He smiled. "Another one of Pop's innovations. I kept tellin' him I needed to figure out a good drainage system for the water when it flowed out the bottom and sides of the pots onto the plastic. He came up with those. They're basically like little rotary sponges that whir around and soak up the excess water. Gotta do what you gotta do to keep the PM away, you know?"

"Ingenious," Betty marveled.

"Pops also rigged up the thermostat so it stays at a nice seventy-six in here and then drops down to sixty-two at night. He also came up with these reflective colored patches that stick on the pots," Peyton proudly said, showing off white, yellow and dark green labels. "White is placed on the light feeders, yellow is for the medium feeders and dark green is for the ladies who need lots of nutrients. It's like eighteen different personalities. You gotta get to know them so you can give them what they need. You give them what they need, and they turn around and give you what you need. So it's a fair deal that works out in the end."

Betty was overwhelmed. "This is incredible."

"This ain't no ghetto set-up, Betty. And this is just half of it!" He carefully clipped a few yellowed leaves off the lower branches of one plant. "Growing cannabis and comedy have one thing in common." He paused a little too long for effect. "*Timing*," he finally said smiling. "Timing of lights, nutrients, watering and especially when the ladies are ready to give up their bud. You gotta keep charts and records of when you gave what to which plant, what strains need more nutrients than others, when it's time to foliar feed —"

"I had no idea it was this complex, Peyton."

"We've taken a sacred weed and turned it into an often demanding goddess. As growers, we plan our schedules around them, we skip vacations, we often invest in better vitamins and nutrients for them than for ourselves, we lose sleep when they're sick, we protect them from others who want to destroy or steal them, and we do anything and everything to make sure they're happy. I guarantee you there are people out there right now inventing new brews, powders, lights and sounds that are meant to make these ladies bigger, better and stronger. I can't explain it. But you'll soon see what I mean. They really do hold some sort of magical appeal over you."

She looked at the eighteen plants and suddenly felt slightly sorry for them. "But...with all the pampering you give them, they never see the sun?"

"No. It'd be too risky to take them outside. That would be asking for somebody to rip them off."

"How sad," she softly said.

He considered the possibilities. "Well, I guess it could be done. I could hang red Christmas ball ornaments on them. From a distance, they might actually look like a tomato plant."

Betty smiled at the visual. She sauntered around the periphery, examining the various leaves and stalks. "Does Pops...enjoy the fruits of your labor?"

"Huh?"

"Does Pops use pot?" Betty replied, straight to the point.

"Oh. Yeah. Of course. He's one of my patients. Not only does it keep his joints moving more freely, he said it puts him in touch with his creative muse. Oh, and please don't call the ladies 'pot.'" He clasped his hands around the top branches of a nearby plant, as if to close off its "ears." They really take offense at that. Just like the Mexican term, 'marijuana,' was hijacked by the government to marginalize cannabis, the same thing goes for the word 'pot.' It's short for *potiguaya*. It's like Doobie Douggie says, 'Every time people call this beautiful plant 'marijuana' or 'pot,' you unknowingly feed into the government's propaganda campaign of manipulation and conditioning they've been selling us for decades.' I love Doobie Douggie. He's a sage of enlightenment and a soldier of freedom for cannabis."

"He's not a wallflower, is he?"

Peyton grabbed the sturdy rootstalk on one plant and began to vigorously shake it back and forth.

"What are you doing?" she asked, slightly alarmed.

"They love this. It kinda mimics the way they bend and sway in a stiff breeze when they grow outside."

"Aren't you afraid of breaking the stalk or a stem?"

"Nah. The ladies need a lot of care, but you gotta remember this is a wild plant and a lot of times, they actually grow better in the midst of chaos." He walked over to another plant and repeated the same method. "Anything you can do to shake or vibrate the root stalk will strengthen the plant and produce a better bud. I know a guy who tortures his ladies. He bends the stalks until they break halfway and then tapes them back together. He also ties string to the branches and pulls the string until the branch bends down, nails it to the floor and lets it stay like that for a day or more. He's brutal but he grows the most incredible herb you've ever seen."

Good God, Betty thought. The Marquis de Sade of marijuana was alive and well and operating with abandon in some Colorado basement. She asked why he used cloth pots, and Peyton informed her that unlike plastic, they breathed better and allowed the roots to self-prune instead of becoming bound to the bottom of the container. "You gotta keep the ladies happy," he said, flicking a speck of caked dirt off a cloth pot.

Betty noted a strange, discordant tone suddenly issuing from the four audio speakers in the basement. "Good God, what's that?"

Peyton checked the clock. "It's six-thirty. Time for a little zither music. They wake up to Zeppelin, mid-morning they get Hendrix, lunch is Pink Floyd, then some down time of total silence – you know, a nap? Zither starts at six-thirty and then we move on to the Allman Brothers, Steve Miller Band and wind up the day before the lights go out at midnight with Country Joe and the Fish."

Betty stared at him. "This is not normal, Peyton."

"Actually, if you spell it differently, it is. As in N-O-R-M-L," he said, explaining the acronym for the National Organization for the Reform of Marijuana Laws. Apparently, NORML didn't heed the message about not using the word 'marijuana' in their acronym. "Hey, the ladies in the bloom room are going to sleep pretty quick."

"*Ly*," Betty corrected. "Quick*ly*."

"Right. So, if you want to see 'em, now's the time." Peyton led Betty to the far corner of the basement where a separate room was built, complete with its own roof. A heavy black cloth covered the entryway. Behind that, about three feet away, was a black door. He turned to Betty. "Get ready," he said as he swept back the cloth and swung open the door.

A brilliant blaze of red and orange light filled the three-hundred-fifty-square-foot space, emitting from four massive, hooded, bloom lights that hung from metal bars.

"Every time I open this door, it's like seeing the Son of God," Peyton said in a reverent tone. "It's almost a religious experience, isn't it?"

Underneath the lights were eighteen plants, between five and six feet tall, all in bloom. The red-orange lights cast an odd color onto Betty's hands, making them appear slightly yellow. She had to steel herself momentarily from the pungent aroma that surrounded and invaded her senses.

"My God, Peyton. One could get high just standing in here."

"Nah. Maybe for beginners like you. After a bit, you get totally used to it."

Betty's head began to swirl, as the scent wrapped around her in an exquisite, sweet bouquet. There was no skunky smell; rather, a fruity aroma with a dash of brie. "What smells like cheese?"

Peyton pointed across the room. "Cheese! For real. That's the name of the plant. It's actually U.K. Cheese. One of my patients, who used to live in England, asked me grow it for him."

Betty walked between the blooming plants and gave a closer look at the heavy, top branch that Peyton explained was called a "cola." Even with the harsh cast of red-orange light, she could detect the glistening resins that frosted across the buds and spread onto the surrounding leaves. It was magical to her – this plant that looked so plain in its vegetative state, had erupted into an imposing beauty. It was hard to believe, she thought, that something could transform itself so naturally and yet so powerfully. There was majesty in each plant. Eighteen individual queens who demanded daily attention and love in order to become the transcendent beauties they were born to be. As Betty looked closer into the shimmering buds, she almost felt as if the plant knew exactly how coveted it was by others outside of its basement home. And with that knowledge, the plant held a harmonious supremacy over humans. "Adore me," she could almost hear the plant saying. "Worship me. Indulge me. Devote yourself to me and I'll make it worth your while." Betty pulled back, wondering if she was slightly loaded. But she couldn't take her eyes off of them. There was nothing remotely evil about them. There was nothing sinful, immoral or corrupt. But there *was* power. Quiet, resolute, vibrating, transcendental, ancient power that calculatingly oozed from each bud.

"You wanna see what the buds look like up close?" Peyton asked.

Betty nodded. He crossed to a table in the far corner of the room and retrieved a microscope and a small pair of scissors. Surveying the various plants and their growth patterns, he settled on one in the center and gingerly cut a small, frosty leaf just over a quarter inch long that grew out of the top cola. Delicately placing it on his palm, he brought it over to the microscope and gently positioned it on the glass specimen slide. Checking the focus, he smiled and handed the microscope to Betty. "Give that a look."

Betty squinted through the scope. She took in a quick breath and turned back to Peyton. "Oh, Peyton. I've never seen anything like that." Returning to the eyepiece and adjusting the focus ring, Betty was mesmerized. It was like a fairyland inside that magnified circle. Against a creamy, glistening white backdrop rose hundreds of iridescent, round heads. Betty soon learned they were called *trichomes* and held dozens of healing compounds. It was like visiting another reality; a world within a world that was both surreal and magical. She moved the leaf just a titch to the left and dozens of new, shimmering trichomes came into view, most of the globular heads clear and a few others slightly milky.

"People don't realize it but you can alter the physical and mental effects of a single plant based on when you harvest it," Peyton instructed. "If you cut it down when the trichomes are clear, the plant has more of an effect on the mind. If you wait until they are all milky, you start to move the effects more into the body. Eventually, if you wait until about half of those trichomes turn amber, you'll get a powerful physical reaction that locks you into the couch or bed. See? That's the art of this, Betty. You can manipulate the strength of the plant based on when you harvest it."

Betty didn't want to take her eyes off the enchanting, magnified scene. Part of her wanted to jump into that exquisite world that occupied the tip of the leaf and roll around in the sparkling landscape. She reluctantly handed the microscope back to Peyton as her head continued to reel with the enthralling, resinous scents. "You know, Peyton, you hear about pot, weed, marijuana, whatever...and you see it in these bags all crushed and dried. But when you see it like this, it's different. And you have to ask yourself why so many people are against it?"

"Aw, now you're gonna get my blood pressure up if we get into the politics of cannabis." He scratched the topsoil of one plant, checking the moisture. "Back in the mid-1800s, on up to around the 1930s, cannabis was a common ingredient in nearly half of any doctor's remedies, usually sold as liquid extracts. They made the extracts for everything from migraine headaches to menstrual cramps. You can still go online and see these cool bottles from the early 1900's with *Cannabis Indica* written across the front. Dude, they even had formulas with cannabis for babies who were teething! Most people *never* thought of cannabis as a way to get high. I'm not saying there weren't people abusing it. There are always going to be people who abuse stuff. Hell, some people still abuse cough syrup." He leaned forward in a confidential manner. "I've heard people even drug their kids with cough syrup."

"Really?" she said, feigning shock. "When did cannabis stop being considered medicine?"

"You can thank William Randolph Hearst and the Dupont Company for starting the bullshit campaign that smeared this beautiful plant." Peyton launched into a concise history lesson, beginning with Hearst's newspaper empire and his vast ownership of timberlands. The strong fibers from *hemp* – the more common name for the non-psychoactive "ditch weed" version of *Cannabis Sativa* – had been used for thousands of years to make everything from paper and clothing, to rope and ship's sails. Hemp fiber was employed as canvases for Rembrandt and Van Gogh, the paper used for the first draft of the Declaration of Independence and the Constitution, as well as the cloth chosen by Betsy Ross to sew the first flag. Labeled a "billion dollar crop" in the 1930s, hemp was poised to propel the United States out of the Great Depression. But Hearst's influence changed the course of history and started the propaganda campaign against the plant.

In 1937, Dupont held the patent for the process to make plastic from oil and coal. Synthetics were the future and natural hemp industrialization, while more cost effective and less invasive to produce, would destroy Dupont's monopoly in the marketplace. Dupont's primary investor in his plastics division was Andrew Mellon. Mellon conveniently became Hoover's Secretary of the Treasury. Even more conveniently,

Mellon appointed his future nephew-in-law and strong pro-
hibitionist, Harry J. Anslinger, to head the Federal Bureau
of Narcotics and Dangerous Drugs. An unholy alliance between the four powerhouses, Hearst, Dupont, Mellon and
Anslinger, was born and exploited. In order for their wealth
and power to continue, cannabis *hemp* had to be removed
from the landscape.

But how? How could they convince the public that a
plant used for thousands of years for fiber and medicine was
suddenly not useful? "Danger and fear," Peyton said in an
ominous tone. "Tell us it's dangerous and make us afraid of
it. Fear sells and compels," he declared. "And there was a shit
load of fear-stained rhetoric they couldn't wait to unleash."
After learning that Mexican laborers smoked "brick weed" –
low potency cannabis that was barely psychoactive and full
of seeds, stems and leaves – Hearst's tabloid-driven, racist-
fueling, agenda-heavy creation of "the evil weed" was established to shock and manipulate the unsuspecting and naïve
masses. "Back then," Peyton added, "if you wanted to turn
people against something, all you had to do was associate it
with immigrants or people who were considered 'low class.'"

Hearst, who believed blacks and Mexicans were inferior,
fused racism with disinformation and the media blitz began. "This is when Hearst and his buddies started calling
it *marijuana*," Peyton informed Betty, "which was purely a
Mexican slang term the field workers gave it." When Harry
Anslinger, who was also an unapologetic racist, discovered
that black jazz musicians liked to toke on joints, he spun a
story about how marijuana smoking would insidiously incite
white women to have wanton sex with black men.

To visually shock the unsophisticated public with the
supposed debauchery caused by "reefer," Anslinger had a
strong hand in the scripting and production of anti-marijuana, propaganda films between 1935 and 1937, including *Marihuana: The Devil's Weed*, *Marihuana: Assassin of Youth* and the
classic, *Reefer Madness*. The films featured "marijuana crazed
youth," who turned into sex hungry, insane, violent, raping,
murdering, nut cases when they smoked the herb. Peyton

shook his head. "I mean, come on. If I vape a little too much of an *Indica* strain, I go to sleep. The last thing on my mind is plotting to kill someone." He pulled a few dead leaves off the bottom of one of the blooming plants. "Have you ever seen those idiotic movies?" Peyton asked. "All the actors playing the 'teenagers' look like they're in their late thirties or early forties. One of the guys even looks like he's balding."

Peyton carefully disposed of the dead leaves in a trash-can. "The whole point was to confuse people, right down to the name of the plant. Medical doctors were used to re-questing *Cannabis Indica* from the pharmacy to add into their formulas, *not* 'marijuana.' So when doctors heard about the dangers of 'marijuana,' they had no idea these jokers were really taking about cannabis, which they all knew was pretty tame." Peyton continued his history lesson, mentioning that when the Marijuana Tax Law was introduced in the spring of 1937 to outlaw cannabis, none of the medical experts fought it because they didn't understand that "marijuana" was cannabis. The Bill was introduced to the House floor by a Du-pont supporter, who was eager to make sure his investment in the plastics industry was protected and that *hemp* would be banned in all forms, *including* medicine.

Once it was banned, the herb stayed under the radar un-til the 1960s when it resurfaced and became connected to the hippie culture. Times were changing and so, as Peyton referenced, "they couldn't tie the plant to blacks and lazy Mexicans anymore." Instead, they created new propaganda, claiming that marijuana made you unproductive and a bur-den on society. A few years later, they spun an unproven story that cannabis killed brain cells. "The irony," Peyton said, "is that some of the cannabinoids actually stimulate new nerve growth in the brain. They proved it on rats."

Peyton's concise history lesson continued. By 1970, with pressure from special interests and hysteria from par-ents who bought into the media's hype against the alleged dangers of cannabis, the Federal government changed the classification of 'marijuana' to a Schedule I drug – the worst possible category to put it in. That label meant it had zero medicinal benefits, was highly addictive and could kill. The only problem was that there had *never* been a single case of anyone dying from using cannabis. Other Schedule I drugs, Peyton noted, include heroin and LSD. "So, you have these harder drugs like cocaine, meth and morphine that are *Schedule II*," Peyton said with a knowing smile. "And yet they say cannabis, a *Schedule I* drug, is a 'gateway drug' to these harder drugs. Don't you just love it? It's all backwards! In this scenario, shouldn't the abuse of cocaine, meth and morphine lead to *cannabis* and not the other way around?"

"Why don't they just change the classification of cannabis to a different Schedule that fits its use?"

Peyton leaned against the wall. "Aw, Betty. Now you're starting to sound like an activist."

"It's an obvious question, don't you think?"

"If they wanted to keep their whole gateway gig going, they'd have to make cannabis Schedule III. But catch this: Getting it out of Schedule I would make it available for Federal research funding. And *that* would quickly uncover all the proven medical and health benefits of the herb that the privately funded foreign studies have already shown. Then the government would have to explain why they demonized the plant for over seventy years, lied to the public and put people in prison for something that was pretty tame in comparison to all the other shit out there."

He paused and let out a disparaging snort. "The more you dig into this, the more you'll realize that everything you've been taught is based on disinformation. The whole thing is a game and a joke, Betty. The government has known since 1974 that cannabis can cure cancer in lab rats. You hear that? *Nineteen seventy-four.* But Nixon, who started the inane 'War on Drugs' wasn't thrilled when he was told that. So he chose to bury the report and continue the ridiculous propaganda campaign against the herb. Don't take my word for it. Look it up." He shook his head. "As if it's the government's job to protect you from a little plant! Like they actually care about your health! If you think the government gives a rat's ass about your health, then *you* must be smoking chemically grown weed," Peyton argued. "It's not their responsibility to tell me how to take care of myself. Why would I want a bunch of strangers whom I've never hung out with, never talked to and who only know me by my social security number, dictate *anything* to me about my well-being? If I wanted to put up with that, I'd go back and live with my parents. They couldn't take care of me and the egg donor doesn't care about the welfare of her own father. That's why I live with him and watch over him."

He examined several colas on a nearby plant. "So now you want to hear the *real* hypocrisy, Betty?"

"Sure."

"Since 1968, the National Institute on Drug Abuse has contracted with a lab on the University of Mississippi campus to grow and harvest cannabis. They literally have *hundreds of pounds* of cannabis in temperature-controlled barrels. It's dried, cured and shipped to the Research Triangle Institute in North Carolina, where it's rolled into three hundred government-approved cigarettes and sent every single month to the last remaining medical cannabis patients the government quietly takes of. There used to be eight people in the program, but I think it's down to four people now. The patients suffer from different problems, like glaucoma, AIDS and MS. So, you tell me? How can the government hand out three hundred joints a month with one hand and use the other hand to write legislation that claims there's no medical benefit to the plant?"

Betty attempted to come up with a reason but failed. "I can't answer that."

"That's because the whole thing is insane! It's like sitting down to a meal with the characters in *Alice in Wonderland*. One person's comment conflicts with the guy across the table, but they both claim they're right. And meanwhile, we're all playing Alice, wondering if we're stuck in some sort of weird dream, and when we wake up everything will be right again." He looked at Betty with a serious expression. "They're all nuts, but they're *also* serious control freaks. Even now, they're quietly putting all their weight behind billion dollar drugs made from cannabis. They know they can't keep up the lies forever, because people are getting smarter. So, now the bastards are gonna cash in on the plant they've been telling us is dangerous and deadly for decades. You watch, Betty. They'll reschedule cannabis down to II or III and then launch one of their big drugs made from cannabis. It'll be for PTSD, anxiety, MS, chronic pain...maybe even the Big 'C.' But before they do that, they'll pull a reverse propaganda campaign and tell the public that cannabis, as a pill or some drug spray, is safe and effective, even though there will be dozens of side effects from whatever they create. There are *always* side effects from Big Pharma's lab creations. You can't patent any plant, Betty. So they'll lie and tell you nature is imperfect, that God made a mistake, and their Frankenstein pills are the ticket to whatever ails you. And I guess that takes us right back to the beginning of this history lesson. Right back to the lies, that plastics were better than anything industrialized cannabis hemp could offer. They're gonna want us to choose the synthetic again over the real deal. And they are gonna do whatever it takes to manipulate and coerce the public into agreeing to that. And you know what? The public might just be dumb enough to fall for it...again."

As if on cue, the lights in the bloom room suddenly snapped off. They stood there in complete darkness until Peyton spoke up.

"I've got my green headlamp around here somewhere. Don't move."

Betty heard him stumbling around the room. "Why green?"

"See how light tight this room is? There's not a sliver of light coming in. That's the way it's gotta be for twelve solid hours. The only light that doesn't alter their dark cycle is a green lamp. Humph, it might be out by my bed. I pop it on when I want to read after midnight when the veg ladies go to sleep. That way, I don't interfere with their natural resting cycle."

"Your world really does revolve around this completely, doesn't it? Do you know what 'myopic,' is?

He continued to fumble around in the dark. "Betty, how could I know what your 'opic' is when I don't know what my 'opic' is?"

Betty explained the definition.

Peyton weighed this new information. "Yeah, I can see how that's dangerous. People who are too consumed by politics, religion, alternative health...I know people like this. They can turn into raging psychopaths. I know a psychopathic, raw-food freak that I keep on a long leash."

"Peyton, you do this 24/7. You work at a dispensary and a grow store and come home to tend your plants. That's myopic."

"Well, I'm just glad the lights are out so the plants can't hear all this," he said with strange sincerity. "These are my ladies. They need me."

"You have a girlfriend?"

He stopped fumbling. There was a slight hesitation. "Why?"

"A boy your age should have a girlfriend," Betty motherly suggested.

There was silence and then he spoke with measured caution. "Betty....how can I say this delicately? I like you and you're pretty hot for someone as old as you are, but I think the age difference between us would cause problems down the road."

"*Not me!* I'm talking about a girl your own age!"

There was another pause. "Oh. Sorry about that. Uh, well, I dated a girl at the dispensary. I thought she was okay, but then I found out she was pretty much a whore. So that was a buzz-kill for our relationship."

Peyton finally gave up trying to find his headlamp. Working their way carefully to the door, they finally exited the blackened bloom room and emerged back into the glaring light and vegetative plants who were now rocking out to The Allman Brothers' "Ramblin' Man." He led her to a smaller area just outside the main vegetative grow area where a smaller, T5 light illuminated nine clones in various stages of development.

"I thought you were only allowed eighteen plants total in a vegetative state?" Betty asked.

"You are. But the law gets kinda grey when the ladies are this small. Some will tell you it's not a true plant until it has four sets of good leaves and a developed root system. Others claim it's not a viable plant until it's a little bigger than that."

"That makes absolutely no sense."

"I know. That's what happens when you have people making laws about cannabis who have never worked with it. What can I say? When you try to regulate a plant, there's a lot that's not gonna make much sense. Sometimes, I think the state kinda makes it all up as they go along." He pointed to three fairly developed plants with medium wide leaves. "That's a new one I'm working with. Her name is Kushberry. I grew her from seed. She's a cross between OG Kush and True Blueberry, and she's supposed to be one of those strains that's rich in CBD. That means she's great for pain and anxiety but doesn't have a lot of the THC effects on the mind."

He wouldn't take any money for the clones. Ducking behind a curtained area where his unmade bed was hidden, he returned with a stack of magazines. "Here are some *High Times* magazines. People like to say they read them for the in-depth interviews, but I read them for the bud porn." He said tongue-in-cheek, opening up the centerfold. "Check out Miss February!" There on the center fold out was an extreme close-up of a very resinous bud, with a kaleidoscope of red and orange hairs. "Isn't she magnificent?"

Yes, Betty silently admitted. The boy really did need a girlfriend.

Peyton gave Betty a piece of paper with Dottie's information on it, along with the required paperwork from the state she'd need to give her. "She's looking forward to meeting you on Sunday. She said one o'clock works for her."

"That's fine. I'll be there five minutes early as usual."

"Cool. You guys are gonna get along real well. Oh, hey, a couple things. First, technically you're not supposed to charge your patients for anything you make or grow for them. According to some people you talk to, you can charge them for the electricity it takes to grow and the cost of nutrients. But the rest is on a donation only basis. But don't worry about Dottie. She's a rich rancher. The second thing is, when you go there on Sunday, you're there to buy a horse."

Betty furrowed her brow. "I'm what?"

"That's what she told me to tell you. Like I said, she wants to keep this on the down low."

Betty had a quiet aversion to horses ever since one bit into her bouffant back in Texas, but she'd play along. "I thought this was all above board, Peyton."

"It is. However, you can't change the perception some people have. Even the people who want to use it. My medical cannabis doc told me she sees hardcore Baptists in her office *after hours*, who show up in disguise and hang their heads, because they can't believe the plant's working for them, and they're terrified someone's gonna find out!" He shook his head. "It's the stigma, Betty, I'm tellin' ya. It's the *stigma* that we got to change!"

"That we *have* to change."

He rested his hand on her shoulder. "I'm so glad you agree!"

He offered to come over the following day around noon to help her set up the grow operation. "Buy several buckets of white paint," he told her. "Everything's gotta be white to reflect the light. Have you figured out the location?"

Betty had given it a lot of thought, and while it was a predictable location, she settled on refurbishing her large basement. Except for the washer and dryer area, she never spent any time down there. It was Frank's domain, but it was built like a bunker. Frank's large gunroom could work for the veg area, while his separate office could be renovated to accommodate the blooming plants. Best of all, the south-facing, sliding glass door that led out to the backyard offered plenty of fresh air for the plants. "It's perfect and discreet," Betty told Peyton. "Oh, and you might want to wear a shirt tomorrow that plays down anything having to do with the herb. My neighbors aren't very tolerant."

Peyton nodded as his cell phone rang, emitting a harsh ring tone of an electric guitar. "That's a Jimi Hendrix riff," he told Betty as he answered it.

Betty wasn't sure who was on the other end of the line, but she could tell by his repetitive use of the word "Dude" in increasing volume and irritation, that whatever he was hearing was not great news. When he hung up, he turned to Betty with a look of frustration. "Well, the sons of bitches are at it again!"

"What's wrong?"

"They closed *Nature's Bud* dispensary today. Kevin got set up by some woman."

Betty's mouth went dry. "What? Are you sure?"

"I don't know. That was how my friend just laid it out. Kevin fucked up and sold herb to a lady without a red card, and then when she asked for some magic mushrooms, he told her he could help her out. *Shit.* I hate it when people don't follow the rules. The rest of us always get lumped in with these guys, and it ruins our credibility."

"Well, that's one bad apple gone, right?"

"Yeah, I guess. Kevin's heart is in the right place but he should have known better." He gave the wall a good pound in frustration. "You know, people have this idea that if they close enough dispensaries, it's going to stop crime. That's only a theory. Out in California, three dispensaries shut down in this one neighborhood and everybody thought it was great. One month later, crime increased in the same area over fifty percent. So, you tell me?"

Betty considered his words. "I think that some individuals have a strong desire to save others from what they think might be harmful. I don't know you can blame them for that."

"If they're ignorant I can," he stated unflinchingly. "If they spout outdated and unproven information to scare people, I can blame them." He took a deep breath and centered himself. "Hey, do you know anything about that bullshit letter to the editor? It was in the paper this past Monday? My buddy thinks the people behind it might have set up Kevin."

Betty tried not to look like a deer in the headlights, standing there clutching her three new cannabis clones and the stack of *High Times*. "No idea."

~~~

She arrived back home safely, after stopping at the hardware store to buy six gallons of the glossiest white paint she could find. The sun was just setting over the farthest hill in Paradox. As she removed the paint from the trunk, Jerry called over to her from across the street. He was standing next to his brother's motorhome, smoking a cigarette and downing a beer. Arnold lay nearby, tethered to a long leash.

"Need any help, Betty?" he slurred.

"No thank you, Jerry. I'm good to go!"

"Home improvements?" he yelled, as his question echoed down the street.

Betty turned, quickly concocting a good lie. "Yes. I'm hiring a young man to help me clean up the attic and give it a fresh splash of paint."

"More power to ya!" he hollered back in an indistinct cadence, as he held his beer can in the air and toasted her with it. "You gotta do what you gotta do to keep your property value up in this economy!"

Between the oncoming darkness and Jerry's muddled senses, Betty was easily able to remove the three new Kushberry clones from the backseat, along with the stack of *High Times*, without her neighbor being any wiser.

She was feeling pretty damn good about her sly maneuver, as she walked upstairs with the three clones and the magazines. "I'm home, girls!" she called out to the three plants secured in her closet. "And I brought you three new sisters!"

Betty rounded the corner, set down the plants and turned to the closet. She dropped the magazines and stifled a shocked scream. There, rolled onto his back under the warm T5 light, was ol' Ronald. And there, protruding out of his partially toothless mouth and slacking jaw was the saliva-drenched, chewed up top stem and leaves from one of the Centennial Blueberry clones.

"Ronald?" Betty fell to the floor in her closet and rested her head on his matted stomach, checking for a heartbeat. His breathing was shallow, but it had been like that for about two years so she wasn't sure if it was anything to worry about.

"*Ronnie?*" she said, fear lacing her voice. "What did you do, sweetheart?" She gently picked the leaf particles out of his mouth. But as she drew one of the larger leaves out, Ronald corralled it with his paw and started chewing it again. "No, no, no, *no!*" A tug of war ensued between the old cat and his concerned mother with the old cat winning the battle. He wasn't dead but he didn't look fabulous. Then again, Betty thought, Ronald hadn't looked dashing for quite some time.

Her head spun with what she should do. She could take him to the Paradox twenty-four hour emergency vet center, but what was she supposed to tell them? She couldn't be open about what he ate, because there was no way to know if somebody there would talk to someone else. That could unleash the news that Betty Craven, stalwart Republican, wife of an honored war veteran and impeccable hostess was growing the "devil weed." She'd have to lie or they'd know what she was doing. But if she lied, what would she say he ate? Pacing back and forth, Betty's heart rate increased by the second. She carefully lifted Ronald off the floor, placed him on the bed and then dashed to her computer in a frantic search for information on cats and cannabis. The first article, "Cats *Love* Cannabis," explained that felines have an attraction to the aromatic plant in all its stages of growth. She then watched a video of a Burmese who had just eaten an entire branch of an outdoor cannabis plant in Hawaii. While she couldn't be certain, it appeared the cat was attempting to hula.

Betty was so focused on the video, she didn't see her stubborn pussycat jump off the bed and head back into the closet. That is until she heard the T5 light swinging back and forth on the stand. Quickly going back to the closet, she found Ronald standing on top of the warm, flat light as if he were surfing. Drool cascaded out of the space where he was missing a tooth as he deliriously hunkered down and rode the cannabis wave. She'd never seen her familial feline acting so uninhibited. So kitten-like. So happy. And yet, she still worried.

Betty dialed Petyon's cell number but got his voicemail. She hung up and paced a little more before she went back to her computer and searched the local telephone directory. She found his name and hesitated briefly before dialing the number.

Chapter 18

"I couldn't take my ears off you."

"Hi, Betty!" Jeff's voice was warm and friendly.

She was taken back. "Hello...How did you know it was me?"

"I'm psychic." He waited and when he heard nothing on the other end. "Caller ID?"

Betty felt stupid for not realizing the simple explanation. "Oh, yes, of course." Suddenly she felt very dizzy. Her mouth went dry.

"So, what's up?"

She sat down on the edge of the bed in an attempt to steady herself. Perhaps, she thought, she was coming down with the stomach flu since her gut kept churning. "What's up...ah...well, Ronald, my cat –"

"You mean Ronald the third."

Betty momentarily lost her momentum. "Yes...the third." As she watched Ronald continue to inelegantly surf the T5 light fixture, she diplomatically explained her predicament, how she and Peyton were going to install the "accoutrements" in the basement the following day and her concern about Ronald's further ingestion and destruction of her new "girls" that evening. After about three minutes, she realized she was rambling. Rambling was not something Betty Craven sponsored. *Ever.* The more she talked with Jeff, the more her stomach felt like an amusement park with the roller coaster and Ferris wheel intersecting around her navel. "I guess I'm just calling you for advice as to what I might do to prevent Ronald from succumbing to his cannabis proclivity."

Jeff chuckled. "God, Betty. You really do enjoy verbose explanations."

"I...well..." Suddenly, she was lost for words.

"Would you like me to come over and see if I can rig up something to keep Mr. Reagan out of the weed?"

Her stomach lurched. "Sure...I'll fix you dinner!"

"I've already eaten. See you in half an hour."

Betty hung up. A strange giddiness briefly overtook her, followed by a drier mouth, more churning in her gut and finally, a sense she was losing control. This was not acceptable. Above all else, she needed to stay in control to maintain the well-worn structure she depended upon. If she didn't, chaos would ensue. And as she'd been lectured many times, structure was essential. Chaos, she believed, bred confusion and unexpected consequences. Taking several deep breaths, she regained her composure. Then she realized Jeff would have to come into her bedroom in order to attend to the girls in the closet. That's when her stomach began churning again, this time with several sharp pangs. What in the hell was going on? She'd never felt this way before. It had to be some sort of...sickness.

The next half hour was a blur, as Betty hurriedly cleaned the room, dusted already dust-free objects and propped pillows on the bed. Then she wondered why she was propping pillows. She was just about to analyze that action further when the doorbell rang.

She greeted Jeff at the front door and welcomed him inside. He was dressed in a weathered, denim shirt that was frayed on the sleeves and neck. His denim jeans looked worse for wear and he wore leather clogs on his feet. He carried a box full of old screens, wood and a few tools.

"So, how's little Doobie doing?" he asked with a grin.

"Please don't call him that," she replied, maintaining a somewhat formal stance. "He's upstairs on the bed sleeping."

"Sleeping the sleep of the innocent?"

Betty felt that damned lightheadedness overtake her again.

"You okay?" he asked.

"I seem to be getting asked that question a lot lately. I'll take you upstairs." She turned as those four words echoed in her head. "What I mean is that I'll take you up to the bedroom. No...wait...let, let, let me be more precise –"

Jeff smiled, as his blue eyes danced. "Betty, I'm here to put a screen around the plants so little Doobie will stay out of them."

"Please...please stop calling him little Doobie."

She led Jeff upstairs and into the bedroom. He set down the box of screening and tools and knelt by the bed, petting Ronald.

"How you doing, ol boy?" Jeff said.

Betty fumbled with her sleeve. "He seems to be quite... relaxed," she whispered.

"Well, instead of Ronald just saying no, he said why the hell not?" He leaned closer and whispered in the cat's ear. "It's okay, Ronnie. Time is slowing down. Your paws are going to feel heavier than normal. You might have a little short-term memory loss, but at your advanced age, you're probably used to that. Sounds are going to be louder, and lights are going to be brighter. But there's nothing to worry about. Just sleep it off, and you'll be back to normal tomorrow."

Betty couldn't help but smile. She directed Jeff to the closet, where he quickly sized up the situation and began to build a temporary screened enclosure. She looked at her clones and realized they really did look like weeds she'd pluck out of her yard in favor of something more beautiful. "Why this weed?" she said out loud.

"What do you mean?" he asked, focused on setting up the frame.

"There are lots of weeds that have been growing for thousands of years. Amaranth, lamb's quarters, bindweed, thistle, the prodigious dandelion...Cannabis can grow in a ditch and isn't exactly stunning."

He stopped what he was doing momentarily. "Well, I guess someone ate it or smoked it, and their consciousness was altered in some way that gave them some sort of...I don't know...understanding they didn't have before." He resumed working. "I know when I used to smoke it, time was held captive; everything that came before and all that was to be were not as important as the present moment." He looked at her. "And in that moment, lies the mystery. One can delve into the *now,* and occupy that space and become one with all the minutia our waking eyes never see."

Betty was in awe. "That's so beautifully said." She turned away, hoping she hadn't lingered too long.

"Maybe the whole point of cannabis is to let us know it's really possible to be present in the *now.* Once you know what that feels like, you can reproduce it without even using the herb." He nonchalantly went back to work. "That's the problem today. Everybody's trapped in their past or terrified of their future. When the truth is, all we have is right now but everyone is betraying it."

Betraying it. Betty was never able to explain the way her son behaved before the drugs took him hostage. But right then, it suddenly became clear. He was always living in the moment and fully engaged in that place with heartfelt abandon. But the tremors of judgment, frustration and rage directed at him by his father tended to make it nearly impossible for him to sustain himself in that space. Worms of self-doubt and self-hatred penetrated his psyche, transforming those moments into sheer pain.

"I like to think I can live in the moment," she declared, "while I'm focusing on the future."

He laughed hard. "Did you hear what you just said? And you said it with such authority! I'll have to remember that one."

Betty joined in the chuckles, even though she wasn't quite sure what was so funny about her statement. She didn't wander far from the closet. While Jeff continued to work, Betty stood close by, effusively discussing her newest Kushberry "girls." She also told him that she was going to meet a new patient who was interested in her chocolates. "Her name's Dottie. That's all I know. Except that she's a bit older than I am." Betty nervously played with her sleeve again as she observed Jeff. He listened to her without interrupting and she wasn't used to that, so she kept talking. "I imagine Dottie and I will have some things in common, given our age." She waited but Jeff didn't respond. "Graduating from high school in the late sixties like we did." And still he said nothing, except acknowledging her with a nod. Finally, she just blurted it out. "When did you graduate from high school?"

He looked at her with his piercing eyes. "Now why on earth would you want to know that?"

"No reason. Just chit-chat." She leaned against the open closet door "When's your birthday?"

Jeff focused on the temporary frame. "In about a month. You planning on baking me a cake?"

"Sure. How many candles should I put on it?"

"You want to know how old I am?"

"Yes."

"Old enough to not care what other people think. Why do I feel like this is a job interview?" He measured the screen. "You want to know about me? Okay. As Phil Ochs sung, 'I'm just a typical American boy from a typical American town. I believe in God and Senator Dodd and keepin' old Castro down.'" He pounded a nail into the frame and continued in an off-hand cadence. "I was raised an Ecopalian. That's an Episcopal with the piss scared out of him. My mother, she was a pistol," he looked at Betty, "so you know what that makes me?"

"A son of a gun?"

He smiled. "You got it. I was a life long Democrat until the day I wasn't anymore. Now I'm a Libertarian. I don't buy into divide and conquer or the us against them mentality. I don't smoke or drink, but I've dated girls who do. I don't believe in organized religion, because I don't want to be told I'm not good enough, pious enough or decent enough to get into that place they call heaven. I think youth is overrated and far too over-worshipped, but I'd give anything to still have the knees I had when I was eighteen." He stood up to unroll the screen. "I love bluegrass in moderation, but I don't like the blues. I don't trust skinny cooks or sleepy baristas. I don't suffer fools, but I sometimes suffer from seasonal allergies. I never had kids but that doesn't mean I didn't give it the ol' college try. I don't have regrets about my past, and I'm not obsessed with my future. I no longer have high expectations or attempt to repeat the same experience twice, but I have learned that the same magic can happen again in the most ordinary places. I believe if people really saw a sausage being made they'd never eat another sausage again. I think you're never too old to fall in love, and if I knew the world was going to get hit with a meteor that would wipe out all life that wasn't hiding in an underground bunker, you know what I'd do? I'd pull up a lawn chair, pour myself a hot cup of coffee and face that ball of fire with a shit-eating grin on my face." He looked at Betty. "Does that cover it?"

Betty felt herself blushing and turned away. "Everything except your age."

He returned to work. "Why does it matter? Are you planning my birthday or something else?"

He obviously wasn't falling for her Texas-style subtlety. "I'm not planning anything." It was pointless to press him further. As she'd heard her father say many times back in Texas, "If you find yourself in a hole, the first thing to do is stop digging."

There was an awkward slice of silence between them until Jeff spoke up.

"Do you have to name your business when you're a caregiver?" he asked, returning to the screen.

Betty leaned back against the doorframe. "I don't think so. But maybe I should. I don't want to call it *The White Violet*, because I wouldn't want there to be any connection between my failed chocolate store and this venture."

"Why *The White Violet?*"

Betty gave Jeff the condensed version, telling him about Frankie and the white violet watercolor he had given her during their last visit.

He stopped working, obviously deeply struck by Frankie's tragic story. "Wow. That makes all this even more of a one-hundred-and-eighty-degree shift for you, doesn't it?" He considered it further. "Good for you. I'm not sure many other women with your experience would ever consider growing pot."

"Cannabis," she corrected him. "I'm not really sure why I'm doing it. Except that I can, so why in the hell not?" She wrestled with what she was feeling. "I think it comes down to the fact that when you've spent your life parroting the words and values of others, you tend to easily ignore the voice inside of you that counters what you're hearing. When you aren't encouraged to have a mind of your own, you readily ride the values of other people and never stop to think whether you actually believe any of it."

Now it was Jeff's turn to gaze a little too long at Betty. "That's a huge realization for you, isn't it?"

She nodded. "Yes. I seem to be having more of those lately." She turned to the clones. "You know, maybe I need to come up with a clever name for my new business."

"Choose carefully," he offered, pounding the first nail into the wooden frame. "I had a friend name a restaurant *Harold's Hideaway*. Nobody could find it. Another buddy called his B&B, *The Secret Garden*. Nobody knew it existed."

She chuckled at his humor. "How about 'Compassionate Cacao.' They use the word 'compassion' in a lot of medical cannabis literature. And here's my slogan: 'We make chocolate you can feel!'"

"I like 'chocolate you can feel' as a slogan. But Compassionate Cacao is kind of boring. Loosen up. Have some fun with the name. I mean, let's get real. I'm the owner of the 'Hippie Dippie Health Food Store.' If you want to keep the sophisticated vibe, call yourself 'Elegant Edibles' or 'Gorgeous Ganja.' How about 'Refined Reefer?'"

"Good Lord, no! This can't be a joke!"

"I know that. But it can sure as hell be fun." He stopped what he was doing and looked at her. "You know what 'fun' is, right? When was the last time you had fun?"

Betty thought hard. "Are we talking random fun or planned activities that include certain fun aspects?"

He let out a howl of laughter. "God, Betty, if anybody needs to smoke a joint, you do."

A twinge of ire ran up her spine. "Well, no thank you. I prefer to ingest it."

"Then you need to ingest a little bit more." A thought crossed his mind. "Hey, I got it. You're a classy woman. You want to operate a classy business. How about 'The Classy Joint?'"

"Right. A play on words."

"When you say it like that, Betty, you suck the fun right out of it." He drove another nail into the wood frame.

She was quiet for several minutes while she watched him work. He seemed so confident. And yet, he didn't take himself too seriously. Such an atypical combination. "Do you think I'm quite foolish for doing all this?"

"No," he said nonchalantly. "I think it's cool." He focused on attaching the screen to a nail. "When I used to see you get up and speak at the town council meetings, I sensed something different about you. You were always prepared and spoke with such measured modulation, but −"

"I won several awards in college for my presentational abilities."

"I bet you did," he replied with a mischievous grin. "But even though I didn't agree with most of what you said at those meetings, you still captured my attention. I couldn't take my ears off you."

Betty felt unpredictably vulnerable. "What exactly did you not agree with?"

He stood up, testing the strength of the improvised barrier. "It doesn't matter, Betty." He moved from the closet and replaced his tools in the box.

"Well," she stressed, following him, "it's just that I'd like to know −"

"Why? So we can dissect it? And then analyze it. And then debate it further? That sounds exhausting." He glanced over her shoulder and smiled. "Is that one of your guiding principles?"

She turned. There was the bold statement from Marilyn Monroe. "ALL A GIRL REALLY WANTS IS FOR ONE GUY TO PROVE TO HER THAT THEY ARE NOT ALL THE SAME." *Shit*, she thought.

Her gut churned. "It was an impulse buy from *The Gilded Rose*. I don't know why I purchased it. I'm not even a fan of Miss Monroe's –"

He put his hand on her shoulder. "It's okay, Betty. You don't need to keep explaining yourself. I hope you figure that out one day."

When he moved his hand off her shoulder, Betty felt strangely empty. "I know you said you already ate dinner, but I can still make you something "

"You don't have to cook for me. I'm good."

Yes, she thought. He was.

"Is there anything else you need done?"

Betty waited a little too long before she answered. "No. That's all. Thank you." She walked him outside to his motorcycle. "Aren't you afraid of falling off this thing and dying?"

Jeff secured the box on the back of the bike with a bungee cord. "God, you really are focused on death, aren't you?"

"You're riding a motorcycle without a helmet."

"Haven't you heard? If you wear a helmet it just means you can have an open casket funeral instead of a closed one."

"That's disgusting."

"Maybe, but it's true. And to answer your question, instead of worrying about whether I'm going to die, I'm more afraid of not living my life to the fullest every day." He straddled the bike. "You really do have issues around death, don't you?"

"Doesn't everyone?"

"I don't know. I haven't talked to 'everyone.'"

She glanced down at his leather clogs. "Do you think those clogs are appropriate footwear for this mode of transportation?"

He smiled and shook his head. "Gosh, Betty. If I didn't know any better, I'd swear you were worried about me."

Her gut began to toss again. "I'm not worried at all. I just think you could have made a safer choice of shoe, that's all."

Jeff cheerfully let the comment slide as he turned the ignition key. "Do you and your friend need help tomorrow setting up your grow operation?"

She was taken aback but quietly thrilled. "Well, sure... you know somebody who might want to help?" Her nervous attempt at humor fell oddly flat. "Noon tomorrow?"

"See you then." He drove away into the darkness.

Betty waited outside until she couldn't hear the sound of his engine any longer. "'The Classy Joint,'" she said to herself. "Sure...why not?"

~~~

Betty tried to eat her evening meal, but her stomach felt tight and anxious. She continued to entertain the possibility she was coming down with something. Sleeping was futile. Melting another small chunk of the cannabis coconut oil, she dipped her finger in the warm liquid and licked it off. She was about to return the oil to the container, when she plunged her thumb into the oil and ingested every last drop she gathered. But she still felt giddy and knew sleep wasn't on the menu. Falling back on her industrious predisposition, she carried the paint buckets downstairs into the basement and began slapping a thick layer of glossy white on the walls of the soon-to-be veg room. By 1 AM, she'd completed the project. Where collectable guns were once stored, there would soon be six young, thriving cannabis plants. There was something quite beautiful and rancorous about that reality.

The next morning she awoke at seven feeling invigorated, even though she'd enjoyed fewer than six hours of sleep. There was so much to do before Peyton and Jeff arrived at noon. After hoisting the flag at her front door and eating a quick breakfast, she spent the next two hours in the basement tossing the remaining plaques, medals and sundry items from Frank's collection into boxes and shoving them in a corner of the basement. It felt good to her; like she'd just lost a few extra pounds of infuriating weight. There was a lot more space in the main room of the basement than she'd realized. She moved Frank's large desk to the side of the room, away from the sliding glass door. It would make a wonderful table for transplanting her girls. Looking down at the battered, olive green carpeting that smelled of tobacco and booze, she decided it had to go. She had to rip him out of there, and she had to do it completely.

After re-checking her "to do" list, Betty showered and dressed. She monitored Ronald several times, but he seemed to be back to his old, albeit lazy, self and none-the-worse for wear. Heading out the door, she saw Jerry and his brother Jack across the street. Arnold was unleashed and on the grass, happily chewing a bone. The men seemed to be packing up the motorhome.

Betty employed her best pageant wave. "Leaving so soon?" she yelled across the street, making sure not to sound too hopeful.

"Yeah," Jack yelled back. "Movin' on!" Arnold started barking viciously, seemingly unprovoked. "Strudel!" Jack ordered the dog, who quickly shut up. He turned back to Betty. "'Movin' on' was another code word we used right before we'd break down a door!" Upon hearing "movin' on" again, Arnold stood up and bore his teeth. "*Strudel!*" Jack demanded.

Something about a grown man yelling 'strudel' to a vicious dog made Betty giggle. After she prayed for her Taurus to start and it did, she continued to smile at the scene all the way to the farmers' market. She spent the next hour carefully perusing the many booths and selecting the perfect fruits, vegetables, baked goods and local offerings. She had everything planned. They'd arrive at noon and start working immediately. They'd break at two o'clock for lunch and then resume working at three. She'd need to make them lunch as well as a hearty snack. The aroma of rotisserie chickens roasting on the grill enticed her. Normally, Betty was not one to rely on pre-cooked fare. She never trusted someone else with that responsibility, given the many seasoning *faux pas* that could easily occur. But it made sense she'd be tired by the end of the day, and knowing that a fully cooked chicken was ready and waiting in the kitchen for her evening repast

sounded divine. She made a point to stop by one of her favorite booths to buy a large bag of beef bones to make soup,
and even treated herself to a container of homemade quince
paste from another vendor who had the same, impeccable,
gourmand appreciation. As far as Betty was concerned,
when one found a consistent source for quince paste, one
was indeed blessed.

The entire experience would have been nearly perfect
had it not been for the damned moccasin clad, tattooed,
strident voices that belonged to the COLORADO ACTIVISTS
4 NATIONAL TOLERANCE. They had permanently hijacked
this community gathering and appeared to be dedicated to
a plethora of causes, blaring on their loudspeakers about everything from freeing Tibet to gay marriage. Betty sighed.
The outdoor market used to so much better, when all she
had to listen to was banjo music and the off-key children's
choir.

When she arrived home, she was shocked to see Buddy
and a male friend of his convened in her driveway. He looked
a bit worse for wear after his spill off her roof. She parked
her car and got out with her bags. Buddy quickly came to
her aid.

"How are you feeling, darling?" she asked him, tentatively eyeing Jerry and Jack across the street.

"Feeling okay, Mrs. Craven. That's Eric," he motioned
to his weather-beaten friend. "He dropped me off to pick up
my truck and get it out of your hair."

She smiled a forced smile toward Eric. "Hello." Turning
to Buddy, she spoke with discretion. "I have your paperwork
inside that you'll need to mail to the state."

"Awesome," Buddy replied, with a thumbs-up gesture.
"Hey, you got any more of those chocolates you gave me on
the ride to the ER?"

"Yes," Betty said, opening the front door and walking inside. "But they're not decorated or wrapped appropriately."
She ushered him inside.

"I don't care about that. I still got some low back pain from when I fell, and I just figured they might help me sleep."

Betty looked him square in the eye. "Darling, I say this to you because I care. Perhaps if you lost a few pounds, there wouldn't be so much pressure on your lower back." She couldn't believe she just said that, but she wasn't sorry one bit. "I bet if you simply cut out sugar and potatoes, you'd be well on your way."

Buddy stared at his enormous belly. "Yep. You're right, Mrs. Craven. Sugar and potatoes. I'll keep that in mind. So, about those candies? Do you have, like...ten?"

"Yes, of course." She started toward the kitchen and then turned back. "You're not planning on sharing these, are you? Legally speaking, they can only be for you."

"Sure."

She waited. "Sure, what? Sure, you won't share them or sure...I'm not clear."

"Sure...They're just for me," he said with genuineness.

Betty nodded and looked out the window at Eric, who was still standing in the driveway. "He doesn't know about our agreement, does he?"

"He knows I work for you on the side, and that I left my truck here when I fell off the roof, and that you're gonna fix me up."

"Fix you up?" she said with an air of indignity. "Hang on a second, Buddy. I'm neither a dating service nor a drug dealer. You shouldn't have said a thing about our arrangement. It's confidential."

"I didn't know that, Mrs. Craven."

Betty let out a frustrated breath. "Safety is imperative, Buddy. Everything is legal, of course." She snuck another look across the street. "But prudence is advised, given the often uncharitable climate around which these operations and exchanges take place. Others might not be as understanding of my altruistic endeavors."

Buddy looked at her like a dog looks at a chemistry book. Baffled. "Sure," he offered. "You want me to wait here or come in the kitchen?"

Betty quickly put ten of the chocolates into a plastic baggie and then secured that into a plain brown bag. Deciding the bag looked plain, she tied a silver ribbon around it, found Buddy's change-of-caregiver forms and headed back into the living room.

"What do I owe you?" He asked, taking the bag.

This was different. Usually that was what she was asking him. "Legally, I can't charge you a specific price. But a donation of your choosing would certainly be valued."

"Huh?"

"I'm just going by what I was told."

Buddy thought so hard, Betty almost swore she heard the gears shifting in his brain. "Well," he finally uttered, "I've paid around five bucks or more a pop for a pain pill from the doc. But they don't touch the pain like your candies do."

"Really?" She was incongruously honored by that news.

"Hand to God." Buddy brought out his wallet and rifled through his cash. "Is seventy-five cool with you?"

"Seventy-five is just fine."

He handed her the cash.

"Mum's the word," she advised him as she walked him to the door.

"Who's mum?"

"This is just between us," she translated. "Mail your paperwork, dear."

He nodded and left. She furtively watched him leave to make sure there was no exchange with Eric. Placated by their departure, she went about putting the food away and making sandwiches. An hour later, she heard loud barking emanating from her driveway. Grabbing a soup bone from the bag, she raced outside. Peyton was trapped in his Prius, while Arnold jumped like a wild beast on his car.

Betty waved the soup bone in the air and strode to the Prius. "Strudel! Strudel!" She launched the bone toward the sidewalk as Arnold fell for the bait. "All clear!"

"Strudel?" he said. "Dude, I'd be pissed too if I was a bad ass dog and someone named me Strudel." He brought out a white plastic, water bottle with a strange chemistry symbol on the side.

"What's that mean?" Betty asked, pointing to the bottle.

"It's the symbol for THC." He walked to the back of the car, opened the hatchback and lifted out a faux-bronze fountain. "I brought you a 'welcome to the fold' gift. It's a solar fountain. I found it dumpster diving at work, and Pops worked his magic on it so it blows water like a son-of-a-bitch. He also rigged it up so you can plug your iPod into the side thingy here, and it'll spew the water up in sync with the music. It's like having a mini Bellagio Las Vegas hotel fountain." As Peyton set it up, he made a point of placing it in the north side of the yard. "In feng shui, you always put your water features in the north sector to encourage the flow of wealth and prosperity."

"It's solar," Betty said. "So wealth stops flowing when it's cloudy or at night?"

"Not sure about that," he said, filling it with water. "I'll have to ask a Chinese person the next time I see one. Okay, get ready for your world to rock!" He set the solar panel inside the fountain top and stood back. An enormous blast of water rose from the center, cascading in ribboned streams and then re-emerging with another surge of energy. "Yeah! Pops is the man!" Peyton exclaimed.

Betty led Peyton downstairs into the basement. He fell silent as he studiously examined the rooms, checking out areas for placing the intake and outtake fans, the best location for the light fixtures and how "light tight" the proposed bloom room would be. "This is great, Betty." He pointed to the sliding glass door. "During the day, you can keep that door open to get more natural airflow in here. You're still gonna have to use a lot of fans though. Remember, fans are _"

"My friend," Betty finished the sentence.

The doorbell ran. Betty nervously reacted. "That's Jeff. He's helping us."

Peyton looked slightly worried. "The fewer people who know about your grow op, the better. You don't show *any-body* your grow op unless you can absolutely can trust them. Is Jeff cool?"

She smiled. "Oh, yes. Very much so."

Chapter 19

"Texas women are not inspired by weak men."

"I brought you some presents," Jeff stated as he walked inside the house and handed her a paper bag. Across his shoulder, he carried a large bag of tools.

"Really?" Betty replied, as her stomach did somersaults. "I should start a grow operation every day." She looked down at the hem of his blue jeans. "Why are your jeans soaking wet?"

"Talk to your fountain out there. I think it's got its own agenda."

Betty peered out the window. The sun was shining brightly on the solar panel and the unit was blowing water higher than Old Faithful. Betty made a mental note to move it toward the center of the yard so it could drench her entire garden. She opened the paper bag and brought out a black plastic bottle of hemp seed oil, a bag of hemp seeds and a pound of hemp seed flour.

"I figured since you were into all things cannabis and you like to cook, why not experiment with the non-psychoactive version of the plant." He explained that the oil was full of beneficial Omega-3, and that while it couldn't be heated, it made a great dipping sauce or addition to salad dressing. The hemp seeds could be ground up and added to smoothies, and the hemp flour could be used half and half with regular flour in any baked goods.

Betty listened carefully and hoped she didn't look too smitten by his gesture. "Thank you so much," she said coyly, her Texas lilt in full swing. So far, this day was starting off quite well.

She introduced Jeff to Peyton, and after some idle chat, Peyton explained his ideas about how to vent the rooms, set up the light and organize the area. Betty brought them sandwiches, which they enjoyed between cutting into walls and securing braces. When she asked them to tear up the olive green carpeting, they were right on it. No questions, no debates, no arguments. How refreshing, Betty mused. They just ripped it off its rusty tacks, rolled it up and dragged it to the trash. Leaving the thin carpet mat underneath, Peyton and Jeff secured two layers of heavy, black plastic to the floor. Thus, Betty didn't have to worry if she spilled water or dirt in the area. Oh, if Frank could see this now, he'd croak a second time from shock.

It felt so good to have activity in her house. Normally, she would have let them continue without her, but she wanted to be part of the renovation. Taking a gander at the room that would eventually hold the blooming plants, she eagerly began to cover the walls with glossy white paint. Betty listened to the back and forth banter between Jeff and Peyton and was cheered by how well they got along. At first Peyton was a bit territorial, but Jeff's ability to observe a situation and figure out a creative solution soon won him over.

They turned on the radio for some background music. At the top of the hour, the national news came on, followed by the Colorado feed. The top local story made them stop their work momentarily. Apparently, the roof on a large grow operation in the garage of a Denver home blew up, leaving the house destroyed, the occupants injured and their beloved pet dead. "While the source of the fire is unknown," the newscaster reported, "there is the theory that too much electricity used to power the grow operation in the garage triggered the explosion."

"That's bullshit!" Peyton exclaimed. "If it was an overload, the power would just cut out. It could have been a bad heater, but it wasn't 'too much electricity.'"

"Are you certain?" Betty asked with an anxious expression.

"Don't worry, Betty," Jeff reassured her. "Even when you add three or four more lights, there's no way it's going to be enough to start a fire. Everything's grounded down here.

They said the fire started in the garage. Who's to say a gas can or some kind of solvent didn't trigger it? For all we know, they had a meth lab."

Peyton nodded. "And they'll never follow up on the story and tell us what happened. They'll just leave the idea hanging out there, so people believe grow ops explode on their own. It'll be another urban legend. Like how the cops pay off people who work at the electric company to red flag a homeowner's bill and contact the cops when they see excessive electrical use that's different from the previous year."

"No, that's actually true," Jeff deadpanned. "The irony is that the cops pay off the snitches with the marijuana that they confiscate. Circle of life."

The jarring voice of Reverend Bobby Lynch blared forth on the radio. He was front and center once again and weighing in on the "marijuana issue" in Colorado. "We are planning a national day of prayer for the children tomorrow," Lynch stated, "to ask God to steer their hearts and minds away from this drug that has become easier to obtain than a bottle of liquor!"

"That's rich," Jeff chuckled, as he continued working. "They're going to pray to God to keep the kids away from a plant that, in essence, God put on this earth. You think God is going to be up for that?"

"Why in the hell are they even asking that idiot for his opinion?" Peyton said, a spark of indignation becoming lit. "Asking him about cannabis is like asking him about forgiveness. He doesn't know shit about either one!"

"He does have a point about children," Betty interrupted. "I never considered how children might glom onto their parents' medical cannabis stash."

"You mean the same way they might glom onto their parents' booze, prescription drugs or cigarettes?" Jeff countered.

"Well yes, I realize that. But their brains are still developing. And I heard once from my son's school counselor that cannabis triggers the brain's reward system, giving the user instant gratification. She made quite a point of telling me that when this happens, the child doesn't learn the necessity of delayed gratification."

"You mean 'fun?'" Jeff asked.

"Hang on," Betty interjected. "There is something to be said for working hard for what you want and realizing it's not going to happen overnight. No pain, no gain."

Peyton shuddered. "God, I hate that mantra. Isn't there enough pain in this messed up world? Do we seriously need to conjure it in order to succeed?"

"Betty, I get what you're saying," Jeff stressed. "But there's got to be a middle ground between suffering and success. If all you do is dwell on the suffering, how in the hell can you enjoy the rewards when they show up?"

Somehow, his comment hit her hard. "Be that as it may, one can't ignore how this cannabis revolution will affect children and their moral compass."

"Betty," Jeff said, "you can't legislate morality or personal behavior. No matter how much you believe it's possible, it's never going to happen. If people want to escape by getting high or drunk or whatever, they're going to do it. Period. The question shouldn't be *what* they're using. The question should be *why* they need to escape. But the good Reverend Lynch isn't exploring that part of the issue. He's just focused a little too hard on saving the children, enough to make you question his agenda."

Betty was intrigued. "What do you mean?"

Jeff punched a staple into the black plastic covering on the floor. "Anyone who digs in and rants like that is overcompensating for something."

"Like what?" Betty asked.

"Maybe he likes to roll a fat one before bed every night," Jeff joked.

"No, really," Betty pressed, "what are you saying?"

"When one doth protest too much about an issue, one doth often have something to hide."

Peyton unrolled the reflective wall covering as he considered Jeff's statement. "Yeah. I know what you mean. When a guy doth drive a jacked-up truck with wheels that are too big and lights flashing all over, he usually has a small –"

"Brain?" Betty interjected.

Peyton smiled and stapled the silver covering to the wall. "I, on the other hand, drive a small car."

Jeff drove another staple into the plastic on the floor. "And I drive a motorcycle."

The three of them continued working away in the basement and made tremendous progress by three o'clock. They took a break under the large canopy elm in the backyard. Betty offered them their choice of tea or coffee, along with a few treats she purchased at the farmers' market that morning. A gentle breeze blew through the yard, as the tree shaded them from the piercing sun.

"Just think, Betty," Peyton said, between bites of an apricot muffin Betty had topped with quince paste, "how far you've come in just one week! I mean, think about where you were on this issue just seven days ago!"

Betty realized that exactly seven days prior, she was seated in her living room, listening to Renée declare her war on the dispensaries. "I'd rather not think about that."

Jeff threw her a knowing look.

Peyton finished the muffin and grabbed another one. "Now, if we can just get more people like you to change their minds, we won't have to deal with the jerk offs who wrote that shitty letter to the editor."

"Wait a second," Jeff intervened. "You're not aware –"

"That what this movement needs is a good ol' Republican to stand up and speak out!" Betty quickly said, shoving a plate full of cookies in Jeff's direction. "Cookie, Jeff?" She turned to Peyton. "I'm talking a moderate Republican, of course."

Jeff eyed Betty. "Okay. Well, why don't *you* become that voice?"

Betty stiffened. "I wasn't referring to myself."

"Why not?" Jeff pressed. "You come to this from an interesting point of view."

"I prefer to work more quietly."

"But that's the problem, isn't it?" Jeff added. "There have got to be lots of people like you who are involved but are afraid to come forward because of the stigma."

"Stigma," Peyton interjected. "Dude, you hit the nail on the head right there."

Jeff turned to Betty. "Maybe when you stop worrying about what other people think, you'll come out of the cannabis closet."

She got up. "Maybe I'll just bring my six plants out for now. Peyton, would you help me bring the light fixture and plants down from upstairs?"

"You need another hand?" Jeff asked.

"No, no, we can handle it." Betty hustled Peyton forward. There was no way she was going upstairs alone and risking Jeff revealing to Peyton that she was one of the "jerk offs" who signed that damned letter.

After corralling the plants and light upstairs, work resumed in the basement for another two hours. Betty was able to slap a good thick coat of glossy paint on the entire bloom room by the time Peyton and Jeff had everything installed. They showed her how to operate the intake and outtake fans, explained how to change the carbon filters and how to adjust the T5 light fixture over the six young plants. Peyton set the timer on the veg light to go on at three in the morning and shut off at nine at night. He advised her to always close the drapes across the sliding glass door at night, so as not to attract too much neighborhood attention from the streaming light. It was closing in on dinnertime by the time they finished cleaning up.

"I have a rotisserie chicken. Would you both please stay for dinner?"

Peyton checked his cell phone. "No can do, Betty. I promised Pops I'd watch the documentary on Tesla: The Man & His Magic."

God help him, Betty mused. This boy really did need a girlfriend. There was an awkward moment when Betty realized the invitation was announced, and now it would just be she and Jeff. Part of her froze but the other part of her melted.

"Guess it's just you and me, Betty," Jeff stated.

She felt dizzy and turned to Peyton. "I'll show you to your car."

When they walked out the front door, Betty noted two things. First, the fountain had subsided to a dwindling Las Vegas squirt, and Jack's motorhome and faithful drug dog were gone. Jerry, however, was across the street, watering his yard and clutching a beer can. If Betty didn't know any better, she'd think those damn cans were soldered to his palm, and he simply refilled them as needed.

"It was fun today," Peyton offered.

"Thank you, Peyton." She lifted her front door flag out of its holder and carefully wrapped it up. "I do appreciate your help."

"How'd you and Jeff hook up?"

Betty was taken back. "Hook up? There's been no hooking up."

"No, how'd you meet him?"

"Oh. Right. At *The Gilded Rose*. He was checking out my Biedermeier."

"I bet he was." He smiled and playfully punched her shoulder. "I like him. I thought he'd be a vegan since he owned a health food store but I'm glad he's not. I'm not fond of vegans anymore than I am of Canadians. I find vegans a strange mix of passive-aggressive frustration that could ironically be remedied by a grass-fed hamburger."

"You have to work through your distrust of Canadians. You can't let one bad Canuck ruin the whole stew."

He looked at her intensely. "Have you actually *met* a Canadian?"

"Yes. Quite a few of them."

"Then you're stronger than I am." He turned to his Prius. "Hey, remind Dottie about how to dose effectively with your candies. I made a cannabis cookie once for a patient who didn't understand she only needed one *bite* and not an entire cookie to kill her pain. She called me from Wal-Mart freakin' out, because she ate two cookies and couldn't fig-ure out how to get out of the automotive department." He opened the car door and got inside. "And remember tomor-row, you're seeing her about a horse."

"I'm seeing her about a horse. Gotcha. Any more advice?"

Peyton settled in his car, pulling his seatbelt across his lap. He considered her question with deep intent. "Yeah. Don't baby your plants. Obviously, you can't ignore them but don't coddle them. The first two months when they're in veg determines how strong and resilient the blooming plant will be. These ladies are hardy by their own nature. You're not dealin' with hothouse orchids. They need love but tough love. You gotta feed them the high nitrogen guanos and fish fertilizers during their veg state, but you also have to allow them to just be and grow. The mistake a lot of newbies make is throwing everything but the kitchen sink at their ladies. It's amazing what can happen if you just allow it, you know? Give them plenty of space, great light and air, warm their feet and they'll dance for you."

"Dance?"

"Yeah. I swear they dance. When the fans flutter their leaves, they move like they're dancing. But even when the wind isn't moving, I've caught them unaware in a fit of glee, shaking their hips to music only they can hear."

"Don't you think personifying them is a little dicey?

"I don't know. Ask them."

She smiled and then remembered a question. "One more thing. I know that changes in light trigger the bud to start blooming, but what triggers the resin?"

"In the wild, the resin forms to allow the pollen from the male plants to stick to the females. But in a controlled envi-ronment – like the way you and I are growing them inside – the females keep producing more and more resin while they wait for the male plant that never shows up. But the ladies never figure that out. And out of their sexual frustration, eventually they turn into spectacular, frosty beauties."

"All dressed up and sparkling with nowhere to go?"

"Well...yeah...until you kill them. Then they hang on a rack in the dark until they're dried up, shoved into a jar and stored away."

"Yes...I can relate." She waved goodbye to Peyton and thought about what he said. How long had she been hanging in the dark and drying up? Well, a light bulb can't change itself, she mused, because it needs the twist of another hand that's willing to help it change. Yes, she thought, with careful preparation, she could launch the exploration of a deeper friendship with Jeff in the future.

And with that idea firmly in hand, she strode with purpose into the house. But she wasn't prepared for what she saw when she returned to the basement. There was Jeff, sitting on Frank's old desk, with his feet resting on Frank's chair, and looking through the box of medals and awards Betty had unceremoniously packed up.

"How did Frank die?" he asked in a sober tone. "Did he have a heart problem?"

This wasn't the genre of conversation requisite to enact her strategy. "No. In order to have a heart problem, first you have to have a heart."

"Okay. So he wasn't a charmer."

She moved toward the box and began putting back the miscellaneous items Jeff had removed. "Frank was only charming if you're partial to an evening with Hitler. Please, I put these away for a reason. I don't want to see them anymore. They mean nothing to me. They never did."

"I get it. He was a tough son-of-a-bitch."

Betty filled the box and carried it back to the corner. "Texas women are not inspired by weak men."

"I can see he wasn't a shrinking violet," Jeff stated, bringing out a photo.

"Where'd you find that?"

"In the desk drawer." He handed it to Betty.

It was a Polaroid photo of Betty and Frank from 1991, taken at a barbeque right after Frank returned home from his year-long deployment during Operation Desert Storm. The ice of contempt was palpable between them. There he was with his regulation haircut, and there she was, leaning away from him and forcing an excruciating smile. She stared at the photo a little too long as the acrid memories washed over her. That day everything changed. That day shaped the rest of her son's tortured life. "I despise this photo." Betty ripped up the Polaroid and threw it in the trash. "Let's go up to the kitchen and I'll fix us some dinner." She started off.

"Why didn't you leave?" he asked, not moving.

"Leave? You act as if options were handed out like Chiclets."

"We all have options. You decided to stay. Why?"

Dammit. This was not part of her plan. "I had no choice! We had a son who needed structure. Come on, let's –"

"How long were you married to Frank before your son was born?"

"Six years. Why?"

"*Six years?* You can't tell me, during all that time, you didn't know things were sour with Frank. You're a smart woman, Betty. Leaving early on in the game was an option. That's why there are hinges on doors."

"Why are you asking all this?"

"I want to know why you do what you do."

She let out a hard sigh. "Leaving Frank was *never* an option. He was the only ticket I was offered."

"And you were afraid if you left him, there wouldn't be any more tickets handed out?"

"You make a commitment. You figure out how to strategize your life and you stick it out, for better or worse. No matter how bad it gets, no matter how many times you want to kill him, you *stick it out*." She centered herself. "Please, let's go upstairs and I'll fix you –"

"Stick it out? Interesting way of looking at life. Do you think suffering is noble?"

Betty was taken back. "Excuse me? You have no goddamned idea!"

"Suffering isn't noble, Betty," he tenderly offered. "Voluntary suffering creates pointless victims. Do you believe if you suffer enough and stick it out, you'll get rewarded down the road?"

Betty gathered herself. "It was expected of me," she said, punctuating each word. "Failure wasn't allowed! I was held to a higher standard. My parents, Frank, my friends, society, they all expect a lot from me."

"Well, pardon my language, but fuck society. As far as your friends, if they were really true friends, they wouldn't expect you to suck it up in a loveless marriage. And as far as your parents, I bet their relationship was just as manipulated, and what's that word you used? *Strategized?*"

Betty began to slightly shake. He was correct. His assumption precisely defined her parents' marital tenure – cold, indifferent bodies of matter, floating from room to room. But she was damned if she was going to admit it. "Look, I was never friends with my husband. Our relationship was more of an agreed-upon tactic of two people coming together, in order to have children and create financial security."

"Wow. When you say it that way, it sounds so scandalous."

She wasn't about to back down. "My adult life revolved around two people; one who couldn't feel and one who felt far too much. It fell on my shoulders to somehow make that work."

"Why on God's earth did you think all that responsibility fell on you?" he gently asked. "Your marriage was doomed from the start."

"Yes, well, someone forgot to tell me that. I was always under the impression that it *was* my job." Resentment colored each word. "I was raised to live the perfect life. You marry the perfect man, you have the perfect child and you live in a perfect house where everyone gets along perfectly. Anything less than that and you're doing something wrong."

He regarded her with compassion. "My God, Betty. They lied to you. Perfection is impossible. Striving toward something impossible is the definition of insanity. I've never met a perfect person in my life or had a perfect meal in a perfect house. I've seen a perfect sunset...at least it was perfect to me. I think perfection is in the eye of the beholder."

Of course, he was right. She knew all that now. But dammit, something inside of her didn't want to back down. "I settled for what I had and saw it through to the bitter of bitter ends. I didn't know that settling was so bad."

"Maybe because it's got the word, 'settle,' in it?" He leaned forward, resting his arms on his thighs. "Why is it more important to you to be right than happy? What has that gotten you?"

She turned away. This sure as hell wasn't going well. That familiar sense of being cornered encroached. But this time, she was the one cornering herself. Turning back, she stood straight as an arrow. "When I was a child, I was taught that one wasn't allowed to have fun or relax until all the work was finished. The problem is that the work is *never* done. So you can never quite unwind. The 'doing' is always on the table... waiting and demanding your attention, like a colicky baby where no amount of walking around or rocking appeases their needs. Those of us who were raised a certain way all carry the cross at the ubiquitous church of hard work. That mandatory toiling ethic hangs the bait of 'fun' out there, but we don't bite, because we don't believe we've earned it. And goddammit, you don't take something you haven't earned."

"So how is that delayed gratification working out for you?" Jeff waited. "Have you had enough pain yet, or do you still think you haven't earned a good life?"

She stiffened. A pulse of anger welled up. "I resent that."

"Good. That's a start."

Betty felt like her boat had lost its mooring. Everything had been perfect and now it was ruined. "Why are you talking to me like this?"

He swung his long legs off the desk and pondered for a moment. "Maybe some of us don't want to end up being the next target in your scope. Frank was an asshole. I get that, loud and clear. But you're still spending a lot of time shooting him down, and that doesn't bode well for future relationships."

Future relationships? Well, slap the dog and spit in the fire, she reflected. If he —

"Is gardening fun for you?" Jeff suddenly asked her.

The question came out of left field. Flummoxed, Betty momentarily withdrew her animosity. "It's comforting. My plants need me, but they also give me a sense of accomplishment. And if I happen to prune them too much or over water them, they still manage to flourish in spite of it. They are forgiving of my weaknesses."

He stared at her with those eyes that could read through her veneer. "They're safe."

She nodded. "Yes. I suppose so."

"Well, let me tell you something." He stood up. "Women who count gardening as their number one, hardcore passion, are in the same league to men as women who have an unhealthy fetish with far too many cats."

She defiantly crossed her arms across her chest. "Did it ever occur to you those women might believe that gardens and cats are infinitely more reliable and less troublesome than a man?"

"Wow. You really were screwed over by ol' Frank, weren't you?" He moved closer to her. "Gardens are great, Betty. I have a garden. And I like to work in it. But I'm not in love with my garden. My garden doesn't sit on the couch and watch a movie with me. My garden doesn't cook dinner with me. My garden doesn't pick me up at the airport at midnight. As far as the cat goes, I don't have one. But if I did, he'd be my buddy, not my focus. It's just an observation perhaps, but when a guy meets a woman who spends more time turning on her tulips and petting her cat than she does paying attention to him, it's not a fruitful start to a long term relationship."

If she had a gauntlet, it would have swung down with gusto. "Well, perhaps that's because some men require far too much attention." She steadied herself. "I think you should go now."

He paused briefly, gently moving closer to her but she inched away.

"I mean it," she stated. "*Go.*"

He regarded her with deep compassion, but she wouldn't make eye contact. "Yes, ma'am."

She didn't move a muscle until she heard the throaty engine of his motorcycle fade into the distance. He was out of line, she told herself. She was right and he was wrong. How on earth could she ever have considered...? She must have gone temporarily insane. Yes, yes, yes, she was right and he was wrong. Her daddy had another saying: "The time to kill a snake is when he raises his head." When a problem rears up, take action.

Betty was right. She just needed to keep telling herself that, even as the familiar hour of lead fell across her heart. Within seconds, that damned syncopated beat started in her right ear. It had been days since it had crept up, and now it felt worse than ever.

She closed the sliding glass door and drew the drapes to block out the generous spill of light coming from the veg room. The last thing Betty wanted were the neighbors knocking on her door and asking why she had a beacon of bright light coming out of her basement. She desperately needed to occupy herself. To move, to *do*, to accomplish something, in order to be worthy of taking in her next breath. Checking on the girls, she felt the temperature of the heat mats that warmed their feet to make sure they weren't too toasty. Reminded of what Peyton told her about shaking the stalks to encourage more strength in the plant, she gently grasped each stalk and shook the plant for about a minute each. Then she had an idea. Two by two, she carried the plants into the small laundry area. She shoved a few large towels into the dryer, and seeing a pair of her sneakers nearby, tossed them in too. She carefully placed the six plants on top of the dryer and turned it on high. Within seconds, they were dancing to the beat every time the circling shoes struck the top of the unit.

Betty stood back and tried to focus, but an overwhelming sense of disappointment and emptiness swallowed her. Her body ached, but not from exertion. The din of loneliness screamed in her face. The need to be right had a price, and she was broke.

It didn't help that the Centennial Blueberry clone, with the half-eaten top stem Ronald had ingested, was not looking as vibrant as her sisters. She turned on all the lights in the tiny room and examined the plant. A dried stream of Ronald's drool could still be seen on one broad sided leaf. She wiped it off with a wet cloth and was about to put the plant back on the tumbling dryer, when she saw something on a lower leaf. No, it couldn't be, she thought. Carrying the plant into the veg room, she held it under the bright light and looked closer. An almost negligible white cloud, the size of a pea, appeared to be forming on a lower leaf. "PM," she whispered, as if saying it too loud would propel it onto the next set of leaves. She wasn't certain but she wasn't going to take chances. She grabbed the powdery mildew spray and squirted a generous blast on the leaf. Waiting a few minutes, she couldn't quite tell if it was gone. She blew on the leaf and waited. Then she waited a bit longer. Nothing. The damned spot was still there. She decided the plant needed to be air-dried; perhaps that would solve the problem.

Carrying the clone out to her car, she got in and placed it on the front seat, securing a seat belt around the center of the two-gallon plastic pot. Once every window was open, she slowly backed out of her driveway and drove to a remote corner of Paradox, a few miles outside of town, where grassy, greenbelt fields lay next to an old asphalt road. She stopped the Taurus and remembered – it was the same place she'd secretly taken Frankie when he couldn't sleep at night as a child or when he suffered from his persistent nightmares. When she was certain that Frank Sr. was passed out or asleep, she'd bundle up her grade school son, put him on the front seat of the car and drive with all the windows down. Frankie would rest his head on the door, hold his arm outside and let the wind blow through his fingers. He wouldn't say a word as they drove up and down that asphalt road in the darkness, but his pain was tangible. And yet, after half an hour, the open air seemed to calm him and wash away his insomnia, until she could return to the house and covertly lay her sleeping son back in his bed.

While Betty sat there on that May night, as twilight succumbed to the darkness, she remembered how she wanted to keep driving on one of those nights so long ago. She had her son and some money, and she could have kept driving. But propriety kept her from doing it. What would people think of her? Somehow back then, the better choice was to endure and hope for happier times. But the happiness never arrived. It just kept being swallowed by resentment and ennui.

And so she drove up that asphalt road with the windows rolled down and watched how the cannabis leaves fluttered against the wind. With each flicker of motion, she hoped it could be washed clean of anything that was trying to destroy it. Without realizing it, she extended her arm outside her window. And she stayed just like that for another hour on that desolate road, even as the tears and regret took over.

Chapter 20

"But you didn't hear that from me."

The drive to Dottie's ranch was a much-needed diversion. Nestled on the front seat of Betty's car was a small cooler that held five beautifully decorated and wrapped chocolates. She didn't want to be too forward and bring Dottie a dozen, but two chocolates seemed inadequate. Dottie lived about forty miles south of Paradox in an unincorporated rural area. The landscape was fairly monotonous, until Betty drove up over a long, two-lane ribbon of highway and descended into a verdant valley. The warm May days and rains had quickly transformed the expanse into a rich tapestry of alfalfa and various grasses, creating an emerald and jade quilt that draped across the panorama for miles.

Betty arrived at the impressive, rusted, iron front gate precisely at 12:55 and punched the intercom button. As she waited for someone to answer, she admired the exquisite, curved, wrought-iron sign that graced the entrance: HAPPY VALLEY HEREFORDS. Underneath, burnt into a slab of wood, the sign read: HAPPY & HEALTHY GRASS-FED COWS SINCE 1980.

"Hello?" a male voice asked, crackling over the intercom.

"Hello," Betty said in her best pageant voice. "This is Betty Craven. I'm here to see Dottie...about a horse?"

"Yes, ma'am. She's expecting you."

The massive gate opened with a slow flourish. Betty drove her beat-up Taurus down the dirt road for nearly half a mile before turning into a cluster of shade trees, crossing a bridge and a slow creek, and arriving at a magnificent, two-story, log house. A large barn stood about a thousand feet past the house, and beyond that, stables and the enormous expanse of land where at least seven hundred cows and calves roamed freely. A stout man in his late fifties approached her, and she rolled down her window. He seemed to observe her with great care and a somewhat worried brow.

"Hello, ma'am," he said, offering his hand. "I'm Hugh. I'm the ranch manager."

"Nice to meet you, Hugh."

He canvassed the inside of her car. "So, you're interested in one of the horses?"

"Yes," Betty said, realizing she hadn't manufactured any suitable story to support this ruse. "But this is just an introductory meeting...with the horse." He looked at her with a quizzical expression. "I don't like to take it too fast." The minute she said that, she wished she hadn't. And before she could fall deeper in the bullshit, she heard the commanding voice of a woman, and saw her quickly walking toward the car.

"Hugh! I got this!" Dottie said with authority, as she approached the passenger side of Betty's car. She opened the door and got in, after Betty quickly moved the cooler into the backseat. "Drive up to the barn and go around the side," Dottie instructed.

Betty complied, but she couldn't help noticing the grave look of concern on Hugh's face in her rearview mirror. "I said exactly what I was told to say," Betty offered.

"Don't worry about it," Dottie replied. "Hugh's a good guy. Just overprotective."

Betty was taken by Dottie's authoritative manner. She had an aura of confidence about her but also gentleness in her eyes. She looked to be around Betty's age or a few years older. Dressed in a pair of sturdy blue jeans, a white ranch shirt and square toed work boots, Dottie softened her outfit with an elegant pair of diamond stud earrings, a turquoise and silver cuff bracelet, and a stunning diamond-and-sapphire wedding ring. Her brown hair was short and wavy with strands of grey. Betty parked around the back of the barn, out of view from anyone who could be watching. "I brought you some...chocolates?"

"Fabulous! Bring them inside."

Betty followed Dottie into the spacious barn. The aroma was a mix of cedar, hay and horseshit but somehow, Betty found it pleasantly intoxicating. Large, open windows allowed the outside air to flow consistently, occasionally fluttering the stacks of papers attached to clipboards hanging from the row of horse stalls. Dottie led Betty to the farthest end of the barn, where a large stall and a huge horse stood.

"I figured if we're going to make this look real, I better bring in an actual horse," Dottie commented, motioning for Betty to enter the stall.

"Do I really have to come in there?" Betty asked, clutching the small cooler to her waist. She realized she'd miscalculated her outfit *du jour*, when she chose a pink, twill dress with appropriate sleeves and matching soft pink pumps.

"If Hugh or one of the ranch hands walk in, it's going to look odd if you're standing out there and I'm in here. Besides, all this hay will muffle our conversation."

Betty briefly flashed back to the indignity in her past when that damned horse rooted through her beautiful bouffant. Trusting that such an ignominy could not happen twice in one's life, and relieved she no longer favored a bouffant, Betty delicately made her way into the stall, closing the heavy door behind her.

Dottie quickly leaned outside the stall door, checking around one more time, before turning back to Betty. "I'm sorry this whole thing has to be carried out in this manner. But my late husband was really clear with all of our workers. No drugs. Period. If they're found with any illegal substances, they're fired immediately."

"Do you let them drink beer when they're not working?"

"Sure. It's beer. It's acceptable." Dottie raised her eyebrows, obviously well aware of the double standard in her succinct statement. "Marijuana is not acceptable."

"I know it's none of my business, but given the way you feel, how do you rationalize what we're doing?"

Dottie bit her lip and studied the ground. "I don't. I'm a hypocrite. But I'm a hypocrite who's done her homework and due diligence." She nervously picked up a pitchfork and traded one lump of hay for another, seemingly needing to keep moving. "I didn't want to believe there was any healing merit to marijuana. I wanted to keep believing I was right. That it was a dangerous drug that should be banned completely. I mean, Christ, I've donated over one hundred grand to the local anti-drug groups and rehab centers. One of them carved my name into a brass plate and nailed it to a bench sitting in the waiting room of an anti-drug awareness group." She shook her head, obviously embarrassed. "There's a rumor floating around that they're going to name a room after me at one of the sober-living facilities just south of here."

Betty looked at her, stunned. "Oh dear."

"'Oh shit,' is more like it." She stabbed a pile of hay with the pitchfork. "But there's the truth, and then there's what you choose to believe. After I started reading and researching the marijuana plant, I had to face the fact I'd been duped by propaganda and well meaning, but ignorant, 'experts.' If you dig really deep, you'll start to see all the lies we've been told. They lie when the truth doesn't fit their agenda. God, I sound like a barefoot leftist, don't I?"

Betty was quickly growing fond of Dottie's no-nonsense demeanor. She set the cooler down and stole a look outside the stall. "What made you start investigating it?"

Dottie stopped shuffling the hay. A mournful cast fell over her face. "My late husband was a big strapping man who always seemed indestructible. But then nineteen years ago, he got MS. I watched the love of my life – my one and only – gradually go from two hundred fifty pounds down to one forty. He tried every cocktail of drugs, spent hundreds of thousands of dollars on experimental treatments that just left him sicker and weaker, until finally he became wheelchair bound. Last year, he fell out of his chair and broke his hip. Nothing touched the pain. *Nothing.* Not even the morphine. All it did was give him constipation. But don't worry. The bastards have a pill for that too."

She leaned the pitchfork against the stall. "Then one day, he had an old friend show up and they hung out by themselves for about an hour. Later when I went upstairs to check on him, he was really calm and incredibly relaxed. I chalked it up to having his friend visit." She smiled. "It wasn't until after he died that I found a jar of marijuana oil capsules hidden in the drawer next to his side of the bed." Her eyes drifted into the distance, lost. "I was confused. Shocked. Bewildered." Dottie turned back to Betty. "Angry! He obviously needed to keep it from me, because he was probably afraid of what I'd think or say. And what the hell, he was right. But I couldn't deny there was something different about him and his ability to get relief after those capsules showed up." She shook off the memory and resumed fussing with the same pile of hay. "That's when I started spending every free moment on the Internet, researching the plant. I downloaded hundreds of pages of medical studies from all over the world, most of which I couldn't make heads or tails out of, but the continuing theme throughout all those dry treatises was that used correctly, marijuana had incredible healing potential."

She walked to the front of the stall and checked to make sure they were still alone. "I hadn't enjoyed a decent night's sleep in almost twenty years." Dottie struggled with her confession. "*Twenty* goddamned years. Do you have any idea what lack of deep sleep will do to your body over that period of time?"

"Yes. I'm acquainted with that issue."

Dottie charted Betty's reaction. "You really *do* understand, don't you?"

Betty nodded.

"So...I tried one of his capsules. And I slept for twelve hours *straight*. Twelve hours of magical, marvelous, deeply restful *sleep*. I didn't think it was ever possible. Then I noticed my joints weren't hurting as much the next morning." She let out a hard breath. "So there it is. I'm addicted to getting a good night's sleep. I'm addicted to pain relief. Welcome to my dilemma. On one hand, I've got a reputation to uphold. On the other hand, I've got to get a decent night's sleep. I D.A.R.E. to keep the kids off drugs, but then I dare myself to contact a kindred spirit like yourself to find a decent edible." She slammed the pitchfork against the side of the stall. "Dammit, this stuff works, but you did *not* hear that from me."

They heard a slight shuffle outside the barn.

"Shit," Dottie muttered. "Hello?" she called out.

One of the ranch hands called out to her, asking a question. After sorting it out, Dottie suggested they go to her office attached to the barn. Once ensconced in the small but well-appointed room, Dottie relaxed. Leaning back in her weather-beaten leather chair, she rested her feet on the desk. Betty sat across from her with the cooler never far from her grasp.

"What else can you make besides chocolates?" Dottie asked in a subdued voice.

Betty wasn't prepared for that question. "I'm not quite sure."

"Don't get me wrong. The chocolate I tried of yours was phenomenal. Better than any pot edible I've eaten."

"It's the honey," Betty offered.

"No, sweetie. It's the pot," Dottie said with a wry smile. She swung her feet off the desk in a decisive manner. "You ought to look into making salves. Did you know the root of the marijuana plant can be ground up, boiled in oil and turned into a terrific topical ointment that dissolves muscle pain? And there's no THC in the root!"

"I didn't know that."

"It's true. Look it up. But you didn't hear it from me."

"Of course not."

"You know what else I learned?" Dottie said leaning forward, eager to share. "If you eat a really ripe mango an hour before you ingest an edible or an oil capsule, the effect of the pot is even stronger."

"My, my," Betty said. "I had no idea."

Dottie edged closer and spoke in a lower voice. "I was never a real fan of mangoes, but I am now. You don't want to overdo it though. After my husband died, I ate a ripe mango, waited an hour and knocked down two of his oil capsules.

Whew. What a ride. I won't do that again, but I did learn something from the experience."

"What's that?"

"Not important. You'll think I'm nuts," she said, turning away.

"No I won't," Betty assured her, remembering her own introductory experience that sent her for a loop.

Dottie considered her words and then leaned forward. "Time is bendable. I know that sounds crazy, but when I was over the top after I took too much, that's what I discovered. The past, the present and the future can fold over each other." She paused, trying to come up with the right words. "And it's like you're witnessing things that haven't happened yet. But you can't remember them when you come out of it. And yet, when they happen...*if* they happen...you have this remote whisper of a memory that you've already experienced this in another place." She looked at Betty. "Oh, Christ. I sound like someone on the lunatic fringe."

Betty leaned forward. "No you don't. I believe you. My son had the gift of accurate intuition."

"Accurate intuition? What in the hell is that? You mean psychic?"

Betty shrugged. "I don't know. He was very sensitive. He saw things other people couldn't or wouldn't see."

Dottie relaxed "Really?" She thought for a long second. "Republican to Republican, how'd you handle that?"

"Not well. I never disbelieved him. But I didn't defend him either." A wash of sadness intruded. "I should have defended him a lot more. I regret that deeply."

Dottie sat back in her chair, clearly more at ease. "Well, I'll tell you one thing. There's a shit load more going on around us than what we think is 'real.' Everything I've ever believed is out the window now. *Everything.* And it's all because of a little plant that I had always condemned. But you didn't hear that from me."

Betty found herself relaxing too, settling back into her chair. "I said to a girlfriend the other day that often the very thing we fight or protest against is exactly the thing we actually need or lack."

She looked at Betty with renewed appreciation. "Yes... *Yes.* That's brilliant! I think the same thing could be said for relationships too. The people we fight against might actually have something we desperately need."

Betty felt an electrical pulse race up her spine. She jolted slightly.

"You alright?"

She centered herself. "Yes." Betty heard the lying chime in her reply. "Well, actually...no."

"Anything I can do?"

"No. It's mine to figure out. But thank you." Betty opened the cooler and brought out the paperwork Dottie needed to make Betty her caregiver. "I filled in all my information," she said, handing it to Dottie. Reaching back into the cooler, she brought out a page from her personalized notepaper. Her name and phone number were embossed across the top in gold print. "I don't have business cards, so I wrote my address on this paper in case you need it. You can call me whenever you need more candy." She instructed her how to fill out the medical marijuana paperwork in blue ink and where to mail it.

"I'll take care of this immediately. Thank you."

"You know, I don't have to name my business as a caregiver, but I wanted to call it something. I decided on 'A Classy Joint.'"

Dottie erupted into a hearty laugh. "I love it! That's fun! You know, the quicker you can get a person to relax and show them you have a sense of humor, the more comfortable they'll be working with you."

Betty suddenly felt more confident. She proudly brought out the exquisitely wrapped chocolates. "I made you five. I hope that's enough for now." She explained about their potency and suggested various dosing options. The last thing she wanted was to get a call from Dottie saying she was stuck in the barn, off her trotter, and couldn't find her way out.

"Seriously," Dottie said, "consider broadening what you offer your patients. Maybe baked goods? Or oil capsules? Or cannabis ghee. Or that salve." She paused. "God, you never would have heard me saying this last year! What do I owe you?"

"I'm not supposed to charge you. Donations only."

Dottie looked at Betty as if she'd just told her the sky was plaid. "Who in the hell made up that stupid rule?"

"I'm not sure."

"So I'm supposed to expect you to do all the work, grow my plants, nurture the plants, process the plants, and then turn it into whatever I want for...whatever I think it's worth? Are Socialists involved in writing the state's medical marijuana laws?"

Betty smiled. "I certainly hope not."

"You're a capitalist, aren't you?"

"Most definitely. I didn't name all of my cats after Ronald Reagan just to have a conversational launching pad."

"*All* of your cats?"

"Every single one."

"Oh, honey, we're going to get along just fine." She opened her wallet and handed Betty a hundred dollar bill.

"I don't have change with me."

"Keep it. How does one put a price on a good night's sleep? It's like putting a price on loss. That's always a steep one. But I don't have to tell you that. Peyton said you were also a widow."

"Yes."

"So you understand what I'm saying." Dottie turned away, lost in her grief. "It's been four months and I still can't clean out his closet. That's his duster and boots over there." She pointed to a pedestal coat rack. "It still smells like him, and I'm afraid if I move his things, they'll lose that aroma." She swallowed hard, as her eyes welled with tears. "It's so hard. But I know you understand."

Betty flashed on the box of Frank's medals and plaques that were thrown into the box in the basement. Any aroma left on them repulsed her. His clothes were long gone too, shoved into a trash bag with the hangers still attached and dragged to the curb even before he was planted six feet under.

"How do you get through the day?" Dottie asked, scratching for answers.

Betty thought about Frankie. It was the only way she could answer the question and not lie. "It's not easy. You keep busy. You take up hobbies. You help other people. But it's always there on the edge of your mind. Forgetting is never easy."

Dottie nodded in agreement and turned back to the coat rack. "God, I miss him." Tears flowed down her cheeks. "My arms ache…literally ache, to hold him again. I know I'll never feel that depth of love for anyone else. I'm not sure how I'm supposed to go on without him." She grabbed a tissue and dabbed at her eyes.

Betty sat back in amazement. Envy surfaced. She wanted to feel what Dottie felt. Not the loss, but the love. Not the sadness, but the passion. But that wasn't safe, she silently counseled herself. That had its own built-in problems, starting with the fact she'd have to give up control. "You know, Dottie, one of the things that cannabis – marijuana – does is it forces you to be in the moment. The past doesn't matter and the future is unmapped. And somehow, that's okay. Because, you can't change the past and you can't strategize your future. I tried and I failed at it miserably. I wasted…" She stopped, realizing she'd never been this forthcoming with someone she'd just met.

"What?"

"I wasted my life." The statement felt like a wall of bricks fell on her. "I'll be fifty-nine years old on July 25th, and I have wasted most of those years."

"You could still have twenty good years left. Maybe more."

Betty pondered that possibility. "Yes…you're right. I could. So could you. The future isn't written in stone. It's written in invisible ink from our own pen."

Dottie smiled. She held up the medical marijuana paperwork. "It's written in blue ink for me. But you didn't –"

"Hear that from you?"

Dottie smiled again, this time with deeper enthusiasm. "I like you, Betty. I especially like the way you think."

~~~

Betty took her time driving back to Paradox. She felt strangely reborn. And with that feeling, there was the unknown. Her future was a blank canvas and it needed paint that hadn't been mixed yet. But for whatever reason, it didn't scare her. She didn't want to rush it but she didn't want to miss it either.

She stopped off at the same dispensary where she'd purchased her Centennial Blueberry clones, and after reading all about the attributes of the available clones that were in stock, she selected three White Russians. The plant was known for its exceptional resin production and high THC – supposedly hitting the scale at over twenty-two percent. However, the dispensary owner told her he liked it, because due to the dense frost it produced, it could be made into "a stupid good salve." Since Dottie encouraged Betty to expand her line of medicinal products, she concluded that those "stupid good" White Russians would be the perfect girls to add to her green family.

When she arrived home, she brought the flag inside and excitedly carried the three new clones downstairs and introduced them to their new sisters. She watered them, checked their leaves and brought in another oscillating fan to ensure optimal airflow. Back upstairs in the kitchen, Betty dove into the large rotisserie chicken she'd only picked at the night before. What she didn't eat, she plunked into a large crock pot, and after adding celery, a large onion, fresh rosemary, a dash of sea salt, and covering it with water, she set it on low to simmer.

Before leaving the ranch, Dottie had requested ten more chocolates. She started to bring out all the materials she'd need, when she glanced up to the darkened room above the garage. Instead of excessively questioning or debating the idea, she tossed all the things she'd need into a large basket and walked the short distance out the back door, across the stone path, and up the narrow stairs that led to the large room.

She turned on a few lights. The room felt cold and unapproachable. She had purposely avoided crossing its threshold, so she wouldn't be reminded of the colossal failure of her cherished chocolate shop. Betty opened a few windows to force the staleness out of the room and then whipped off all the protective covers on the commercial equipment from *The White Violet*. After brushing off the dust, she washed everything down with a damp rag. After an hour, she had everything plugged in and humming. Excitement bubbled under her veins. She felt like the maestro to this purring symphony of stainless steel. With a long handled spoon as her baton, she put together the chocolate base in the melter. Setting the cannabis-infused cocoa butter into a smaller melter, she waited patiently for it to liquefy. The room still felt somewhat dead and staid.

She flicked on the radio and heard the first strains of a sad selection from *La Bohème* on the pre-programmed classical radio station. As much as she usually adored the soothing strains of that beloved opera, something inside of her rebelled against it now. Punching buttons on the radio, she arrived at a classic rock station that was in the middle of Van Morrison's "Brown Eyed Girl." Betty twirled back to check the melting cannabis butter. Stirring it in rhythm with Van Morrison's voice, she purposely allowed some of the liquid to splatter over the side of the saucepan. Without giving it a second thought, she wiped it up with her finger and sucked it off. Van Morrison gave way to ZZ Top and "Sharp Dressed Man." Betty turned up the volume and grabbed another wooden spoon in order to play the drumbeat on the tempering unit. In between riffs, she checked and stirred the green medicine, each time wiping up the splatters with her fingers and licking them off.

By the time The Rolling Stones took over with "You Can't Always Get What You Want" and then The Hollies stepped to the plate with "Long Cool Woman In A Black Dress," Betty had long since kicked off her pink pumps, with each shoe falling on an opposite side of the room. She hadn't had this much fun since...well, since never. And that feeling was punctuated when Steppenwolf's "Born to Be Wild" blared over the speakers. Another song and another dip of her wooden spoon into the cannabis butter, with the residual drops falling into her mouth.

Two glorious hours passed, and the radio continued to churn out one classic rock hit after another. The chocolate slid into the moulds in a perfectly-timed ballet of precision, as Betty blissfully added the measured doses of the canna cocoa butter. The room felt light as her body vibrated on its own frequency. Betty didn't give a damn about anything except watching the exquisite splendor of honey melding with velvety cocoa and infusing with cannabis in a harmonized masterpiece of confectionary magnificence. She fell into that moment, captivated. The buzz deepened in her body as tentacles of energy grew from every cell inside and radiated like rays of brilliant light from the summer sun. Journey's "Don't Stop Believin'" crested and dissolved into Robert Palmer's drum driven "Bad Case of Lovin' You." Five-dozen dazzling chocolates filled with cannabis and still safe in their molds rolled off the small conveyor belt and rested on a tray that Betty quickly transferred to the freezer compartment. The bowl of green butter was empty, save for the oily residue Betty promptly licked out of the bowl.

It was nearly nine in the evening and Betty felt alive for the first time in forever. Robert Palmer sung, "Doctor, Doctor, Give me the news, I've got a bad case of lovin' you!" as Betty suddenly understood a deeper meaning in those lyrics. She twirled and shook her hips to the tune as if nobody was watching. The music was crisp, the lights were sparkling and the man standing outside the glass door, with those dancing blue eyes, was captivated.

Chapter 21

"He was drawing your life..."

Betty turned and saw Jeff. Slightly out of breath, she stood frozen, held lovingly in his gaze. That now familiar bolt of electricity shot up her spine, sending a flush across her cheeks. Her heart softened as she felt the cannabis oil take the edge off. Locked into the moment, there was nothing else that mattered except right now – no past and no future – just that miraculous instant she inhabited without fear.

The music continued in the background, as the drumbeat pounded in unison with her heart. He opened the door and walked toward her. Drawing her to his chest, he held her for what seemed like an eternity. When he finally pulled back, he cupped her face between his hands.

"I can't stop thinking about you, and I couldn't handle the way we left it last night."

She dove in and out of his eyes. "I know. Same here."

"You've never met the right man, Betty."

A pulse of excitement vibrated throughout her body. "Maybe that's because I spent too many years with the wrong one."

He smiled. "I've never met anyone like you."

Her body was buzzing and alive. "Really? Don't you get out and about much?"

Jeff chuckled. "Oh, hell, Betty. I think I'm falling in love with you."

Now her head was spinning in a delicious orbit. "I've never cooked you a full meal. How could you be falling in love with me?"

A smile lit up his face. "I don't know. It doesn't make sense, does it?"

"No," she whispered, transfixed. "But I don't care." She grinned impishly. "I'm not sure my mother would approve." He pulled away a few inches. "Am I the one your mama warned you about?" She pulled him back to her. "Most definitely." "Don't worry. Those warnings were exaggerated on purpose. She saw the same rebel streak in you that I see. It's like you've been waiting all these years to explode."

"Uh-huh," was all she could get out, still drawn into his eyes.

He leaned closer to her. "You need a man who makes you think. You need someone who frustrates you, in a good way. But most of all, you need someone who keeps you honest."

Her heart pounded as the room swirled in sensuous circles. There was a slight second of fear as his lips touched hers. But as he tenderly kissed her, the trepidation dissolved into the kind of passion she had never before experienced. Each kiss intensified every cell in her body, igniting a heat that swelled and grew, as his hands moved eagerly across her body. Their breathing rose and fell in unison. Betty never wanted anyone as much as she wanted Jeff and she gave in completely.

"It's been a long time for me," Betty whispered.

"Don't worry. It's like riding a bike."

"It's been even longer since I've ridden a bike."

Turning off the lights and music, they raced down the stairs, into her house and upstairs to the bedroom, stopping along the way several times to steal an eager kiss. Ronald jumped off the bed as they disappeared under the sheets. Probing kisses were only slightly interrupted by frantic removal of clothing, which sailed across the room in every direction. There was a moment, lying there naked, when Betty felt embarrassed, suddenly aware of those extra pounds around her belly and waist.

"It's all right," Jeff whispered, exploring her body with his lips. "You're beautiful."

He rolled on top of her and she locked onto his gaze. How incredible it was to see herself reflected with such love in another's eyes. He kissed her and then moved his lips to her neck. A bolt of energy went down her spine.

"Oh...dear...God," she managed to utter, as all other words were pointless.

His hands caressed places on her pale skin that no one had ever visited. With each discovery, a part of her that had been dead became awake and transformed. She arched her back as she felt him inside. Moving her hands across his square, tanned shoulders and down his muscular back, she felt protected and safe for the first time in her life. Neither the past nor the future was as important as that second and the next one after that. Rising and falling as one, they merged in exquisite harmony until Betty didn't know where she began or ended. And at the point where every sensation crested, their bodies responded as one and he fell back into her arms. She held onto him, never wanting him to move. They continued to hold each other for several blissful minutes, hearts fused in a breathtaking denouement.

Jeff nestled next to her and they spooned their bodies as he cupped his hand over her breast. A few more minutes of silence slipped away and then he spoke.

"I'll be fifty-four in one month."

"Is that so?" she whispered.

They rolled out of bed two hours later and shared the shower. At first, Betty haltingly agreed, but the combination of his skin pressed against hers and the hot, pulsating water quickly won her over. She gave herself to him again, and they made love as the water beat down in a warm frenzy. A spark had been ignited within her; one that had been waiting for decades to find its flame. Now lit, it engulfed and dominated her. The pleasures of touch and form, of curves and muscle became insatiable. There was beauty and inventiveness that captivated her, leaving Betty exhausted and hungering for more. In that instant, she realized that this is who she really was. This is what she was born to feel and experience. Life was meant to be inhaled deeply, not tentatively suffered in shallow breaths stitched with fear. Life's flavors were there to be sampled and the ambrosia imbibed without inhibition.

Love didn't require pain or fear or regret. It didn't need to be questioned or analyzed. Love just *was*.

And even though Betty didn't utter a word to explain how she felt, Jeff somehow understood exactly what was unspoken. He stood behind her as the water beat across their bodies and cupped her breasts in his palms. "You've heard about how people find old paintings in their attic, and the picture looks unremarkable? But then, they start to chip away at the top layer of paint, and they find this incredible masterpiece underneath. That's you, Betty. You've been hiding all these years underneath a canvas that's rich and sensual. You're like a sexy Rembrandt. Like *Bathsheba at Her Bath*."

Betty thought about the image and turned to him. "I'm a woman with a large gut, bathing herself?"

"You're *zaftig*, Betty."

"That's a diplomatic way of saying 'fat'?"

He held her closer, cradling her in his arms. "Let it go."

Those words stopped her. It was the second time Jeff used those specific words. "If only..." She nestled her head in his chest.

"You know what I think someone needs to do?" he asked. "They should take two cannabis plants and cross them. And the new strain that emerges should be desired by everyone but only available to one. That singular strain would be able to help you sleep and dream in Technicolor. It could relax your senses but also invigorate your mind. When you ingested it, you'd be able to step back and observe, allowing light to inhabit the dark corners. And then, whenever you were ready, it would give you the courage to step forward and not be afraid to voice your opinion...or stand up for someone who couldn't speak for themselves. That's the kind of plant I wish someone would create. And if they did, they would have to call it 'Betty.'"

She looked at him and realized she had no words to express what her heart felt. All she knew in that blessed second was that you know you're connected to someone when you look into their eyes and you feel as if you're seeing yourself for the first time. Betty buried her head in Jeff's chest as the warm water cascaded down her body.

"I wish I was brave enough to find you sooner," she said. "I wasted so much of my life." She looked up at him. "You're everything I've ever wanted and everything I never knew I needed."

As the clock struck midnight and the neighborhood went dark and into slumber, Betty and Jeff headed to the kitchen. With Betty wearing a clingy bathrobe and Jeff opting for a towel wrapped around his waist, they agreed that a chocolate crêpe wrapped around peanut butter and whipped cream sounded divine. Jeff helped whip up the egg base while Betty improvised a decadent cocoa and peanut butter mélange.

Setting the bowl to the side, Jeff crept behind Betty. "I remember all those times I saw you get up to speak at the town council meetings. Your voice was always really sexy, even if you were just talking about the need for a new speed bump on the main drag. You were always well dressed but *so* covered up. I kind of wanted to know what you were hiding under all that fabric."

"Someone told me it's called a *zaftig* body."

He leaned closer, whispering in her ear. "You've heard of a moveable feast? How about a moveable tryst?"

Betty softly chuckled at his clever bend of the English language. "I don't want to kill you."

"I think that'd be a great way to die. Can't you see the article in the *Paradox Press*? 'Jeff Carroll was found dead in bed. Rigor mortis apparently started in an isolated area a few hours prior to his demise' –"

She playfully swiped his shoulder. "That's terrible!"

He wrapped his arms around her waist, seductively inching his hands under her robe. "Later in the article, just to be accurate, it could say, 'Mr. Carroll was apparently engaged in activity at the time of his death with local, Elizabeth Cragen.'"

She turned to him, smiling. "I'm never going to live that one down, am I?"

"When are you going to tell Peyton that Cragen is Craven?"

"Oh, don't ruin this moment. Let me just linger here a little longer. We don't even know for sure if he's read the names. Anyway, I don't want to think about that letter or telling Peyton or..."

"Your friends?"

Betty buried her head in his chest. "It's impossible. I couldn't do that."

"You can't keep this operation a secret forever."

She looked up at him with bold determination. "You bet I can! I read in the book you gave me that you never, ever, *ever* show anyone your grow operation. The fewer people who know, the fewer people to talk about it. Besides, you said yourself it's important to keep this low profile."

"I'm not talking about alerting the media. I'm talking about your friends."

She shook her head. "No. They're never going to find out. I can be quite formidable when I need to be, and my friends will never know what's behind that door. Believe me, I've planned this whole thing out. That's one thing I did learn from Frank; figure out everything that can go wrong and circumvent it before anything happens. I assure you that whatever I set out to do in this life from now on, I will do *well*. If I decide to be a stripper, I will be an award-winning stripper!"

"Well," he kissed the top of her head, "good luck on that one, doll."

"Doll? I don't like that pet name."

"What did Frank call you?"

"I believe it was, 'Come here,'" she deadpanned. "But it never sounded as romantic as that when *he* said it."

"Did you ever get him back in your own little way?"

She thought. "Yes. I used to put regular coffee in his decaf cup at night just to give him the jitters all evening long."

"Whew, Betty. And the black ops assassins haven't offered you a power gig?"

She gave Jeff's backside a playful smack. "How complex do you want this filling?"

Jeff started toward the living room. "Life's complicated enough, sweets. We don't need a filling to exacerbate it."

"'Sweets'?" Betty said, shaking her head. "I don't think so." She heard him ruffling through a bookcase in the living room, and her thoughts turned to all those nights she purposefully got Frank jacked up on caffeine so he couldn't sleep. She suddenly realized that in her passive/aggressive need to get back at him, she'd ironically made her own life worse. The better option would have been to give him something calming, so she didn't have to deal with his caffeine-driven pacing all night long.

Jeff returned to the kitchen carrying the white violet print and an old scrapbook. "This could have some value," he said as he sat down at the table.

"I could never sell that," Betty assured him, pouring the crêpe batter onto the hot pan. "It has too much meaning."

"Why white violets? Was that a flower that meant something between you and your son?"

"Not at all. I have no idea why he felt so strongly that I needed to have that. But he was quite insistent that day." She stopped, her heart moving back in time. "He was very purposeful the last time I saw him. He wanted to be upstairs by himself, then he walked outside to the big elm and finally he gave me that print. Told me to 'pay attention.'"

"Pay attention to what?"

"I don't know. He was probably high at the time. It was also part of a vision he'd had and wanted to share with me. I went along with it so he would feel good."

Jeff stared at the white violet print before gently placing it on the table and opening the scrapbook. "What's this?" He turned the scrapbook toward her and pointed to a back page. It was a photo of Betty standing on stage, accepting a blue ribbon. Next to her was a ten-foot-tall mullein stalk in full flower.

"That was a joke! I was always entering the proper rose and lily competitions at the State Fair. Judi dared me to enter the 'Tallest Weed' competition and I took the challenge. I figured I'd just use my secret fertilizer on it and off to the races we'd go."

"What's the secret?"

She tested the crêpe and flipped it over. "Beans."

"Coffee?"

"No. Llama." She added a small handful of hemp seeds to the peanut butter and whipped cream blend before carefully spooning it onto the crêpe.

"Llama?"

Betty turned and simply stated, "Shit." She folded the crêpe. "Their feces look like large black beans. Thus, llama beans." Betty explained how the beans never burn the plants, and how they can either be top-dressed on the soil or made into a garden "tea" by soaking one cup of beans to every five gallons of water and leaving the mixture out in the hot sun to brew. "It yields a quite interesting bouquet after two days in the blazing sun, but when your plants drink it in – Katie, bar the door – they explode! My girls downstairs will soon enjoy the same potent concoction."

"So when you tell your friends about your new venture, you can blame Judi for challenging you to the tallest weed contest and using the gateway weed of mullein to get you hooked."

"Would you stop it?" she admonished playfully. "It's none of their business!"

"When you do tell them, can I be there? It'll be like reality TV, except it'll actually be real."

"*Jeff?*"

"*Betty?*"

"Your crêpe is ready," she said, brushing off the banter.

She served the crêpes on two bone china plates with a raised floral edging she kept for special occasions, and then joined Jeff at the table. He complimented her heartily after his first bite. Turning the pages in the album, Jeff skimmed the various photos of Frank, Sr. and stopped on a page devoted to Frankie. Besides the photos, there was also something that looked like a partially torn page from a sketchpad.

Jeff really looked at Frankie's photos, as if he were trying to figure out the boy.

"He was a gentle kid, wasn't he?" Jeff asked.

"Very much so. I'm sure Frank thought he was gay."

"Was he?"

"No! He had a girlfriend when he was sixteen. She was artistic like he was and slightly eccentric." Betty flashed back on the girl. "She had blond and purple hair and was actually quite pretty, even with the multiple piercings and tattoos. But there was a genuine sweetness to her. Frankie absolutely adored her. She might have even…" Betty paused briefly. "She might have been able to rescue him. However, his father banned her from our house. So that broke up their relationship."

"Didn't you have a say?"

"I was conspicuously silent. Something I'd unfortunately honed to perfection."

Jeff resumed looking at the photos. "He's got a different vibe to him. Almost enigmatic."

Betty nodded. "I know. I saw it from the moment he was born. I couldn't explain it, but I embraced it. He was different. *Very* different. He was able to see things at quite a young age that others couldn't or didn't want to see." She stared at a shot of Frankie. "I think his father recognized that. And I think it scared the hell out of him."

"Why?"

"Because Frank Sr. enjoyed being a mystery and there was only room for one of those in our home. When your lifetime career is all about being tough and inscrutable, and your own son can see behind that façade, it tends to create a rather explosive potential." She took a bite of the crêpe and was in heaven for the third time that night.

"What's the torn drawing?" Jeff asked.

Betty didn't answer right away, attempting to be engaged in her dessert. "I salvaged that," she quietly said.

Jeff examined the drawing more closely. "Who drew this?"

"Who do you think?" Betty asked, taking another generous bite.

He removed the torn paper from the underside of the plastic. "Look at this," he offered, turning the white violet print around to face Betty. He placed the torn drawing next to a section on the print. "This part of the drawing is almost identical to that part of the white violet print."

Betty stopped eating and analyzed the two. "You're right," she said, stunned. "But that's impossible. Frankie drew that picture when he was ten years old. And he found this antique print in the dumpster five years ago." She leaned closer, carefully comparing the childhood drawing closer against the print. "It's like a copy. I don't get it." Her thoughts traveled back to that traumatic night almost nineteen years ago. All those drawings on the wall...they made no sense, and yet...

"What is it?" Jeff scraped his fork against the dish to pick up every morsel.

"I don't want to ruin this night."

"You can't ruin the night. It's already morning. Tell me."

She regarded Jeff with slight apprehension. "I've never told anyone this before."

He reached out and placed his hand over hers. "It's okay. I want to know."

Betty put down her fork and gathered her nervous memories. "For as long as I can remember, I wanted to be a mother. I thought I'd be quite good at it. I love to take care of things and nurture them. But I forgot that part of nurturing is protecting those you love from people or situations that could harm them." She hesitated, struggling somewhat. "And so because I didn't do that, I failed at being a mother. I should have told his father to leave him alone. Blame it on how I was raised. Say please and thank you. Always look your best. Don't criticize. If you have nothing good to say, say nothing at all." She rolled her eyes. "What they forgot to teach me is that it's all right to go against the grain and speak up if it will keep you or someone else from getting hurt. If I'd learned that one lesson, I could have saved my son. In retrospect, I really didn't want to be a wife – only a mother. Unfortunately, the two were not mutually exclusive where I came from."

She looked off to the side and smiled. "But I kind of got my wish of just being a mother when Frank went to the Persian Gulf back in 1990. He was going to be gone for a full year and everyone was so worried about me. But I was secretly in heaven. The year he was gone was the best year of my life, because Frankie finally calmed down. His stomach-aches went away. His nervous anticipation vanished. Even the nightmares stopped. He finally felt free to do what he enjoyed and to do it with abandon. One of his passions was drawing, but Frank didn't think it was a manly pursuit."

"So you signed him up for art classes?"

"Damn right I did," she declared proudly. "He was only nine when he started the class, but the teacher was aston-ished by his talent. They let him draw whatever he wanted, and he got better and better. Pretty soon, his entire bed-room was wallpapered with his pictures. Even the ceiling was covered. And I'm not just bragging...they were *incredible* drawings for a child his age." She paused, recalling the past. "I didn't always understand them, though. There wasn't a central theme. In fact, nothing he drew made much sense, but they were all really well done."

"What kinds of pictures did he draw?"

"Well, he drew a picture of the house I grew up in back in Houston. He must have seen a photo of it somewhere. He had a few drawings of chairs and furniture from our house."

"Like what?"

"Oh, let's see. It was so long ago." She forced herself back in time. "I used to have chair with a needlepoint seat in the living room. It sold for a song last weekend at *The Gilded Rose*. He drew a picture of that chair from various angles. Oh, and that Biedermeier? Yes, he was fascinated with that for some strange reason. He must have had twelve drawings of it in his room."

"I was fascinated with your Biedermeier, too," Jeff added with a sly smile.

Betty returned his smile but contemplation quickly took hold.

"What is it?" Jeff asked.

"Why that chair? Why the Biedermeier?" Betty quietly mused.

"What else did he draw?"

Betty visualized her son's bedroom. Suddenly, a memory surfaced. "Motorcycles..."

Jeff looked at her incredulously. "Really?"

Betty seemed far away. "Yes. I'd forgotten about those. It was the same motorcycle drawn from various angles." She continued to remember. "Then there were all the sketches of white violets and even a..." She stopped.

"What?" he asked with great interest.

"A...mullein stalk."

"Your tallest weed?"

"Yes...But he drew that years before I won that silly contest."

"What else?"

"As it got closer to the time when his father would return from the Middle East, his art became darker. Even his teacher was concerned enough to make an appointment with a counselor. I think Frankie wore down every black, brown and red pencil in the box." Her face sunk. "They were very disturbing. There were dozens of them, all with a boy a little older than he was, either sitting in a hole or lying in a cemetery." She recalled another drawing. "I never forgot the one with the giant."

"The giant?"

"Yes, he drew himself, very small, lying in a bed. And standing over him was a giant man with his arms reaching out to attack him. Obviously, the giant was his father." She continued to recall more of Frankie's artwork. "There was another one that didn't make any sense. It was a boy lying on a bench in some city..." Her voice trailed off. "Oh, my God..." Color drained from her face. "He was found dead on a bus bench in Denver. He was drawing...his life." The realization astonished her.

"He was drawing your life too," Jeff added.

"You believe me?" she asked, still not sure of her discovery.

"Of course, I believe you. There are people out there with gifts we can't explain. Sounds like Frankie was one of them. Where are all these drawings? I'd love to take a look at them."

She pointed to the torn page in the scrapbook. "This one is all that's left. The night Frank came home from Desert Storm, he walked into Frankie's bedroom and saw all the drawings covering the walls and ceiling. He erupted. I'd never seen him so vicious. He tore every single one off the walls and ceiling and burned them in the fireplace. And I didn't do a damn thing. I just stood there holding Frankie and waiting for his father to stop screaming. Then he yelled at me and told me I'd coddled our son when he was away, and he would have none of that. Frankie was crying and I tried to comfort him, but Frank Sr. got between us and told me our son would never be a real man if he expected comfort whenever he was hurt." Betty lowered her head. "And so I let him go and his father just kept yelling at him. At one point, he grabbed Frankie and slapped him across the face. All I can remember is the way Frankie looked at me right at that moment. It was as if...as if he was begging me to speak up. But I couldn't. I didn't know how."

Betty turned the scrapbook toward her. "I found that torn drawing behind his bed. I guess it'd fallen back there when Frank went ballistic in his bedroom. I hid it in my bureau and after Frank died, I put it in this scrapbook. After that night, Frankie's stomachaches started again and his anxiety was off the chart. Nothing I could do or say seemed to help. And two years later, when he was twelve, he started smoking pot and drinking." She looked at Jeff. "And the rest...well, you know the rest. The coroner wasn't sure if it was suicide or an unintentional overdose. I wanted to tell the man that it was suicide, and that my son started killing himself the day his father returned from Desert Storm. But, as usual, I kept my mouth shut. If you can't say anything good..."

Jeff reached across the table, clasping her hands in his. "Can you finally accept that your kid's drug problem was a symptom of all that emotional shit and not the cause of it?"

Betty felt as if a weight suddenly fell from her shoulders. "Yes." She considered it. "It's like the chicken and the egg. What came first? The pain or the pill?"

"The pain always comes first. And we can spend the rest of our lives either overcoming it or killing it."

"Or killing ourselves?"

He sat back. "Not me. Remember? I'm in the health business. I prefer to watch people thrive, not just survive." He got up and held out his hand to Betty. "Speaking of which, I need to be at the store in fewer than nine hours. Come on. Let's see if we can catch a few hours of sleep."

She smiled. "You can sleep when I'm dead."

Chapter 22

"...It's the journey that can stall us."

He was drawing your life.

Those words reverberated in Betty's head as she awoke the next morning. Was that even possible? It was one thing to casually admit Frankie had second sight; it was quite another to take the plunge and realize there was concrete merit to his predictions. Could a child so young and perceptive have the ability to telegraph points in the future on a sketchpad? If she only had those drawings now, she could verify it. But then what? Could she show it to anyone besides Jeff? Maybe Peyton. But certainly no one else. They'd argue about the meaning of the drawings and find every conceivable excuse to chalk it up to coincidence. A thought crossed Betty's mind that perhaps by Frank burning them, he unintentionally ignited those images into reality.

What an odd thought, she said to herself, rolling over and finding Jeff gone. The sound of the shower assured her he wasn't far away. Propping up her pillow, she turned to the sunny window that looked out to the backyard. The tap-tap of the old canopy elm got her attention. Not every impression by Frankie burned up that night nineteen years ago. The curious carving he left on that tree was now starting to make more sense.

Jeff opened the bathroom door and walked into the bedroom. His hair was loose and wet, making him look a bit rough. But when he smiled at Betty, any perceived edginess melted away. "Good morning," he said softly. He whipped off the wet towel and crawled across the bed toward Betty. "I had an idea. I can be back around six with dinner, and we can take a ride on my bike up to the lake."

"I don't ride on the back of motorcycles."

"Bad experience?"

"No. I just don't do things that have the potential to kill me."

"So you don't cross streets? Or drive a car? Or get up on ladders?"

She put her hand over his mouth. "I'm not riding on your motorcycle. But you can still bring dinner and we can eat it here."

"Here?" Jeff pointed to the bed.

"Sure. You can eat your whole wheat crackers in my bed any day." She leaned over and kissed him.

"God, Betty. It's been a long time since a woman has kissed me the way you do."

"Maybe you needed an older woman?" she whispered.

"The same way you needed a younger man?"

Betty grinned and got out of bed, donning a heavy cotton robe from the closet. "I'll make you breakfast."

He got off the bed and collected his clothes from around the room. "You don't have to cook for me. I'm a big boy. I can figure it out."

"I want to. I like to cook."

"Okay. But don't turn me into your latest project."

It was staggering to Betty how much Jeff could read her intentions, even before she had a chance to formulate the perfect stratagem.

She walked downstairs and raised the flag outside the front door. Turning to Jeff's motorcycle parked in the driveway, the thought briefly crossed her mind that there might be chatter in the neighborhood as to who owned that bike. She hated idle gossip. So intrusive. Just then, the little five-year-old girl who lived next door rolled past her house riding her tricycle. Betty drew the robe tighter around her body and waved to the child. She stared a little longer at the motorcycle before turning to go back inside. Jeff was leaning against the credenza, pulling on his boots. His hair was combed and pulled back into a neat ponytail. Even though his clothes had spent the night draped across furniture and the carpet, he still looked well put together.

"That was fast!" Betty exclaimed.

"I'm not enamored with mirrors."

She started toward the kitchen and turned. "Have you ever considered cutting off your ponytail?"

"Have you ever considered shaving your head?" He put his arm around her, gave her a quick goose in the rump and followed her into the kitchen.

Half an hour later, as they were wrapping up breakfast, the front doorbell rang. Betty froze slightly and darted out of the kitchen. When she saw the Prius in the driveway, there was a sigh of great relief.

"Peyton!" she said, ushering him inside. "It's rather early for a visit. Is everything all right?"

He wore his usual low-slung blue jeans and a black t-shirt with white lettering that read: C.O.D. = CANNABIS ON DEMAND. "A-okay, Betty. I'm on my way to work and thought I'd drop by and tell you I got a thumbs-up phone call from Dottie. She's crazy happy to be working with you! And I got a new patient for you to contact." Peyton's eyes drifted behind Betty. "Okay. This is awkward."

Betty turned to see Jeff standing there.

"Hey, Peyton," Jeff said casually.

"Hey, there."

The silence was heavy and clumsy for a few seconds.

"Whew," Peyton finally said. "I just had a flashback to when I was six years old and walked in on my folks –"

"*Okay*," Betty interrupted. "Why don't you go down to the girls' room and see the new sisters I brought home last night?"

"Cool," he headed toward the basement door, giving a rushed goodbye to Jeff.

Jeff walked over to Betty and kissed her. "See you to-night, Boopsie."

"Boopsie?"

"Yeah. A take on Betty Boop. I'm auditioning it."

"No, no. It sounds like you're saying *Boob*sie."

"That's got potential," he said with his usual dry humor.

Betty shook her head, smiling when she heard Peyton's roar from downstairs.

"Oh, fuck! *Betty*! Come here!"

Betty furrowed her brow. "God, he sounds just like Frank."

She kissed Jeff again and quickly went downstairs. There was Peyton looking shell shocked, holding the three White Russians clones.

"These weren't on the list I gave you, Betty!"

"So what? Dottie said she wanted me to make her a salve and apparently that's a great strain for that purpose."

"Oh, no denying it. It's got tons of THC but it's also known for being a PM magnet."

Betty gathered her thoughts. "Oh, dear. Well, I'll return them."

"No, that's pointless. They've been introduced into your environment. The PM is already in the room and the vents." He set them down on Frank's desk and calmed down enough to think clearly. "Here's the plan. I come and show you how to do a sulfur burn tonight. You gotta do it when the lights go off. So, that's nine o'clock –"

"You can't sulfur the girls tonight."

"Betty, we gotta get on this immediately. I told you how PM can wipe out your entire crop if you don't stay vigilant."

"I understand that. But it's not happening tonight."

Peyton regarded her with an irked expression. "Why?" There was a self-conscious silence between them. "Oh, okay. You and he have plans."

"Now, hang on a second, Peyton. I understand this is important, and while I might have gone off your list and purchased a strain you don't recommend, waiting one day to sulfur this area won't change anything. I understand about priorities. And that's why I'm saying that you and I can do this tomorrow night."

He looked crestfallen. The old Betty would have hugged him and cooked a heaping portion of his favorite food, with enough leftovers to provide lunch for several days. But the new Betty stood firm and offered some advice. "In the meantime, pull up your pants. They're drooping again."

"Maybe I like them this way."

"Are you planning on being single the rest of your life?"

"Huh?"

"There's hip and there's horrible. When I can see the part of your body that only your mother and a mirror have gazed upon, it's time to purchase a pair of pants that fit and a belt that ensures that outcome."

He made a weak attempt at staring her down but it was pointless, given Betty's height and commanding posture. Finally, he spoke up. "You gotta re-pot all these plants in five-gallon containers," he instructed with a terse tone. "Use the nitrogen seaweed and guanos in the water to feed them. We gotta get them growing as fast as possible. They usually only light feed the clones at the dispensaries. And foliar spray them with the B-vitamins only. If we're gonna sulfur, you can't have anything oily on the leaves. Oh, and don't forget to pH the water. God only knows what kind of crap is in your water."

Betty didn't move. "I'll take care of it today," she calmly replied.

Peyton seemed a bit lost. "Well, okay, then. Here." He handed her a piece of paper. "That's Doctor Dave's info. He's your next patient."

"Don't these people have last names?" she implored. "They worked so diligently to earn their degrees. Why must everyone refer to them in the same way a three year old would?"

"Got me. He was a trauma doctor in Vietnam. I think he's got more things to think about than what people call him."

"He's military?"

"Yeah. He was an Army surgeon. He's like sixty-nine but he's real fit. He's been a friend of Mary Jane since the war." Peyton intently stared at Betty. "A military guy is okay with you, *right?*"

"That's fine," she replied.

Peyton looked around the room. "You gotta get some tunes in here. The ladies grow better with music. Supposedly, it makes their root stalk grow really fat."

They walked back upstairs. There was still an uneasy undercurrent coming from Peyton that Betty continued to ignore. He stood by the front door and took a gander around the room. Gradually, his edge softened. "It's getting lighter in here."

"Brighter?"

"No. Lighter. It's not as weighty. Like you just threw some bricks out of the room and the room is diggin' it."

By noon, Betty was still in the same robe she donned when she woke up. For three hours, she'd been glued to her computer downloading music. But this wasn't just any music. *This* was for her girls. Plants, it turns out, really do need music and specific sounds that are conducive to growth and vitality. As sound vibrates, Betty learned, it creates either harmonious or inharmonious wavelengths that affect not only plants, but pets and people. Many people have studied this intriguing science and determined that plants thrive best when exposed to rhythms that mimic the human heartbeat. Top of the list were waltzes, with Strauss' *Blue Danube* the favorite selection of plant enthusiasts worldwide. Baroque music was also popular, with Bach's Adagio from Brandenburg Concerto No. 6 and Barber's Adagio for Strings, op.11, the two top picks.

Vivaldi's Spring and Summer pieces lent an uplifting mood to the grow room, according to one classical music aficionado, while the more meditative Larghetto from Lute and Harp Concerto op. 6 allowed plants to "wind down" and remain stress free. Staying away from anything jarring or driven with too many discordant drum beats was essential, as this pulse was counter to the natural human heartbeat and thought to stunt plant growth and even increase the likelihood of compromising the health of the plant, leaving it open to opportunistic diseases.

But perhaps the most fascinating sound that plants adore is the sound of chirping birds. More specifically, chirping birds at *sunrise*. Apparently, scientists discovered that the stoma – or pore – on the leaf surface naturally opens with the sound of waking birds. Once the stomata are all open, anything sprayed on the leaf surface at that time is more readily absorbed and utilized by the plant. Thus, a sunrise rain would theoretically hydrate a plant more so than an afternoon rain. Foliar feeding plants when the stomata had their collective mouths open and hungry would also be more beneficial.

Yes, Betty learned, someone who had a lot of free time made a recording of birds at sunrise and then duplicated and layered it repeatedly, until it sounded as if one were in a forest and three billion birds were rousing simultaneously. Thanks to computer manipulation, the creator of this incessant chirping was able to incorporate an ebb and flow in the recording so one didn't feel as if they were listening to a scene from "The Birds" for the duration. She watched videos where gigantic speakers were placed in fields of corn and this persistent chirping was broadcast across the acreage thirty minutes prior to sunrise. Then, when the stomata were wide open, the water and feeding sprays commenced, dousing the corn as the recording of the chirping birds continued in a melodic manner. After thorough coverage, the corn sat waving in the wind, embraced by two more hours of birds chirping their little beaks off. The proof of this experiment impressed Betty. The cornstalks in the fields that had been exposed to the chirping birds were taller, the ears were heavier, the leaves remained greener and the pest population was negligible. One farmer noted that "the bugs just jumped off the corn." After half an hour of downloading and listening to a chirping bird CD, Betty was ready to jump off the corn too.

Armed with her symphonic CD arsenal, Betty located a large boom box that had belonged to Frankie and situated it in the basement so her girls could benefit from the penetrating waves of green music. For thirty minutes, she dutifully blared the chirping birds sequence, bathing her clones in a dense aura of synchronized aviary harmony. Somehow, she was able to tune it out after about twenty minutes. Locating a stack of five-gallon plastic pots, she carefully re-potted the girls in the rich, organic soil. She top-dressed them with worm castings and scratched a small amount of nitrogen-rich bat guano into the soil around the rootstalk before giving them a light water feeding of nitrogen-targeted seaweed and fish fertilizer concentrates. As the musical tweeting and cheeping continued, Betty filled a spray bottle with liquid B-vitamins and painted the tops and bottoms of each leaf with the solution. Once she was done, she stood back and looked at her transplanted beauties. They looked like sad, little dogs left out in a downpour. Certainly, plants known to attract powdery mildew were not best served by leaving them dripping wet.

Betty devised a plan. She dug up an old red wagon that was stored in the garage, placed three pots at a time in the wagon, and wheeled them out the sliding glass door and into the warm sunshine and steady but calm wind. She'd learned that direct light wasn't a good idea after cannabis plants had been foliar sprayed, so she arranged them, one by one, in a circle under the stippled light and protective cover of the large elm tree. She stood back to admire her brood, when a honeybee made pinpoint contact with her ring finger. Betty let out a little yelp as the burning sensation began and steadily increased. She raced inside and into the kitchen, where she was able to gingerly remove the stinger and hold her hand under cold running water. After several minutes, she thought about the cannabis infused coconut oil and decided to try an experiment. Cutting off a small chunk of the frozen slab, she melted it between her hands and then generously covered the entire swollen finger with the oil. She lavished her arms and face with the leftover droplets and debated the rest of her day, when her peripheral vision caught sight of a figure in the backyard. With her heart racing, she didn't hesitate as she bolted out the kitchen door. She stopped short fifteen feet later.

"Hi."

Betty secured her robe around her waist. Her neighbor's five-year-old daughter was sitting cross-legged on the grass, under the elm tree, seemingly mesmerized by the nine cannabis plants waving in the gentle breeze. "Hello, sweetheart." Betty calmly moved toward her. "What are you doing here?"

The child looked up at her. "My ball went over your fence." She pointed to a large, red ball nestled in the grass.

Betty's heart was still racing, but she was doing everything possible to act nonchalant. "You better go home, darling, before your mother comes looking for you."

"What's that called?" the child asked, sweetly pointing her finger toward a plant.

"That's called..." Betty hesitated. "That's called Centennial Blueberry."

The child appeared transfixed. "And that one over there?"

"That's called Kushberry."

She looked up at Betty. "They're pretty."

Betty took a slow breath. "Thank you."

The child stared a little longer before casually getting up, grabbing her ball and walking out of the back gate.

Betty wasn't sure what just occurred but she wished it could always be that easy.

~~~

An hour later, with the girls sufficiently dry, Betty put them back under their grow light. She'd gotten an enthusiastic call from Lily at *The Gilded Rose* that her table runners had sold. Dressing in a brightly colored floral summer shirt and skirt, she raced out of the house, and after saying a quick prayer to the automotive gods, zoomed over to the consignment store. Instead of being able to roll a bowling ball down the aisles without hitting anyone, today the store was teeming with customers. Lily motioned to Betty, telling her she'd be with her shortly. From the corner of her eye, Betty noticed Yarrow outside, smoking a cigarette. She walked outside and sidled next to the girl.

"Hey," Yarrow said in a friendly tone.

"Hello. We've already met each other informally," Betty stated in a friendly voice. She extended her hand. "My name's Betty Craven." Betty noted that the usual black streak down the center of Yarrow's hair was gone, lending a softer and prettier look to her face.

"Hey, Betty. I'm Yarrow." She shook Betty's hand in a loose grip.

"Oh, you have to improve on that," Betty suggested.

"Huh?"

"Your handshake. You want a firm grip. Not too intrusive but not like a dead fish. It should be confident but absent of arrogance."

Yarrow looked at Betty, not quite sure what to think. "You okay?"

"Yes. I'm quite well, thank you."

Yarrow tossed her cigarette to the pavement and crushed it. "Well, I gotta get back –"

"Your hair looks nice without that skunk stripe down the center. You should keep it like that."

"Yeah? You think?"

"Yes. Most definitely."

"It's Monday. I usually dye it blue on Mondays, but I ran out of coloring."

"Is that right? Well, the money you didn't spend on coloring, you could invest in a new hairstyle. Something fresh that makes your eyes pop."

She nodded. "Yeah. I've been thinking about that."

"I can give you the name of a wonderful stylist."

"Cool."

"I thought you were going to Canada on a trip." Betty saw that the girl was confused. "Lily mentioned it to me when I was here last."

"Oh. Yeah, well I decided not to. I have a lot of anxiety about flying."

"Terrorism?"

"Hell, no. I don't want to be radiated in a naked body scanner and have my private images analyzed by fat men drinking diet sodas."

Betty considered her concern. "So, it's not the destination that gives you pause, it's –"

"The getting there that does."

"Yes. Good point." She leaned against the building. "Well, that could be said for a lot of things. It's not so much where we're going, it's the journey that can stall us."

"I hear you."

"Sometimes, if you have someone in your life who is supportive and shares common interests, it can soften those anxious edges and make the journey a lot easier."

"Yeah, I suppose. It's just me and my mom, though. And she's always working."

Betty smiled broadly. "So you're saying you don't have a boyfriend?"

Yarrow shook her head.

"Well, I might be able to help you with more than just a new hairstyle."

~~~

Betty pocketed seventy-five dollars from Lily for the two table runners and stopped off at a hardware store to purchase a pair of digital thermometers that connected to a remote sensor. She figured this way she could monitor the heat in the veg area from any room in her house. The next stop was twenty miles outside of Paradox to *The Lazy Llama Ranch*. She needed some fresh beans, and the pile just inside the pasture gate looked top-notch. Shoveling the black beans into several trash bags, she secured them in her trunk and headed back to the house.

As she turned into her driveway, she was planning the rest of her day when a car pulled in behind her. Looking in the rearview mirror, her jaw tightened.

"Judi!" Betty said, pulling the handle to release the trunk.

Judi looked anxious as she approached the Taurus. In her hands, she carried the borrowed tablecloth. "Hi, Betty."

She glanced at the plastic trash bags in Betty's trunk and backed away from the pungent scent. "That smells like shit!"

"That's because it is shit, darling," Betty replied, heaving one of the bags onto the driveway.

"Shouldn't you wear gloves when you handle that?"

"Maybe. But I'm living more dangerously these days," she half-joked, lugging another large bag of beans out of her trunk.

Judi observed her. "You look different."

"Do I?"

"Yes. Strangely different."

"Strangely good or strangely bad?"

Judi regarded Betty more closely. "Different."

"Hmmm. I have absolutely no idea what could be the cause of that." Betty relocated the final bag from her trunk and closed the lid with a good slam.

"Here," Judi offered, handing her the tablecloth. "I wanted to return this to you as soon as possible. I hate it when people don't return things after they borrow them. Everyone at our party loved it by the way. They kept telling Roger how it made the table look so classy."

She smiled. "Is that right? Well, I've been told I have a classy joint." She dragged one of the larger bags closer to the front garden. "Keep the tablecloth."

Judi looked confused. "What?"

"Keep it. I don't need it."

Her back went up. "Oh, so now you're giving away stuff? This is one of the signs, Betty."

"Of what?"

She hesitated and then spoke. "Suicide."

Betty stopped what she was doing and tried not to look too shocked. "You have got to be kidding me."

"Hey, half of Roger's patients are suicidal. He's told me all about the signs."

"If half of his patients are suicidal, perhaps he needs to make adjustments in their treatment options."

"He does! He adjusts their meds! Listen, I want to help you get over whatever in the hell is bothering you. That way, we can go back to the way it was."

Betty felt a primordial surge, but she didn't want to release it too fast and shock Judi. "I'm not sure that's possible."

Judi approached her, grabbing Betty's arm tightly. "Okay, you're scaring me. If you're not suicidal and you don't have cancer, then what in God's name is going on?"

Betty calmly looked at Judi, part of her wishing she could tell her and the other part wishing she'd leave.

"Look," Judi expressed with shallow breaths, "I'm sorry about what I said at lunch the other day. I didn't mean to slam your son in any way."

"My son? His name is Frankie."

"I know that. I just...I..."

"It's messy, isn't it? That's why we don't talk about him, right? Addiction is not a polite, dinnertime discussion. Best to just keep silent and pretend it doesn't exist."

Judi caught the connotation of Betty's statement and stiffened. "I didn't think you'd want to talk about him, given the way he was found."

"I talk to Frankie every day. And sometimes I hear him speak back. I'm not ashamed of him one bit. I'm as much to blame for his death as anyone."

"You didn't put the needle in his arm."

"No. But I did keep the father in his life."

Judi furrowed her brow. "What in the hell are you talking about? Frank Sr. was fabulous! An incredible provider, a man of integrity, a patriotic American –"

"Right." Betty needed to stop her before the drumbeat of the *Battle Hymn of the Republic* began playing. "He was also a man with a lot of problems."

This stunned Judi. "Who doesn't have problems?"

"He drank far too much." There. She said it. And for whatever reason, there wasn't a shred of remorse or regret.

Judi pursed her lips. "Yes...well...there are worse things than that."

Betty checked her watch. "I need to get going."

Judi nodded and turned back to her car. "Hey, if you have to go out again, avoid the east side of town. They've got Lake Road taped off."

"What happened?"

"Oh, it's no big deal. Some guys with guns broke into this couple's house and kicked in their teeth, trying to steal their pot plants."

Betty froze. "What?"

"I know. I know. What do these people expect? Rumor has it that the couple are marijuana 'caregivers.'" She rolled her eyes. "Yeah, right. Whatever. You play with fire, you're going to get burned. Just a bunch of stoner losers. No need to lose sleep over it."

Chapter 23

"The art of forgetting becomes one's savior."

Betty debated canceling Jeff's visit that night, but then she realized how incredibly relaxed she'd been all day. She needed another calming dose after hearing about the break-in from Judi. His response, when she told him about the armed home invasion, was in keeping with his nimble flexing of the English language. "People who live in glass houses shouldn't get stoned."

They also had no place to hang their artwork, Betty thought, as her mind drifted momentarily. But after an appetizer of lovemaking and a delicious dinner of free-range lemon garlic chicken on a bed of arugula and pine nuts, drizzled in an olive oil and lime dressing, the upsetting news of the day didn't seem as dire. Finishing off the meal with a decadent coffee crème brûlée, Betty couldn't have cared less if the scale said she was one or two pounds heavier. She was getting quite fond of diving into the sensuous side of life. Her only regret was not commencing it sooner. All those wasted nights of allowing fear to chart her course did nothing but guarantee loneliness and grief.

As Jeff lay sleeping beside her that night, she listened to the sounds of the night outside her open bedroom window. She realized that the evening wasn't the enemy any longer. Where before it fell like a mournful companion, forcing her under the covers to escape the clutches of the unknown, now the night was just the night. It didn't own her or hold her hostage. Instead of cowering under the sheet, she allowed the warm, late spring air to caress her bare legs. She decided it was favorable to start a love affair when the weather was warmer. She could wear less clothing, which was quicker to remove. The windows could be wide open, allowing the breeze to blow across her body as she lay on top of the tangled sheets. She could hear the birds and the rustle of leaves on the trees, and make the connection that the life outside was as vibrant as she felt at that moment.

She also concluded that relationships later in life are often more real. In youth, you're looking for a partner to start a family. Eliminate that criteria and the pressures that go with it, and suddenly you're looking for someone you get along with and who shares common ground with you. While Betty wasn't certain what common ground she and Jeff enjoyed, somehow her heart told her he was someone she needed. And it seemed he needed her. The mere fact that they could be in the same room and not feel the need to constantly talk was a sign of how comfortable they'd quickly become with each other. Then there was the way he seemed to understand her like no one else ever had. That kind of vulnerability was new to her. Peyton also appeared to have a certain ability to bore through the façade. It was as if the loving husband she'd never had and her second imperfect son had simultaneously come into Betty's life to release her from her self-imposed, staid ways. As each new day dawned, with the breath of transformation hovering nearby, she felt the need to throw off more shackles.

And yet, when she awoke the next morning, angst – her more common bedfellow – noticeably drifted perilously close. As she lay there longer, watching the sun weave its way across the large window and illuminate the bedroom, she felt a quiver of skepticism. Her mind quickly started to spin webs of doubt. Was she guilty of repeating old patterns in new forms? When the honeymoon wore off, would she discover that Jeff was just as controlling as Frank Sr.? Perhaps she should have pushed her heart toward someone more... conventional. There was safety in convention and none of the embarrassments of explanation that she despised. Convention hadn't worked for her, and it certainly didn't entice happiness out of its cloistered shell, but it was dependable in its bland, predictable way.

She gingerly turned toward Jeff. He was still sound asleep. Would he be insulted or understand her quandary? Betty quietly slipped out of bed and donned her robe. She snagged an old copy of *High Times Magazine* from the stack Peyton had loaned her and padded quietly down the stairs. Seated in the kitchen with her strong cup of coffee, she flipped through the magazine. Advertisements with nubile, long-haired girls lying naked with their nipples and nether regions covered in cannabis buds got her attention. It seemed that ninety percent of the ads featured a nude or scantily clad, buxom girl, whether they were selling glass pipes, carbon filters or organic nutrients. Yes, it became clear to Betty that cannabis growing was indeed a "boy's club," and that club clearly required a steady stream of sexually desirable females to prop up their products.

After reading a few short articles on "How to buy the best fan for your grow room" and one on a born-again Christian tattoo artist who "loved to smoke the herb," Betty noted an ad with "420" prominently displayed. She recalled how the grow store where Peyton worked closed at "4:20," and how Dr. Jan's nurse chuckled when she told her she had a "4:20 appointment." The mystery was solved when Betty read the small print under the ad. It seemed that "4:20" was code for the time each afternoon when students involved in the cannabis culture would stop to light up. *High Times* referred to "420" as a "ritualization of cannabis use that holds deep meaning." So deep, in fact, that April 20 was also designated as the day when many students collectively "light up a doobie" on college campuses everywhere.

She heard the upstairs shower water draining through the old pipes and realized Jeff was up and about. Betty brought out the eggs and milk and was about to whip up an omelet when she noticed her next-door neighbor, Crystal, peering over the back gate. She darted out the back door, securing her robe tightly around her waist and tried her best to casually greet the woman.

"Good morning!" Betty said with a stiff smile.

"Hey, little Miss Green Thumb!"

Betty regarded Crystal with caution. "What do you mean?"

"Sophia told me all about your new endeavor!"

Betty froze but maintained her posture. "I don't know... what?"

"Berries! You're growing berries! How fun! And how brave are you?!"

Right. The child heard the word "Blueberry" and "Kushberry" and she understood "berry." Why in the hell growing berries was brave was beyond Betty. Going to war or running into a burning house to save a person requires bravery. But she kept smiling the whole time. "Oh, well. You know, something to keep my old fingers busy."

Crystal started to unlock the gate. "Can I see them?"

"Oh, actually they're in pots and they're inside. And they're small. Quite small."

She seemed disappointed. "Oh. Shoot. Well, another time perhaps." She started off and then turned back. "Hey, just wonderin'. The motorcycle?" She pointed to Jeff's ride in the driveway. "Are you riding now?"

"God no!" Betty said with a chuckle. "No, no, no. I don't ride motorcycles." There was an awkward patch of silence. "It belongs..." she hesitated, feeling her chin tremble, "to one of the men who is helping me out. Sometimes, they leave their trucks or...motorcycles..." The more she talked, the less her words sounded genuine.

"Oh. Well, I hope one day I'll get to see whatever wonderful renovations you're doing. Your kitchen is to die for."

Betty nodded and after another effusive gush of chatter, they parted. Returning inside, she peered through the front window and watched as Crystal got into her Lexus and drove away.

"Hey!"

Betty turned, startled. Jeff moved toward her and kissed her passionately.

"Good morning, babe," he said with enthusiasm.

"Morning."

He cocked his head. "Something wrong?"

She shook her head. "No. Not a thing. I'll start breakfast."

~~~

After Jeff left for the store, Betty called Dr. Dave. He picked up after the second ring and expressed how much he liked the sample gourmet chocolate Peyton had given him. They arranged to meet near a lake located thirty miles west of town. "Wear something casual," he said to Betty, after telling her he'd like another ten of her chocolates. "It's still a little muddy around the water's edge."

Betty didn't ask Dr. Dave why he insisted on meeting at a lake and not his home or office. Searching for something casual to don, she settled on a pair of soft green linen trousers and a cream-colored summer sweater top with three-quarter sleeves. It was as casual as Betty got. In truth, the trousers were more akin to casual-with-a-chance-of-brunch-at-the-club. But she hoped they would work for their muddy lake meeting.

Dr. Dave's directions were perfect. Once Betty hit the rural dirt road, she traveled along the lonely ribbon of dust and rocks, keeping a keen eye out for the road markers he gave her. Arriving at the final one, she pulled her car off to the side and saw the silver Toyota Highlander he had described, parked under the shade of a large Aspen grove. She removed the cooler that held the candies and traipsed through the new grass, until she came to a short hill that descended and opened up into a pristine, glass-topped mountain lake. The only sounds were the birds chirping and the water lapping softly around the edges of the muddy bank.

"Hello?" Betty called out, her voice echoing into the bluebird sky.

"Hi!" Dr. Dave called back.

Betty shaded her eyes against the arcing sun and spied the good doctor around the bend, fly-fishing about one hundred feet out into the lake.

He removed a fat cigar from his mouth. "I put some chest waders under that aspen tree on your left!" he called out to Betty.

Betty regarded him with a confused gaze. "You want me to come out *there*?"

"Yeah!"

This was certainly different. She set the cooler down under the breezy shade of the aspen trees and struggled into the waders that covered her body from chest to toe. She reasoned that the good doctor was still a bit paranoid from his time in Vietnam and needed a seriously discreet location in which to discuss his medical cannabis usage. Once dressed in the unforgiving rubber suit, Betty walked out into the water, ignoring the occasional sucking sound her feet made when she hit a pocket of air and mud. The closer she got, the better she could observe the doctor. His skin was rough and hardened by the sun; his short wavy grey hair was neatly combed and secured under a green baseball cap with the insignia of a medical institution embroidered on the front. He looked to be about her height with a square, stocky build. One thing was for sure – he was focused intently, almost in a meditative manner, on casting his line back and forth.

She finally arrived by his side. The smell of cigar smoke clung closely, like an earthy perfume. Betty extended her hand. "I'm Betty Craven."

He kept the cigar perched between his lips and shook her hand. "Doctor Dave. Nice to meet you." He sized her up. "You're not what I was expecting." He cast his line.

"What were you expecting?"

"Maybe more of a Bohemian."

"You ate one of my chocolates, and you seriously thought a Bohemian was capable of creating that?"

He laughed. "You got me on that one."

"If you don't mind me asking, why are we meeting out here? Are you that concerned about people finding out?"

"I don't give a shit what people think." He cast his line into the water. "This is my office. This is my refuge. This is my sanity. This and Mary Jane."

Betty took a gander around the pristine locale. "I can see your attraction to it. Peyton mentioned you were a surgeon in Vietnam? My late husband was career military."

"I'm sorry," he said casually.

"Yes. Thank you." She wanted to fill the empty space. "He had a lot of...issues."

"Yep."

Doctor Dave was a man of few words, she reckoned. "If he knew I was growing the plants, he'd have one helluva fit."

"Well, good thing he's dead I guess." He cast the line, this time further.

It was obvious to Betty that Dave wasn't wrapped up in posturing himself in platitudes or polite chitchat. "Do you still practice as a surgeon?"

"Here and there," he puffed on his cigar. "I mostly do a lot of consulting."

"Do others in your profession know you partake of the herb?"

"You mean, do they know I smoke doobie? Yeah, they know. And if they ever give me shit for it, I remind the bastards that most of them haven't met a pain pill or sleeping pill that they don't love. And if they keep arguing the point with me, I tell them to pull their heads out of their asses and do some research."

No, Doctor Dave didn't give a damn about what anyone thought of him. Suddenly, the formerly taciturn physician became quite talkative. He spoke about how too many of the popular pain medications create detachment, whereas cannabis encourages introspection. "I realize now," he offered, "how scared people are of introspection. Of focusing and delving into what's in front of you and seeing it from a new perspective." He whipped the fly line behind him and cast it forward. "Drugs and alcohol let you tune out. Pot makes you tune in. But you have to be open to hearing the message." He puffed on his cigar. "Maybe that's why the Feds keep it illegal. You ever think of that?"

Betty shook her head. "Not really."

"Well, you see, this is the kind if shit one ponders when one tokes." He said it with a smile, but it was laced with sincerity. "I don't think the powers-that-be want a pensive populace. All those people questioning their lives, and why they do what they do. The usefulness or use*less*ness of it? I'm not saying progress is the enemy. I'm not saying work and diligence are worthless. It's a question of whether the things you have been programmed to do, believe, become and repeat are useful to you. We're all just puppets in this insane play, unless we choose to cut the strings and actually think for ourselves. That's what pot does for me. It saved my life. That's not an exaggeration, Betty. It saved my fucking life." He turned around, seeking out a new section of the lake to cast his line. "Forty years ago, I had a noose tied so tightly around my neck, and then one day, I realized I was the one who put it there. I could hang myself or I could remove the noose and use that same rope to pull myself back into some scrap of sanity." He let the line lay on the water a little longer. "You can't simultaneously control people, while offering them guaranteed freedom as their birthright. You can pass all the laws you want, but in the end, people will find a way to do whatever it takes to get from here to there in their minds. Even a man in a solitary cell, with nothing but the four cement walls around him, can imagine himself out of that hell hole, running free in the open air and warm sunshine. He can shift his consciousness to another place by repetitively humming a single sound, holding his breath, spinning in circles. And nothing anyone does, short of killing him, will stop him if that's what he chooses to do."

Betty thought about it. "There will always be those who need to toe the line."

"Of course. Those same ones believe the lie when they're told they have no power. They trust that someone else knows more about their needs than they do. They think their noose is a trendy necktie."

Betty shifted in the muddy lake bottom. She found herself wanting to argue with the good doctor, and she didn't know why. Part of her wanted to play the devil's advocate, but she stopped short when she glanced over at the cooler holding her cannabis chocolates. Any argument she came up with would be as solid as the mucky soil beneath her feet.

"I'll let you in on a secret, Betty. Everyone thinks memories are so important. I disagree. There's grace that comes with forgetting some things. I'm not talking about dementia. I'm talking about the ability to not hold the past so close to you that it suffocates the present moment. There's a knack to forgetting one's pain. Mary Jane makes that goal more attainable."

Betty couldn't connect to Doctor Dave's idea. "I would never want to forget my past or the people in it."

"What about the pain?" He released the fly line again. "What if those unbearable memories prevent you from moving forward and finding pleasure? Would you change your mind then? I watched kids as young as eighteen take their last breath on a dirty, gut-soaked stretcher in the middle of a chaotic firefight. I saw guys with their legs and arms blown off. All they had left was a torso and head, and right before they died, they'd tell me to let their mother know they loved her." He puffed on his cigar. "There were thousands of those kids, and I was able to save ten, maybe twenty percent. I was expected to suck it up and keep doing the same thing every day, even though I knew the next day would be worse. All those dead bodies kept stacking up in my head until finally, their voices haunted me. I couldn't tune them out. What good did that do me? *Tell me.*"

Betty felt a chill down her spine. "I can't answer that," she said somberly.

"I never got shot, but I was as much a casualty as the guys who did." His cigar needed a tune up. He patiently re-lit it in contemplative silence. "There's a quote from Albert Schweitzer that I have framed on my desk. 'Happiness is nothing more than good health and a bad memory.' With the help of Mary Jane, I found that contentment through the slow murkiness that dissolved all those young faces from my mind. Memory can cripple us, Betty. The art of forgetting becomes one's savior. Forgetting allows a respite from pain and regret — two chains that occupy every second and weigh you down. Forgetting is a gift one should never refuse, if within that is the promise that all the mind clutter will stop controlling and owning you."

They talked for another hour, moving only a few yards in the water the entire time. Finally, the beating sun forced Betty to depart. Doctor Dave instructed her to put the chocolates and caregiver paperwork in a large cooler he had in the backseat of his SUV. There was a one hundred dollar bill waiting for her in a white envelope in the cooler. When Betty asked him what strain he would like her to grow for him, he gave a slightly self-conscious smile. "AK-47," Dave stated.

~~~

When Betty got closer to town, she called around to various dispensaries until she found one that had three AK-47 clones for sale. All of them were over one month old and beginning to develop into beautiful girls. After securing them discreetly on the floor of the backseat, she reasoned she would soon need another ounce or two of sweet leaf shake in order to keep up with her patients' requests. She quickly took a detour home, dropped off her three new girls under the veg lights in the basement and grabbed ten cannabis chocolates. Boxing them up and setting them in her cooler, she was back on the road in fewer than ten minutes.

Rolling into the parking lot of Louie's Lube 'n' Tube, Betty parked in the shade, removed the box of chocolates and walked through the side steel door with the gold wheel decal. The place was purring with activity. She glanced around until she saw Louie standing under a hoisted truck.

"Louie?" she said.

He turned, and when he saw Betty, his face froze. "Hey." Skittishly, he looked around. "You're not supposed to be in here. Insurance rules."

The greeting was certainly nothing like their first visit. "Of course. I understand. Could I have a word with you please? Outside?"

Louie instructed a mechanic to check the air filter on the truck and then walked outside with Betty.

"I'm sorry to bother you during business hours," Betty stated before handing him the chocolates, "but I wanted to thank you for your generosity and give you a little taste of my efforts."

He took the box but seemed a bit distant. "Okay. Thank you."

"I also need to engage in another transaction with you. I'd like two more ounces of the sweet leaf shake please."

Louie looked lost. "I don't have any."

"When will you have some?"

He casually tilted his head toward the far end of the automotive yard and she followed him. "I got out of the grow business. I sold all my plants to a buddy and did the same thing with the bud and shake I had sittin' around."

Betty wasn't sure she was hearing this correctly. "I just saw you last week. What in the hell happened between then and now?"

"Well...to be honest..." He hesitated for a second. "*You* happened."

"*Me?*"

"Yeah. You." He scratched his head, trying to come up with the right words. "You got me thinking. You asked how I handled it, havin' kids in the house and all. I had a long talk with my wife and we both agreed it was time to fold it up."

Betty stood there in stunned disbelief. "Well, I'm so glad I could be of service to you. Now, where in the hell am I going to purchase more shake?"

"I have no idea. Maybe the street?"

Her jaw dropped. "*On the street?* Excuse me, but do I look like someone who purchases cannabis *on the street?* I need to know how it's grown, what the strain is, whether it's covered with mold or pesticides. Do you actually think that some poorly educated, street corner, drug-addled lackey can acquire that information for me? I think not!"

"Uh, you know, technically, I am 'the street.'"

"Present company excepted," she quickly said.

"Ma'am, I hear you. But I can't help you. What about Peyton?"

She was still fuming as she tilted her imposing stature closer to Louie. "He won't be harvesting his current crop until July. I can't wait until then! I have patients depending on me to deliver quality cannabis chocolates in a timely manner! What do you think I'm running here? Some fly-by-night operation?" Betty realized she'd temporarily lost both her manners and her mind. She pulled away from Louie and took a moment to calm down. "I'm sorry. That was unacceptable."

"It's okay, ma'am. Just my two cents, but maybe you should lay off the Sativas and move more toward the calming Indicas."

The whole way home, Betty berated herself for wasting one of the ounces of shake she originally purchased from Louie, in the coconut oil infusion. Sure, she could use that one for making salves, but if she'd used the entire amount of shake in the cocoa butter, she'd have an extra forty-eight dosed candies to hand out. Unfortunately, she knew she couldn't substitute the coconut oil cannabis in her chocolates because of the odd soapy taste it imparted. At this rate, she only had seventeen cannabis chocolates left. Her balloon of enthusiasm quickly burst.

Betty made a point of stopping by the nursery to pick up two raspberry and two blueberry bushes. She had no interest in them, but she figured it was important to cover her bases and at least have them, just in case Crystal wanted to see how "brave" she really was.

She spent the rest of the day in her front yard garden, tending to the mass of weeds and pruning what she'd ignored for over a week. As the sun grew hotter and the solar fountain continued to spew arcs of water into the flowerbeds, Betty contemplated every possible way of obtaining more shake. But nothing she came up with allowed for the degree of discretion she needed. Jeff called mid-day to check in, which cheered her up. However, he wouldn't be over that night, since Peyton and she would be heading down to sulfur the basement. When he said goodbye and she hung up, a striking loneliness took hold. Betty tried to push it away, but it was clear she truly felt something for him. Throwing all the unconventional drivel to the side, he was quickly turning into a good habit.

She wrapped up dinner early that evening, put the dishes away and checked the girls several times before turning on the chirping birds CD for them to enjoy. After installing the remote thermometer in the veg room, she wandered back into the living room, figuring she'd kill time and read an old *High Times* while waiting for Peyton's eight-thirty arrival. But even a scintillating Q&A interview, with a former cop who was fighting for cannabis reform, didn't help her forget she would soon have nothing to offer her patients. Putting down the magazine, she dozed lightly. But she was strangely aware she was falling asleep and conscious of the sounds in the room. Her body relaxed, but she still felt the soft couch under her body. Suddenly, she felt a wooden surface against her back. She opened her eyes and found herself in the attic. A dim lamp was the only source of light in the darkened room. There was slow movement in the corner of the room, and she watched without fear as Frankie emerged from the shadows. He looked somewhat different this time. He was still thin, but his face didn't harbor the usual scars of drug abuse as it always did whenever she had seen him before in these altered states. He looked down at her and smiled. Then, for some odd reason, he walked to the narrow part of the room, where the ceiling slanted, and placed his palm against the wall. Without taking his eyes off Betty, he tapped his fingers repeatedly on the wood. She heard his voice whisper in her head, "Pay attention." There was more and in that moment, she understood him, but when she awoke, the information evaporated.

Betty turned to the clock and realized that half an hour had passed, even though she felt as if it had only been a minute. The air prickled around her, as if Frankie's essence was still close by and waiting. Getting up, she turned around in a full circle, expecting to see her son without the fog of sleep, alcohol or cannabis encouraging it. "Frankie?"

Silence.

And then her feet, as Emily Dickinson wrote, "mechanical" went round and upstairs to the attic door. She opened the door, turned on the light and made her way up the narrow steps. After switching on another lamp, she stared at the spot where Frankie's hand rested in her strange vision. Moving carefully to the slanted ceiling, she told herself this was ridiculous, and yet she peered closer. Betty brought the lamp toward her and illuminated the rough wood. She was just about to turn around when she noticed a gap where two panels of wood had been joined together. Finding a lone ballpoint pen lying nearby, she jabbed it into the thin slit and was easily able to pry one panel away from the wall. She removed the second panel and found a cavernous hole, rife with cobwebs and cakes of dust. Taking the shade off the lamp, she poked the lightbulb into the cavity and saw a reflection. Betty reached in and felt a firmly wrapped, brick-shaped object. She withdrew it and sat on Frankie's bed. The object was covered in two inches of thick plastic. It took her ten minutes to slice through and remove the plastic, and when she did, she found a latched, metal box. Unhooking the latch, she stared in stunned disbelief.

Inside the box was a vacuum-sealed pound of premium cannabis bud. The label read: L.A. CONFIDENTIAL/NORTHERN CALIFORNIA – 2005.

Chapter 24

"...He had a fight with a hammer and the hammer lost."

Betty brought the pound of buds down to the kitchen and cut open the airtight plastic bag. To her shock and amazement, it still retained a fairly strong, skunky aroma with a hint of pine. She brought out one of the dense, dark green buds and clearly saw the frosty maroon red hairs. Some of the smaller buds weren't as aromatically pungent, so she set those aside. But after carefully rooting through the bag, she ended up with almost seven ounces of incredibly pungent cannabis. Once it passed the smell test, she needed to figure out if there was still some kick left to it, after spending five years in the dark, airtight storage. Betty carried a bud to the stove and gently lit it on the burner. After blowing out the flame, she held the bud to her nose and inhaled one good ribbon of smoke. It took about one minute before she felt a smooth but relaxing buzz creep from her head to her toes. She may have only been able to salvage seven ounces out of the pound, but cannabis bud was a lot stronger than sweet leaf shake, so she factored she could use less and still obtain the same medicinal effects.

Betty immediately looked up the L.A. Confidential strain on her computer, and found to her delight that it was a three-time Cannabis Cup winner for best Indica strain and boasted a stunning eighteen percent THC. It was also used mainly for pain and insomnia – two issues she was sure all of her patients would benefit from. Obviously, after five years in hiding, the THC content might have been compromised. But if the smoke test was any indication, Betty knew she had a reprieve from worrying about how she was going to take care of her patients.

It was nothing short of a strange, almost mystical discovery. And then she remembered the last time she saw Frankie alive, when he insisted on going up to his old room alone. She recalled the backpack slung over his shoulder, which she only now realized held the brick of cannabis. But where in the hell did he get such a huge amount of herb? And why was he secreting it away in their home? There was no way to explain it except that somehow, Frankie did this for a purpose she wasn't prepared to understand. And if she couldn't explain it, there was no way she was about to bring it up to Peyton. She diligently wrapped up the useable bud and hid it in her bedroom closet, next to Frankie's box of ashes.

Peyton arrived with a bag that held a tub of yellow sulfur crystals, a metal-handled burner and two green headlamps. They still had half an hour before the lights went out in the veg room, but Peyton wanted to get everything set up. Putting the items on the living room table, he explained the whole process. Sulfur burning had to be done with the lights off, because if light hit the leaves during the process − or even a few hours afterward − there was a risk of burning the leaves, turning them black. The leaves also had to be free of oils, such as those natural substances used for pest control, as that would also destroy the plant, essentially denuding it, leaving only a lonely stalk. While sulfuring cannabis plants was extreme, so was the potentially devastating effects of PM, especially when one's intention was to make medicine out of the mature plants. As Peyton described it, the sulfur burner was hung over the plants, and after it was filled with the yellow sulfur crystals, the burner was plugged in and allowed to warm up, until a slow, smoky vapor that smelled like decaying eggs wafted through the enclosed space. There was no way to be in the room during the process, but after about three hours when the smoke dissipated, one could return to the room wearing a green headlamp and remove the burner. The entire process made Betty as nervous as a whore in church. But the thought of losing her girls worried her more. They went downstairs and were instantly greeted with the incessant chirping birds CD.

Peyton put his hands to his ears. "Sweet baby Jesus! Make it stop!"

"I can't!" Betty said, talking over a particularly high-pitched, starling sequence. "It opens the stomata! I figured it would help the sulfur absorb better."

"For real?"

"Yes. For real."

"What about music?"

"Oh, they get that too. They start the day with chirping birds. Mid-morning they get Vivaldi's Four Seasons, lunch is a series of energetic Strauss Waltzes, then a bit of down time for their nap. Baroque starts in the late afternoon and then we move through Beethoven and Bach, before we end the day with a calming Mozart compilation and a final restful Suite Number 3: Air on the G String. It's one of my favorite Baroque pieces. You know what they say, Peyton. If it ain't Baroque, don't fix it."

He looked at her with a confused expression. "I'm still fixating on the G String." He noticed the temperature sensor on the wall. "What's that?"

"That's synced to two digital thermometers upstairs. One is in my bedroom and the other is in the kitchen. That way I can remotely keep tabs on the temperature."

"Geez, Betty. You've taken this to a whole new level. It's like you just adopted a Cambodian orphan, and you're worried it's gonna suffocate in its pillow. You sure you don't want to install a baby monitor just in case they call out in the middle of the night for a cup of water?"

"This is coming from a young man who sleeps with his plants?" she countered with a gentle smile, turning the volume down on the chirping birds. "Did you hear about the caregivers who were assaulted in their home and had their plants stolen?"

He nodded. "Yeah, dude. It sucks. They obviously showed their grow op to the wrong person."

"Well, that's not going to happen here. But I do think we need to take precautions. From now on, when we're talking on the phone or between us, we won't use the word 'plants.'

Instead, we'll talk about 'the girls.' So if I say the girls are hungry, it means I'm feeding them. Or when I say the girls want to see you, it means come over. If I say the girls need a little special attention, that means we need to amend their nutrients. Make sense?"

"Yeah. Sure. One problem though, Betty. Instead of people assuming you're growing cannabis, they are gonna assume you're running a brothel."

"Well, just as long as I don't get screwed either way," she said with a wry smile. "Speaking of the girls, before the lights go out, I want to get your opinion on this one." She pointed to the partially top-chewed Centennial Blueberry plant that Ronald trashed. "What do you think? Is she going to make it, or did Ronald permanently stunt her?"

Peyton examined the plant carefully. "Nah. He just super-cropped her. That's cannabis speak for 'high tech pruning.' Instead of a top cola, you'll get three or four top ones. People do this on purpose to create more of a canopy bush effect, so that light can penetrate down to the lower branches better."

"Okay." She looked at the plant with a scowl of displeasure. "But this branch looks like it's deformed. I'm just concerned it's not going to rally to the occasion. It's already stunted compared to the others and difficult to prop up. And look over at this leaf –"

"Betty, Betty, Betty. You're freakin' out over nothin'. Remember? This is supposed to be fun."

"Right. Fun."

"No, I'm serious, Betty. *Fun?* The plant's gonna make it. It may not look perfect but it's worth keeping around." He set the plant down and put a reassuring hand on her shoulder. "Dude, I can see how attached you already are. It happens to all of us. These plants...these *girls*...they capture your heart in a very strange way. But you gotta stop worrying so much about the little stuff." He leaned forward, whispering to her in confidence. "They can feel your stress, and that's not doing them any good. They just want to chill, you know? Listen to some tunes, drink some water, eat some food, be talked to in a soothing manner and grow to their greatest healing potential."

She contemplated his guidance. "Good advice." She peered down at the lopsided plant and a brazen idea formed. "I'm going to call that girl Helen. She's got a lot of issues."

Peyton started setting up the sulfur burner. Betty looked around the room and felt a deep sense of connection with her young flock.

"You know, Peyton. You're right. I really think I might have found my niche."

He looked up. "Oh yeah? I didn't know your niece was missing."

An hour later, after feeding Peyton a light but suitable snack for that time of evening, Betty gave him a large bag of llama beans. One would have thought she'd given him a glow-in-the-dark watering can by the look of excitement in his eyes.

Betty realized something drastic had to be done. As far as she was concerned, he needed companionship as soon as possible. "Are you free for lunch tomorrow?" she asked him.

"Yeah. It's my day off. But tomorrow's my scheduled pre-flip, foliar spray on the ladies who are heading into bloom."

"Yes, of course it is. But you're meeting me outside *The Gilded Rose* at noon. I'll write down the address. It'll be *fun*. Trust me."

And as it turned out, it was fun. After lunch the following day, Betty nonchalantly suggested a post-meal visit to *The Green Wellness* dispensary where Yarrow just so happened to be working as a bud tender. She also just happened to have a new hairstyle, thanks to Betty's dependable stylist. And not so strangely, it just so happened that Peyton and Yarrow hit it off, like two cannabis plants under the same grow light. When she left them at the dispensary, she had a strong feeling her second imperfect son would soon have something else to occupy his free time.

~~~

The days passed quickly, and before she knew it, summer was in full swing. By early July, Peyton told Betty it was time to flip her plants from veg into bloom. But first, he showed her how to clone them. Choosing the most vigorous and healthy plants that had the densest growth patterns, they spent a hot summer afternoon carefully cutting the best specimens from the lower branches, dipping them in cloning solution and securing them in wet peat plugs. From there, they placed the cuttings in a large, water-filled cloning unit with multiple jets that, when turned on, sprayed the peat to encourage root growth. She kept track of each plant and which "mother" it came from, by affixing handwritten labels made out of masking tape to the edges of each plug. The only plant they didn't clone was White Russian, not wanting to continue the powdery mildew problem.

Of all the original "mother" plants, the Kushberry ones had grown like they had something to prove, measuring an astounding three feet. "Helen," the Centennial Blueberry plant that Ronald "supercropped," had also taken on the look of a lush, healthy bush, with a discernable canopy filled with dozens of beautiful nodes that would eventually transform into even more outstanding buds. With each passing week, Betty invested more time and money in her stable of twelve girls. Seeing her electric bill that covered the first month of growing, she realized that, as the saying goes, experience ran up big bills and so did those grow lights. In an attempt to conserve energy, she snuck the girls outside to wave in the soft breeze under the large elm tree. They always seemed happier and infused with vitality after a day in the sun. That treat would become less viable once they began blooming and growing taller. The heady scent of the developing buds would require them to be held captive inside.

Thanks to Betty's matchmaking, Peyton and Yarrow had formed a great friendship that turned into something more serious in late June. It seemed to be the perfect coupling, even though Peyton still had no idea she had Canadian blood running through her veins.

Betty still had only three of the five patients allowed by Colorado law. But Buddy, Dottie and Dr. Dave certainly kept her busy making chocolates. She even experimented making several salves, using the cannabis coconut oil infusion, and found it to be a great hit with her trio. Buddy especially was hooked on the salve and was convinced it was helping relieve the spasms in his lower back. Dottie even used it on a few of her horses, and she said they seemed to benefit from daily applications. The trick, she told Betty, was keeping the salve tucked away so no one else would find it. After several visits to Dottie's ranch to deliver chocolates and more cannabis salve, Betty noticed that Hugh, the ranch manager, was becoming increasingly concerned, hovering close to the barn every time Betty arrived. As for Doctor Dave, Betty met him every Wednesday *in* the lake, wading out to chat, before leaving the chocolates in his cooler. The three of them were a joy to work with – even Buddy slowly let down his usual, pulled-back demeanor and was more at ease with Betty.

It was, as Betty began to call it, her summer of love. She had her girls she adored, and she had Jeff who adored her. She knew when she gave him a key to the house, he was more than just a passing infatuation. When he wasn't there or she wasn't at his house outside of Paradox, she felt as if a part of her was missing. It was such an odd feeling, because their relationship "on paper" continued to make no sense to her. But the Betty that had been buried for too many decades gradually emerged, bonding with him in a sensuous, arousing celebration that made her feel young and in bloom. And yet, she continued to keep their relationship a secret from her friends. Betty told herself it was because she was private and the bond between them was sacrosanct. But deep down, there was more to the exclusion of his name than she wanted to admit. Even their overnight getaway to Glenwood Springs for his birthday in June was fraught with creative deception, when Judi unexpectedly showed up at the house and saw Betty's overnight bag by the door. She appeased Judi by telling her that she used the bag to store winter blankets. Betty knew this subterfuge couldn't go on forever. But then she told herself if she could successfully hide the girls, she could also continue to hide the man. What she couldn't hide, however, was the way she was changing. She brought out photos of Frankie and propped them up around the house. For the first time, she allowed her grey roots to grow out a little longer before coloring them. The soft adagios still played in her bedroom, but she discovered that listening to the local classic rock station, while driving with the windows rolled down, made her feel alive. And every single night, right before bed, she took upwards of a half-teaspoon of the cannabis-infused coconut oil.

On the local news front, the fallout from Renée's letter to the editor continued, as local anger toward the number of dispensaries in Paradox and the surrounding towns created an antagonistic atmosphere. When one of the dispensaries had their front room destroyed by a Molotov Cocktail thrown through their storefront window, Renée kept the blaze burning by writing yet another letter to the editor, thanking the arsonist who "took care of business." It was such an odd thing for Renée to do, Betty thought. But she noticed that Renée's fervor had intensified with the summer heat, turning her into a cannabis Carrie Nation, swinging her pen like a hatchet. She was manically gleeful when the law-abiding dispensary, with no signs of criminal activity, was forced to shut down. Even the woman known as "Elizabeth Cragen," who signed that blistering letter in early May, would never have preened or taken credit for the destruction of someone's business. While it angered Betty, she kept her mouth shut.

As expected, the righteousness of the Reverend Bobby Lynch hadn't slowed down either. In June, he launched a summer camp through his church where children spent two weeks in a remote rural setting and endured daily lectures on the "talons of Satan, promiscuity, drinking and marijuana." After hearing him bleat on about his camp one evening on the local news, Betty wondered whatever happened to hiking, swimming, sitting around a campfire eating s'mores, and making keepsake boxes out of pine cones and twine.

But Reverend Lynch still had Doobie Douggie to con-
tend with. For every story featuring Lynch, there were two
highlighting the latest adventures of the grey-haired, wheel-
chair-bound cannabis reformer. Some members of the public might not have endorsed Douggie's behavior, but they
couldn't ignore his in-your-face determination to "free the
weed." Draped in another flag made with hemp fabric and
emblazoned with large cannabis leaves, Douggie rolled over
to the state capitol, lit up a joint and spent thirty minutes
explaining to the local Denver news organizations how the
herb could cure everything from epilepsy to cancer. It was
when he dared to mention the "C" word, that the capitol
security asked the cops to remove him. As Betty watched
them wheel the crusader away, she marveled at the fact that
he never looked like a victim. He might not have been able
to walk, but he could stand up to anyone at anytime and
outthink them all.

When it was time to purchase the bloom lights, Betty
gathered together all the money she'd saved from the sales
of her chocolates as well as the consignment cash, and found
she had just enough for the two, thousand-watt sets she
needed. She opted for the best quality unit available at the
grow store where Peyton worked, and then adding the required high phosphorus nutrients, blackstrap molasses and
foliar sprays necessary to help trigger the girls into bloom,
the bill came to just over twelve hundred dollars. "That's a
helluva lot of chocolates," Betty thought to herself as she
secured the huge boxes in the backseat of her Taurus. Back
at the house, Jeff built two sturdy support frames to hang
the hooded lights, and then together they secured the units
to the immovable structures. While Jeff checked the bloom
room for any light leaks, Betty prepped the girls, removing any yellow leaves and large fan leaves that obscured bud
nodes, treated them with the necessary organic foliar sprays
and phosphorus-rich food and finished with a top-dressing
of rich humus. All the while, the chirping birds CD played
in the background. At one point, Jeff handed Betty a couple
vintage CDs featuring the humor of George Carlin.

"I figured they might enjoy a break from the tweeting and the classical hits, and benefit from Carlin's acerbic wit," he joked.

Once the girls were spaced perfectly in the bloom room, Betty set the timer on the twelve and twelve cycle and plugged in the lights. It took several minutes for the lights to warm up and glow to their brightest spectrum, but once they did, Jeff and Betty stood back and admired their handiwork.

"So now the fun really begins," Jeff commented.

Betty nodded. "Yes. I suppose this is when it gets serious."

"Not too serious I hope." He wrapped his arm around her shoulder.

She leaned into his broad shoulder. "I don't think I could have done this without your help. Thank you."

He kissed the top of her head. "I'm enjoying it. It's different. I wouldn't want to miss a moment of any of it."

"There's still enough space in here for a few more plants if I get my full patient load."

"I might be able to help you with one of them. I talked to a longtime customer at my store. Her name's Jean. She could definitely use some good cannabis. I'll take you over to see her tomorrow if you'd like."

The prospect of working with another person, who might become a long-term friend, cheered Betty tremendously. "That's fantastic! Yes! Of course I want to meet Jean. What's she like?"

"She's wonderful. Great spirit. Down to earth. I know you two will get along. She's married to a former judge."

"A judge? Good lord! And he's okay with this?"

"Yeah. It was actually his idea. He just wanted to make sure he found the right person to work with."

A sense of pride engulfed Betty. The idea that she was the right fit for someone who needed her services excited her, and she couldn't wait to meet Jean. Betty was just about to ask more about her prospective patient, when she heard a man's voice calling her name. She froze momentarily.

"I think whoever it is, is in the backyard," Jeff offered casually.

"Would you mind staying here and holding down the fort while I check?"

Betty quickly walked out the sliding glass door and into the backyard. There was Buddy at the kitchen door, looking rather lost. "Buddy!" She turned back to the basement area with a look of concern and then moved toward him. "I wasn't expecting you. Are you in need of more chocolates?"

"That's what I came here to talk to you about, Mrs. Craven." He scuffed the grass with his big work boot. "I just got some crappy news. My boss had all the guys do a random piss test and I failed."

"Well of course you did, darling. You're averaging at least one chocolate every night." She stole a quick glance back to the basement's sliding door.

"Yeah. I know. But he doesn't care whether it's medical marijuana or recreational. Pot is pot to him. He has a zero-tolerance policy for all drugs. The way he explained it to me, is that his lawyer says his insurance company doesn't cover anyone using heavy equipment who uses pot, because it's an illegal drug. He told me if I was hurt on the job and tested positive, I couldn't be covered by worker's comp."

"Were you fired?" Betty asked, terribly concerned.

"No. Just demoted. I'm now a flagger, directing traffic around the worksite. Huge pay cut, but at least he didn't give me the heave-ho."

Betty felt somewhat responsible for this unfortunate turn of events. "Perhaps if I called him and explained everything. I wouldn't use my name, but maybe I could –"

"No, ma'am. That would not be a good thing. You never know what kind of mood he's gonna be in. He pops Vicodin by the fistful for his nerve pain. Last week, he had a fight with a hammer and the hammer lost. It was ugly." Buddy scuffed the grass again. "Anyway, I just wanted to come over and tell you that I can't afford the chocolates anymore. I'm gonna have to quit and see if my insurance will pay for some painkillers from the pharmacy. Thanks for everything." He turned to go.

Betty felt a growing anger swelling inside that she tried to tamp down. "Buddy, wait! This is ridiculous. You have your red card. You went through the process, and you are legal. You have a doctor's recommendation, for heaven's sake! What am I missing?"

"Uh...it's a Federally banned substance?"

"*And?*"

Buddy looked at her perplexed. "And that's about it. It kinda trumps anything the states are doing. It's the Federal lawmakers. They make the laws."

"That's it? Oh, for God's sake. This makes no sense. Lawmakers, my ass. Just because a cat gives birth in an oven doesn't make her babies kitten biscuits!"

"Huh? What's a kitten biscuit?"

"Never mind." Betty fumed.

"You okay, Betty?" Jeff called out to her.

She turned and found him standing in the sun behind her. Her mouth went dry.

"Who's that?" Buddy asked.

"I'm fine," she said to Jeff. She took Buddy by the elbow and moved him toward the back gate. "He's a friend. Listen, I don't care if you can't pay for the chocolates. I'll still make them for you if you want me to."

"That doesn't seem right, Mrs. Craven."

"Well, how about this. Let's do a trade. You work on my roof, and I'll make you all the chocolates you want. If you do another drug test and fail, you can't get demoted any further than a flagger. If you get fired, you'll find another job. But at least you won't get addicted to pain pills or deal with the nasty side effects. Is that a deal?"

He nodded. "Thank you." He walked to the gate and then turned back to her. "You know, if someone had told me six months ago you were into this, I never would have believed it."

"Well, darling, six months ago, I wouldn't have believed it either."

Chapter 25

"Stuart went on a road trip."

The following day, Jeff and Betty drove fifteen miles north of Paradox to meet Jean. She was still furious about what happened to Buddy and couldn't stop talking about the injustice toward him during the drive.

"Instead of preaching to the choir," Jeff said, "why don't you write another letter to the editor. But this time, have Betty Craven sign it instead of your alter ego, Elizabeth Cragen."

"Are you nuts? Did you drink too much carrot juice again?"

He chuckled. "Why not?"

"You are *seriously* asking me this question?"

"Babe, you know what? You can't keep all of this a secret. And I mean, *all* of it."

She sat back. Betty knew exactly what he meant. He wasn't stupid. However, she kept telling herself that her personal nondisclosure was purely to guard her privacy.

Betty was relieved they arrived at Jean's house before they could discuss it further. She cradled the cooler as they walked to the front door of the modest, one-story brick house and rang the bell.

"I think Jean's going to be the perfect person for you to get to know," Jeff said.

The door opened and a grey-haired man in his mid-sixties greeted them. "Hi, I'm Arthur," he said, shaking Betty's hand. "You must be Betty."

"Pleased to meet you," Betty replied, her manners on point.

Arthur waved them inside and into the light-filled living room. "I'll get Jean."

Betty was admiring a painting above the fireplace when she heard Jean's voice behind her.

"Hello, Betty."

Betty turned. Thanks to her pageant training, she was able to keep her smile firmly in place, even though her heart was imploding. Jean stood there, about five foot seven inches tall and probably no more than one hundred pounds. She was likely in her early sixties, but looked far older with her face drained of color and dark circles cresting underneath her eyes. Her head was covered in a stylish purple scarf that couldn't hide her bald head. Betty felt Jeff's reassuring, warm hand on her back, which gave her the courage to speak up.

"Jean. How lovely to meet you," Betty said, moving gently toward the woman and shaking her hand.

They all sat down in the sun-drenched room, and after some congenial chitchat, Arthur explained the situation. Jean had terminal brain cancer, and after two unsuccessful surgeries and numerous medications that made her unable to function, he took a friend up on an offer and brought home several joints. Before she finished the first one, her pain was nearly gone and she could finally get four straight hours of sleep. After doing his own research, he learned that edibles were a better choice because of their strength and the fact that they stayed in the system longer.

"Jeff told us when we were at his store last week, that you make some pretty damn good edibles," Arthur stated with enthusiasm.

Betty felt as if she were melded to the chair.

"We brought you some of them," Jeff piped up, gently nudging Betty.

Betty did her best to snap out of it. "Yes! Right." She opened the cooler and handed the elegantly wrapped box to Jean. "Each one is rather strong. You might want to split them in half or even smaller."

Jean complimented Betty on her artistic prowess and opened the box. "I know I don't weigh much," she replied without a shred of awkwardness, "but from what I've read, if you're in a lot of pain and dealing with an aggressive cancer, a higher dose is needed to even feel it." Without giving it a second thought, Jean popped a whole chocolate in her mouth. "Wow! These taste fantastic, Betty. Jeff was right!"

"Thank you." She felt lost. "It's the honey."

"Did you bring the paperwork we need to fill out?" Arthur asked.

"Yes," she said, clumsily pulling the caregiver forms out of the cooler and handing them to Arthur. "But maybe it would be a better idea for you to see how you like the chocolates before we commit to anything?"

Jean smiled. "I don't like them. I *love* them. Sign me up."

Arthur handed Betty a small envelope. "I hope this covers it and the next batch?"

Betty opened the envelope to find four crisp one hundred dollar bills. "This is far too much."

"No, it's not," Jean said.

After a half hour of discussion, Jean excused herself, saying she needed to rest. After she left the room, Arthur walked them to the front door and asked if Betty could grow the G-13 strain for his wife. "It's quite the urban legend," he offered, stating that he'd done his research. "Supposedly, it was a strong, government-created strain that someone covertly released. Not sure if that's true, but G-13 was in one of the joints she smoked and it worked quite well."

Betty agreed to grow it for Jean. "I hope you don't take this the wrong way, Arthur, but Jeff said you were a retired judge. Did you ever send someone to prison for cannabis?"

A look of regret covered his face. "Yes. I did. I made an oath to uphold the law. But if it's any consolation, I always gave the accused ample opportunities to reform or go to rehab before sentencing them to any time."

"I see," Betty said quietly. "It's quite a different reality we live in now, isn't it?"

"Yes." His eyes misted over. "It sure is."

Jeff drove the Taurus back to Paradox, while Betty sat staring out of the passenger window. The silence was thick between them until Betty piped up.

"Pull over! I need to get out."

Jeff slowly moved the sedan to the side of the road where a large swath of rural, grassy acreage stretched into the distance. Before he could put the car in park, Betty opened the passenger door and got out. She tore into the field, shallowly breathing the entire way. Her head spun as the July sun beat down on her head like a hard rain. Jeff finally caught up with her.

She spun around toward him. "What in the hell was that?"

"That's a woman who needs your help. She's sick."

Betty regarded him with a perplexed expression. "She's *dying!*"

"So you only help people who have the potential of outliving you?"

"I've had enough death to last a lifetime. I cannot watch another person die a horrible death." Tears welled in her eyes. "This scares the shit out of me!"

He faced her. "I know it does."

"So what was your point? Force me into something I can't handle?"

"No. Show you that you're stronger than you think you are."

"You're *wrong*. I'm not strong. If that were true, I would have spoken up years ago and made a huge difference in the life of one person."

He grasped her shoulders gently but firmly. "Betty, stop living in the past. That night did not determine who you are or what you're capable of now."

"It determined Frankie's fate."

"No. He determined his own fate! Hell, it seems he understood his fate when he was ten! He drew it! You and I are living right here, in this moment. Your husband's dead. Your son is gone. You have no excuses for not following your path."

"What path?" she asked with a slight twist of anger.

"You were meant to do this, Betty. It's your purpose in life. You're damn good at it. You *truly* care about people. They can depend on you and trust you. And those plants in your basement? I'm a little jealous of your girls." He said with a soft smile. "I watch you with them, and I see how much you love and dote on them. This is your calling. Maybe it'll turn into your passion. But it'll all go to hell if you let fear take over and tell you that you can't do it."

"Oh, come on. Growing cannabis? Making chocolates?"

He looked her straight in the eye. "*Helping people*, Betty. Giving them something beautiful and allowing them to believe they can get through another day. Do you have any idea how powerful that can be for someone who is sick or hurting...or dying?"

She turned away.

Jeff pulled her back toward him. "You don't have to pretend to understand their pain. You *know* what real pain feels like. They see that in you, and they know they can talk to you and not feel alone."

Betty shook loose of his hold and walked a few feet away. Her gut churned from anxiety as tears inched down her cheeks. "I can't do it," she softly said. "You can't say any of this is my purpose."

"If you don't believe me, then listen to your son. He told you years ago. And I bet if you still had those drawings, there'd be one of a purple scarf on a bald headed woman. He reached out to you with his drawings, and I bet he's still reaching out to you until you're strong enough to let him go."

She was dumbstruck. This was the third time Jeff said it. She couldn't help but recall the last lines of that damned poem that clung like a heavy cloak against her heart. "*This is the Hour of Lead, Remembered, if outlived, As Freezing persons, recollect the Snow, First – Chill – then Stupor – then the letting go.*" Betty turned to him, sadness etched in every pore. "I can't... let him go."

He drew her toward him, holding her tightly. After a few moments, he pulled back and draped his arm around her shoulder. "You know that park in the west side of Paradox on the river? Love Park? Everyone thinks it's a place to make out, but it's named after Stuart Love. He died on that river saving the life of a little girl who was drowning. There's more to the story most people don't talk about because it's kind of weird, but I heard it straight from the family who lives on the river and experienced it firsthand. They said that after Stuart died, he hung around the river because he didn't know he was dead. He went from house to house, until he decided to stay with this one particular family. They told me Stuart didn't scare them. He just liked to open and close doors, walk up and down the hallway and rattle a few pans. Eventually, they got used to him...started calling him by name, until he was part of the family. They went on vacation to visit the in-laws and damned if Stuart didn't tag along."

"You're kidding me."

"I'm not kidding. Hand to God. Stuart went on a road trip. They couldn't shake his ghost, and they couldn't figure out why he was sticking around them and no one else who lived on that river. But the longer he stayed with him, the more they realized something. They realized each member in that household started to change for the better. The edges around them softened. Where there'd been anger, now there was forgiveness. Where there had been regret, suddenly there was acceptance −"

"Wait a second. You're using a ghost story to −"

"It's not a ghost story, Betty." He looked at her with compassion. "There's more to it. And there's more to this world than meets the eye. And there's more to you than you thought until a couple months ago. Somewhere deep down inside of you, you *do* know that. You're gradually remembering the reason you were born. Sometimes we fight against who we really are, because the reliability of the well-worn mask is too damn comfortable, even though it suffocates our potential." He kissed her. "If you just get out of your own way, babe, there's nothing you can't do."

Jeff dropped her off at her house and returned to work on his motorcycle. Her mind was still aflutter as she checked on the girls. In the bloom room, she delicately checked the bud nodes in search of any sign of growth. Peyton assured her it would take two weeks or longer before the first cluster of white hairs appeared, signaling the formation of a bud. But Betty wanted to believe that, like herself, her girls were high achievers and sought to bloom as early as possible. Walking into the veg room, she was cheered to see the Centennial Blueberry, Kushberry and a few of the AK-47 clones had developed a thick clump of white roots reaching nearly five inches into the cloning machine. Peyton's suggestion of "over cloning" to compensate for losing a few in the process was good advice, as two of the AK-47s set aside for Dr. Dave were looking a little sad. It was time to get the clones into pots. Taking a quick inventory of her nutrients, she figured she could use another bag of worm castings and humus, along with several bags of organic soil. She searched for a piece of paper to jot down the items and came up empty handed. Upstairs, she grabbed a sheet of personalized notepaper with her named scripted in gold-embossed lettering next to her phone number and wrote down all the necessary items under the words: CANNABIS SUPPLIES. She added the three G-13 clones Jean's husband requested, along with titanium trimming scissors, in anticipation of helping Peyton harvest his crop the following week. Drawing a line under that, she figured as long as she was out and about she'd visit the farmers' market, so she listed everything from arugula to brie, even though there wasn't much of a chance she could possibly forget to buy brie. Somehow, all this planning and prospect of "doing" calmed her nerves as she set out that late afternoon.

The Taurus was running a little throaty, which set her on edge. But by the time she purchased the G-13 clones at a dispensary outside of Paradox, and secured all of her items at the grow store, the old car seemed to be happily purring. Betty arrived at the farmers' market, list in hand, and grabbed a plastic basket at the front community table before dodging the megaphone cacophony that had become a regular nuisance, thanks to the strident members of the COLORADO ACTIVISTS 4 NATIONAL TOLERANCE. Checking her list, she went from booth to booth, chitchatting with the vendors and feeling the tremors of that day gradually melt away. By the time she had the basket filled with her farm-fresh treasures, she was able to step back and realize she could indeed work with Jean, and perhaps get past the anticipated fear.

Betty set her basket on the front table, carefully removing each bag, when she heard someone call her name. She turned and saw Judi, Renée and Helen entering the market. Her stomach clamped down in an unexpected *thud*.

"Long time no see, stranger," Judi said, her tone a little testy.

Betty set the empty basket back onto the stack. "Oh, it hasn't been that long."

"Damn near a month since I last saw you at the house," Judi replied.

"I'll see your month and raise you a week," Renée countered. "The last time we crossed paths was right after the A.A. potluck in early June."

Betty was still amazed how Renée always seemed to time events in her life in relationship to the various A.A. or other addiction meetings that continued to rule her daily existence.

Helen piped up. "I can't really remember when I saw you last," she scowled. "Ever since I had that damn nasal polyp removed, everything's a blur."

Betty suddenly felt as if she were back in Texas in 1969, being confronted by the insufferable girls who didn't win the Homecoming Queen title. From somewhere deep inside, the cattiness she had long abandoned re-emerged. "Well, Helen, at least you're enjoying that beautiful scarf Renée so generously gave you."

Helen adjusted the green and black, paisley sheer scarf around her neck. "Yeah. I dropped some food on it the other day but I can't find the damn stain in all this confusing design."

Yes, Betty mused. Naming her difficult plant "Helen" was a good choice.

Renée bristled. "Enough with the scarf, for God's sake," she mumbled.

Several vendors moved toward them, returning baskets to the table. The shrill voice of one of the activists blared forth on the megaphone, drowning out any chance of further conversation. It was the first time Betty was actually thankful for the group's timely intervention.

"I do expect you to see you at Roger's annual summer party in early August!" Judi yelled above the ruckus. "Please don't disappoint me on that one." Her voice was visibly desperate. "It's a goddamned tradition, like it or not! But we also have your birthday before that."

The megaphone chanting by the activists gained auditory steam. Betty had already promised to spend her birthday with Jeff at his house. Now was the perfect time to launch that announcement. And yet, she faltered. "I'm going out of town for my birthday weekend," she yelled above the noise. "Couple nights away to...reflect."

The women looked at Betty as if she just told them she was heading to Trinidad, Colorado for a sex change operation.

Helen leaned closer to Renée and spoke in a stage whisper. "What in the hell is she doing?"

"Ditching us!" Renée declared, grabbing a basket and heading into the market.

"Bitching us?" Helen asked, also grabbing a basket and following Renée.

It was just Judi and Betty. And the incessant blare of an undernourished broad screaming on the megaphone about tolerance.

Judi slid a basket toward her and moved closer to Betty. Her face was shaded in sadness. "I liked the way our friendship used to be. What happened to the Betty I've always loved and depended on?"

Judi walked into the crowd as a group of families descended around Betty, grabbing baskets and making their way into the market. In the midst of the crowd and unremitting noise from the activists, she thought she heard her name called out. Betty turned but all she saw was an ocean of people. She started to walk out when she reached for her list. In that instant, she realized she'd left it in her basket. Her heart began to pound as she thought about what was written on that list, along with her gold-embossed name and phone number shining at the top. Betty pushed through the crowd to the table but someone had taken her basket. She stood there, shell-shocked, as her worst fear was taking form. Which one of them grabbed it and saw that list?

Jeff called later to check in. She didn't tell him about the debacle at the market, because she knew exactly what he'd tell her and she didn't want to hear it. But there was also a bit of shame involved that she didn't speak up and tell her friends about him. Perhaps because of that, she told Jeff she wanted to be alone that night. But as night approached and twilight swallowed the light, she wished she hadn't been so hasty in asking for solitude. That vexing sense of being unmoored wrapped around her body, as her worries were set adrift in murky water. The phone rang and she checked the Caller ID, desperately hoping it was Jeff again. But the return number showed only: PRIVATE. She let it ring through to voicemail but the moment her recording said, "You've reached the Craven residence," the caller hung up. It wasn't unusual to get hang up calls but then again, it wasn't normal for Betty to leave a handwritten list in a basket outlining "Cannabis Supplies" with her phone number and name on it. She started to walk away when the phone rang again. She stood there nearly dazed as that damned word, PRIVATE, glared on the Caller ID. Betty reached for the phone and then pulled away, letting it go to voicemail again. And just like the first time, the minute her voicemail recording began, the caller quickly hung up. Her mind did somersaults, going over the possibilities of who could be on the other end. Her friends' names all showed up when they called, but surely Judi and Renée knew how to switch it over to PRIVATE if they wanted to hide their name. But why would they do that? Perhaps the person who picked up the list was harassing her? Paranoia suddenly arrived on time and decided to stay for the night.

Betty checked all the doors and locked all the windows as a hot wind blew outside. It was, as they say in Colorado every summer, "the warm before the storm." She puttered around the house, looking in on the three new G-13 girls and telling them how beautiful they were. Before the lights went out at eight o'clock in the bloom room, she dutifully checked for any sign of a bud, even though it had only been seven hours since the last time she looked.

Pellets of rain began striking the sliding glass door as Betty bid her girls a goodnight. As she firmly closed the bloom room door, a clap of thunder hit hard above the house. Twenty minutes later, as she was leaning over, transplanting the clones into their pots, a deluge began to fall that drowned out the adagio playing in the veg room. By the time Betty got back upstairs in the kitchen an hour later, the wind was whipping violently, sending gusts of perhaps 40 mph across the backyard. The old canopy elm stood strong, but several of the larger branches bent against the raging storm. When she walked into her bedroom, the largest branch that always tapped her windowpane was making creaking noises that sounded like an old bureau scraping against a wooden floor. There was a blinding flash of lightning, followed by a huge boom of thunder and the lights went out. Betty inched across the bedroom until she found the flashlight in her bedside table. Outside, it was like a war zone as smaller branches from the elm tore off the tree and slammed against the house.

Betty swung the flashlight to the bed where Ronald slept quietly. Checking him, she saw he was sound asleep, unaware of upheaval just a few yards outside his domain. Betty slid under the covers, bracing herself for each pounding crack of thunder. One particularly shocking explosion of sound was punctuated by a punishing fracture that caused Betty to sit upright in bed. Turning on the flashlight, she cast it toward the window. Something looked different, so she got up and moved toward the window in measured steps. As the glare of lightening flashed across the backyard, Betty saw the damage. The old branch on the tree had cracked off the trunk and was lying across the backyard. Little by little, more of the smaller branches followed suit, piling up like dead soldiers on the suburban battlefield. There was nothing she could do but stand there at the window, watching the destruction unfold, hoping the old tree wouldn't come down completely.

It took another half hour before the storm subsided to a continuous rain. Betty retreated back to her bed, clutching the flashlight as if it were her only beacon of salvation. Somehow, she finally fell asleep but hovered close to waking as the sounds of hard rain occasionally roused her. About two hours later she awoke, and in the coal black room, saw high-beam streams of light crisscrossing above her head. Throwing back the covers, she grabbed her flashlight and found her Beretta Tomcat in the bedside drawer. Her heart pounded, as a million thoughts raced through her mind, none of them cheerful or ending well. She turned off the flashlight and inched toward the large window in the bedroom, peered out and saw three figures in her yard shining their lights into the basement. The power was still out, and her head reeled with the genuine possibility that some nefarious group was using this opportunity to break into her house. Visions of Molotov Cocktails and marauders, intent on stealing her plants and assaulting her, spun through her mind. Straight away, she told herself that someone of ill repute had found that list with her phone number, called the number to see if she was home, figured out where she lived and decided to make their move.

She glanced down again and clearly saw the three figures moving around her yard. They were dressed in all black. The glint of one of their flashlights appeared to show the quick image of a gun.

"Go around the front!" she heard a male voice announce.

Betty's gut clamped down. One of her worst fears was happening. She could dial 911, but then the jig would be up, and it would be plastered all over the papers that Betty Craven's house was broken into by thieves trying to steal her cannabis plants. The mere thought of that story on the front page of the *Paradox Press* sent her downstairs, Tomcat at the ready and waiting like a vigilante for them to break down her front door. Just when she thought her heart couldn't stand it any longer, she heard footsteps walk across the garden pathway and up to the door. She braced herself against the credenza, raised the gun and said a prayer.

Chapter 26

"You can't be sure until it's dried and cured."

Betty held her breath as the shadow of one of the intruders crossed in front of the front door. She steadied the .32 with both hands. Suddenly, one of them pounded rapidly on her front door five times.

"Police! Open up!"

Betty froze. What in the hell was happening?

"Police!" a man's voice yelled.

Betty laid the Tomcat on the credenza and walked to the door, opening it slowly.

Three cops stood outside, flashlights cast toward her face. She moved her hand to her eyes, to shade against the extreme glare. "I'm Betty Craven. What's going on?" she asked breathlessly.

"We got a 911 call regarding a domestic disturbance," the officer stated.

"That wasn't me," she said, but her voice was shaky and scared.

"Ma'am, if you need some help, please tell us," the second officer demanded, shining his flashlight into the living room window.

"No, really sir. I didn't make the call."

"Are you Theresa Hamilton?"

Betty's mind spun for a moment. "No...Jerry and Theresa live across the street." She pointed to Jerry's house.

The lead cop turned around. "Sorry to bother you, ma'am. With the power out, it wasn't easy to see the address."

With that, they turned and walked with great purpose across the street to Jerry's house. Betty strolled toward her driveway and watched, as the scene unfolded against the red, blue and white flashing lights atop the police cruisers.

In astonishment, she watched the cops drag an extremely drunk Jerry out of his house, in nothing but his ball cap. She couldn't hear exactly what he was yelling, but she could tell his words were slurred. "Bitch" and "slut" were two of his favorites, as the officers cuffed him. His wife, Theresa, stood in the front door light, holding her hand over her left eye and bawling.

"Keep him away from me!" Theresa screamed, her voice echoing into the damp, summer night. "I'm filing a restraining order, you son-of-a-bitch!"

Betty stared in disbelief. As she walked back inside, the irony that she wasn't the only one on the block with a little secret didn't escape her.

The following day she called Jeff, who promised he'd show up after work with his chainsaw. Fortunately, the power came back on by 2:00 am, allowing the grow lights to pop back on so they didn't go off their cycle. Betty adjusted the timers and breathed a sigh of relief that everything – at least at that moment – was copasetic.

Buddy was also called into action to replace missing shingles on the roof from the wind and tree damage. When Jeff arrived, Buddy was still there, diligently repairing a bent gutter crushed by the tree. Betty went out to meet him and was shocked to see him drive up in an old Ford pickup with a bashed-in passenger door.

"You own a truck?" she asked, kissing him as they walked through the back gate.

"No. I just rented it to impress you," he replied with that familiar sly smile, as he carried the chainsaw into the backyard.

Buddy looked up and nodded to Jeff, wiping his brow.

Betty put her arm around Jeff. "Buddy, I didn't formally introduce you before. This is my very good friend, Jeff." She kissed him quickly on the lips as if to punctuate her statement.

"How ya doin'?" Buddy said before going back to work.

Jeff fired up the chainsaw and leaned closer to Betty, speaking above the roar of the saw. "See? That wasn't so hard?" He kicked a branch out of the way. "'Very good friend,' huh? Baby steps, Betty. Baby steps."

Betty insisted on giving Buddy twenty chocolates for his long hours of labor, figuring he'd be in need of pain relief and a good night's sleep after climbing around all day on her roof. Jeff stayed the night, and that wonderful feeling of being moored to a safe harbor resonated within her. They made love before dinner, and then sat out in the backyard, amidst the freshly cut logs, and enjoyed an orgy of organic offerings from the farmers' market. Twice, she nearly mentioned the missing list to him, along with the strange hang-up calls, but stopped short each time. Instead, she regaled him with tales of her false bravado, as she crept downstairs with the Tomcat the previous night. After a space of silence as they watched the sun set behind a luminous cloud, Betty finally told him about finding the pound of cannabis stashed in the attic.

"I saw Frankie in a dream," she related with hesitation. "I see him a lot that way. He placed his palm right over the area in the wall where the cannabis was hidden."

Jeff took her hand and kissed it. "It's almost as if he purposely put it there so you would find it later. Kind of like he knew you'd be needing it."

"How is that even possible?"

"I've stopped asking questions like that, babe. The older I get, the more I question how much free will we really have. When you look back on your life, you can easily see the points that led you toward the things or people that brought you closer to your purpose. I think a lot of us have a soul's purpose in this life. Somewhere deep down we recognize it, but I think we fight against it in order to maintain some mind-numbing social standing, or to carry out the expectations of others. I've always felt that when a person is depressed or restless, it's because an inner voice is trying to bore through and tell them they're off track and not paying attention to the reason they were born. When you're doing what you love and it loves you back, you know it in your heart. The mind will screw you every single time, and will make you question what your heart knows is right."

"Frankie told me to 'pay attention' when I saw him before he died. He says the same words to me when I dream about him. I'm just not sure what I'm supposed to be paying attention to."

Jeff looked at her. "You're not?"

"If you know, please tell me."

He chuckled. "I'm not in control of your destiny."

She looked into his eyes. "Are you part of my destiny?"

"I don't know. You haven't told me yet."

~~~

Two weeks later, Peyton called Betty to let her know it was time to harvest twelve of his plants. "It's going to be a long day," he warned her, after asking her to show up at eight in the morning. She was there five minutes early as usual, and along with her pristine titanium trimming scissors, she brought breakfast crêpes and a cooler filled with arugula and pine nut salad, a roast beef and red pepper quiche and *non*-cannabinized chocolate cake. When Pops unpacked the cooler to put the food in the refrigerator, he did a little jig of joy.

"That's a high compliment, Betty," he told her. "Pops usually does that dance only when the new phone book shows up."

He brought her down into his basement and into a separately draped area, cloaked in darkness. Peyton explained what he had done during his pre-harvest ritual. He took the plants earmarked for harvest and flushed them thoroughly with fifteen or more gallons of water, to pull out any accumulated salts in the soil. He then gave them a tablespoon of blackstrap molasses, mixed in one gallon of water. (Betty recalled that during the entire bloom cycle, it was beneficial to add a regular treat of molasses to the nutrient regimen. It built a thriving herd of microorganisms in the soil, which returned the favor by unlocking the available nutrients and nourishing the developing buds.) After Peyton doused the soil with the blackstrap molasses rinse, he waited three days, keeping them under the bloom lights. He explained that this helped trigger the final thrust of sugars in the plant. After that, he put the plants into a completely darkened room, which hovered between sixty-eight and seventy degrees Fahrenheit, for forty-eight hours. During that time, he deprived them of water. While it sounded torturous, Peyton explained it put the cannabis plants into "survival mode." They know they are about to die, so in a last ditch effort to excel, they release an increased amount of resin into the bud and surrounding leaves. "It's like the last gasp before death," he told Betty. "And in that gasp they give up everything, so we can benefit from their sacrifice."

"Sounds religious," Betty offered.

"Nah. It's *spiritual*. Everything about this plant is spiritual. And magical. Haven't you noticed that, Betty? How the magic – all the stuff you can't explain – tends to seep into your life the more you nurture and use the cannabis plant?"

"Yes," she said softly. "Actually, I have noticed that."

"Isn't that a beautiful thing? You can't explain it to anyone who hasn't had the good fortune of knowing this plant from birth to death. It reminds me that there's a loving God. I don't think you can be an atheist and grow good cannabis. I can always tell if I ingest cannabis grown by an atheist. It still might work, but it's missing part of its heart. Does that make sense?"

Betty nodded. "Amazingly, it does."

In keeping with Peyton's reverence for his cherished plants, he demonstrated how he brought each one out separately, and before removing the first branch, thanked it for everything it had given him and everything it would provide to others who were in need.

"It knows it's about to die," he whispered to Betty, getting somewhat emotional. "But it's not afraid, because deep down it knows, from the moment it's born, it has a noble purpose in death." He turned back to the four-foot-tall, fragrant, resinous beauty. "Thank you. You've been a faithful friend. I hope I've been the same to you." And with that, he clipped several of the lower branches off the rootstalk.

Betty actually felt herself choking up as his clippers cut through the hard, fibrous stems. There was such finality to it all, but the necessary death heralded a fruitful afterlife.

They carried the plant upstairs, and seated under the brilliant rays of the summer sun in Peyton's fenced backyard, they proceeded to patiently trim the sticky buds. First, they removed the larger fan leaves. The leaves closest to the resinous buds often had a generous spray of white "sugar" on them, compliments of whatever the buds spit out. Peyton set those aside, along with the healthy larger fan leaves, for one of his patients, who found that extracting the juice from the leaves and drinking it in shot-glass doses reduced her lupus symptoms. "There's no high from the juice," Peyton told Betty. "Even if you juice a raw bud, there's no high. You gotta use heat to convert the THC into its psychoactive form."

The trimming lesson continued for the first hour. There were new terms to learn. A "tight trim" removed nearly all the smaller leaves that protruded from the individual buds, going so far as to painstakingly work the tips of the scissors around each resinous flower. A "loose trim" was more forgiving, leaving the sugar-saturated leaf tips around the bud, while removing any dead or dying growth. Peyton always opted for a loose trim, because he didn't want to miss any of the strongly beneficial compounds found in the surrounding leaf tips.

Then there was "wet trimming" versus "dry trimming." Wet trimming was what they were doing – harvesting the plant and immediately cutting and pruning the buds, as opposed to cutting the plant down by the rootstalk and hanging it to dry, before coming back a week or more later to trim. Peyton had done one dry trim in his life and said he would never do it again. "It's like trying to cut through a kudzu patch in Florida, in the middle of August. Good damn luck!"

As with anything Betty put her mind to, she quickly picked up the proper technique and proudly showed off her buds and "their cute little haircuts." It took them nearly ninety minutes per plant to meticulously trim and hang the stems in an outdoor shed Pops helped Peyton build expressly for drying the buds. They dropped the fresh, healthy fan leaves into paper bags and stored them in the refrigerator for delivery to Peyton's lupus patient. As the hours passed, one thing became blatantly clear to Betty: it was like working at *The White Violet*, surrounded by chocolate. At first, you think to yourself how incredibly wonderful it is, and then the reality of making and handling all that chocolate becomes somewhat overpowering and an assault on the senses. She felt the same thing after six plants and nine hours of head-down labor. The novelty wore off fast, and the reality of how much work was involved became clearly apparent. She only took breaks to grab some food, use the bathroom, stretch and remove the brown "finger hash" that accumulated on the edges of her titanium blades and fingertips. Peyton showed her how to carefully roll the brown, gummy concentrate off her fingertips. Then he employed a clean razor blade to remove it off the used blade. Finally, he gingerly rolled the sticky resin into a ball, placed it into a plastic baggie and labeled it. Ingesting or smoking that, Peyton assured her, was not for beginners, as it had a higher THC and CBD content. However, if someone needed heavy pain relief, it was the quickest way to "get from point 'A' to hallelujah."

Peyton illuminated Betty with the critical final process of drying and curing the bud. After hanging in the darkened shed for up to ten days, the bud was ready when the stem could be easily snapped. The dried buds were then meticulously snipped off the stem, placed in glass mason jars no more than three-quarters full and stored in the dark. "Light and air are two enemies of dried bud," he instructed her. But there was more. Once a day, the jars had to be "burped," which entailed gently shaking the dried buds back and forth, and then opening the lid for several minutes to allow any moisture to escape. If the bud was too dry, one could place a single, healthy, fresh fan leaf in the tightly sealed jar overnight. Another option was to put an apple slice into the sealed jar. The next day, the apple would be removed after it had imparted both moisture and a pleasant scent to the curing buds. But nothing was guaranteed until the cannabis was completely cured, which could take up to five months for certain strains, or as few as three weeks for others. "You can't be sure until it's dried and cured," Peyton advised Betty, rattling off one of his original cannabis rhymes.

"These are so beautiful, Peyton," Betty exclaimed, bringing out her cell phone. "I'm going to take a photo."

"Uh, no way, dude. No photos, ever. No matter how legal you and I are, you don't want to risk the wrong people finding those photos and hassling you."

Betty nodded and put away her phone. His comment brought back the sobering realization that someone out there had her cannabis list and contact information. She briefly considered telling Peyton the troubling tale but refrained.

"I swear the only people who look forward to trimming these nuggets are old hippies living in the Emerald Triangle," Peyton related, skimming a sticky, BB-sized ball of resin off his scissors with the blade. "Those dudes live for harvest season every fall. But when you grow indoors and you got your rotation in full swing, you're trimming four or more times a year, so it's more like a job." He took a quick bite of Betty's chocolate cake. "But then I look on the bright side and see this as an opportunity to get all Zen and let my mind travel." He held his stem closer to examine the top bud. "You know that saying, 'if life gives you lemons, make lemonade?' Well, is the lemonade sweet? Because if it isn't, why is sour lemonade going to quench unhappiness? And another thing, I know a fool and his money are soon parted. But I think it's because a fool and his money are soon partied out. And why don't they have greeting cards for bartenders? Or plumbers? It's an untapped market. These are the kind of things I think about after a few hours of trimming."

After several minutes, Betty piped up. "What do your parents think of all this?"

"My dad just shakes his head in disgust and disappears into the garage. My mom pretends it doesn't exist. Just like she pretends I don't exist. Just like she pretends Pops doesn't exist."

"Why?"

"Because we're different and that scares her. We see the world through cannabis eyes, in different colors and shades, and she can't relate to it. Pops was always considered an odd fellow, but his inventions gave my mom a pretty decent life growing up. She was always embarrassed by his eccentricities. In my family, the originality skips a generation, so she knew going into it that I had the potential of being just as peculiar as Pops. And when that became obvious to her, she didn't handle it well. If you're different in my family, you're considered difficult. You require more attention, and my mom and dad weren't able, or willing, to offer it. My parents didn't want me to stand out. They just wanted me to fit in. But I couldn't do that. I was labeled 'A-D-D', whatever in the hell that is. Personally, I think some chemist made up the disorder, so he could score some big money off all the leftover 'speed' in his lab."

He admired his bud handiwork and picked up the next stem. "So I got to experience all the crazy drugs the FDA allows kids to take – all the ones that dull your senses and make life feel like one monotonous TV test pattern. By the time I was fifteen, I thought that if this was what life was all about, what was the point? Then some dude at school gave me a joint, and suddenly everything changed. I realized I wasn't difficult. I didn't have a learning disability. I was as creative as Pops, and if you put the right project in front of me, I was unstoppable." He put down the stem and turned to Betty. "You see, cannabis just expands who you really are and what you can understand. If you're creative and clever, it can take you to another level. But if you're stupid and shallow, there's a good chance you'll just be more stupid and shallow. That's why it's not for everyone. But when it's the right fit, like it was for me...shit...it's like gold. But it came with a price. The more I rebelled against the humdrum, boring life, the more my parents pushed me away, until I said, 'that's okay.' I'd rather live my life honestly, than spend it adapting to what others think I should be."

Betty took a break from trimming. "How in the hell did you figure that out so young?"

He grinned. "I'm different, remember? We tend to understand things at a younger age than others who live inside the box."

Betty contemplated his words. "I can't argue with that one, Peyton. Well, I guess as the old saying goes, what doesn't kill you makes you stronger."

"I tend to think that whatever doesn't kill you, makes you bitter and overly cautious. But that's just me." He stood up, snipped another stem off the plant and sat back in his chair. "I've come to look on myself like a cat, Betty."

"A cat?"

"Yeah. I think there comes a time in every cat owner's life, when they look at their cat and say, 'I wish you could do more. All you do is catch mice, sleep, take a dump, drink water and eat. Too bad you can't lift heavy objects, drive me to the airport or fix me a meal.' And the cat thinks, 'I do what I do. This is who I am. This is what a cat *is*.' They're not out to prove they're anything but who they are. And most importantly, they don't give a shit what you or I think. They just go along catching mice, sleeping, take a dump, drink water and eat. They're comfortable in their fur and make no apologies for what they can't or won't do. That's me, Betty." He turned to her. "And I never thought I'd find another cat just like me. But then you introduced me to Yarrow." He leaned closer, speaking in confidence. "She calls me her 'honeydude.' She thinks like I do. We share some of the same fears, but she's determined to overcome them. So that makes me want to overcome mine too. I can be myself around her, and it makes me feel like I'm finally home. You know what I mean?"

Betty's eyes misted over. "Yes. I do."

"If it weren't for you, Betty. I never would have met her. Thank you."

She placed her palm on Peyton's arm. "No, Peyton. Thank you for giving me a chance to make it right again."

Betty didn't get home that night until after nine o'clock, and after checking on her girls with only the surreal light of the green headlamp, she was ready to head to bed when a car pulled up in her driveway. She peeked out of the front window just as Renée walked across the front path. It wasn't like Renée to show up unexpected, unless of course, she was the one who found Betty's list in the basket. Betty's heart did a little sprint as she opened the front door.

"You and I need to talk," Renée curtly said, striding into the house.

Betty closed the front door and prepared herself for the worst. "What is it?"

Renée started to speak, when she sniffed the air around her. "My God, Betty! It smells like pot in here!"

Betty froze. She'd sort of rehearsed what she'd say if this ever happened. And yet at that moment, she couldn't recall any of her clever retorts. "Pot?"

"*Yes. Pot.*" She moved closer to Betty. "Is it coming from you?"

Many women had a signature perfume that defined them. Betty suddenly realized that instead of Chanel No. 5, her twelve, long hours of trimming bud had obviously imbued her with Cannabis No. 1. She swallowed hard and started to speak, when Renée impatiently interrupted her.

"Aha!" Renée exclaimed, walking to the credenza. She swept up the complimentary lighter, with the smiling cannabis leaf Betty had been given when she purchased her first clones, and held it in the air. "This belongs to him, doesn't it?"

Betty felt that familiar sense of being cornered. It had been awhile since she'd experienced the sensation, and it wasn't setting well with her. "Him who?"

"Oh, for chrissake, Betty! You know exactly who I'm talking about!" She moved closer. "Peyton! Your little mentoring project? He's been here and he's been smoking grass, and you obviously weren't even aware of it!"

Something about Renée's tone emboldened Betty. "Perhaps...or maybe it's because I'm growing pot in my basement!"

Betty tried to decipher the strange look Renée shot her direction. It wasn't shock, but it wasn't appreciation either. After what seemed like an eternity, Renée pursed her lips and spoke up.

"That's not even remotely funny, Betty. Not one damn bit." She turned away, lost in her own world. Gradually, she came back into herself and looked around the living room quickly. "Your house feels different. Lonelier."

"Really? I think it feels more buoyant." Betty sauntered to the couch. "What is it you wanted to talk to me about?"

"The damn scarf I gave to Helen on her birthday! I don't understand why you insist on all the passive/aggressive digs."

"All two of them, you mean? And I certainly wouldn't characterize them as passive/aggressive, Renée. I'd color them more like a Texas jab with a pointy tip."

She ran her fingers nervously through her hair. "Call it whatever in the hell you want! I've got a lot on my plate right now, Betty. I don't need the added stress of your negativity toward me." There was definitely an increased restless intensity surrounding Renée. "As I was just saying to Cindy D. tonight at the meeting, it feels like time is speeding up and we're losing our ability to fully experience anything, because the next thing happens and then the next and so on." She seemed to be rotating in her own manic orbit. "How in the hell do you process anything anymore?" She looked up at Betty with desperation.

For some strange reason, Betty felt compassion for her irksome friend. "Maybe you should stop trying to process or experience everything, and just allow it to take its course?"

It appeared for one brilliant second that Renée was actually considering the idea. But then, her mouth turned down with a peevish expression. "*Allow it?* My God! That's it? That's your advice?!" She let out an exasperated sigh. "I can't *allow* it! Life is a fight, for God's sake. You, more than anyone, should understand that! If you don't fight, you can't overcome. And you have to overcome so much. All the shit that crowds inside your head and keeps you awake at night. All those voices telling you that you're no fucking good? That you'll never amount to anything?" She stared at Betty, slightly shaking. "You know what I mean, right? The stuff that makes you want to..." She stopped quickly and pulled herself together, as she walked across the living room.

As far as Betty was concerned, it didn't appear that Renée's nearly thirty-years of sobriety or weekly A.A. meetings had made any positive impact. She gave her a chance to calm down. "Renée, do you think it's possible to become addicted to A.A. meetings?"

Renée turned around. "*What?* What are you talking about?"

"I was just wondering. Do you think that's possible?"

"Are you all right?"

"I'm fine."

"No, really. Are you okay?"

Betty smiled and shrugged her shoulders. "Yes. Why wouldn't I be okay?"

"You're asking odd questions."

"Why is that odd?"

"I don't know. It just is."

"So? You think it's possible?" Betty asked.

"Is *what* possible?"

"Being addicted to A.A. meetings?"

Renée threw her hands in the air. "I don't even know how to answer that question! I'll ask my sponsor and see what she says."

"You still have a sponsor? Seriously?"

Renée caught sight of all the photos of Frankie that were on the credenza and propped up around the room. Betty observed, as her friend appeared overcome by them. "Why in the hell do you have all of these out?"

"Because I hid them in the drawer for too many years. He wants...he needs to be celebrated and not denied."

Renée silently took in several of the shots. She peered closely at the one on the credenza that Betty had taken an eraser to so long ago. "Is that a –"

"Joint? Yes. That's a joint between his fingers."

Renée picked up the photo and gazed at it with what looked like trepidation. "How do you stand it? Look at him. So much heartache. Like a wall that can never be climbed." She turned to Betty. "You need to put all of these away. Why voluntarily put yourself through hell again?" Renée set the photo facedown and walked to the front door. "He could never be enough, could he? I know the feeling."

Betty stood there for several minutes after she left. Emotion balled in her throat as she moved to the credenza and turned over the photo of Frankie. The familiar grief began to swell again, but right before it overtook her, the phone rang. She walked into the kitchen and checked the Caller ID. There was that damned PRIVATE staring back at her. She started to pick up the phone, but let it go to voicemail. And on cue, whoever was on the other end of the line quickly hung up.

Chapter 27

"As I've grown older, I prefer to state my age in Celsius."

"Our girls are becoming women!" Betty enthusiastically told Peyton. He was the first person she called, right after opening the bloom room door and spying a spray of white tendrils a little over a quarter inch tall. They only appeared on the Kushberry plants, but they'd always been ahead of the curve, towering in height nearly twelve inches over the other girls in the bloom room. But then Betty noticed the telltale sign of an emerging series of buds along the top nodes of the Centennial Blueberry plants.

It was official. The cannabis' plain-Jane, weed-like, vegetative appearance was beginning its powerful transformation into a potent, budding plant. Betty marked the momentous day on her *High Times* calendar. And as she said to herself, one never forgets the first time they see the buds forming on their first homegrown cannabis plant. She desperately wanted to capture the moment on film but reminded herself of Peyton's warning about taking photos of her girls. Instead, she would etch the moment into her mind's eye and hope that age and mental decline later in life would not erase it from her memory bank.

It was the Wednesday before her birthday weekend, and she had a lot to do before Saturday, when she'd meet Jeff at his house for a two-night visit. She started out mixing up a new trashcan full of llama bean tea. Then, she transplanted her young clones into two-gallon pots and foliar sprayed them with B-vitamins, kelp and a wee bit of enzymes. After that, she fed her blooming girls with the phosphorus-rich bat guano liquid and blackstrap molasses. Betty mused she was busier than a cat trying to cover up its crap on a marble floor. The remainder of the day was spent making sixty of her gourmet chocolates, each with their trademark decorative silver and gold swirls she'd perfected with artistic precision. Thankfully, Peyton gave her nearly four ounces of potent, sweet leaf shake in exchange for her long hours of dutiful, trimming labor. With almost three ounces left of the valuable L.A. Confidential bud she found in the attic, Betty felt confident she'd have enough to fulfill her patients' needs until her first crop of girls matured.

Buddy dropped by early in the day to continue work on the initial roof project that seemed to be going on *ad infinitum*. Finding several more integrity issues in the roof near the front of the house, Betty came to the conclusion that her aging house was quickly becoming a dark hole into which she threw money – or in Buddy's case, cannabis chocolates. As John Muir stated, "When one tugs at a single thing in nature, he finds it attached to the rest of the world." Similarly, tug on one thing in an old, deteriorating house like Betty's, and you'd easily trip over ten more things that needed to be upgraded. She boxed up twenty-five of the chocolates, all fully decorated, and handed them to Buddy as he left.

"You don't have to waste one of your fancy boxes and ribbons on me, Mrs. Craven."

"*Betty*," she insisted. "Please call me Betty from now on."

He looked a little uncomfortable. "Uh...okay...Betty."

"And that box and ribbon is not wasted on you, Buddy. Everyone deserves to be given something that helps to remind them there's still elegance and graciousness in this unsettling world. It's like a cup of chamomile tea in the middle of a battle zone."

The next day, she arrived at Jean's house as requested, with a cooler full of fourteen chocolates. Arthur met Betty at the door and told her that Jean wasn't having a good day and had retired to bed. Then Jean called out to Betty from the upstairs bedroom and asked her to come and see her. Betty would have normally bowed out, but found herself walking up the stairs, in spite of her unease.

Jean sat up in bed, her head covered with her jaunty purple scarf, and held her arms out to Betty. "Betty! I'm so glad to see you!"

They hugged, and Betty sat on the edge of the bed. "You just like me for my chocolates," she joked.

"I like you both." She looked over Betty's shoulder, where Arthur hovered in the doorway. "It's okay, hon. Why don't you lie down? Betty can keep me company."

Arthur smiled a sad smile and walked downstairs.

Jean teared up. "He's trying so hard to stay strong." Wiping her eyes with the bed sheet, she sat up a bit more in bed. "I'm not having a good day."

Betty tapped the bed. "I can go and come back later –"

"No, no, no!" She held her arm. "You're afraid. I get it. But it's okay. I'm not dying today, Betty." Jean released Betty's arm. "You can double the strength on the next batch. I'm doing two of your candies now to get the same pain relief."

Betty helped Jean with the pillows behind her back. "We should contact your doctor."

"What's my doctor going to do? Pump me full of morphine so I'm constipated for a week? No, thanks. Your chocolates are working beautifully, and they don't shut off my plumbing!" She nestled comfortably into the soft pillows. "I don't want to be out of it. Even when it's time, I don't want to be pumped full of anything. I want to feel the ride at the end. That way, I can open my eyes on the other side and know it's not a hallucination...that I really, truly finally cut the cord and took the leap."

Betty did everything to maintain her composure. "You're so very brave."

"This is not bravery, Betty. This is just part of life. Do you tell a mother who just gave birth how brave her baby is? Birth and death, it's all part of the deal each time we agree to give it another shot." She reflected for a moment. "It's not the dying, you know? It's the living...that's when you've got to be brave. I should not have been so afraid. I should have spoken up more. I shouldn't have cared so much about what people thought of me. When you're forced to lie in a bed like this, all you do is think. And that's what you think about. All the 'should have's.'"

Betty rested her hand on Jean's arm. "Don't 'should' all over yourself. That's what my friend...Jeff...that's what he tells me all the time."

Jean smiled. "You're right." She smiled a mischievous grin. "And I know that Jeff is more than a 'friend.' When the two of you came by here the first time? It was clear as a bell. You two make a great couple. You and he have an extraordinary connection."

Betty felt somewhat overexposed. "Well...uh..." She traced the carpet with her foot, unable to put two intelligible words together.

"Look at you! You're like a schoolgirl. I love it! That's beautiful, Betty. Hey," she tapped her on the leg to make eye contact. "Don't ever lose that. It's worth more than all the money in the world."

"He and I come from very different walks of life," Betty said with a self-conscious shrug of her shoulders.

"So? Who cares? Arthur and I came from opposite sides of the fence. He was very straight-laced and I was a free spirit. But over time, he grounded me and I lifted him up. So it was a good pairing. We have the same deep connection you and Jeff have. That's why I worry about Arthur after I'm gone." She lost herself momentarily before shifting her focus. "You know, I was reading this article the other day about the top five regrets of the dying. The number one regret? Wishing they had more courage to live life true to themselves and not the life others expected them to live."

The comment hit Betty hard. "Is that right?"

"And I emphatically agree. We need to be the gatekeeper of our own destiny. To waste one's life doing what others expect of them and denying one's own dreams..." Jean paused, reflecting on her thoughts. "No one ever understands how the soul can hurt when you're pushing yourself into shoes that don't fit."

Betty nodded. "Amen."

Jean turned and looked out the window, as sunlight washed the bedroom in a soft glow. "When you're young, you pray for material things. Then when you're a little older, you pray for money, success and to find love. Then life happens and you get sick or have an accident, and you pray for health. And then, if it all turns to hell, you have your dark night of the soul. You feel outside of yourself and fear rules your every move...that's if you can even make a move, because you're so paralyzed with apprehension. And so you pray again. But this time you pray to feel peace. Just sweet peace. If you're smart, you realize you should have been praying for that since the beginning, because without peace, there is no success or good love or health. And all the 'stuff' you started out praying for? That's pointless. But you only really understand this when the world falls apart around you. Enlightenment, Betty. Too bad it usually has to come with such a steep price."

~~~

Friday night, Jeff called Betty to tell her he had a surprise for her birthday weekend. "Pack comfortable, casual clothes and shoes," he advised her. Jeff then emailed her a remote address, along with a MapQuest link to the location. She was to meet him there at 11:00 in the morning the following day. After studying the directions, Betty had no idea where she was going. All she knew was that it was nearly thirty miles southwest of Paradox and appeared to be nestled in a semi-rural, mountainous area. Part of her wished they could just keep the birthday festivities at his house, but another part of her wondered what in the hell he had planned.

She'd already arranged with Peyton to check in twice a day to feed and pet Ronald and take care of her girls. It was one thing to have a pet that needed to be cared for when one went on a vacation; it was certainly another hurdle altogether when you also had a bevy of thriving cannabis plants needing constant attention. Clearly, this commitment put the *kibosh* on lengthy vacations, unless one had a trusted friend to take care of the green beauties. "Thank God for

Peyton," Betty said to herself, realizing other people in her situation weren't as lucky to have someone so faithful and discreet. After handing Peyton a spare house key Saturday morning, she tossed her two bags into the Taurus and set off to destinations yet unknown. Even without the benefit of visiting the location for a dry run, Betty still arrived five minutes early. But when she put the Taurus in park, she wondered if she'd made a wrong turn. After ascending a two-lane, asphalt road for nearly two miles and only passing four houses, the road turned to dirt and ended in a cul-de-sac that overlooked an astonishing, panoramic, mountainous landscape. The air was sweet and warm and so still that Betty could hear the sound of a creek in the distance. Within a few minutes, another sound fused into the silence, growing with intensity as it moved closer. She turned to see Jeff on his motorcycle, driving down a narrow, one-lane road that fed into the cul-de-sac. Behind his seat was a hard-shell saddle trunk.

"I should have known you'd beat me here," he said, leaning over and kissing Betty. "Where are your bags?"

"In the backseat," she said apprehensively.

He got off the bike to retrieve her luggage.

"Hang on!" she said with hesitation. "Where are we going?"

"Up the dirt road I just came down."

She peered toward the road. "That's driveable. Come on, let's take the Taurus."

Jeff locked the Taurus and was already halfway to his bike with her two bags. "Nah, it can get kinda soupy where the shade hits the wet dirt." He attached her bags to the back of the trunk with a bungee cord. "Get on," he said, motioning to the Harley.

"I'm not getting on that, Jeff." She held her ground.

"Well, if you don't, you won't experience the next great adventure in your life."

She peered up the desolate road. "Unless there's a five-star resort perched at the top of that hill, with linen tablecloths, napkins and monogrammed fluffy towels, I don't see this progressing any further."

He screwed his face into an extremely pensive expression. "Hmmm. Linen tablecloths and fluffy towels – that's a pretty unlikely possibility given this territory. I'll tell you this: there's no five-star resort up there, but there's a ten-star view." He got on the bike. "Elizabeth Cragen doesn't ride bikes. Betty Craven tries it at least once." He tipped his head toward the roomy seat. "Come on, Betty. Give it a shot."

Anyone else...*anyone else*, and she would have said a re-sounding "no." But his subtle charm and calming manner drew her in each time. It was pointless to fight it. With great care and anxiety edging close, she straddled the sun-blasted, black leather seat and wrapped her arms tightly around his waist. "Go slowly, please."

"Aw, can't I do some cool stunts I've been practicing?" he asked her, his voice obviously dripping with sarcasm.

They drove up the dirt road softened by a top layer of decomposed aspen leaves. The densely packed forest featured chalky-barked aspens that stood like thin sentinels and co-mingled with the occasional aromatic spruce tree. The scent of the high mountain woods intoxicated Betty's senses. Above her head, the brilliant, cloudless summer sky shone like a sapphire. She held tighter onto Jeff's waist and rested her head against his back. There was something so terrifyingly calm about it. God, it was comfortable. So exquisitely natural. However, just as she was falling into the moment, Betty wondered if it was okay. Where was the struggle in this relationship? Isn't that what life was all about? Continuous struggles that had to be overcome, and once conquered, the next challenge was introduced? How could this much happiness be self-sustaining? She was about to leap into the next level of anxiety, when he interrupted her dark projections.

"Hey, I came up with a couple riddles. What do you call a pre-owned Prius?"

The distraction was enough to bring her back to her senses. "No idea."

"A Previous!"

Betty smiled. "Well done!"

"What's another way to describe a really loud, protest march?"

Betty tried to figure it out and gave up. "Tell me."

"A din of inequity!"

She laughed. "I love it!" And she relaxed. All the conflicting voices in her head shut up, and the peace and quiet allowed Betty to take a breath and rest in that moment with abandon.

About one mile up the road, Jeff slowed and crossed a wooden bridge on the right hand side that sheltered a twenty-foot-wide, slow-moving creek. The landscape quickly opened, as they drove up a short hill and then came to a stop. There before her was a secluded expanse of nearly two grassy acres, edged with the meandering creek. A large tent, big enough to fit six adults, stood thirty feet from the water. In front of the tent, a stone barbeque pit waited patiently, along with two cushioned, Adirondack chairs. A pair of fishing poles tilted against the tent, next to two creels and hats. Next to the tent was a brass towel rack that looked completely out of place in this rustic setting. Draped over it, were two fluffy, monogrammed towels. On a flat piece of grassy ground closer to the creek, a small, round table sat covered in a crisp, linen tablecloth and two sharply folded linen napkins. A single copper lantern graced the center of the table, along with a bottle of unopened wine.

Betty was in awe, as she slid off the Harley. "What is all this?"

"Happy birthday, babe," he replied, moving around the bike and planting a passionate kiss on her lips. "I've got three coolers of food and drinks sitting in a cold mountain spring up on that ridge," he said, pointing to a shaded spot on the north side of the property. "There's a king-size, blow-up mattress inside the tent, that's more comfortable than the bed at your house. And *if* we get rain, there's a covered wooden shelter over that ridge we can retreat to. Did I forget anything?"

She couldn't stop taking it all in. "Nobody has ever taken the time to do something like this for me. I'm speechless."

"Are you happy?"

Betty nodded. "Beyond happy, if that's possible." She suddenly realized something. "How on earth did you get everything up here with only your bike?"

"I used my truck."

She pointed back to the road they just traversed. "But you told me –"

"I know exactly what I said. Now you can always say you rode a Harley for the first time, on the day before your fifty-ninth birthday. And best of all, nothing bad happened to you."

The old Betty would have become piqued by his sneaky strategy. But the new Betty was overwhelmed by his creativity and tasteful élan.

The property, he related, belonged to a friend who owned a summer retreat about a half-mile away. It was a homestead in the late 1800s, which morphed into a popular hunting camp, until twenty-five years ago when his friend purchased the land. Betty could easily see how anyone could fall in love with this exceptional slice of heaven.

"You hungry?" Jeff asked, moving toward a cooler on the other side of the tent.

"Not really."

"Okay, then." He brought two large water bottles out of the cooler and held his hand out to her. "Come on. Follow me."

They walked hand-in-hand over a gentle slope and across a spruce-shaded patch of ground that hugged the creek. The sound of water was everywhere, filling the air with a moist, earthy resonance. A series of steps, roughly carved into the side of the hill, ascended about another thirty feet higher. Moving in front of her, Jeff started up the steps, never letting go of her hand. The reward for the steep climb was enough to set Betty's mouth agape. Protected by a curved rock wall was a pristine thermal pool that stretched in a twenty-foot radius and overlooked miles of untouched forest and grassland.

Jeff held her close. "Isn't this one of the coolest places you've ever seen?"

She nodded as she took in the expansive view. "And rare as hen's teeth."

He took off his shirt and threw it across a rock. "Let's get in."

"But I didn't pack a bathing suit."

"You've never skinny dipped?"

Betty blushed. Perhaps it was the memory long ago when she was thirteen and crept over a hill in rural Texas during a vacation, only to find a teenage couple skinny-dipping in a river. Part of her thought it was offensive and part of her wished she could know what it felt like to be so free. She turned back to Jeff who already had his boxers off and was edging into the water. "This is private, right?"

"I know the owner. It's completely private."

With that, Betty undressed, carefully folding her clothes and setting them on a flat rock. She stepped into the thermal pool; the warmth penetrated every cell of her body. The freedom of being naked in that comforting heat enveloped her. Jeff pulled her toward him and kissed her. Amidst the sounds of birds, the steady breeze and the slow moving creek below, they made love.

"I love you, Betty," Jeff softly offered in the afterglow.

She rested her head on his chest. His words echoed in her veins, but she still hesitated.

"It's okay, babe," he gently said. "You don't have to respond."

Five minutes passed, with only the symphony of nature filling in the silence.

"I don't know how to get past it," she finally said in a tentative voice.

"Past what?"

"The fear. All the pain." She looked at him. "I think something is changing, though. I seem to be more open-minded than I used to be. I can look at the same situation and find new solutions I couldn't see before. And I understand what calmness feels like now. Not all the time, but feeling it even once is a big step for me. When you've been trained to wait for the other shoe to drop, it's mystifying when you fall for a barefoot lover."

He kissed her wet head. "I think whatever anyone does to handle pain should also allow them to move forward, and take part in life, instead of constantly focusing on keeping the pain away. Eventually you have to let go, move beyond merely coping and shift into the art of living. You can do it, Betty. All you have to do is allow it, and your life will instantly change."

That night, Betty enjoyed another new experience – raw oysters. A spicy, green salad filled with artichokes and hearts of palm came next, and after they finished their meal with a delicate tiramisu, the evening was capped with a roaring fire and another soak in the thermal pool before retiring to the roomy tent and blissful sleep."

The following morning, Jeff awakened Betty with a hot cup of coffee. He slid back under the sleeping bag. "Happy fifty-ninth birthday, babe."

"Fifty-nine," she mused quietly. "That's fifteen when you convert it to Celsius. As I've grown older, I prefer to state my age in Celsius. It's not as jarring."

He chuckled. "I talked to a gentleman once at my grandfather's nursing home. He was celebrating his one hundred and tenth birthday and I asked him what was the best thing about turning that age. 'Three words,' he said. 'No peer pressure.'"

It was clever retorts like that, that kept Betty enthralled. The spin of a word or a quick-witted mind was as sexy to her as a confident lover. The morning moved gracefully into the afternoon. They fished, made love, hiked along the many trails, soaked in the hot pool, made love and napped, before taking a strenuous stroll from the tent to the table by the creek. Betty enjoyed a glass of red wine, while Jeff poured himself a sparkling glass of spring water. The monogrammed towels hung across the low branches of a mountain mahogany shrub.

"You know, turning fifteen degrees Celsius wasn't as difficult as I expected," Betty announced with a serene grin. "I'd like to send a thank you card to your friend who owns this place. It was terribly generous of him to let us use it for my birthday."

Jeff sat back in his chair. "Well...you know my address..."

Betty was bowled over. "What? You said he owned a retreat –"

"He does. He fell onto hard times and needed some quick cash. I made him a ridiculous offer on this land, thinking he'd turn me down and he didn't. Signed the papers almost two weeks ago."

"My God! Just like that?"

"Just like that."

She sat back. "Wow. Are you going to build up here?"

"I don't think so. I kind of want to keep it as a camping retreat. But, you know, the soil here is incredible...Really rich humus and with that spring and the creek, plenty of water to irrigate. I'm thinking that right about there," he pointed to a semi-shaded plot, "would be the perfect place to grow a dozen or so cannabis plants next summer."

"Are you getting your red card too?"

"No, babe. The garden would be for you."

Betty looked across to the proposed plot. Her imagination immediately soared with visions of eight- to ten-foot-tall cannabis "trees" blowing in the wind. And then, as quickly as the visions ballooned, she let the air out. "Next summer is a long way off."

"It'll be here before you know it." He rested his hand on hers. "Hey, did you notice the monogrammed towels?" he asked.

"Of course."

"'C' for Carroll. But for that matter, it could be a 'C' for Craven." He leaned across the table toward her. "Move in with me."

Betty flushed nervously. "What? I...I...I can't. I have a house –"

"That's falling apart around you. You can't sell it until you pound a lot of money into it. Maybe it's time to think of other possibilities."

Her head was spinning, and she hadn't had a sip of wine. "We've only known each other fewer than three months. And part of that time wasn't in the religious sense –"

"We're good together, Betty," Jeff declared. "I love you. And I think when you push past all your fear and those damned voices in your head, you'll realize you might just love me too."

She felt herself falling and out of control. A haze of discordant thoughts raced through her head. "I can't...answer you right now."

Jeff looked a bit dispirited but nodded. "Think about it. That's all I ask."

She helped him pack up what was portable enough to carry on the Harley before eating an early dinner and heading down the aspen-lined road as the sun set that night. It was difficult to walk away from the magnificent beauty but part of her wanted to run fast and far, until she was safe in her reliable bubble of conventional predictability. It was all happening too fast. She began questioning every bit of progress she'd made. Maybe it was just delayed teenage rebellion. Perhaps she'd wake up in a few days or weeks and wonder what in the hell she was thinking. There was a peculiar comfort in the conformist's life. It expected nothing except allegiance to tedium and repetition. But this newer life she'd adopted had no boundaries, no fences, no chains. It expected her to trust in the unknown and leap into her future, without calculating whether she'd land on rock or clay. She had the power to erase every second of these last three months and retreat back into the dependable arms of disappointment.

They kissed goodbye and Betty set off down the twisting mountain road. With only her darkened thoughts to keep her company, her trip home was a long one. But the farther she drove, the more she felt his presence in that car. He was seated next to her, like he was when she'd sneak him out of the house as a child. But this time he wasn't resting his head on the door and holding his arm outside the passenger window to calm his troubled mind. He was staring straight ahead, fists balled and angry as hell. She never recalled feeling such ire coming from him before.

With her mind preoccupied, she turned onto the wrong road as darkness sucked the last bit of light from that warm July night. She drove another few miles before she realized she was lost. There she was on a rural, two-lane road and completely unable, for some strange reason, to find her way back. The more she tried to figure out a solution, the more confused she became. She was just about to turn the car around one more time, when the engine coughed like she'd never heard it hack before.

"Oh, God, no!" she exclaimed, her heart racing. "Please, please, *please*," she begged her Taurus, petting the dashboard, as if that would soothe the throaty irritation. "Not here! Not now!"

But the ol' sedan had other plans and stuttered to a quick, inglorious stop. Betty turned on the hazard lights and reached for her cell phone, but there was no service. Her mouth went dry. She got out of the car and peered down the ribbon of road in front of her. No houses or lights anywhere. She could walk back in the direction she came from, until her cell phone hooked up with a tower. But then, she thought, what if she just kept walking and her phone was still searching for service? Betty felt the walls crash around her. She turned back to her car and was just a few feet from it, when the headlights of a vehicle crested a distant hill and moved toward her. She stood in front of her car and waited, until a four-wheel-drive, black truck with exceptionally bright headlights cruised to a stop more than forty feet from her. She felt a shiver bleed down her spine, as the occupants remained inside for what seemed like an eternity. Gradually, both the driver and passenger doors of the truck opened. Two burly men ambled toward her. The driver was in his mid-thirties, over six feet tall, probably tipping the scale at close to three hundred pounds, and sporting a shaven head. As he moved closer, she could see he carried enough ink on his muscular arms to fill a small-town newspaper. His compatriot was a bit shorter but matched his friend in height, circumference and attitude.

For a birthday that started so beautifully, Betty was beginning to think it wasn't going to have a happy ending.

Chapter 28

"What in God's name is a 'Betty Bullet?'"

"Hey," the driver said in a remote tone. He tossed a look to his friend who started to move to the rear of Betty's car. "How you doin'?"

Betty stood as straight as possible and locked her knees so she wouldn't collapse from fear. She swung her left arm into the air with her palm out to halt their progress. "Stop right there!" she said in a resolute voice.

The men froze.

"My name is Betty Craven!" she yelled with razor sharp elocution. "I am the widow of the late Colonel Frank Craven. He was an extremely irrational man, who surrounded himself with other irrational men, as he served our great country on the battlefield. If I am found dead in a ditch and only my teeth are recovered, they will *still* be able to easily identify me by my exceptional dental records. And when news of my death is broadcast, the loyal men who served with my husband will extend the code of *semper fi* to their Colonel's wife and will rise from *every* corner. The two of you will be hunted down, not only by my ghost, but also by my husband's band of angry veterans, who all suffer from severe gout, enlarged prostates and night terrors. When they find you, your demise will be unforgiving and quite painful. Please ruminate on this before you take another step toward me."

The men looked at each other and took two huge steps backward.

"Uh, lady," the driver finally said. "This here is a tow truck. My name's Bert and that's my brother, Ernie."

Betty furrowed her brow. "Bert and Ernie? You've got to be kidding me."

"Unfortunately, I'm not. Our parents had a twisted sense of humor. Now, if you take a look at the side of our truck, you'll see it says, 'Bert 'n' Ernie's Tow Service.'"

Betty scooted just far enough to the right to read the panel on the side of the truck. Yep. It was a tow truck. She relaxed just a bit. "Well, you have to admit. That was a bit strange. My car breaks down and then you happen down this road within minutes?"

"Well, not really," Ernie piped up. "Our house and auto repair shop are just two miles from here. I don't think that qualifies this encounter as being Twilight Zone-ish or anything. That's not to say it didn't start off a little spooky, though."

Bert lifted the hood of the Taurus as Ernie brought over a high-powered flashlight. "I can't really see it good enough out here. We can tow you back to our place and check out your car. If we can't figure it out, maybe a friend can come get you?"

Betty considered calling either Jeff or Peyton. She didn't want to put out Peyton anymore than she already had that weekend, and she was still struggling with the unexpected turn of events with Jeff. "I don't have anyone I can call."

"That's okay," Bert offered in a casual manner. "You could borrow one of our beater cars or trucks until we fix your rig."

The two men moved their truck into place and secured the tow hitch to the Taurus. Betty quickly retrieved her purse from the front seat, along with her two bags of luggage, and started toward the tow truck when she heard Ernie sharing a quiet joke with his brother. She swore she heard her name whispered.

"Excuse me, but you just said, 'Betty.'"

Ernie looked up at her, visibly embarrassed. "Oh, ma'am, it's just a little private joke between my brother and me. It's got nothin' to do with you."

Betty stood there like a third wheel. "Tell me the joke. I like jokes."

Bert glanced at his brother. "I'm not sure you'd under-stand it, ma'am," Bert stated, checking the connection of the tow hitch.

"You think I'm too conservative, right?"

"Maybe." Ernie offered. "It's not in your...realm of...I don't know how to say it."

"Just tell me the joke, dammit!" Betty demanded, tiring of their evasiveness.

Bert stood up. "It's not a joke. It's a saying we got be-tween us when we're ready to get home and unwind. We say, 'Time to put the feet up and shoot a Betty Bullet.'"

Ernie stifled a guffaw.

"What in God's name is a 'Betty Bullet?'" she demanded.

The men exchanged worried looks. Bert spoke up again. "It's the greatest little chocolate you ever had in your entire life! They're full of some sort of incredible pot."

"*What?*" Betty said, eyes widening.

"You see?" Bert quickly stated. "I told you that you wouldn't approve."

"We get them and we melt them down," Ernie interject-ed, "and then pour them into these moulds that look like .38 special ammo. You know? A *bullet?*"

"Bullet," Betty nodded. "Yes, I'm clear on that part." She found herself slightly shaking. "Why 'Betty?'"

"'Cause we heard it's the name of the hot chick who makes them," Ernie said, smiling like a little boy.

Well, if the Twilight Zone-ish effect hadn't kicked in ful-ly, it was now running full throttle. Betty's head swam, un-able to fully comprehend what was happening. "Stop! Stop what you're doing, please."

The men did as they were told.

"Ma'am?" Bert said, "We didn't mean to upset –"

"Where did you get the impression she was a 'hot chick?'" Betty asked pointedly.

The men turned to each other.

"Uh," Ernie stammered, "'cause all the girls I've ever known who know how to cook with weed are super hot."

Betty gained her composure and extended her hand. "Let me introduce myself again. My name is Betty Craven. And I'm the 'hot chick' who made those chocolates."

They just stared at her, dumbfounded. For nearly one minute, she watched as they mutually attempted to comprehend this information.

"You messin' with us?" Bert said.

"No. I am not."

"Prove it," Ernie stated.

"I make them with the finest high altitude honey kissed from the bees, a titch of cinnamon, a wisp of ginger and a moderate dollop of the best Madagascar vanilla beans in the world. They melt in your mouth like ambrosia. And when that chocolate hits your stomach, the angels sing."

Ernie looked like he wanted to drop to his knees. Bert was equally shell-shocked.

"Oh, my God," Ernie stuttered.

"Our dad is gonna freak the hell out when he finds out we're towing the Betty's rig!" Bert exclaimed.

"*The* Betty?" she queried.

"Excuse my language, ma'am," Bert continued, nearly hyperventilating. "But you're not just an icon in our family. You're a fuckin' icon!" He grabbed her luggage. "Please have a seat in our truck!"

And so there she was, pressed between them in the center front seat of the large truck. Bert and Ernie reached across and fist bumped each other and then motioned for Betty to lift her fist so they could both touch it.

"Damn! It's like meetin' Cheech!" Ernie effusively gushed.

"Or Chong!" Bert added.

Bert slid in a CD and Joe Cocker blared "Feelin' Alright" into the warm night air as they enthusiastically made the short trip down the road to their repair shop and home. One by one, Bert and Ernie's entire family greeted Betty with the kind of veneration set aside for the Pope or Mick Jagger. After offering her every kind of food and beverage imaginable,

Bert took Betty by the arm and explained he would be honored if she would take a look at the "family grow op."

She agreed, silently hoping they didn't want her to bless it. While Ernie fiddled with her Taurus, Bert led her across the large compound and into a remodeled Quonset hut that held over fifty huge cannabis plants in full bloom.

"How many plants are you allowed to grow?" she asked.

"Allowed?" he asked. "I don't understand." Apparently, Bert hadn't gotten the memo from the State of Colorado yet. "We've been growin' in our family for generations. It's in our blood. I never understood how anything could be illegal that came from a seed."

"Aren't you worried about people finding out?" she asked cautiously.

"Nah. Two of the local cops and a county judge are my best customers."

They spent the next hour giving her the grand tour. Betty got a few new tips on pruning and staking the blooming plants, to encourage better growth of the top cola. All in all, it was an unexpectedly successful side trip. And even though she had to drive back to her house in a "beater" Pontiac with a bad muffler, she couldn't help thinking that, for all that happened, her fifty-ninth birthday ended well.

But there was that little niggling detail of how Bert and Ernie happened upon her chocolates. All they could tell her was "a friend knew a friend who kinda knew a friend" who either gave or sold them the treats. She sorted through the possibilities of people who could have shared her chocolates. There was Peyton, but she'd only given him a few chocolates here and there. However, he did admit to selling the remainder of his Aunt Peggy's chocolates that he'd melted down and mixed with his own cannabis butter. That accounted for at least thirty-five chocolates. Then there was Peyton's pal, Louie at the automotive shop, who sold her the sweet leaf shake and then decided to get out of the business. She gave him ten chocolates, which he might have given to someone else. And there was Buddy — she had certainly given him a tremendous number of chocolates in exchange for his dutiful labor. That was the extent of her suspects, as she knew that Dottie, Doctor Dave and Jean certainly wouldn't part with their edible stash. All told, there could have been as many as ninety chocolates bouncing around out there from buyer to seller. And somewhere along that path, *her* first name surfaced as the creator of the cannabis cacao concoctions that apparently made grown men weep in ecstasy.

While professional pride took a front seat, the back seat was filled with agonizing anxiety, fear and foreboding. How long would it take before someone she knew ran across a "Betty Bullet" or "Betty Buzz" or whatever stoned alliteration someone invented? As she pulled into her driveway right before midnight, with the Pontiac's muffler waking up every dog and cat on her street, her mind was in a dither.

Once inside, she dropped her bags at the door, carved a good teaspoonful of the frozen coconut cannabis oil out of the container and let it melt in her mouth. Sleep would salvage her troubled mind and the oil would make sure of that outcome. But then the phone rang. It was past midnight and the only calls one ever received at that hour were not usually jovial. Checking the Caller ID, there it was again. "PRIVATE." A wellspring of resentment issued forth and she picked up the phone.

"This is Betty Craven!" she announced in the most officious voice she could muster. "What do you want?"

"Betty..."

Betty dismounted from her high horse. "Who is this?"

"Who in the hell do you think it is?" Her words were slurred and she spoke softly.

"Judi. Are you all right?"

"Of course, I'm all right. Why wouldn't I be all right?"

"Why are you calling me so late? The Caller ID didn't show your name."

"Huh?" She seemed to be having a difficult time focusing. "Oh, I'm on Roger's home office phone. He set it to private so his patients can't track him down. Listen, I was going to leave a message. I thought you were gone for your birthday weekend."

"I was away. I just got in now."

"Uh-huh."

"Judi, what's going on?"

"I wanted to wish you a happy birthday before the day was over..." her voice trailed off before she dropped the phone. It took her a long ten seconds to retrieve it and come back on the line. "I gotta talk to you in person about something I found out."

Betty's mouth went dry. "Tell me now."

"No...I'll see you around ten tomorrow morning."

"You mean today. Tomorrow is today."

"Humph...tomorrow is today...tomorrow is today... That's deep, Betty."

"No, really. It's past midnight."

"Oh...Right...See you today." And she hung up.

Betty hung up and ran her tired fingers through her hair. Noting the red blinking light that signaled a message, she hit the PLAY button.

"Hey, babe," Jeff said. "Just wanted to make sure you got home okay. Love you."

Betty stared at the phone and hit the PLAY button again. She closed her eyes and fell into the embrace of his comforting voice. And yet, she still struggled.

She climbed the stairs and found her stalwart Ronald resting on his favorite pillow on the bed. He lifted his chin just enough to feel her tickle his jaw before he fell back into slumber. "You doing okay, ol' fella?" She gradually felt the edge of the cannabis oil take hold and slid under the covers. As sleep quickly took over and her body melted into the mattress, she swore she heard Frankie whisper in her ear.

~~~

"So, how was your weekend of reflection?" Judi asked, as Betty directed her toward the kitchen the next morning.

"Quite reflective, actually." Betty offered her a cup of coffee.

Judi handed her a two-foot square box with a huge bow planted in the center. "Happy birthday."

Betty unwrapped the gift to find a bevy of gourmet nuts, expensive truffle oil, caviar and canned delicacies from around the globe, all tucked into a sturdy, large, utilitarian, metal mesh tray. She was taken with the offerings, many of which she adored. But the more she eyed the mesh tray, the more she realized it was the ideal tool for drying cannabis bud. "I love it! Thank you!"

After a few minutes of awkward chitchat, Judi took a deep breath. "Listen, I think I have a buyer for your chocolate making equipment."

Betty's gut clamped down. "Oh?"

"Based on what I know you paid for it, I think you'll be happy with their offer."

Betty turned to the sink. "Would you like some breakfast?"

"No. I ate."

She glanced back at Judi. "Really? You look hungry."

"I'm not hungry. Anyway, I gave the guy your phone number, and he should call you today or tomorrow."

Betty's mind went blank. She noticed Judi's outfit, along with the linen pants she seemed to live in. "I *do* love those pants. You really scored –"

"Scored? That's not usually a term you would use."

"Oh? Humph."

"Why are you being evasive about the equipment? I thought you wanted to sell it." She let out a hard sigh. "Jesus, Betty. I'm trying to help you. I'm trying to be your friend. Why...why is this becoming so difficult lately?"

Betty saw the true distress in Judi's eyes. For the first time, she also saw the pain that hung there. She walked back to the kitchen table and rested her hand over Judi's arm. "I'm sorry, darling. I don't mean to be evasive. Thank you for putting the word out regarding my equipment." A thought dove into her mind. "But I actually already have a buyer who is interested. I met her this weekend, in fact."

"Where?"

"Where?"

"Yeah. Where?"

"Ouray. The hot springs?"

"You went to Ouray hot springs for your birthday and you didn't invite me?"

Betty was perplexed. "I didn't know you liked hot springs."

"I *love* hot springs. I was born to soak in a hot spring! I used to carry a travel guide that notated every hot spring in Colorado. *That* is how much I love hot springs."

"I had no idea. Well anyway, I met a woman there and mentioned about the equipment, and she was quite interested."

"You're soaking in the Ouray hot springs and you bring up your chocolate making equipment? Really? How does that just slip into the conversation?"

Betty started to come up with another fabrication when the phone rang. She crossed over to check the Caller ID on the phone but couldn't find where she'd left the receiver. Two more rings and the voicemail came on.

"Hey, Betty! It's me, Peyton!"

Betty pushed every button on the phone unit in an attempt to mute his voice, but instead, she pushed the button that increased the volume.

"Wanted to make sure you got home from your getaway," Peyton continued.

"Peyton?" Judi said. "Isn't that the kid Renée said you're mentoring?"

"Everything looks good at your place. Did a little watering since some of the plants looked dry..."

"*He* was your house sitter?" Judi asked, incredulously.

"No, no, no," Betty breathlessly offered, still hunting for the receiver. "Just popped in here and there."

Peyton continued. "You might want to check Ronald out. He seems kinda out of it. He was makin' a whistling sound when I was talking to him yesterday morning."

"*I* could have taken care of Ronald for you," Judi stressed.

"Oh, and one thing before I forget," Peyton pressed on. "I had a little chat with Helen on Saturday afternoon...."

Oh God no, Betty thought, feverishly trying to figure out how to stop this nightmare, short of unplugging the phone and throwing it through the kitchen window.

"I think you need to keep an eye on her, Betty. Ever since Ronald took a bite out of her, she doesn't seem normal...whatever normal is for Helen..."

Judi looked at Betty. "Ronald bit Helen? I never heard this!"

"I also noticed some white patches on her," Peyton added.

"White patches? *What*? Why was Helen here on Saturday when you were gone?"

"I'm not sure what the white patches are, to be honest with you," Peyton offered, "but I think it's gotta be some kind of nutrient deficiency."

Judi furrowed her brow. "So now this kid's a doctor?!"

"Where's the goddamned phone?!" Betty yelled as she tore into the living room searching for it.

"Please don't get worked up like you always do and think she's gonna die," Peyton said in a reassuring voice. "She's probably fine, but she'll always be high maintenance. Maybe she just needs a big –"

"Peyton!" Betty quickly said, as she found the phone and cut off the voicemail. "How lovely to hear from you! I have a friend here right now and can't talk, but let's connect later on today, okay?"

Peyton hesitated. "Geez, Betty. You sound kinda like you lost your mind."

"You have no idea!" Betty said. "Talk to you soon." She hung up and walked back into the kitchen.

Judi was waiting with her arms folded. "Helen needs a big *what?*"

"Dose of vitamins." Betty rested the phone on the cradle. "She has seemed a little out there lately, don't you agree?" She was trying desperately to keep her voice modulated and free of the high pitch that often signaled deception.

"Helen has *always* been out there and disagreeable. But if you think she's sick, you should confide in *me*, not that kid! I could talk to Roger and he could prescribe –"

"No! I'm sure it's nothing to worry about –"

"White patches? Where are these patches? I've never seen them!"

"You're sure you don't want anything to eat, honey?" It was evident to Betty that the layers of deceit were earning interest by the minute.

Judi got up and started for the front door. "Roger's annual summer party is *this* Sunday. Three o'clock. Our house. I expect you to be there for me."

Betty didn't want to go, but the look on Judi's face disarmed her. "I'll bring something."

"You don't have to bring anything." An odd sadness came over her. "Just bring yourself." There was a heavy pause. "*Please.*"

Betty nodded. "I'll be there. Hey, you said you wanted to talk to me in person about something you found out?"

"Oh, right. Thought you should know there's a rumor going around that someone in your neighborhood is growing pot."

Betty steadied herself against the kitchen sink. "Who?"

"I have no idea. But you might want to keep your eyes open. That kind of crap attracts the kookiest people."

Chapter 29

"You're searching for that rope."

Several days passed and Betty's anxiety didn't abate. Even with the regularly nightly doses of her trusted cannabis oil, she found her head swimming during the day. The lies were stacking up like old bricks, one on top of the other. One wrong move and it would all come down in a jagged heap. How could rumors about a grow op have gotten out? Then she wondered if there could possibly be someone else in her little enclave, surreptitiously doing the same thing in their basement? But if not, and the rumor was about her, how in the hell did that information leak?

And Helen and her "white patches"? Every time Betty remembered that, her anxiety peaked again. But she saved the greatest angst for Jeff. He called twice before she finally got back to him. She was polite and thanked him profusely for a lovely birthday weekend, but she knew he wasn't stupid. Betty wasn't giving all of herself. She was pulling back, allowing fear to take over. And every time she felt herself holding back, she detected a little voice in her head saying, "Are you nuts?"

When he finally showed up on Thursday, saw the beater Pontiac in her driveway and then discovered the story behind it, he was clearly upset she didn't call him to pick her up that night.

"I wasn't even halfway back to Paradox," he told her. "It was no big deal. I could have come and gotten you!"

"It's one thing to catch a ride on your bike to go up a short hill," Betty said, slightly flustered. "It's quite another hanging on for dear life for almost thirty miles."

He observed her carefully, his face slightly troubled. "What's going on, Betty?"

She couldn't say it, so she opted for something else. "My name is apparently now synonymous with cannabis." She explained the peculiar evening she spent with Bert and Ernie. "And rumors are flying that 'someone' in this neighborhood is growing pot!"

He listened, but she could tell he knew she wasn't being completely forthcoming. "Well...okay...so it's time to come clean with your friends."

"Jeff, are you out of your mind?" Her tone was harsh.

"Actually, no. I'm not. Don't you have enough stress right, now nurturing these plants and keeping up with all your patients' needs? Why add to it by continuing all this secrecy?"

"You know the answer."

"Yeah, I do," he said with a somber tenor. "You're searching for that rope."

"What rope?" she questioned, feeling the tinge of resentment.

"You jumped off the cliff but you landed on a ledge, and now you're looking for the rope so you can climb back up to the top instead of seeing if you can fly."

"Please don't assume you know everything that's going through my head. You don't. You have no idea."

His blue eyes traced hers with a subdued gaze. "Don't do this, Betty," he said quietly. "Remember what you felt like three months ago? You want to go back to that? Mrs. Elizabeth Cragen? *She's* safe, isn't she? Nobody knows who she is. She can smile, even when she's dying inside. She can laugh, when all she wants to do is cry. And she can crawl under the covers and hide, until her house falls down around her."

"Stop it, please."

"Goddammit, Betty," he said, slight ire building.

"You're upset. Maybe you should go."

He let out a sigh. "I have to work on Saturday doing inventory. How about on Sunday we go out and —"

"I can't. I promised Judi I'd attend their annual summer party."

"Right. Judi. She was in the store recently picking up lunch."

Of course, he knew her. This whole relationship started over a jar of "Mama's Muscle Mojo" that Judi enthusiastically endorsed. He seemed to be waiting for an invitation to join her at the party, but that wasn't going to happen.

"Let's talk next week when everything's calmed down, okay?" she stated, feeling the pain of her false smile.

The next day, she got a call from Jean's husband Arthur, asking if Betty could whip up fifteen more chocolates with double strength doses in each one. Betty's heart ached at his request, knowing it wasn't a good sign that Jean needed another batch so soon. When she told him she couldn't drive out to their place until Monday, he offered to come to her house on Sunday to pick up the order. Betty stayed up late that night, making Jean's chocolates. While she was at it, she made a platter of thirty regular chocolates for Judi's summer soirée.

Betty spent the entire morning on Saturday tending to her girls. All of the ones in bloom were showing their beautiful buds and starting to exude a scent that resembled a mixture of fruit, berries and skunk. As unappealing as that sounded, Betty loved to breathe in the aroma. There was something revitalizing about it, coupled with the calming hours spent spoiling and talking to her girls. Her front garden might not have had the same crisp, blue-ribbon gleam it usually enjoyed each summer, but her basement full of "weeds" shone like a silver cup. At night, their wide leaves tended to slightly droop as if to signal sleep. But each morning, they lifted upright like chalices, eager to drink in the light. She did spend a little extra time with Helen, the Centennial Blueberry that looked like it was developing into a low hedge, thanks to Ronald's intensive chew trimming. She noted the vague white patches on a few of Helen's leaves Peyton had mentioned on his voicemail.

Out of curiosity, she walked into the veg room and brought Helen's young clones into the main room, where the natural light made it somewhat easier to check the leaves. To Betty's dismay, there was another small white patch on one of Helen's clones. Taking it just outside the sliding glass door, she tried to discern, under the blaze of sunlight, whether she needed to intervene with a spray or resort to another sulfur burn. After debating for another twenty minutes, she decided to bring the young clone upstairs to the kitchen, where she could spend the day soaking in the natural solar rainbow rays that filtered through the custom windows with handcrafted etching. The seven-inch-tall progeny in the one-gallon, black-plastic pot seemed to enjoy the special attention as she caught the heat and colorful reflections whirling melodically around the kitchen. Betty gathered the two separate trays of frozen chocolates and carried them outside and upstairs to the large room above the garage she'd jokingly started calling *"The White Violet, Le Deux."* With the precision of an electrical engineer, she patiently decorated each chocolate with refined silver and gold swirls. In the background, Colorado Public Radio's classical station played a rousing Strauss waltz. She was so deeply engrossed in the moment that she didn't hear the car pull up behind the beater Pontiac. Nor did she hear the knock on her kitchen door. However, she did hear someone calling her name, just as the kitchen door slammed.

Betty raced to the window and peered around the corner. There was Helen's old sedan parked behind the Pontiac. She dashed down the stairs and tore into the kitchen. Out of breath, she stood there in shock as Helen sat at the kitchen table arm's length from Helen *the clone*, which stood proudly in a brilliant beam of sunlight.

"Helen!" Betty exclaimed. "I didn't hear you drive in, darling."

"I have to talk to you. Could you sit down?"

Betty took a seat across from her, peering over the top leaf of the cannabis plant. "What is it?"

"Do you know what it feels like to be my age?"

"No."

"It sucks. I hate it. Something is either leaking out of me or it's backed up and can't get out. Everything hurts,

including brushing my hair. I can't hold thirteen playing cards in my hands anymore, because my fingers are all
twisted from arthritis. That killed my bridge game every
Wednesday afternoon. The side effects from all my pills are
now worse than the symptoms I had when I started taking
them in the first place. I can't sleep through the night so I
doze through the day. Are you getting the picture?"

"I'm not sure." Betty scooted the plant a few inches to
the side. The shock of carrying on this conversation across
a table that held a cannabis plant was beginning to pale in
comparison to Helen's sudden garrulous spurt.

Helen leaned forward. "I don't have a lot to look forward to!" she yelled, pounding the table with her fist. As she
brought her hand back, she hit the black pot and acciden-
tally tipped over the cannabis clone.

Betty jumped up, but Helen stood up and righted the
pot.

"I've got it!" Helen admonished, dragging the one-gallon
container toward her with her crooked, arthritic fingers, and
putting back the clumps of wet dirt that fell from it. "What
I'm trying to get across to you is that I live for Judi's annual,
idiotic, summer party. I mark it on my AARP calendar every
goddamn January. I buy a new pair of orthotics just in case
I have to stand too long in the buffet line. I can't remember the people from one year to the next but that's okay,
because all they do is drone on about insipid things I don't
care about. I get to sit in a chair, eat moderately good food,
drink average cognac and forget for three hours that any day
now it'll be time to tune the harp and cue the organ music
for my funeral!" She plugged the last clump of dirt in the pot
and pushed it away from her with indifference. "And now *you*
want to take that away from me!"

"Me? What are you – ?

"I got a call from Judi yesterday that I should take it easy
and not bother coming on Sunday. I pressed her further and
found out *you* told her I'm *dying!*"

"*Dying?* I said no such thing!" Betty scoffed, even though
she knew Helen had been planning her own funeral since

she turned twenty-one. "You could have lots of life still in you, dear. Imagine all the medical wonders on the horizon. You could live to be one hundred. And you know the advantage of that, Helen? No peer pressure!"

Helen screwed her face into an ugly scowl. "Is that supposed to be *funny*? Live to *one hundred*? Are you kidding me? If I live to eighty, drag me out behind the barn and shoot me!" She stood up. "Oh, and white patches?" she grimaced. "What are white patches? The only white patches I know about are the ones in that skin condition Michael Jackson had. Do I look remotely like Michael Jackson to you?"

"No, darling. You're much shorter." Betty tried to stifle a smile. Something about the entire scene and elderly umbrage was becoming so hysterically incongruous, that Betty wasn't sure how long she could contain herself.

"This is not funny, Betty!" Helen roared. "I'm going to that damn party and you're not stopping me!" She leaned over the clone, brushing her shirt against the tips of the leaves. "You're going to call Judi, and tell her that I'm just fine. That you misjudged my health. You make it clear to her that I'm not going to pot!"

Betty snorted an unexpected laugh.

"When in the hell did I become such an amusement for you?!" Helen exclaimed.

Betty got up and moved Helen toward the door. "I'll see you tomorrow at the party." Helen wasn't even out the door before Betty collapsed into a fit of giggles.

The next morning, Betty boxed up the chocolates for Jean, adding a few extra decorative flairs to the ribbon to brighten her spirits, before setting the box in her freezer. Turning her attention to the thirty plain chocolates for Judi's party, she arranged them on a platter lined with a silver satin cloth that had once graced the shelves at *The White Violet*. Seeing the cloth brought her back to the bittersweet memories of her chic chocolate shop. That memory spurred the image of the antique white violet print, which in turn prompted the recollection of Frankie's torn drawing showing a near carbon copy of that section in the watercolor print. She could ignore it all she wanted or attempt to explain it away, but the fact remained that somehow her young son's pencil drawing predicted the appearance of that watercolor. Betty wandered into the living room and picked up the framed print that still rested on the credenza next to his photos. Why this print? It had to have some sort of meaning to Frankie for him to give it to her during their last visit. The mere fact she chose to name her chocolate store *The White Violet* leant credence to the idea that, for whatever unknown reason, the enigmatic watercolor held some significance.

She spent the following morning weeding in her front garden and attempting to bring it halfway up to its usual splendor. But to her dismay, Betty noticed many of the perennials she had lovingly and patiently cultivated throughout the years were struggling. Some were dying and others were stunted. Looking closer, she couldn't see any root rot or infestation taking hold. But one by one, her treasured, prize-winning flowers were disintegrating in front of her stunned eyes. The ring of her phone interrupted the sad scene. Checking the Caller ID, Betty saw that it was "Bert 'n' Ernie's" calling. Her ol' Taurus was ready to be picked up, and according to an effusive Bert, "it was now running like a rabid cougar on the prowl." He also announced he wasn't charging her, because the "honor of caressing her engine" was payment enough. Worship was one thing, Betty told herself, but a fair exchange for prompt, excellent service was essential.

"If you won't take my money, would you take twenty-five chocolates?"

Bert starting weeping like a little girl, which Betty took as a "yes."

The clock was ticking down to the three o'clock start of Judi's party, and the ghastly thought of showing up in a Pontiac with a muffler that announced her arrival four blocks away was not appealing. Thus, with her characteristic verve and shoulder to the grindstone mentality, Betty effortlessly melted, poured and froze the chocolates for Bert and Ernie. She kept a watchful eye out for Arthur who promised he'd show up to collect Jean's order. But by 1:00 when she was ready to go, there was no sign of him. She set a cooler with Jean's chocolates by the back door in the shade and left a message on his voicemail, directing him to their location. With Bert and Ernie's chocolates in tow, she blew out of her driveway in the Pontiac, setting the neighborhood dogs on point, and drove with gusto to pick up her Taurus.

Since it was a Sunday, the forty-five minute journey was relatively quick and free of traffic. When she arrived, she was shocked to find fifteen new people waiting to meet her. It was just a tad disarming, given their somewhat odd attire. One woman wore a garland of fresh cannabis leaves strung around her neck, which she ceremoniously bestowed on Betty. A man wearing a Bob Marley tie-dye t-shirt wore hoop earrings, through which a small, dried cannabis bud hung. They were a peculiar bunch of folks, Betty decided, but they were also extremely kind and munificent. When they weren't expressing their heartfelt gratitude for her "green talent," they were eagerly inviting her to visit *their* grow ops and the use of their "premium shake" if she ever ran out and was in need. What started out with a bit of a circus milieu, developed into a relaxed discussion that revolved continually around the cannabis plant. Betty became so involved in the various conversations that time slipped by too quickly. But when she glanced at a clock, and saw it was 3:30, she jumped up from the hemp-clothed futon and dashed to her car.

Betty Craven was *never* late to her destination. And now, for the first time, her excuse was that she was engaged with an uncommonly gregarious group of ganja aficionados. No, that story wasn't going to float, she pondered as she put the pedal to the metal to see what her overhauled, rabid-cougar engine could do. As the clock closed in on 4:20, however, she suddenly realized she'd left the party chocolates at her house. She pounded the steering wheel in frustration and made a quick turn back to her home. This wasn't like Betty. She wasn't scatterbrained and tardy. What in God's name was happening to her, she scolded herself.

Arriving at her house, she dashed from the car and through the back gate. Arthur had thankfully shown up to retrieve the cooler. That was one less thing to worry about, she reasoned, as she went inside to collect the chocolates. As she quickly removed the platter of chocolates from the freezer, her attention was drawn to the blinking light on her phone. Punching the button, she heard Arthur's voice.

"Hi, Betty. I can't make it over to your house today. I need to stay here with Jean. If there's any way you can come to our place tomorrow, we'd appreciate it. Thanks."

Betty momentarily froze. Her first thought was that Jean might have taken a turn for the worse. That grave realization was followed by the question of where in the hell was the cooler of Jean's medicated chocolates? No sooner had that thought troubled her already frenzied mind than the phone rang. It was Judi, and she wasn't happy.

"Where are you?" Judi asked in a slurred voice.

"I'm just leaving now," Betty replied, carefully placing the frozen platter into a quilted casserole carrier.

"You're never late! *Ever*! Why now? Why *today*?" Judi's voice was growing irrational.

"I'll just grab the chocolates and be there in a jiffy!"

"We've already got your chocolates ready to go on the table!" Judi announced. "Helen was running a little late, so I told her to stop by your place. She found the cooler at the back door. All that's missing is *you*!"

Betty grabbed the counter to steady herself. "I'll be right there." She hung up, as her life flashed before her eyes. It was closing in on 4:30. Dessert would be served at any moment. "Shit!" she screamed, racing out the door with the platter of chocolates. It was official. Helen could foul up a two-car funeral.

Chapter 30

"You've never seen a good death, have you Betty?"

Betty forced her newly repaired car to work for its supper, as she floored it nearly all the way to Judi's house. She double-parked, grabbed the quilted casserole carrier and raced to the back of the house. Slipping quietly past a few guests and edging into the large, empty kitchen, she spied her cooler. The lid was off and the elegantly wrapped box and ribbon were carelessly tossed on the granite-topped island. Retrieving the box and ribbon, she dropped it into the cooler and kicked it closer to the door that led into the living room. Peering into the crowded room, all she could see were the backs of guests, chatting and eating off paper plates. Leaning around the corner, she eyed the dessert table covered with the antique tablecloth she given Judi. There, proudly featured in the center, was a silver platter and the cannabis chocolates.

Betty crept to the table, picked up the platter and whisked it back into the kitchen. She had to think for a second how many chocolates she made for Jean. Fifteen. Yes, fifteen. She counted the remaining chocolates and ended up with nine. *Oh, dear Lord*, she thought, swallowing hard. Betty frantically transferred the nine cannabis chocolates into their box in the cooler, lifted the plain chocolates off her platter inside of the satin cloth and spread them as beautifully as she could on Judi's silver platter before anyone saw the subterfuge. She had to ferret out the six remaining chocolates or somehow find which unsuspecting partygoers were about to feel some unusual effects.

Betty adopted her best pageant walk and smile and strolled back into the living room, silver platter in hand. Moving around the periphery of the room, she tried to scope out any discarded or uneaten chocolates. But the minute she considered that possibility, she realized how highly unlikely that scenario would be, given the rapturous ecstasy her chocolates tended to induce. And yet, as dumb luck would have it, she spied one lonely chocolate on a dessert dish stationed on a small table. Like a magician trained in the art of sleight of hand, Betty collected the cannabis-infused chocolate and replaced it with a plain one from her silver party platter.

"One down," she said to herself. "Five to go."

Betty walked around the room, first asking the guests if they'd had a chocolate yet, before offering them one from her platter. No one mentioned anything about already eating one, but there were guests scattered around the house and property. One person might have eaten two. And there was no way to know who might have already enjoyed one and left early. That latter possibility nearly sent her head spinning, when she heard a woman's voice behind her.

"I'll have another chocolate!"

Betty turned and took in a little gasp. It was Helen.

"Why are you shocked to see me?" Helen asked her. "I thought I had your blessing to be here." She took one chocolate off the platter. "I think you need to check the expiration date on your ingredients. The first one I ate tasted like a lawn with the septic tank flooding." Helen sunk back in her chair and popped the chocolate into her mouth.

Betty felt as though everything slowed down at that point. The panic and realization of what could soon transpire – how she could potentially be both exposed and held accountable all in one breath – gripped her hard. The scandal would linger forever in Paradox, with her reputation tarnished permanently. She was just beginning to picture the throng of journalists camped in front of her house, when she felt a tap on her shoulder. She turned to find Judi staring at her with steely resentment.

"What in the hell are you doing, Betty?" she asked her, clearly unsteady on her feet. "I didn't hire you to serve chocolates." She snagged a white-shirted catering waitress and

handed the young girl the silver platter. Grabbing Betty by
the arm, she pulled her toward the bar in the far corner of
the living room. "An hour and a half late!" she said with a
drunken sneer. "And I have to call your house and chase you
down like a rebellious child!" She spilled her drink across the
bar. "Oh, shit! That's the second time today!" She twisted
the top off another bottle of whiskey.

"I really do think you've had enough, darling," Betty cau-
tioned, momentarily forgetting the impending disaster.

"You don't get to make that decision today," Judi said,
pouring three fingers of scotch into her glass. "I serve the
guests the fruity shit." She pointed to a round table near the
front door. "I keep the good stuff for myself."

Betty peered across the room at a punchbowl that held
a frothy orange liquid. "What's that?"

"Some kind of fermented mango juice the caterer guaranteed would be the showstopper for my party."

Betty was glad she had a bar to hang onto at that moment. She instantly recalled Dottie's assertion that if someone ate a really-ripe mango an hour prior to consuming
cannabis, the effects of the herb would increase. *Fermented
mango?* Yeah, that would get the party ball rolling pretty fast,
leading up to the real showstopper.

"What do you want to drink? Bourbon?" Judi asked.

Betty's head swirled, trying to figure out how to stop this
nightmare without risking her reputation in the process.
"Actually, I don't want anything. I'm..." She looked around
the room. "I'm not feeling that well. I think I'm having a
reaction to..." Betty honed in on her target. "To those strawberries over there." Betty scanned the room and realized
that nearly every plate had a large strawberry or two on it.

"Strawberries?" Judi replied in a flippant tone. "What
are you talking about?"

"Pesticides," Betty blurted out.

"Huh?"

"They heavily spray conventionally grown strawberries
with lots of pesticides. It's been all over the TV. Haven't you
heard about it?" She said it so convincingly she almost began

to believe it was the top story on the evening news. "They use over thirty-five chemicals on that poor, little, innocent red fruit. They mentioned that the effects of those chemicals after ingesting them are almost immediate. There's dizziness, confusion, extreme fatigue, a slight buzzing in the head –"

"Really? You just described how I feel for the first ninety minutes of every single morning. Try again, Betty."

"I'm serious, Judi," she casually observed Helen across the room. She was still glued to her chair and showing her usual disinterest in everything. "I really don't feel top shelf. Unless those strawberries are organic –"

"*Organic?* Excuse me, but look at this crowd." She gulped the whiskey. "You think I'd waste organic strawberries on these pill poppers? They're all so over-medicated, their livers operate in another zip code and their brains have all turned to Swiss Cheese. *Expensive* Swiss Cheese, mind you, but it's still cheese with gaping holes. They don't care about organics or free-range! Go on! Ask them! Bet they'll tell you that a free-range chicken is chicken you don't pay for!"

In the midst of potential chaos breaking out, Betty realized that something was terribly wrong with her friend. She'd always noticed her propensity to occasionally drink too much in the past, but there was something else. Betty couldn't believe she'd been so blind to it. "If you detest them so much, why do you keep hosting this party?"

She was silent, studying the amber reflections in her cut crystal glass. "Because...you just do. You just keep doing the same fucking thing, day in and day out until you drop dead. You do it because it's what you've always done. End of story."

Betty regarded her with compassion. "Maybe you should rethink that mindset."

Judi stared at her with glazed eyes. "Rethink...that... mindset? What in the hell? What's happened to you, Betty? Who in the hell are you? You've changed. I can't sit across from you anymore and dish about all the stupid things in the world that don't matter. I can't count on you to indulge me in a harmless game of gossip. It's not fun anymore." A shadow of grief engulfed her. "You're my only real true friend in this world. You're the only one I can always depend on and trust with everything. All the rest of them are just cushions to keep my life at arm's length. But you've abandoned me for some reason, and I don't know what I've done." She gripped Betty's arm. "Tell me what I've done so we can put this behind us and get back to normal." She twisted the cap off the whiskey bottle again and poured herself another three fingers of booze.

"I think you should slow down."

Her tone instantaneously flipped. "And *I* told you that wasn't your decision!" She sloppily poured the whiskey into her glass.

Betty felt the sting of a memory rise up. She'd had this same drunken argument too many times in the past, with someone who could turn meaner than a sack of snakes, faster than green grass through a goose. She knew from heartbreaking experience it was better to back off than fuel the fire with sensible suggestions.

"Frankly," Judi took a sip, "I think I should speed up the adult beverage consumption, so I can handle the remainder of this red hot mess. In about half an hour, we'll move to the portion of the afternoon where they all take turns thanking me for putting the party together, and complimenting us on what a 'fantastic home' we have for entertaining. Then they'll drone on about how the partners are going to expand the practice next year, so they can kick some serious ass! Honestly, Betty, I'd have a strong drink if I were you. You gotta fortify yourself for that part of the festivities. I never really saw the big business of medicine until I married a doctor. I thought I was married to someone who actually wanted to heal people. What a stupid cow I was. Medicine is a business, Betty. And business is *very* good."

"*Judi,*" Betty stressed, equally worried for her friend as she was for the four remaining unsuspecting guests. "I'm not disregarding or ignoring anything you're telling me. But I'm really not feeling well at all, and I do think we need to seriously consider the fact that others might begin to experience some of these symptoms –"

"*Good*. I hope they drop like flies drenched in Raid. At least it'll be one of the more memorable parties I've thrown. One by one, to watch these self-important fucks fall over. I can't wait."

"I'm not kidding! Perhaps I could ask for everyone's attention and explain the possible issue with the strawberries –"

"Betty, put down the crack pipe and consider what you just said. You bring up to these people that there might be a 'possible issue' in which they might start to feel sick, and everyone's going to start believing they're sick. *Everyone!* Even the ones who haven't eaten the goddamn strawberries. Ever heard of the placebo effect? It's real! I've seen it in action. Roger ran out of anti-depressant samples for his patients two months ago, so he gave them placebos until the new shipment arrived. Every single one of those bastards reported back to him that those pills changed their lives and cured their depression. If that wasn't a total mind fuck, I don't know what was!"

Betty was just about to question how feeling better was a "mind fuck" when Helen approached them. She stood there, with arms outstretched, captivated by a small crack in the ceiling.

"Aren't words interesting?" Helen said, eyes as glassy as a still mountain lake. "Like the word 'therapist.' If you make it two words, you get 'the rapist.' And Santa. Flip the letters around and you get 'Satan.'" She stared blankly at the women. "What do you think that means?"

They regarded Helen in stunned silence for a long thirty seconds.

"Pesticides." Betty finally whispered to Judi.

Judi observed Helen through inebriated eyes. "Your little friend, Peyton, was right," she whispered back to Betty. "I think we need to keep an eye on her."

Helen laid down on one of the couches and promptly fell into such a deep sleep that Judi's Persian cat was able to groom himself while balancing across her chest. An hour later, Betty noticed the portly husband of one of the office receptionists staring a little too long at the floral centerpiece. The remaining guests that unknowingly drew the short cannabis straws that early evening included an eighty-year-old retired doctor and an X-ray technician. Both of them seemed unaware of the cause for their sudden disorientation. As their respective partners helped them to their cars and the party broke up, one of the catering waitresses sidled next to Betty, grinning like a seasoned pro.

"So, who made the chocolates?" the waitress asked, visibly enjoying the buzz.

Betty put a protective arm around her and pointed across the room. "See that elderly lady over there sound asleep with the Persian on her chest?" Betty sighed. "She brought them."

Once she knew every edible had been accounted for, Betty grabbed her cooler in the kitchen and said goodbye to Judi. Their parting was awkward, as Judi was slumped across a leather chair in the den, mindlessly channel surfing with the sound on MUTE. Even though the catering waitress was well aware the chocolates were spiked, she thankfully kept mum. Betty insisted on driving the girl home and helping her into the house.

"That ol' lady sure knows how to cook with weed!" the girl declared, as Betty helped her to the couch and left only after she fell into a deep sleep.

Driving home, Betty realized there was one thing to be grateful for – Renée wasn't at the party. According to Judi, Renée decided at the last minute to ditch the party in favor of having bad coffee with her sponsor. If she had attended and eaten one of the cannabis-laced chocolates, her savvy, drug-discerning taste buds would know exactly what was causing the strange effects, and she'd have quickly honed in on the source.

Betty whipped up the balance of the double-strength chocolates for Jean, re-boxed them and alerted Arthur that she'd bring them over to their house early the next day.

On the hour-long drive to their house on Monday, Betty had a chance to reflect on the previous day's confusion. It was another close call that she somehow evaded. But one thing was apparent – the opportunities for being discovered were ramping up exponentially. Her double life she'd been able to keep separated was beginning to overlap. It was obvious that her underground popularity – something she had no control over – had usurped her calculating and cautious strategy. She was in the unusual position of being a cannabis "rock star" on one side of the fence and a vague, unknown commodity on the other. Judi was right when she said, "Who in the hell are you?" Betty couldn't answer that. She wasn't her old self, but she wasn't committed to the new Betty either. She floated somewhere in the middle ground, with not even a toe pointed in either direction. And yet, here she was, parking in front of a terminally ill woman's house and delivering fifteen super-charged cannabis chocolates to her bedside. The dichotomy was palpable.

Betty didn't want to linger too long by Jean's side. She was sliding downhill fast, and there was nothing Betty could offer her except a few soothing words and a genuine smile. Death, that onerous bedfellow, was slinking closer to Jean. However, as much as Betty wanted to keep her at arm's length, she couldn't do it. She felt compelled to assist her with anything she needed, even though the reality of Jean's impending demise was kicking Betty in the teeth. She'd certainly progressed from her stilted visit with Peggy on her deathbed, but the part of her that held back, allowing fear to dictate the next move, was still present. The only thing clearly evident was that Jean was truly benefiting from the cannabis chocolates. There was an undeniable comfort watching as the herb took hold and washed the pain from Jean's gaunt face. As her suffering subsided, the grace of the plant took over, infusing Jean with a calm dignity and philosophical approach.

"You've never seen a good death, have you Betty?" Jean asked her.

"I didn't know there was such a thing," she whispered.

388 Laurel Dewey

Jean softly smiled. "They happen every day. I plan to go 'gentle into that good night."

When Betty returned home, there was a message on her voicemail from Jeff. Apparently, there was a Hoedown/Carnival/Barbeque at Love Park in four days on Friday night. It was something different, he mentioned on his message, and he wanted to know if she'd go with him. "Something different," she said to herself. And that's when she realized it was all "different." Nothing was predictable any longer. Any control she thought she had was gone. The roller coaster of change was moving so quickly now, and she was starting to resent it. Yes, she told herself, it was one thing to be bored out of her gourd and want a little excitement to mix things up. But what had thinking outside the box done for her except create more confusion, more fear and a greater desire to hide?

Freedom, it seemed, had a precipitous price. It required one to remove the safety nets and accept that failure was as much a possibility as wild success. It demanded continual adjustment and reassessment of all the old paradigms that were comforting but not typically healthy. It stipulated that one frequently travel outside one's constrictive comfort zone and navigate in that space, trusting one's abilities to shore up their confidence and make it easier each time. Liberation from one's past was a journey, not a destination. The tender ego needed to release its chokehold on propriety and admit it made mistakes. In short, that long metal rod that had been placed up one's nether regions and held one's spine in a rigid, inflexible position had to be surgically removed. The only surgeon who could successfully do the operation was oneself, and the only scalpel needed was courage.

But like so many who needed that procedure, the fear of removing their self-imposed rod and choosing to support one's spine with experience, knowledge and blind faith overwhelmed the senses and easily overrode the extrication of the steel stick. And that is where Betty Craven was stuck – between a metal rod and a very hard place. So she stood there after listening to Jeff's voicemail and stared into the void. She wasn't dead yet, but she hadn't been born either. She was just drifting in a swell of uncertainty, desperate for the safety of convention, yet tempted by the appeal of independence. She couldn't help but recall Jean's words to her during their second visit. "Enlightenment... Too bad it usually has to come with such a steep price."

She dialed his number several times, hanging up each time before the call went through. Her hands were shaking and her gut felt empty and hollow. Betty could feel panic nipping at her heels and working its way up her body. Soon, it would engulf her and paralyze progress. Just before it reached her heart, the phone rang. It was Jeff.

"Hey, babe," he said. "I've gotten three calls in a row from you with a hang up. What's going on?"

What in the hell – she thought. *She* never heard a dial tone. Wonderful. Now, it was even more awkward. "Something's wrong with my landline. I never heard a dial tone so I hung up." Her voice was halted, absent of any warmth.

"Okay..." he offered. "Did you get my message?"

"Yes. A hoedown, eh? I usually don't attend functions with the word 'ho' in them." Betty chuckled nervously at her tense reach for humor.

"It's a very laid back event. We can just walk around, grab a bite to eat and if you don't like it, we can go."

He was so accommodating. "Okay," Betty said, wondering a split second after she spoke why she agreed. "Why don't I meet you halfway? In case parking is difficult, we'll only have one car."

"Yeah...finding a place to park a motorcycle is always one of my pet peeves."

She noted something different in his voice. A mild exasperation; an edge forming where there had always been softness and acceptance. Was her self-fulfilling prophecy finally coming to fruition? Suddenly, she wanted to regain control of the situation. "You know what I'm talking about," Betty assured him, doing everything possible to "church up" her tenor. "It's just easier traveling in one vehicle."

Jeff agreed to meet her in a mall parking lot about a mile from Love Park at five o'clock on Friday night. She haphazardly invited him for dinner on Wednesday, but he told her that he still had lot of inventory to finish that week. When she hung up, she felt as if she'd just played a tennis game with a savvy person who knew how the game was going to end before the first serve.

~~~

Love Park was just beginning to fill up with visitors when they arrived on Friday night. The sounds of fiddle and banjo music greeted them as they walked up the grassy berm that surrounded the park. Fragrant waves of fatty smoke wafted nearby, signaling a long row of food vendors. Jeff took her hand in his.

"You know," he said, "I never finished telling you the story of Stuart Love and his ghost."

They started walking into the center of the park when Betty heard her name called. She instantly released Jeff's hand and turned around.

Judi and Renée stood there, each juggling several cardboard trays of food and drinks. The two women regarded Betty with quizzical expressions.

"Well, hello," Betty replied, feeling her blood pressure track up twenty points.

There was a surge of heavy silence, in which her friends traced Jeff's body up and down.

"Jeff?" Judi finally said, securing one of her trays under the other.

"Hey, Judi. How's it going?" he replied in a comfortable manner.

"Going well, thank you," Judi offered, a bit pulled back. "Rotary Club has a booth here. Roger is holding down the fort so we could get some food for everyone."

Betty remained silent.

Jeff eyed the heap of barbeque and sundry items on their trays. "Looking forward to trying out the ribs again this year."

Renée looked baffled. "Are you and –"

"Yes," Betty interrupted her. "I want to try the ribs too! Can't wait!"

Jeff glanced at her.

Betty pointed to their overflowing trays. "You better get those back to everyone before you drop them."

But nobody moved. And even though there was lively music playing and people happily chatting and children laughing all around them, the wedge of gracelessness was blatant in their orbit, drowning out the carefree *joie de vivre*.

"Yes," Judi finally said. "Enjoy the evening."

Judi and Renée quickly walked away and into the park.

Betty started off toward the periphery of the festivities and then stopped ten feet later, when she realized Jeff hadn't moved. She turned to find him staring at her, with eyes she'd never seen before. They weren't angry or on the verge of rage. Instead, they were guarded and rimmed with dejection. "You coming?" she asked, feeling the appearance of that false smile grip her face.

"You let go of my hand," he said.

"Did I? Oh, I...I didn't realize I did. Come on. Gotta grab those ribs!"

He didn't move a muscle. "I was always under the impression cannabis makes you more tolerant. More introspective. More forgiving. You seem to be fighting against that too."

The minute he said the word "cannabis," Betty's gut clenched and she moved toward him quickly. "Please don't mention that word here so loudly," she implored.

"Which one? Forgiving?"

Her spine stiffened. "Very funny. You know exactly what I'm –"

"You asked to meet me halfway here today. That's so my bike isn't seen at your house anymore. Can't have the neighbors asking too many questions, can you?"

"Why are you –"

"Here's the irony. I'm meeting you halfway, but you're not even halfway in this relationship anymore."

The whole thing felt like a dream to Betty. Her perfectly manicured world was being held together with staples and rusty paper clips. She looked at Jeff and her heart still craved his touch. But she still stood there lost. "Please," she begged him. "Don't do this."

"You're doing this, Betty. Not me." An unexpected stern tone laced his words. "Is this just a game for you? Am *I* a game? Is the pot a game? Are we both just distractions on your way back to a sensible life?"

Betty glanced around at the crowd. "Don't make a scene. Please."

"I'm not making a scene. I'm simply asking you a question." He looked her straight in eyes. "Do you care about me?"

"Yes. I care a great deal for you."

"Great." He took her by the hand. "Let's go down to that Rotary booth where your friends are hanging out and make a formal introduction."

Betty pulled back. "No!" She shook off his hand like an impudent child.

Jeff stared at her in stony silence.

"Look, Jeff, you know I'm a private person. I don't flaunt my life in front of people. I never have and I'm not starting now."

"I'm not asking you to flaunt anything, Betty. I'm simply asking you to acknowledge to your friends that I exist and that we exist as a couple. Why is that so hard for you to do?"

She wasn't going to rummage through her usual box of excuses. "Please don't do this. *Please.* Let's just go along and continue our day and −"

"And then what? What happens tomorrow, Betty? Or next week? How are you going to explain me away then?"

"I think that's rather harsh, don't you?"

"No. I think that's rather honest, actually." His eyes misted. "I understand you, Betty. I bet I understand you better than all of your friends and family combined. And I've always accepted you, even when you couldn't accept yourself. But I wasn't blind either. I was completely aware of your attempts to keep me hidden away. I put up with it, because I hoped that your basement garden and the people you were helping would mellow you...that you'd wake up one day and realize it's okay to be happy. That it's okay to feel something besides regret and grief every damn second of your life. But it seems you haven't yet communed completely with those basement plants. If you had, they would have shown you how to release it all...that I'm not a risk or a threat to your future...that every decaying thing or thought you keep holding onto is crumbling." He moved a step away from her. "I know you're scared of death, Betty. But there you are, dying in front of me." He turned and walked out of the park.

Chapter 31

This is what it felt like to die, she told herself.

Betty stood in place for several minutes as the world around her collapsed on cue. Retreating to a shady spot under a tree, she tried to sort out what to do next. But after half an hour of indecision, she gave up and walked to her car. It was then she realized that Jeff had a mile to walk to his motorcycle. She drove along the roads that led back to the parking lot but didn't see him. When she arrived at the parking lot, his bike was gone. She stared blankly into the spot where they left it and wondered if it was all real. Had she only imagined the last three months? Was it all a dream and would she lay her head on her pillow tonight and wake up tomorrow back in early May? Contemplating that bizarre notion, Betty felt a defined sadness surround her. Suddenly, just the thought of going back to how it was became viscerally repugnant. Sitting there in that car, she felt abandoned and more alone than ever. "Help me, Frankie," she whispered through her tears. "Help me, please."

When she got home, there were two messages on her voicemail, both from Arthur. Jean wanted to see her immediately and she didn't need to bring any chocolates. Betty arrived at their doorstep a little over an hour later, as the late summer sun hovered low like an orange orb in the western sky. Arthur greeted her with sad eyes and led her back to Jean's room. He took a seat on Jean's left side while Betty walked around the bed and sat opposite him. Jean's eyes were half-closed and her breathing was shallow.

Betty held Jean's hand and spoke quietly to Arthur. "I shouldn't be here. This is your time with her."

Arthur pressed Jean's hand to his face. "It's okay, Betty. She told me she wanted you to be here."

Jean tried to speak. She opened her eyes a little more and made contact with Betty. It was almost imperceptible, but Betty heard her clearly. "Don't be afraid."

Betty swallowed hard, but she couldn't stop the tears.

"Thank you..." Jean said softly, "for everything..."

Betty held onto Jean's hand tightly. "You're so welcome, darling."

Jean turned her head and gazed into Arthur's eyes. She mouthed the words, "I love you."

"And I love you too, my love," he replied, choking up.

They didn't move from that spot for another hour. As the sun set behind the far mountains, and twilight put that August day to bed, Jean slipped gently behind the luminous veil that separates the worlds.

Arthur released her hand and collapsed on his wife's body, sobbing uncontrollably. Betty placed a reassuring hand across his back as the toll of the day gripped her heart. She realized that within the tragedy, Jean had given her the gift of witnessing a "good death." There was enigmatic beauty and a sense that as Jean left her besieged body, she was re-born and made new as she walked back into the light.

The next day, Betty still couldn't shake the scene. She retreated to her girls and spent two hours repotting some of the veg plants into larger containers. As she'd come to expect, within half an hour of coddling them and telling them how beautiful they were, they returned the favor by soothing her troubled mind. These "weeds," she realized, almost had a sentient knowing that they somehow transmitted to Betty along unseen currents. She stood back and admired them for all they were and all they would one day become. There was nothing cruel there; nothing caustic nor evil. Somehow, they understood their purpose in their short lives and they preened quietly, knowing the sweet control they had over their often-bewildered masters.

Jeff called mid-day, but she didn't pick up. He left a message saying he'd heard about Jean's death and that Betty was with her when she passed. He didn't litter his message with placating homilies about death. Instead, he seemed to understand every emotion she was going through at that moment, as if his heart had eyes.

Changing out of her gardening clothes, she donned a casual dress and headed to the farmers' market. The prospect of perusing cheese and heirloom fruit buoyed her momentarily. But when she arrived, nothing excited her. Even the first delivery of Palisade peaches didn't trigger her culinary imagination. She was in a daze, floating aimlessly from one booth to another, sampling the jellies and fruits but unable to discern their flavors. This is what it felt like to die, she told herself. Taste is one of the first senses to go. But hearing is the last one. And it was easy to hear the blaring megaphone issuing forth from the COLORADO ACTIVISTS 4 NATIONAL TOLERANCE. Without carefully constructing a well-thought approach, Betty walked across the parking lot and stood in front of their booth.

"Do you have any idea how loud you are?" Betty asked them. "Every time I come here, I have to ignore all you bleating hearted liberals."

The tank-topped, skinny woman with the megaphone set it down on the table. "We got a right to express ourselves!" she countered. "Last time I checked, it's still a free country."

Betty looked up at their banner that hung above their table. "Did any of you ever notice that if you remove the number four, your acronym spells 'C.A.N.T.?'"

The women looked a bit taken back by this information. However, one of the more antagonistic members moved forward to defend their group.

"That might be so. But we are *unified!*" the woman gloated.

"That's all well and good, my dear. But I don't suggest you change your group's name to the Coloradans *Unified* 4 National Tolerance. *That* acronym would be far more odious than C.A.N.T."

Another woman stepped forward. "We're not taking the word 'Activists' out of our name. It's not a dirty word, honey. You may not like it. It may offend those who are sensitive.

But I'd rather be getting attention for something that makes people uncomfortable than for sitting back and bitching about things and doing nothing." She grabbed another megaphone. "You want to live in a bubble? Be my guest. But there better always be people like us who carry the needles that burst that bubble."

And with that, the woman turned on the megaphone and continued her rant. But Betty couldn't hear a word of the noise. Nor could she hear her name being called across the parking lot. Hearing was the last to go before the death knell. She realized, standing there, that she had indeed died. And like her friend, Jean, it was a good death.

She arrived home empty handed and stood in the bright sunlight, amidst what was left of the old canopy elm tree in the backyard. She walked to the large trunk and stared at those two words Frankie carved so prophetically on the tree. "Okay," Betty whispered. "But I'm terrified."

Walking inside the house, she called Judi, Renée and Helen, asking them to come to her house later on that Saturday afternoon. When they each asked what was going on, she gave them all the same answer. "It's time for a good talk."

The women arrived nearly simultaneously and Betty gathered them anxiously in the living room.

Judi looked as nervous as a snake in a wheel rut. "Are you dying?" she asked, her eyes fixated like brown orbs on Betty.

Betty carefully considered her question. "Yes."

The women looked deeply troubled. Even crusty Helen seemed distraught.

Betty quickly continued. "But it's a necessary death."

"What?" Renée questioned her, almost in shock.

"If I'm..." Betty replied, trying to figure out the right words, "lucky enough to have a useful death and the three of you can allow yourselves to know me when I begin again..." Her voice trailed off.

"Wait a second," Renée said, walking toward Betty, "are we talking about six feet under death or existential death?"

"The latter," Betty quickly replied.

The three women released a sigh in unison.

"Has this got something to do with Jeff Carroll?" Judi asked pointedly.

"Who's Jeff Carroll?" Helen asked Judi.

"Apparently, Betty's boyfriend." Renée answered.

"Boyfriend?" Helen exclaimed, clearly disgusted. "*Ech*! Teenage girls have boyfriends. Grown women have husbands or dead husbands!"

This was already getting out of control. "No! It's got nothing to do with Jeff," Betty interjected, then realized she misspoke. "Let me rephrase that." She steeled herself. "He's part of it...a big part of it...but I don't know what the future holds there. And that's not why I asked you to come over. I want to show you something. It means a great deal to me, and it will be in my future for as long as possible. Follow me."

Betty led them through the living room and down the basement stairs. The scent from the open bloom room door was evident to perceptive senses like Renée's, before they even reached the bottom step.

Renée nervously piped up. "*Betty?* Please tell me this isn't what I think this is!"

Betty stood in the main room of the basement as the women gathered around her. Both doors to the veg and bloom room were wide open, displaying the plants blowing freely amidst the fans and the blast of bright lights surrounding them.

Judi's mouth dropped open. Helen screwed her face into an ugly expression. Renée steadied herself against Frank's old desk.

"Holy shit!" Renée exclaimed.

Betty took a deep breath. "These are my girls." She turned to the plants. "Girls? Meet my friends."

"Oh, my God," Judi said, inching closer to the bloom room. Turning to Betty, she was overwhelmed with shock. "*Oh, my God!*"

"Really, now," Betty offered, "it's not *that* big a deal!"

"Not a big deal?" Renée declared. "I shouldn't even *be* in this room!"

"Oh, please Renée, spare me," Betty said. "You've seen worse things on Christmas morning!"

"I'm feeling dizzy," Helen griped, grabbing a chair and sitting down.

Betty rested an assuring hand on her shoulder. "It's the trichomes on the buds, Helen. The resins are still developing and they put off a heady scent."

"I'm going to pass out," Helen insisted.

"Put your head between your legs, darling." Betty instructed. "Just like gas, it'll pass." She turned to the other women. "I can bring out the little microscope and let you see what the trichomes look like when they're magnified. It's like a fairyland!"

"I don't want to see it," Renée stated.

"Why?" Betty asked.

"Because this is five kinds of wrong, Betty! What in God's name got into you?"

"It's just a *plant*, Renée," Betty quietly said.

"A plant with an agenda!" Renée countered.

"No, dear. It's people who have the agenda about this plant. And frankly, I've grown quite fond of this endearing weed."

Judi wandered into the bloom room, gazing around at the plants in stunned silence.

"Are you drunk?" Helen asked, lifting her head from her lap.

"Maybe she's high?" Renée queried, checking Betty's eyes.

"I'm neither drunk nor high!" Betty's voice raised a few octaves. "These plants have been a saving grace for me. They've taught me a lot −"

"Taught?" Renée interrupted. "You've got to be kidding me! Taught you what?"

"Compassion," Betty announced. "Seeing beauty in something that is erroneously labeled as ugly. I admire their ability to withstand the slings and arrows and grow in spite of it. They only demand dedication and love, and in return, their fruits provide insight I've never experienced before."

"So, you *are* loaded!" Renée spitefully pronounced.

Betty's back went up. "No, Renée. I don't get loaded. I get introspective. And that's far more dangerous than getting loaded. And if you'd been at Judi's summer party last week and eaten one of the chocolates Helen mistakenly brought to her house, you would have experienced that deep introspection for yourself!"

Renée regarded Betty with a look that bordered on shock and horror.

Judi walked out of the bloom room and glared at Betty. "You fed my guests pot chocolates?!"

"Just four of your guests, Judi...And one of your caterers who requested my business card."

Judi's mind traveled back to that day. "Oh, dear God... That's why old Doc Gordon told me he felt like an astronaut floating through space! I thought he'd downed too much of that mango punch! Pesticides on strawberries, my ass! Jesus, Betty! Somebody could have gotten hurt!"

"Helen looks normal to me," Betty said succinctly.

Renée nearly choked on air. "She ate..."

"What?" Helen asked, totally out of the loop. "I ate what?"

"She didn't!" Judi exclaimed.

Betty turned to Judi. "Do you really think she figured out that if you flip the letters around in the word 'Santa,' it spells 'Satan,' without a little nudge from the bud?" Betty looked at Helen. "How did you sleep last Sunday night after Judi's party?"

"Like a log," Helen grumbled.

Betty shrugged her shoulders. "I rest my case. No harm, no foul, ladies." She needed to lighten up the mood. "No one has ever died from cannabis. *Ever.* You can't overdose on it! If you try, you just go to sleep and you might wake up a little groggy but after one cup of coffee, you're good to go!"

"Well, in that case," Judi sarcastically stated, "let's put it in the city water system!"

Betty shook her head, "Hey, dude," she softly admonished.

"*Dude?*" Judi sharply replied.

Betty looked at her. "I didn't say 'dude.' I said 'Jude.' Your name is Judi. Jude? Get it?"

"When have you *ever* called me 'Jude?'"

"Nobody's ever called you 'Jude?'" Betty asked, trying to coyly sidestep her slip of the tongue. "That's hard to believe."

"Are you sure you're not high?" Judi stressed.

"Please stop assuming that because I am not responding in the manner in which you are accustomed, I must be high! How can I get across to all of you that this endeavor is not the horrible thing you think it is? Because of this enterprise, I've met many people who I normally would never have be-friended –"

"Peyton!" Renée exclaimed. "Oh, my God! You weren't mentoring him! He was mentoring you on pot!"

Betty turned to Renée. "It was a two-way street, Renée. Trust me. And he's just one of many I've learned from." She took a needed breath. "I'm a caregiver. That means I grow for various people and make edibles for them. One of them is a doctor. One is a Republican!"

The women collectively gasped.

"And one of them died of cancer last night," Betty said, her throat catching. "I only knew her a short time, but she taught me a lot. She taught me that fear is wasted energy and that no matter how grim the situation is, there can still be grace and humanity, even as the world seemingly falls apart around you."

"That's quite poetic, Betty," Judi remarked. "But you cannot convince me that this weed has any consistently proven medical value. If it did everything they claim it can do, don't you think people would be screaming from their roof tops and demonstrating its 'healing' effects, so we could all see it for ourselves?"

"Judi, the proof *is* out there! Open your eyes as I did and do the research for yourself! Listen, a lot of people who use cannabis would love to scream openly about it, and some of them do. But most people keep it a secret, because they're afraid of the social stigma, losing their job, losing their family's respect, looking foolish, being called a 'stoner,' being marginalized –"

"Oh, my God Betty!" Judi interrupted. "You're not just drinking the Kool-Aid, you're *making* it!"

"No! It's true. I'm not working with people who are lazy or stupid! How can I make you understand?" she pleaded.

"Jesus, Betty!" Judi exclaimed. "*Enough!* Have you forgotten what marijuana did to your own son?"

Betty bristled. "I know what pain did to my son. I know what hostility and depression did to my son. I know what ignoring his problems and forcing him to be someone he could never be did to my son. But I have no damn clue what marijuana has to do with any of that!"

"For God's sake, Betty!" Renée contemptuously erupted. "Marijuana is a gateway drug! And Frankie proved that!"

"Bullshit!" Betty yelled. "The way I see it, marijuana is only a gateway drug when the gates are closed at home! And the gates of affection at this house were locked down when it came to Frankie's father!"

"God rest his soul," Helen dutifully said.

"No," Betty retorted, "God *damn* his soul!"

"Betty! How dare you!" Judi shouted.

"I mean it! I grew so tired of the platitudes and well-meaning gestures during my supposed mourning period! Strange how I never got any of that thoughtfulness from anyone when Frankie died! Was his death just not clean enough? Was it too embarrassing? Not polite teatime chat-chat?" A fountain of remorse wrapped in rage erupted. "He was my son, goddammit! My only child! And his life, while imperfect, still mattered. His death, while disturbing, still deserved compassion. Doesn't it make more sense to examine why we have so much pain in this world, instead of attacking those who attempt to quell it with whatever is in their reach? I pity all of you. You think the crust is unsightly, but that's what holds the bread together. How lovely it must be to believe you're so much better than everyone else, just because you haven't sullied yourselves!"

"Hey!" Renée bellowed. "I've sullied myself plenty! I've been down that dark hole, Betty!"

"But have you learned anything?" Betty questioned her. "Have you stopped the chatter in your head long enough to ask yourself the bigger questions? Like, 'why do we choose to do what we do?' I've asked myself that question a lot these past few months. Why do we blindly go about our lives, unconsciously and monotonously creating the same problems and the same outcomes? Do we do it for family? Religion? Our country? Whom do we choose to sacrifice and for what purpose? Do we do what we do because we want to be liked? Because we don't want to be alone? Because we don't want to disappoint? Because to *not* do it would show us to be fallible? I've grown to admire those who choose to stop their own destructive machine. They are freer than the ones who never question. To stand toe-to-toe with your greatest fears, to feel your pain and still emerge from it on the other side in one piece and wiser, is like seeing a new sky and feeling fresh ground underfoot." She took a meaningful pause. "I'm a much better person since I've gotten to know this plant."

"*What?!*" Renée exclaimed.

"It's true," Betty stressed. "I *am* better. I can feel a change inside me. I still have a long journey, but at least I'm on the road. And you know what else? I'm happy."

The women appeared to glower in unison.

"*Happy...*" Helen mocked. "Happiness is for those unacquainted with the rigor of reality. Good God, Betty –"

"You got a lot of nerve!" Judi interjected, sharply aiming her vitriol toward Betty.

Betty suddenly felt as if she were the only temperate voice in the room. "I'm not clear, ladies. Do you prefer me miserable and disheartened? Is that less of a threat to all of you?"

"Wow, Betty," Renée stated, "that was nicely put!"

Betty straightened her dress. "I'm tired of being nice. Nice got me nothing. Nice prevented me from saving my son!"

"So...growing pot is your own personal 'fuck you'?" Renée asked.

"No, Renée. It's my *thank you*. I don't know everything about it, but I want to learn. Maybe I'll be able to teach others to grow it or how to cook with it. Or maybe I can just serve as an example of someone who was born and raised in Texas, always voted Republican, is patriotic to a fault, still believes in good manners, but also happens to have a green heart when it comes to cannabis. I can tell you this much; I will never be the same from now on. And the more I cast off all those tired opinions I carried for so long that didn't belong to me, the less my back aches from the weight. I can tell you this with certainty. There's nothing more liberating than releasing a limiting belief."

Renée turned and glanced at the cannabis plants blowing back and forth. She looked preoccupied and troubled. "I gotta go call my sponsor!" She raced upstairs and out of the house.

Helen heaved her body out of the chair and headed to the stairs. "You're out of your mind," she groused.

It was just Judi and Betty and stone cold silence. Finally, Judi spoke up.

"Why is it you suddenly think you can do whatever you want?"

Betty contemplated the question. "Because if I don't do what I want for the first time in my life, I'm no good to anyone. And I'm fifty-nine. I've earned the right to do whatever the hell I want."

Judi waited, expecting more. "That's it? That's your answer? Is that how you explain yourself?"

"No more explaining. It's simply a statement of fact."

Judi was at a loss. "Well, must be nice..."

"Oh, it's more than nice. You should try it sometime."

Judi turned frosty. "Fine. Grow your pot. Just don't expect anyone to cheer you on for it!"

"I don't expect to be cheered on for doing this. I just thought maybe..."

"Maybe what, Betty?" she asked tersely.

"That real friendship wasn't conditional."

Judi arched her an eyebrow. "Really? You must be smoking a lot of weed if you think that." She brushed past Betty and trod up the stairs, slamming the front door on her way out.

Yes, right, Betty thought. That certainly went well. She gathered herself together and went upstairs. Ronald was in the kitchen, drinking sideways from his water bowl.

"How are you doing, Ronald darling?" Betty asked him.

He gazed at her with his old, tired eyes. Picking him up, she cuddled him tenderly. "You did a marvelous job pruning our first little clone. I never really thanked you properly for that." Ronald purred and nestled his head into Betty's chest just as the phone rang.

Setting him down gently, she checked the Caller ID. There was that PRIVATE again. "Enough," she whispered and picked up the phone. "This is Betty Craven!"

"Uh...hi...Betty..."

The male voice was unfamiliar. "Who is this?"

"I...uh...found your stationary with your name and phone number in a basket at the farmers' market..."

Betty grabbed a kitchen chair and sat down. "I see. Are you the one who has been calling me and hanging up?"

"Yeah...right...um, I didn't know what to say on your message."

"What do you mean?" She felt her body shaking slightly.

"I kind of gathered from your list that maybe...uh...maybe you grew the herb?"

"Well, that's quite the assumption, isn't it?"

"But you do, right?" He pressed. "The reason I ask is, I have a red card and I'm looking for someone to be my caregiver. I wondered if that is something you do?"

Betty's head spun. "I don't...I...This is very inappropriate. I don't know you –"

"I knew your son!" he blurted out.

Betty felt the floor go out beneath her. "What...what do you mean?"

"Frankie? I knew him. I was with him when he died. I carried his body to the bus stop. I think we need to talk."

Chapter 32

"It all makes sense now."

His name was Greg Boswell. He lived north of Paradox and worked as manager for an organic farm that supplied restaurants with greens and produce. He asked if Betty could meet him that evening, as it was his only night off. She didn't want to, but she felt a strange pull at her heart and acquiesced. Right before she left at six o'clock, Peyton pulled up in her driveway.

"I was in the neighborhood," he told her. "I want to check up on Helen."

"Helen?" Betty asked, her mind preoccupied. "She stormed out of here. Well, as much as Helen 'storms' any-where –"

"No, Betty. Helen the plant?"

"Oh. Right. Is there a problem?"

"I don't know. Mind if I check?"

"Of course, not. You have a key. Lock up when you leave, darling."

He looked at her more closely. "Are you okay, Betty?"

She gathered her senses. "I don't know. Ask me in a couple hours."

Betty had agreed to meet Greg in a diner north of Para-dox. She brought a copy of the medical marijuana patient paperwork, even though she had no intention of formalizing their relationship as his caregiver. And yet, she noticed the more she resisted, the more an unseen hand kept pushing her forward.

She got to the diner just after six thirty. The place was packed and she realized that in her flustered daze, she'd forgotten to ask Greg what he looked like. Just then a tall, beefy man with dirty-blond hair, who looked to be in his mid-thirties, stood up from a booth in the rear of the diner and waved at her. The closer she got, the larger he became. He was like a giant, she told herself, close to seven feet tall, with long arms and huge hands. When he shook her hand, she could tell not only how calloused his hands were from the farm work, but also how much strength he possessed.

"Hi, Betty," Greg said nervously. "Can I call you Betty?"

"Yes, of course." She briefly looked around the diner.

"I know it's crowded, but it's okay. We can talk freely. Nobody's gonna hear us."

She suddenly had a revelation. "I don't care if they do." She settled into the booth. "How did you know what I looked like?"

"Our farm has a booth at the outdoor market. You buy your arugula and mixed greens from us. But I didn't make the connection between your name and your face until I found the list you left in the basket. I called out your name, but you couldn't hear me because of those women yelling over their megaphone. Same thing happened the other day when I saw you over at their table. I'm glad you finally picked up the phone."

"Forgive me, but you can't help but stand out in a crowd. I don't know why I've never seen you at your booth."

"I usually hang around the produce truck, unloading and loading boxes. I leave all the schmoozing to the farm interns who enjoy bantering with customers more than I do. I'm not a real people person. That's why I prefer hanging with my plants."

She managed a weak smile. "Yes. Cats and plants. A loner's best friend."

The waitress arrived. Greg ordered a ham sandwich. Betty wasn't hungry but Greg insisted she get something, so she settled on a cheeseburger and fries, figuring "when at a diner...."

"Frankie was a loner," Greg asserted. "But I don't have to tell you that."

Betty played with the edge of her napkin. "How long did you know him?"

"On and off, maybe eighteen months. We crashed at a lot of the same places. Shoot up, get high, disappear...you know..."

"You were a heroin addict too?"

"I guess. My D-O-C was Oxy."

"What's D-O-C?"

"Oh, sorry. Drug of choice. I got hooked on Oxy straight up. When I couldn't get enough from ingesting, I shot it up my arm or snorted it."

"You didn't stop first at cannabis?"

He chuckled. "No. I went right to the hard stuff. My gateway drug was a shitty life." He sat back calmly, with a contemplative appearance. "Frankie talked about you all the time. He used to mention about some big tree in your backyard. There was a swing and you guys would sit out there when he'd come over. He never talked about his dad, except to say he died of liver failure brought on by his alcoholism."

Betty looked at him, incredulously. "Wait a second. His father didn't die of liver failure until *after* Frankie's death."

Greg shrugged. "That's what he always told me."

"But that's impossible. How would he —"

Greg leaned forward. "Frankie was really different, but you know that. He told me you were the only one who understood how different he was." He took a quick sip of water. "Frankie could see things others couldn't. We nicknamed him 'Sy,' short for 'psychic.' He thought that was cool. I'll never forget the first time I met him, he said, 'Happy to meet you again.' I told him I'd never seen him before, and he said he drew me when he was ten years old."

Betty's heart pounded hard. "Oh, my God. You were the giant?"

"The giant?"

She nodded. "He drew a picture of a tall man with long arms, reaching out to him while he lay in a bed. I assumed it was his father."

Greg was stunned. "Holy shit...wow...he never told me that part."

Betty leaned forward, touching Greg's hand. "I have to ask you something, and I want you to tell me the truth. Did Frankie overdose on purpose or by accident?"

"Neither."

Betty felt her body begin to shake. "What?"

"Maybe it was more like a conscious accident? He'd been totally clean for three straight days. He went off everything cold turkey, even though we kept telling him it wasn't a good idea. But he said he didn't want to go the Methadone route and that 'it was time.' But those last three days of his life? They were a kick. The first day, he was at his dealer's house when his dealer got shot and killed. Frankie told me he hid in a closet under a bunch of blankets. That's where he found the boxes full of one-pound bricks of Humboldt's best grade pot. He also found cash. Five grand! So he stole it, along with a brick of weed. I understood stealing the money but not the weed, 'cause he didn't smoke anymore. But he told me he needed it."

Betty's mind spun. "He needed it? Why?"

"He said something about having to give it to someone who was going to be really happy to find it one day."

Betty sat back in the booth. The hair on her arms prickled. "And the cash?"

"That was the best part. We got ourselves a room in a decent three-star motel and stayed there. It sure beat the dives we were used to. I went out and scored some Oxy, and he told me he was going to visit you. I came back on the third day and found him in bed having a seizure. It was bad, but he could still talk and he kept saying, 'Pay attention,' over and over. After awhile he was barely conscious, but right before he died he got real calm...and then it was as if he thought of something funny, because he kinda smiled and said 'Cragen.' That was the last thing he said."

Betty's eyes filled with tears.

"Hey, I'm sorry, Betty. I didn't mean –"

"No. It's okay. It all makes sense now."

"I guess I just needed you to know your son didn't die on that bus stop. He died in a bed in a decent room, with clean sheets and towels. I covered him in a blanket and carried him to the bus stop bench later that night. I didn't know what else to do. That was the worst night of my life. But you know what they say. You gotta hit rock bottom and then re-build from there. As crazy as it sounds, Frankie stayed with me the whole time. I could feel him beside me. He always told me I was gonna get clean and that he saw me working with plants. When I went to rehab and did the sober living stint, I interned at a CSA farm. Frankie was right. It made all the difference. Something about being one with the dirt and watching things grow was healing. It saved my life."

She touched his hand. "I know." She wiped her tears. "You said you wanted me to be your caregiver? If you're clean and sober, how do you justify using cannabis?"

"I used pot to help me get off alcohol. I couldn't have done it without the herb." He paused, struggling for the right words.

"Just say it, Greg. You don't have to worry about wheth-er it's right."

"Thanks," he said with a smile. "I don't abuse it. For some reason, I don't want to. I'm not in this to get high. I'm just trying to stay sane."

She nodded. Opening her purse, she handed him the pa-perwork. "I'd be honored to be your caregiver."

They sat and talked for three more hours, until Greg said he had to get back to the farm and prep for the outdoor market the next day. When she asked him what strain he wanted her to grow, he wasn't particular. "I don't need my world rocked," he offered. "Grow me something that takes the edge off and puts the world in perspective."

When Betty walked out of the diner, the warm summer wind was whipping wildly. Before she was halfway home, fat pellets of rain began to fall until a massive deluge ensued. The Taurus hydroplaned on the waves of water that filled the side streets. Thunder and lightening quickly followed on the heels of another powerful downpour that fell horizon-tally, making it nearly impossible to see ten feet in front of her car. Branches from the tree-lined streets dropped like toothpicks across the flooded roads, as the wind angrily wailed.

The storm was still raging when she got back to her house just after ten o'clock. She was soaked as she walked inside and headed upstairs. That's when she smelled something odd. It was like rotten eggs and it was coming from the basement. Her mind raced with every possibility, including a fire in the grow rooms. In her frantic rush, she didn't see the note Peyton had taped on the closed basement door. Instead, she flung open the door and was met with a wave of sulfurous fumes.

Boom!

Betty backed up, feeling the house shake and hearing glass shatter downstairs. The roar of the storm outside was menacing. She ran into the kitchen, grabbed a towel to put around her nose and mouth, and headed back to the basement door. Frantically flicking on the lights, her mind was still not registering what was happening. Through the fetid waves of fumes, she made it into the basement, turning on all the available lamps in the veg room and main area. She could instantly feel moisture hitting her body. That's when she noticed the smashed side window next to the sliding glass door and the enormous trunk of the elm tree punching through it. The wind swirled into the main room, tossing papers and rolling empty plastic pots across the floor. As the chaos continued, Betty's disconcerted mind didn't see the spitting smoke from the sulfur burner mingling with the light on the plants' delicate leaves.

She quickly opened the sliding glass door and ran outside, desperate to inhale fresh air. Her eyes burned and teared. All she could faintly see was her beloved old tree lying across the yard. The surging rain chased her back toward the sliding glass door. It was only then she finally looked inside and saw the sulfur burner hanging from the chain above the plants in the veg room. The lights were all on and the chilling realization hit her that light and sulfur were sworn enemies. Covering her mouth and nose with the towel, she tore back into the basement and struggled to remove the red-hot burner from its chain. However, between the fumes and the heat she couldn't grasp it and had to run outside repeatedly to refuel on fresh air, before racing back inside for another futile attempt. On the fourth try, the smoke was clearing out through the open door. That's when she saw the damage. One by one, the leaves on her beloved girls were curling and turning translucent. She screamed like a mother watching her children die, gathering the pots as quickly as she could, before hustling them outside the sliding glass door. Once they were out of the room, she was finally able to remove the sulfur burner and set it outside to let the rain suffocate the nauseating coals.

It took her almost an hour to completely rid the room of the stench and lingering smoke. She kept the door to the bloom room closed, but she knew the lights were already out in there. As the storm subsided, she walked outside to check her veg girls. It was nothing short of a nuclear holocaust. One by one their leaves continued to curl, and there was nothing she could do to stop it. All the months of careful nurturing and labor were being destroyed in front of her. "Why?" she plaintively asked. All she could do now was return them to the aired out veg room and let them linger in the dark until morning. As she stood in the darkened basement, that familiar tightening in her jaw reappeared. Her neck began to spasm, and as if on cue, her right ear fluttered in that damned syncopated beat. She grabbed her ear. "Oh God, not again!"

It wasn't until she walked back up the stairs that she saw the note Peyton taped to the basement door. "Started sulfur at 9:15. Helen's clones needed it, so all of them in the veg are getting a dose too. DON'T GO INTO THE BASEMENT UNTIL MORNING." And there was a P.S. "Hung out with Ronald. You need to check on him."

Betty's heart began to pound, as she raced up the stairs and turned on the light in her bedroom. There was Ronald, curled up on the bed. She stood in the doorway, wanting to move forward, yet petrified of that queasy feeling in her gut. "Ronald?" she softly asked. When he still didn't stir,

Betty reluctantly walked over and sat on the edge of the bed. "Ronald, darling?" She touched his head but he didn't respond. Kneeling by the side of the bed, she looked at him more closely. His body was still slightly warm, but he had slipped peacefully from this world. A swell of emotion hit hard, as she crumbled to the carpet. Those familiar walls moved in tightly around her, as the impact of so many losses enveloped her. Finally, she worked up the courage to touch him again. Cradling his limp body in her arms like a baby, she rocked him back and forth. "You were a good cat, Ronald the third. Thank you for being a loyal friend." Once she got her wits back, Betty found a box and towel, and placed his body inside. She would take him to the emergency vet's office the next day and have him cremated.

But for now, the familiar darkness that had followed and shrouded her for so many years seized her body. She'd come so far and now it was all falling away, bit by bit, friendship by friendship. "You gotta hit rock bottom," she recalled Greg telling her earlier that evening, "and then rebuild from there." But how? Everything seemed meaningless to her. What was the point of her three months of enlightenment – of intense love and heartfelt satisfaction – if all of it was destined to be shattered in the end? The same feelings that hollowed her soul the night Frankie died reemerged. On that night, five years earlier, she'd wandered into the backyard and lay on the ground under the elm tree, begging God for answers. She felt the wet dirt beneath her palms and the kiss of the leaves as they fell across her aching body. And somehow, when she awoke in the same place the next morning, she was able to get up and keep going. It was as if the earth had infused her with enough strength to continue.

So, guided by that memory, Betty walked back to the basement, feeling her way in the coal darkness, and walked into the pitch-black bloom room, closing the door behind her. There, amidst the intoxicating buds, she lay down and prayed to the same God. Then, as slumber overwhelmed the pain, she finally let go. For the first time in her life, Betty Craven let go.

~~~

The bloom lights burst on at eight o'clock the following morning, quickly awakening Betty. Even with the fans blowing and the intake and outtake fans turned on, her head swam from the dizzying aromas. She looked up at her girls swaying back and forth and smiled. She checked their leaves and buds; the distinguished sparkling residue of sulfur that had been sucked in by the fans could be seen. But except for the disagreeable, rotten egg odor that was evident on closer examination, they all seemed to be holding up well. The other girls in the veg room, however, were not as fortunate. Helen's clones were all but dead. Only one, surrounded by blackened leaves, had a complete center stalk. Most of the remaining clones had lost their entire top-half, with only a few lower branches barely alive. But something ignited inside of Betty. Instead of falling into a crevice of gloom, she was determined to turn this all around. Even against the sorrow of losing Ronald, Betty felt a budding strength overtake her. As it moved through her, she realized the spasm in her neck was gone, her jaw had loosened and the perplexing flutter in her ear had disappeared.

She called Peyton and he came over immediately. After telling him about Ronald's passing, she told him about the girls. It wasn't clear which news hit him the hardest. After examining the plants, he almost started to cry.

"Some of these are gone, Betty."

"They're quite resilient. You've told me that before."

"They can't come back from the dead."

"Look at the stalks!" she said, pointing to one of the Kushberry girls that only had a thin stalk left. "They're strong! They have a lot of willpower. I just need to figure out how to reboot them!"

"Reboot? They're plants, not computers." He glanced around the room, shaking his head. "I can't help you on this one, Betty."

She walked out into the main room as Peyton followed. Even though she'd swept up most of the debris, the occasional glass shard was still evident where the tree trunk burst through the window.

"When is Jeff showing up with his chainsaw?"

Betty felt her stomach tighten. "This is a job for a tree service."

Peyton regarded her carefully. "Did you tell him about Ronald and the girls?"

"Not yet. Watch your step, dear. There are still small glass shards −"

"Why not?" he pressed her. "He liked Ronald."

She searched for a proper lie that wouldn't confuse the issue, but quickly realized how the process was already tiring her. "I just haven't, Peyton." She turned on the radio to the classical station, as the top of the hour news began. The lead local story was another solo protest by Doobie Douggie along a stretch of highway near his home. Apparently, the "Pope of Dope," as the reporter disparagingly referred to him, had wheeled himself out onto the overpass that crossed the highway from his home and hung an enormous, red flag from the bridge, decorated with a huge, bright-green cannabis leaf. The man, as always, loved to wave his many flags. However, the visual distraction caused several minor accidents as well as gridlock. As Douggie was cited for the disturbance, he wasted no time and launched into a loud rebuke of the policies that made his venerated plant illegal.

Betty turned to Peyton. "That's it! If anyone knows how to fix this, he does."

Peyton followed Betty back up the stairs. "You've gotta be kidding me! Did you suck up too much sulfur into your lungs last night?"

"I know exactly where that highway is. It's right near Dottie's ranch. It's a small area. I bet she knows where he lives."

"Betty, you cannot just show up at this guy's house and expect him to welcome you! He's kinda out there. You know what I'm sayin'? He's smart as hell but −"

"Peyton, I don't give a damn if he's one wicker chair short of a summer patio set. Nobody knows cannabis like Douggie. When I have a problem, I go to the source!"

"He carries a gun, Betty. *A gun?*"

"I have a gun too, Peyton. Should I bring it along?" She marched into the kitchen, with Peyton right on her heels.

"Betty, he's like a rock star. He's really private. He's a grower, not a shower. You won't get past his gate!"

"Yes, I will." She brought out her cacao powder and plain cocoa butter.

"What are you doing?"

"I'm going to make him some chocolates. With honey. You can catch more bees with honey, you know?"

"Betty, you're not hearing me! Douggie is not like the rest of us. He doesn't believe in daylight saving time. He thinks it's a government conspiracy to throw off the flowering light-cycle of his blooming cannabis plants! He has a target of Nixon's face he shoots, with Nixon's nose as the bulls-eye. This is not the kind of person who allows anyone to just show up unannounced!"

She stopped what she was doing and turned to Peyton. "Fear doesn't motivate me anymore, Peyton. So I suggest you put on an apron and start stirring."

Three hours later on that Sunday afternoon, Betty was on the road. With Ronald tucked into a box on her backseat, she stopped first at the 24-hour emergency vet's office outside of town and carried her dearly loved cat inside. She made the arrangements to have him cremated, said her tearful goodbye and left.

Her next stop was Dottie's ranch. When she got to the gate, Hugh, the ranch manager, answered the intercom and buzzed her inside. Before she rolled to a stop, he was right there waiting for her, with a terribly worried expression.

"I need to speak to Dottie right away," Betty told him, getting out of the car.

"Wait!" He said, touching her arm. "I gotta ask you something and you gotta tell me the truth. Does Dottie have cancer?"

Betty studied the man's eyes, filled with panic and worry. "No, Hugh. She doesn't have cancer."

"Then why do you keep bringing her marijuana?"

Betty stopped dead. "I'm not bringing Dottie –"

"I found one of those chocolates in her office and ate it. I could taste the pot right away. Look, we all care a lot for her, and she's not the same since her ol' man died. She's like family to all of us. And if she's dying, I need to know about it." He was shaking and riddled with apprehension.

Betty put a reassuring hand on his shoulder. "She's doesn't have cancer, Hugh. You have my word on that. She's just trying to figure it all out. And I guess my chocolates might help with that desire."

He nodded and seemed to relax a bit. "She's in the house. I'll get her." He turned to walk away and then turned back to Betty. "Thank you for helping her."

Once alone with Dottie, Betty asked about the infamous Douggie. Dottie rolled her eyes and pointed up the highway. "You can't miss his house. It's about five miles from here, at the end of a dirt road. Keep your windows down. You'll smell it before you see it."

Betty followed Dottie's directions and easily found the pot star's house. She parked her car and carried the cooler of chocolates to his modest front gate. A boxwood hedge, towering six-feet-high, surrounded the front yard. She started to open the latch on the gate, when she heard the distinctive *click* of a pistol being cocked.

"Now, who in the hell do you think you are?"

Chapter 33

"Did you ever watch a movie when you were high?"

"I'm Betty Craven," she replied, holding out her hand.

Douggie didn't move a muscle. Wearing his frayed "Legalize the Weed" t-shirt, he sat in his wheelchair – sans his usual protest flag – and with steely eyes never allowed his pistol to move a hair off his target. "So what?"

"Please put your gun away," Betty said with a relaxed smile. "I didn't bring my little Tomcat, so you can't show me yours if I can't show you mine."

Douggie's long mane of unruly grey hair blew in the wind. "Who in the hell sent you here?"

"I sent myself. I have a very serious gardening problem, and I need your expert assistance." She handed him the cooler. "I brought you chocolates as a gift."

Douggie lowered the pistol and opened the cooler. Holding one to his nose, he gave it a good whiff. "These aren't loaded."

"Of course, not. Why would I bring you cannabis chocolates? That would be far too predictable, wouldn't it?"

He popped a chocolate in his mouth and let it melt across his tongue, the whole time never taking his eyes off Betty. "Shit...those are good."

"It's the honey," she said with a grin.

He silently sized her up and then tilted his head toward the back garden. Wheeling himself forward along the brick path, Betty followed close behind. "You sure as hell don't look like the assholes who usually show up here."

"Why, thank you...do you like to be called Douggie or Doobie Douggie?"

"Neither," he barked, skillfully rolling his chair over a few bricks and leading Betty around a sharp corner. "That's just the name some stoner kid came up with. I've had a lot of names over the years. 'The Captain of Cannabis,' 'The Wizard of Weed,' 'The Rustler of Reefer,' 'The Gardener of Ganja.'"

"So what do you want me to call you?"

"Use my real name. Frank."

Betty stopped in her tracks. "*Frank?*"

He wheeled his chair around. "Yeah? What's it to ya?"

She shook her head in stunned amazement. "Everything. You wouldn't believe me if I told you...Frank."

With Betty close behind, Frank rolled down a short brick path, through another gate and did a wheelie down a short ramp leading into an enormous, prolific, outdoor cannabis garden. Rows and rows of healthy, vibrant cannabis plants filled the space, sunk into the rich soil and surrounded with compost. Most were well over eight feet tall, each one easily spanning five- to six-feet across.

"It's kinda like the Disneyland of cannabis, huh?" he asked her. "All of them, E-Ticket rides!" He jutted his thumb in the air to accentuate his point.

One by one, Frank introduced her to each of the plants. She lost count after number twenty-two. Occasionally, he'd grab a nearby hose and spray a few plants that looked thirsty. It all seemed so natural to Betty, except most people didn't water their garden with a hose in their hand and a 9mm tucked in their waistband. After the tour, they wandered over to a sheltered patio where it looked like Frank spent most of his time. There was even a single bed in the corner, sheltered by a sheet of plastic.

"Are you so nervous you have to sleep out here all summer?" Betty asked.

"Nah. If people are dumb enough to bust in, my Sig will do the talking. I sleep out here because they protect me from myself. They remind me. They always remind me."

"Remind you of what?"

"Whatever's important at the moment. So why'd you come out here?"

Betty explained her terrible sulfur mishap, told him she was a caregiver and how people were depending upon her to come through for them.

"Well, now you know what a farmer feels like when his corn crop gets wiped out by a tornado or pestilence."

"I suppose I do," Betty contemplated.

"I feel for them when that happens, but I don't think the farmer would give me the same respect if it happened to my crop. But that doesn't mean both that farmer and I are not expert gardeners."

"You don't understand, Frank. I can't fail again."

"Sweetheart, if you're afraid of failing, you better get the hell out of this game. You have a long list of people who came before you and failed badly. Some of them went to prison for growing this damn plant. Some of them lost everything – lovers, wives, parents, friends...all because they loved to grow and learn everything they could about this little weed." He leaned forward in his chair. "It's a passion, Betty. Not an addiction. But try explaining that to all the people who scream and tell everyone how dangerous it is. I can't believe they're dredging up the same Nixon-ian bullshit about brain damage and the lack of motivation syndrome. Do you think it's possible to have a garden this big and not have a functioning brain and a tremendous amount of motivation to keep it alive and thriving? All the anti-cannabis speeches are filled with such inaccuracies, it makes me want to puke. It's incredible how much ignorance can be expressed with such insane confidence! But somehow, they pull it off!" He offered a joint to Betty who turned him down. He lit up and inhaled deeply. "You know what you don't hear on the news? You don't hear about how you can juice the fresh leaves, just like you would do with spinach. There are all these enzymes in the leaves that can cure anything from Crohn's Disease to arthritis." He reached over and uncovered an old wheat grass juicer. "I drink a shot a day." He opened up a zippered leather pouch and brought out a plastic baby syringe, filled with a dark green, tar-like substance. "And then there's this. You're looking at the crème de le crème, Betty. A guy out of Canada named Rick Simpson developed this method for extracting the resins into a thick oil. You concentrate one pound of cannabis buds down into *two ounces* of this stuff. We're talking holy shit potent! But it's curing the incurables. Cancer, diabetes, epilepsy, you name it. Some choose to run for the cure. I prefer to grow for it!"

"That's quite a statement."

"It's true, Betty. But there's no money in it! Cannabis is the people's medicine! If weed were legal, the price would drop like crazy. Everybody and their cousin would be growing it and making what they needed out of it. Now, can you see how the powerbrokers in charge don't want that to happen? They'd lose control of their medical monopolies. When one plant can do the job of five or more drugs, there's no profit in it. The profit is in our pain. The profit is in prolonging our misery. The profit is in handing us false hope, that their pills, shots and poisons are better and healthier for us than something nature provides. I happen to find that line of thought disgusting. That's why I take every opportunity to discredit all those inbred, mono-celled drones, who insist upon making false statements about this plant. But sometimes I wonder why I bother. Nothing creates a pointless debate like an inaccurate supposition."

"I think it's the stigma that gets in the way of intelligent conversation."

"The stigma was manmade!" he bellowed, taking another quick hit before snuffing out the joint. "Political fraud meets Hollywood! Two whores in the same bed, trying to bend over John Q. Public. It doesn't matter if it's *Reefer Madness* or some botoxed TV drug-addiction doc spouting the 'dangers of weed.' It's two cheeks on the same ass."

Betty smiled. "Same church, different pew?"

He leaned forward. "*Exactly*. And if they're not trying to scare you, they throw out the morality issue. I never understood that one, Betty. Who in the hell ever said cannabis had anything to do with morality? They've foisted that false doctrine on us, ever since Harry Anslinger swore it made white women want to screw black men. That's not to say the right strain can't make sex incredible." He winked. "So I've heard. There's nothing moral or immoral about it, for God's sake! It's a plant. Why don't we ban the iris flower, because Georgia O'Keeffe made it look a woman's genitalia? That painting still freaks out a lot of people...especially men."

Betty leaned toward Frank. "I don't think that's what most people are afraid of, Frank, when it comes to cannabis. They're afraid of addiction –"

"Oh, hell, don't get me started, Betty. They've already proven that addiction theory to be wrong." He wheeled over to a small table, where an automatic coffee maker sat, with its carafe filled to the top with the darkest brew Betty had ever seen. "You want to talk about addiction? Let's start with coffee." He poured himself a cup and offered her one. "Don't worry. Just like your chocolates, it's only loaded with caffeine." She nodded and took a cup. "If I miss a day without four strong cups of Joe, my hands shake like a Parkinson's patient. But the few times I've gone without my herb, after all the years of smoking and eating it, all I do is miss it. But I'm not flailing like a fish on the concrete, having a goddamn seizure!" He took a sip of the coal black coffee. "Look, there's impulse control versus addiction; habitual versus addiction. Cannabis can be habitual and if you suffer from the inability to handle your impulses, you just might feel that you can't live without your herb. But those assholes who believe that are the same ones who *always* blame others for the tornado of shit that constantly hits them and how they can't catch a break!" His singsong tone mimicked a whiny brat. "Spare me! Unfortunately, somebody never sat those pricks down when they were little and gave them a solid foundation. Taught them about cause and effect, the consequences of their actions, and that you don't usually get everything you want the second you want it!"

Betty was quite surprised by Doobie Frank's perspective. "Careful there, Frank. You're starting to sound like a social Conservative."

"Aw, fuck labels! All I can tell you is it fries my fritter when ignorant people blame this beautiful herb for their inability to pull their head out of their own ass! It's not the herb, Betty – it's the loser who happens to be using the herb. The jerk-off showed up first; the herb just happened to meet him on his muddled journey. Guaranteed Betty, that fool would act the same whether he was one toke over the line or not. It's not addiction when it comes to Mary Jane. If some idiot suffers from impulse control, that's a helluva lot different than the crack head down on his knees, sifting through the shag carpet, looking for a leftover rock he can plug in his pipe." He scooted his wheelchair closer to her. "I'll let you in on why I really think the big boys want to keep the weed illegal. You ready?"

"Ready." She took a sip of the burnt brew and had to think lovely thoughts so she wouldn't spit it out.

"Did you ever watch a movie when you were high?"

"No. Can't say I have."

"Well, give it a shot sometime. You won't be able to focus on the story, because all you'll see is the 'acting.' Doesn't matter if it's good acting or bad acting. It's the 'acting' you won't be able to get past. You'll easily see the lie in the actors' performance – the pretending to be someone else. Now, take that understanding and watch a political debate when you're high. Oh, hell! You won't be able to get through the introductions, guaranteed! When they start lying and telling the audience what they want to hear, you'll see how insidious those pricks are. It's as if the herb removes the blinders and the truth is exposed." He wheeled back a few inches. "So you see, I don't think it's the plant they're really afraid of. It's the *power* of the plant that scares the shit out of the people who want to ban it. They don't want a world of people collectively questioning their governments, their churches or their educational systems. They want us docile! You start becoming one with the weed and it will shine perspective on aspects of your life you never saw before. Hell, you'll wake up one day and say, 'Why didn't I notice that?' Weed punctures the darkness and gradually exposes you to your own shadow and the collective shadow governing all of us. You start to realize there's more to life than the grind and the pursuit of crap that puts you in debt and prevents you from getting in touch with what's really important in here." He pointed to his heart. "They want you to keep running on their wheel that goes nowhere, because that's what the machine demands. The machine needs to be fed by each of us. And they own that damn machine, Betty! However, when you wake up and see that the machine has nothing to do with your greater good, you elect to step away from it. But the owners of the machine don't want that to happen, because they need reliable slaves to do their dirty work. And that, sweetheart, is why cannabis is so dangerous." He leaned closer to her. "*It makes you think.*"

Betty silently took in every word. "I know, and for some of us who opted to borrow our beliefs from others, it's quite an awakening."

Frank sat back. "Damn! It's refreshing to sit across from someone who looks like you and loves the herb. If everyone looked like you, instead of the trolls who usually come 'round, I'd build a pool and have lots of parties."

"Well, Frank...you are so kind to say that."

"I mean it! I wish there were more like you! Well-dressed, well-spoken, educated –"

"I'm a Republican."

"Even better! *I love it*! The cannabis movement needs people who don't look like they need a bath or spell cannabis, c-a-n-u-b-u-s-s! The problem right now? We have too many dubious people filtering into this medical marijuana business from the illegal side. They might have a dispensary or a grow op, but they always have that creepy vibe, you know? They don't walk; they skulk. It's from spending too many years doing dark-alley weed deals. If we're going to get the public-at-large to understand what this plant can do, you don't want to put some skinny Rastafarian dude with dreadlocks on TV or some chick with stained teeth who looks like she does the ho stroll down at the truck stop." He snapped his finger in the air. "Betty! You could be the poster girl for cannabis reform!"

"No, no, no, Frank."

"With your good looks and your ability to communicate clearly, you'd be worshipped by weed growers and users everywhere!" He smiled, showing his obvious crush for Betty. "I'm worshipping you right now."

"Now, now Frank –" she said a little taken back.

"You married?"

"No."

"Boyfriend?"

Betty took a breath. "I'm not sure."

"Not sure?"

"It's complicated, Frank."

"Bullshit. It's not complicated Betty, unless you want it to be." He pulled back. "Sorry. I didn't mean to get too personal with you."

"No. It's okay. I've been known to complicate a lemon sorbet."

He raised his coffee mug. "How about a toast?"

Betty reluctantly lifted her mug. "To what?"

"To non-conformists like us!"

A peculiar sense of pride engulfed Betty. "To non-conformists!" She clinked her mug against his.

"To all those who conform in order to feel safe," he continued, "understand that safety is only a perception and has its limits, whereas independence is infinite!" He slugged down a healthy gulp of java.

Betty took a dainty sip and started to speak.

"One more toast!" Doobie Frank interrupted. "Here's to always listening with your heart. Because when you do that, you'll always hear the right answer."

Betty felt a lump form in her throat. "Amen." She took another genteel sip and checked the time. "About my plants?"

"Oh, right. The reason for your visit." He grabbed a pad and jotted down a name and phone number. "This guy makes a fresh compost tea that's so alive, you can almost feel its heartbeat. It's got tons of beneficial microorganisms in it and other stuff."

"What other stuff?"

"Magic, Betty. *Magic*. Spray the tea full strength on your plants every three days. Water them with it too. Don't feed them anything else, except some liquid B Vitamins and a small amount of powdered minerals. That'll help them get over the shock of the sulfur. This guy's got everything you'll need." He handed her the slip of paper.

"Anything else?"

"If any of the plants are halfway decent, remove all the dead leaves and branches. If the top of a plant was hit hard, chop it off. It'll just slow down the growth of the rest of it. Whenever you can, bring them outside and put them some-place where they can get dappled shade. Right now, you want to limit as much direct light and heat as you can. Let them grow out seven inches or so and then clone the best branches. That way, you can continue the genetics."

Betty made mental notes. "Good ideas. Is that all?"

He thought. "Time. As with most things in life, Betty, time tends to either cure it or make it worse. You should probably see some new growth starting within a week or ten days. If you don't, well I guess it was time to say goodbye to that particular plant." He looked out at his lush garden. "Just like I'm going to have to say goodbye to all these beautiful ladies in fewer than two months, when harvest season starts. Life and death. You get more used to it when you work with nature."

He rolled his wheelchair out to her car to see her off. "You ever need any more help, you can come over anytime," he said with a coy smile.

"Thank you, Frank." She got into the car.

"Anything. I mean it."

"There is one thing. Jeremy Lindholm? The producer of that documentary you appeared in? If you ever talk to him again, tell him Betty from the merry-go-round said 'hello'... and a heartfelt 'thank you.'"

She headed back on the road, buoyed by a sense of pur-pose once again. Turning on the radio, she searched for a classic rock station, but stopped on a local news station when she heard a familiar name mentioned on their top

story. It seemed that the morally uptight Reverend Bobby
Lynch, who did everything "for the children," had been arrested for "inappropriate contact with several seventeen-
year-old boys" from his congregation. Betty was momentarily shocked, but then she recalled a comment Jeff made
about Lynch months before. "When one doth protest too
much about an issue," he said, "one doth often have something to hide."

Wasting no time, she called the fellow with the "magic"
tea and arranged to purchase a five-gallon bucket, more liquid B vitamins and the powdered minerals that looked like
they'd been mined from pristine, glacial rock. After loading
everything into her backseat, she quickly headed home. As
she turned into the driveway, she was shocked to see Renée
sitting in the shade of her front doorway. Betty hauled the
heavy bucket from the car as Renée stepped forward to help
her.

"This is unexpected," Betty stated, keeping her tone formal and distant.

"Yeah...I know..."

Betty noticed something odd about Renée. Although
she was still preoccupied, she had a conspicuous calmness
Betty had never experienced before. "I didn't think you'd
ever grace my doorstep again."

"I gotta talk to you."

"Help me drag this bucket to the basement door," Betty
instructed, feeling quite bold in her demand.

Renée was still orbiting in her own space, but she
stopped when she saw the fallen elm tree. "Oh God, Betty.
Your favorite tree. I'm sorry." And she meant it.

"Thank you." Betty perched her backside on the hori-
zontal trunk. "If you've come here to convince me that I
shouldn't –"

"No, it's not that at all." Renée sat next to Betty, swinging
her large purse onto her lap. "I came here to make amends.
It's Step Nine of the program. Making amends?"

"Oh, Renée. You've marched up and down those steps so
many times, your thighs must be burning."

She actually smiled. "Yeah, I hear you. I'm still not very good at it after all these years, I guess." She opened her purse. "I gotta show you something." After dumping a mass of contents onto the grass, she sorted through the heap and held up a decorative glass pipe. "I guess you know what this is."

Betty closely examined it. Smelling the resin-soaked bowl, she kept a poker face. "Smells like some kind of Kush." She handed the pipe back to Renée.

"Cocoa Kush." She shook her head in shock. "You got a good nose there."

"*Cocoa* Kush? Well, that would be an interesting one to add to my potpourri of plants. The pure Kush strains are more *Indica* in their effects. They tend to calm the mind, which I know you need."

"I don't get it," she said, anxiety reappearing, "you're supposed to be traumatized and disgusted by my duplicity. God knows I am!"

"Yes, I guess I should be," Betty calmly said. "But then, I really don't want to 'should' all over myself anymore. Am I traumatized?" She checked herself. "No, can't say I am. Shocked? Nope. It actually explains a lot."

"Step Nine says we are to 'make direct amends to such people wherever possible' –"

"Stop," Betty said, placing her hand on Renée's arm. "I don't need to hear what your book tells you to do. I only care about what *you* feel. And there's no right or wrong feeling."

Renée looked mystified. "After everything I said to you – after everything I did – I can't believe you have this kind of compassion."

"It comes with the territory. As my dear friend, Peyton, told me once, 'We're all just unmade beds, searching for the perfect comforter.'" She smiled. "And I believe he was high when he said it."

"Well, I'm a California king sized, unmade bed. I'm a walking hypocrite. I pound the pulpit by day, while I light up in my closet at night and take the two quick hits I allow myself. It's my only vice and I know it's wrong, but it seems to help me calm down and get perspective, if only briefly. But the next morning the guilt kicks in, and I'm back pounding on that pulpit. It's exhausting, Betty."

"Then stop fighting it."

"I can't! Besides, I gotta keep fighting the good fight!"

"Why?"

"Because, I have to be better than this!"

"Better than what?" Betty quietly inquired.

Renée sighed. "Just *better*."

Betty gave her comment serious consideration. "I used to think the same thing. Always striving for perfection – always reaching for the unreachable. If you want to go crazy, give it a try. If you want to stay sane, let it go."

Renée stared off into the distance. "You know what I wish I could do?"

"What's that?"

"Figure out how to just be." She turned to Betty. "You know? Just *be*."

Betty patted her arm in a reassuring manner. "You and everyone else, Renée. If we could all get the noise to stop, perhaps we could figure it out."

Renée rested her head on Betty's shoulder. "Thank you." She gathered her items from the lawn, tossing them back into her purse.

Betty eyed a peculiar looking plastic baggie with strangely shaped brown nuggets inside. "What's that?"

"Oh, it's an underground favorite. They call them 'BB's' or 'bullets.' They're made of chocolate."

"Well, I guess I have something else to tell you too."

~~~

After Renée left, Betty brought all the veg girls outside onto an area of shaded grass that hadn't been hit by the fallen elm debris. With painstaking exactness, she followed Doobie Frank's advice and removed all the dead or nearly dead leaves and branches, and even cut off seven inches of blackened growth from the top of two plants. After she was done, her girls looked naked and vulnerable. One of her favorite Kushberry plants, that had been such a vital and fast grower, now only had a single stalk. But she couldn't bear to destroy it. Betty filled her large plastic spray canister with the "magic" compost tea and diligently saturated each plant, including the underside of all the leaves. When each plant was dripping with the earthy-smelling brew, she treated each girl to a healing cupful.

Standing back, she stared at her bevy of beauties in their weakened appearance and felt nothing but love for each and every one of them. In all their stark imperfection, Betty saw beyond their defects and cheered them on with gusto. "You can make it, girls. Carry on."

The plants were too wet to put back inside and Doobie Frank did mention that giving them as much shaded exposure to the outdoors would be beneficial in their fragile state. She washed out the canister and turned to look at the devastation surrounding her from the fallen tree. Checking out the roof, it was evident that more damage had occurred, wiping out most of the hard work Buddy had completed. But in that same instant, something changed within Betty. She didn't give up; she gave in. She realized whatever was going to happen would happen, and there was nothing she could do to prevent her fate from being drawn to its completion.

Walking the length of the large elm trunk, she came to the uprooted point and the spot three feet above it where she could still easily see Frankie's carved words. Running her fingers across the deep crevices of the two words, she swore she could feel his spirit move through her. Somehow he knew, on that final day of his life, exactly what she would need in the years to come. No two words had ever haunted her so desperately since his death. But in that moment, those words awakened her again and, infused with that sensation, she didn't fear the possibilities of failure or loneliness. She didn't question how he understood the kind of power that Emily Dickinson poem held over her. But somehow, he knew enough to carve the two last words of that powerful work into their favorite tree.

"LETTING GO."

Chapter 34

"This belongs to you, Betty."

The first thing Betty did was take photographs. *Lots* of photographs. She dragged out several of her blooming plants, that showed impressive bud development with dense, frosty crystal formations, and set them in the bright sun. Like a proud mother, she set her camera lens on "macro" and captured dozens of outstanding shots, using the sun's rays to reflect the pinpoints of sugar resting heavily on the main top cola. True, Peyton told her never to photograph any of her girls, fearing the "wrong" people might find them and harass her. But none of that concerned her anymore. Just like her prized flowers that graced the front yard and whose photos blanketed the hallway walls, Betty felt it was only fair to give the same consideration to her basement girls. After downloading them on her computer, she finally decided on her favorite and printed it out on premium photo paper. She removed an old print of a blue-ribbon-winning yellow rose of Texas from a frame in the hallway, Betty eagerly replaced it with a vibrant close-up of "Helen's" glistening top bud.

Walking back into the kitchen, she turned around and silently canvassed the living room. She felt like a foreigner, detached from the area and all of its belongings. Grabbing a box, she began going through the drawers and cupboards with a judicious eye, leaving her emotional attachment at the door, and selecting numerous items to take to Lily at the *The Gilded Rose*. Hours passed and Betty's unexpected quest to rid herself of the excess baggage filling her house took on epic proportions. She felt driven by a mysterious force that demanded an unapologetic assessment of what was necessary to keep versus what was intrinsic to her happiness. The disparity between those two grew wider as the hours passed.

Knickknacks and collectables she'd always thought were important no longer held their allure. Antique tablecloths and tea sets she'd enjoyed for decades also seemed to lose their glimmer. As night fell, Betty's systematic approach became even stronger, almost ruthlessly electing to either dispose of or box up more items that carried no special feelings. After prowling through the attic late into the night, she effortlessly got rid of half the packed storage boxes that had been reverently protected under a sheet for more than ten years. Instead of finding the process depressing, she found it invigorating. She was still awake at 2:00 A.M., after only taking a short break for a bite to eat and an iced coffee to buttress her motivation.

Letting her mind wander as she worked, she felt pangs of sadness erupt when she collected all of Ronald's things and ceremoniously placed them into a bag. But when she allowed her mind to drift to the human relationships she'd lost over the last few days, the only person that tugged at her heart was Jeff. He hadn't called again, after leaving the message of condolence on her voicemail. The ball, she surmised, was in her court, but she was hopelessly lost as to how to serve it back. If only he didn't understand her as well as he did, perhaps it would have been easier to approach him. But she wasn't an enigma to him, and the bare vulnerability that came with that fact was overwhelming. Still, her damned pride surfaced each time she considered picking up the phone. No, she told herself, she would do nothing. And in the mere act of doing nothing, she convinced herself, she was doing something. That type of warped logic seemed to make sense at 3:00 in the morning, when her head finally hit the pillow.

She awoke just past nine, with enough vim and vigor to keep her ritual of removal on track. Without losing any momentum from the previous night, she went about the house with renewed purpose. After checking on the state of her girls, and finding no discernable change for better or worse from the compost tea, she fixed herself a quick breakfast crêpe and got back to work. Striding into the living room, she lined up the packed boxes by the front door and started upstairs when she spied the white violet print on the credenza. She carried it to the dining room table and stared at it for what seemed like an eternity. Perhaps it had value? Maybe Frankie gave it to her because he knew it was worth something; the same way he purposely hid the pound of cannabis in the wall of the attic. She knew now he wouldn't just give her that print on their last visit if it didn't carry certain significance.

"Pay attention," he kept telling her that day. She removed the print from its antique frame in an attempt to locate a possible famous autograph or hidden note he might have slipped between the print and the heavy cardboard backing. But she found nothing. Replacing the watercolor back into its frame, she set it upright and stared at it again. And then her mind drifted to the two words on the elm tree. Perhaps, she considered, the whole point was to release it, and maybe something positive would come through that act. She set it upright in one of the boxes by the front door, just as she heard the sound of a car pulling into her driveway. Peering out the front window, she saw Peyton and opened the door to welcome him inside.

His happy-go-lucky countenance took on a dire appearance when he saw all the packed boxes around the room. "What's goin' on, Betty?"

"Out with the old, Peyton," she nonchalantly said. "Sometimes, you get weighed down by all the things that you believe matter. I decided to lighten my load a bit more."

"A bit?" he queried, scanning the room. "You get rid of much more in here and it's gonna look as homey as a motel room."

He was enthused to hear about her trip to Doobie Douggie's house. Over an omelet and cup of hot chocolate she made from scratch using her fine chocolate and cinnamon, she regaled him with her adventure. But when she confessed that Douggie's real name was Frank, and that his true personality was a tad softer and not as intensely erratic as his public persona, Peyton seemed disappointed.

"Dude. Bummer. This is like finding out that John Wayne couldn't ride a horse or Jackie Chan uses a stunt double."

"Well, Peyton. People aren't always forthcoming with their true nature." She decided now was as good a time as any. "I have two confessions to make to you."

He looked a little freaked out. "Should I be seated in a sturdier chair?"

"No, I think you can handle it from that one," she said, pushing her plate to the side of the table. She debated which one to start off with. "That letter to the editor back in May? Did you read the names of the people who signed it?"

"I glanced through them, but I didn't recognize any of them."

"Well, the first one was Elizabeth Cragen." She took a breath. "That's me."

Peyton stared at her, momentarily expressionless but then became increasingly concerned. "Oh my God, Betty. Dude, are you on the run! Do you have a buried past? Are you in the FBI's protective custody – ?"

"No, no, it's nowhere near as romantic as that. 'Cragen' was a typo. Elizabeth is formal for 'Betty.'" She felt silly stating too much of the obvious. "*I* signed it, Peyton. Elizabeth 'Betty' Craven signed that letter."

His eyes studied the table. "Well, that's because you didn't know any better. And it makes what you've done since then even more special."

Betty sat back in her chair. This must have been what it felt like to Renée, seeing the lack of disgust in Betty's eyes, when she uncovered her clandestine pipe. "That's a very mature response."

He grinned. "I hope it's not too mature. Yarrow said she likes the goofy side of me, so I can't lose that part. What's the second thing you wanted to confess? I hope it packs more of a punch."

"You know Frank Sr. was career military. But what you don't know is that my father was also military. He served in the air force – the Royal Canadian Air Force, to be precise. My mother held British citizenship. My parents moved to the States in early 1951, after he left the service and agreed to relocate to Houston to work as an engineer for the aerospace industry. I was born that summer. So, while I'm not Canadian, I'm close enough to the well to fall into your anti-Canuck heap."

Peyton took it all in, allowing his mouth to slightly fall open. "So, what you're saying to me...is that you were an anchor baby? Oh, God, Betty. Talk about a stigma."

"Anchor baby?" Betty exclaimed. She dutifully explained the process in which her father's work Visa allowed him to continue living in the States, and eventually, how both her parents became U.S. citizens.

He listened carefully but Betty could tell he was struggling with the concept slightly. "Did you keep it a secret because you didn't want people knowing you came from snow backs?"

"My parents were not 'snow backs'!"

"It's okay, it's okay. It's all starting to make sense now. The first generation born to immigrants typically feels they have to excel over and above their peers. That must be where you get your drive. I kinda see the same thing in Yarrow. You know, her mom's from Canada. When you set me up with Yarrow..." he stopped suddenly. "Oh, wait a minute...hang on a second...you set me up with her on purpose to prove me wrong about Canadians!"

She smiled. "Maybe."

"Wow, it's exactly what I've always said. Your people are really slippery and passively devious!"

"*My people*?!"

He paused a moment before breaking into a big grin. "Ha! Gotcha!" He couldn't let it go. "Canadians are so easy to screw with."

Peyton checked out the girls before leaving. But on his way out, he saw the white violet print in the box by the front door. "You're not throwing this out."

"No. I'm taking it to *The Gilded Rose* today."

He picked up the framed print. "But this means something to you, Betty."

She shrugged her shoulders, somewhat sadly. "I don't know if it does anymore. Maybe it's time I set it free."

He thought deeply as he gently replaced the print back into the box. "Is that the same thing you did to Jeff?"

She felt her back go up. "That's not something you need to be concerned about, Peyton."

"So you *did?* Geez, Betty." He walked back into the room, clearly upset. "You set me up with Yarrow, because you didn't want me to be alone!"

"I set you up with Yarrow because you're in your mid-twenties, and I didn't want you to turn thirty and realize that the only substantial relationship you had during that time was with an aromatic bud."

"So, how is that different for you?"

She tried to come up with a good answer but failed. "I don't know."

"Does your conscience allow you to love him?"

Taken back by his poetic question, Betty said, "I think my conscience is on board. It's just that my heart hasn't fully bought the ticket."

He looked at her with deep consideration. "You're afraid of getting hurt again?"

"No, actually I'm not. I know he's not going to hurt me. Maybe that's the problem." The epiphany was nearly overwhelming. "When you get so used to pain, it's difficult to get used to pleasure."

After Peyton left, Betty spent most of the afternoon finding more treasures to take to Lily's store. Her mood became more contemplative as the hours passed. When she took the metal sign off her bureau with the Marilyn Monroe quote, she realized Marilyn left out an important part. While it was true that many women are looking for one man to prove that they're not all the same, in order to maintain that sought after relationship, the woman has to be willing to accept that happiness is not a luxury but a necessity.

Arriving at *The Gilded Rose*, she parked her car as close as possible to the front door, so she could unload the many boxes. Yarrow happened to be strolling down the street from the dispensary and offered to give her a hand.

"Betty's here!" Yarrow announced, walking up to the front desk.

Lily welcomed Betty and enthusiastically combed through a few of the boxes, oohing and ahhing at each piece. Yarrow hung around the front desk, enamored with the various items as well. While Betty would have been offended three months ago by the girl's bold interest, she now enjoyed watching her admire each new thing she uncovered. Lily maintained her impeccable manners and professionalism as she chatted with Betty, telling her how thankful she was to have Betty's treasures available for her discerning clientele. Yes, Betty thought, Lily was one of the last women on this planet with true refinement and a born sense of good taste.

"I'm sorry to hear about you and Jeff breaking up," Yarrow announced. "Peyton told me all about it."

Betty stared at the girl, taken back.

"Yarrow!" Lily chided, "That's none of our business."

Our, Betty thought. Since when had she become coffee klatch conversation?

Yarrow wouldn't be silenced. "Why? *I* think he's a great guy. He's always really nice when he comes in here –"

"*Yarrow!*" Lily admonished again. "Enough," she said with a soft but firm voice.

Several awkward moments followed. Betty needed to lighten the mood. "You sound like mother and daughter."

"Well," Yarrow replied, "that's because...we are."

"Excuse me?"

"That's my mom," Yarrow explained, as if Betty was a little dense.

"Yarrow," Lily warned, "watch your tone."

Betty tried to gather her muddled thoughts. "I'm not shocked that you have a daughter, Lily. I guess I'm just –"

"Shocked that I named her after an invasive flower?" she asked with a broad smile, enjoying the joke she just made.

Betty attempted to regain her poise. "No...actually, yes."

"Well," Lily said, lifting a few items from a box, "chalk that up to my days living on a commune in Northern California."

Living on a commune? Was Betty dreaming? "I can't even imagine you living on a commune, Lily."

"Humboldt County," Lily stated.

Betty did the math. Lived on a commune in Humboldt County. Named her daughter Yarrow. "So that's why you don't mind her working at the dispensary."

"Huh?" Yarrow said, with a twist of her face.

"Yarrow –" Lily said with a warning tone.

"What?" Yarrow asked. "She's cool, mom. Trust me. Betty grows."

Lily and Betty simultaneously dropped their jaws.

"Yarrow!" Betty exclaimed.

"*Betty?*" Lily exclaimed.

"I...I..." Betty was too confused to come up with a suitable lie. And what was the point anyway? "She's right. I dabble."

"Well, I'll be damned," Lily chuckled. Almost immediately her body relaxed, and she instantly became more comfortable with Betty. "Who'd have thunk it? Betty Craven! You're the last person I'd think would –"

"I know, I know. My avocation doesn't necessarily match my face. But she's right." Betty felt so free suddenly. "I grow cannabis. And I love every minute of it. Well, most minutes, at least."

Lily stopped processing the items for a moment and leaned on the front desk. "You know, this store is *my* avocation. I adore beautiful antiques and all the wonderful finds buried in people's attics."

"You mean 'vocation,' don't you?" Betty asked.

"Not in this economy. This place hasn't turned a profit since 2007 when the economy went to hell." She took a moment and then continued. "This store is my avocation. The dispensary down the street is my vocation."

Betty steadied herself on the desk. "You run a –"

"No. I own it. It's the only way I can keep *The Gilded Rose* afloat. We were one of the first dispensaries to open in Denver when the state allowed it."

Betty needed to check herself. "Well, isn't this a twist?"

"Sure is," Lily agreed. "But I don't see the two businesses as being that different. I like to connect patients at the dispensary with the right strain for their needs, and I like to connect customers here with the perfect antique that brings beauty into their lives. Healing and beauty. I think they make the perfect duet."

Betty nodded. "I couldn't have said it better myself."

Lily turned back to one of the larger boxes that Betty brought to her. "Hey, Betty. I remember this. You bought this here." She lifted the Marilyn Monroe metal sign from the box. "I had it sitting on your Biedermeier."

Betty turned to where the Biedermeier was still waiting patiently for the right owner. Her mind unexpectedly drifted back to that day in May that seemed so long ago. She felt her heart catch just a wee bit. "Yes...I remember that day well."

Lily handed the sign back to her. "This belongs to you, Betty."

Betty reluctantly nodded and took the sign. But before she left, she cast one last, lingering look at the white violet print, before silently wishing it a somber goodbye.

It was getting cloudier, and the wind shifted to the west heralding another summer storm, when Betty finally left *The Gilded Rose.* Traffic on the main roads back to Paradox was already backing up as usual, as it neared five o'clock. It opened up when she was about two miles from home, but then it suddenly choked down again. Coming to a standstill on the four-lane road, Betty strained outside her window to see if she could figure out what was causing the delay. Dark indigo clouds hovered above her, as a warm wind rushed across her face. Creeping a little closer, she finally saw the spinning police lights and an ambulance parked nearby. "Oh, dear," she whispered, always hating to see someone else's automotive misfortune. She tried to change lanes but no one let her through. Inching closer, she could see the damaged vehicle in question – a white Lexus, slammed sideways on the passenger side into an electrical post. As Betty rolled even closer, she saw the whole demoralizing scene. There was her friend, Judi, standing next to the police car, handcuffed and almost unable to stand up without wobbling. Betty stared in disbelief, as an officer put her friend into the police car and drove away.

An hour later, Betty was staring in continued disbelief at the beverage offerings available in the front waiting room of the Paradox police station. How could anyone stand to pour artificial cream from little plastic containers into their cups, hoping it would mollify the taste of the swill they called "coffee?" She heard an officer's voice behind the door that led down the hall to the holding cells.

"This way ma'am."

The door opened and Judi walked into the waiting room. When she saw Betty, she froze and turned back to the officer.

"Mrs. Craven?" the officer said. "I need you to sign this, and check off the box that you paid Mrs. Hancock's bail amount."

Judi visibly shrunk in mortal humiliation and did everything possible not to make eye contact with Betty. After Betty signed the document, the officer informed Judi of the involved process she would need to go through in the future.

"Do you understand everything, Mrs. Hancock?" the officer asked her.

Judi began to shake. "Yes," she said almost inaudibly. "I do."

Betty walked to her Taurus, with a conspicuously silent Judi behind her. The short ride to Judi's house was thick with tension, but none of it came from Betty. Not a word was spoken during the short drive, and the silence continued as Betty parked in front of Judi's house and turned off the engine. After what seemed like hours, but was only minutes, Judi fumbled with her purse and brought out her checkbook. With her hands still shaking, she signed a blank check and handed it to Betty without looking at her.

"Thank you," Judi whispered, shame filling the void.

Betty noted that Judi wrote the word "fundraiser" on the memo line of the check. "Fortunately, I had the cash saved up from my cannabis chocolate sales," Betty delicately announced.

Judi shook her head, burying her face in her hands. "Shit." She opened the passenger door and stepped out, closing the door. But when she reached the wrought iron front gate, she stopped.

Betty leaned over toward the open passenger window. "Judi?"

Judi turned, with tears falling freely down her narrow face. She knelt down by the passenger door, grasping the edge of the window. "I've always envied you. I always thought you were so perfect." Finally, she made eye contact. "And I was right." She paused briefly. "Well, except for one thing. You're too proud."

The comment took Betty by surprise. "I thought you were going to say –"

"I saw Jeff today at his health food store," Judi blurted out. "I love his juice bar. Well, I guess I love anything with the word 'bar' in it. When I asked him about the two of you, he told me your relationship was 'uncertain.'"

Betty felt terribly exposed but maintained her composure. "Yes, well –"

"He gets you, Betty. Did you hear me? He *understands* you. Do you have any idea how rare that is?"

Betty bit her lip. "Yes. I do."

"He's made you a better person, if that's even possible. And I hate you for it. And I love you for it. Does that make sense to you?"

"Yes."

"Good. So stop fucking it up, would you?" Judi said with growing conviction.

"But what about 'on paper'?"

Judi snorted contempt. "I married 'on paper.' You married 'on paper.' What did it give us? That paper had everything we thought we wanted, except one thing – love." She stood up and leaned back into the window. "Burn the paper, Betty. That's all it's really good for." She let out a hard breath and turned around. With reluctance in every step, she walked through the front gate and disappeared through her front door.

Hard pellets of rain swept across the tree-lined street. By the time Betty returned home that evening, the downpour swept diagonally under the orange glow of the streetlamps. Retreating into her emptier house, she felt a deep hollowness. Even though the air was warm outside, she felt chilled to the bone. A loud clap of thunder broke, followed by a sharp blast of lightning. She checked on her girls just before the timed lights went out in the veg room, and then headed to bed. But the rain was relentless. As she lay there in bed, she felt like a guest in her own home. She was almost half asleep when she heard a loud pounding sound coming from downstairs. Startled, she sat up in bed and then grabbed her Tomcat. Edging around the bed, she crept through the door and out into the hallway. The pounding had stopped, and now she heard the sound of the front door knob jiggling, as if someone were trying to break in. Betty moved quickly and quietly down the stairs, her Tomcat extended in front of her. Her heart raced, the closer she got to the door. As the thunder and lightening melded into one, she heard a click and the front door opened. She raised the gun and took aim.

Chapter 35
Letting go.

"I've got a gun!" Betty screamed, her back against the wall.

"Betty! It's me!"

She flicked on the wall switch. There was Jeff, his leather jacket and hair wet from the downpour. She wasn't sure whether she was shaking from the fear of what she thought was going to happen, or from seeing him again.

He set a large brown paper sack on the floor and strode to her with great purpose as Betty lowered the pistol and dropped it on the stairs. Cradling her face between his palms, he kissed her passionately. She melted into his body and the missing part of her returned.

Jeff pulled away just a few inches, still framing her face with his hands. "You were born to lead a different life, Betty. You should have seduced more men. You should have drunk in more passion instead of taking sips to quench your thirst. You should have inhaled life until your lungs burst. You should have given fear a reason to run from *you.*" He pressed her body against the wall. "You should have challenged your friends and confounded your enemies. You should have pounded the shit out of every conventional belief, until you beat the safety out of them. You should have laughed more and grieved less. You should have devoured each opportunity and consumed every challenge." He moved his hands to her shoulders. "But more than anything, Betty, you should have risked happiness because you deserve it." He pulled her toward him, kissing her deeply.

She held him tightly and then rested her head on his shoulder as the realization finally hit. "You're everything I truly wanted and never knew I needed." She grabbed him tighter. "I love you."

"Thank that pain in your neck. Without that pain, we never would have met." He pulled back a few inches. "I got you something." Walking over to the door, he picked up the brown paper sack. "What's that stupid saying? 'If you love someone, set them free. If they come back, they're yours.' I think the same principle applies to this." He handed Betty the paper bag. "Your second son came into my store and tipped me off," he revealed to her.

She opened the bag and choked with emotion. It was the white violet print. "'Letting go.' That's what Frankie carved into that old elm. I thought maybe if I got rid of this, something good would happen."

"And something did," he said with a smile.

"So he knew even this would happen?"

"I'm not sure. But out of curiosity, I did look up the meaning of the white violet."

"And?"

"The exact words I found? 'Let's take a chance on happiness.'"

Betty's eyes filled with tears.

"That's all your son ever wanted for you, Betty. As he was letting go that day, he wanted you to do the same and discover what made you feel alive for the first time."

She stared at the white violet print. "When I met you at your store the first time? You said something to me. You said, 'It's the fighting that got you to this point. It's the letting go that matters.'" She looked up at Jeff. "I knew right then we were supposed to be together because I felt my heart jump. But I couldn't stop the fight in my head. I didn't want to fail again."

Jeff pulled her toward him again. "I will promise you this, Betty. I'll never ruin you for another man."

"I don't want another man," she whispered. "I just want you."

~~~

Several days later, Betty collected Ronald's ashes from the vet's office. When she returned home, she set the box of his remains on the credenza. Gazing at the white violet print propped up against a few books, she scooted her favorite photo of Frankie holding the joint closer to the print. But she decided something was missing. She crossed down the hall and removed the framed close-up photo she took of the glistening bud and proudly displayed it next to others on the credenza.

Betty took Ronald's box of ashes up to her bedroom and lovingly set them on the shelf in her bedroom closet next to Frankie's remains. Walking over to the bedroom window that looked out on the debris field that still lay scattered across the backyard, she made a decision. Collecting the two boxes of ashes, she went downstairs and into the yard and stood at the base of the elm tree where the roots were exposed. With great reverence, Betty first opened Ronald's box and scattered his remains against the roots of the tree. She said a little prayer for her faithful feline, wishing him well on his journey.

She took a deep breath and opened up Frankie's box. Betty wanted to say something meaningful but words failed her. She dug her hand into the plastic bag that held the ashes and clutched a large handful. "I know it hasn't been easy to be the main reason someone else needs to keep on living. So, I want you to be free, sweetheart."

Betty lovingly spread Frankie's remains in the roots of the tree, and with the final handful, pressed them into the words he carved on the trunk. When she was done, she sat on the grass in the shade. Without any drink or cannabis to influence the moment, she felt him walk behind her and sit next to her. He was whole again. The scars of abuse were gone, and his eyes were clear and content.

"Your future is bright, mom," he softly said.

"I know, Frankie. I can finally see it too."

~~~

Six weeks passed quickly, filled with activity. All of Betty's girls, except for two of them, recovered enough to either grow to fruition or else be cloned into new plants. She easily met a new patient to take Jean's place and complete the full five she was allowed. Betty never discovered who released her chocolates into the vast underground market, but it didn't matter anymore. Her popularity soared, and she was asked to visit various community groups to tell her story. While she first cringed at the idea, she finally agreed. She always started her presentations with the same introduction. "There are two things I can't stand: ignorance and hypocrisy. Right now, they run rampant in the cannabis field. When you're ignorant about a subject, your opinion about it is built on vapor. But if you're brave enough, you'll find the truth and it will find you."

Betty said those exact words on that September afternoon as she stood in front of an overflowing, attentive crowd at *The Happy Mountain Retirement Center.* On their own, a group of seniors who lived in the building got their red cards and set up a non-profit cannabis collective that allowed members to cultivate small grows in their closets. However, the many challenges of nurturing a decent plant plagued them, just like anyone else new to this often-challenging endeavor. So on that day, as the aspen trees pitched a brilliant, yellow-leafed glow into the main room of the retirement center, Betty spent ninety minutes giving some important pointers to the dedicated group and entertaining them with stories of her various mishaps in her quest to grow the best bud. When she was done, it was obvious she'd made the residents of *The Happy Mountain* even happier, and perhaps more confident in their attempt to grow their own bud.

She was packing up all of her props, including an antique teacup and saucer she always brought along, when she looked at the far back row of the seats and saw Judi. They hadn't spoken since Betty dropped her off at her house that night. Betty walked over to Judi, with box in hand. "Do you mind if we go outside?" Betty asked her. "I have another appointment I need to get to."

Judi nodded and followed her into the parking lot. "What's the teacup for?" she asked Betty.

"To always keep it civilized," she replied with a gentle smile.

They arrived at Betty's car, and Judi handed her a wrapped package that felt soft and pliable.

"I got those for you," Judi said.

Betty opened the present and found a pair of the linen slacks she'd always admired on Judi. "I love it! Thank you, darling." Betty embraced Judi. "But you said they were sold out —"

"Yeah. I lied. Those aren't linen. They're made out of hemp. I was worried if I mentioned I was wearing hemp cloth, it would become the butt of everyone's joke. I just wasn't ready to be a punch line."

"I will wear these pants with a smile in my heart," Betty confessed, placing them into the box. She checked the time. "I'm sorry I don't have more time, but I have to get across town to the *Cottonmouth Café*. They're hosting me to do a cannabis cooking demonstration."

Judi smiled. "I love it. Good for you." She hesitated and then spoke. "Hey, listen. Roger and I are divorcing."

Betty stopped. "Oh, Judi. Because of the DUI?"

"God, no. My drinking doesn't bother him. Don't you know? There's a pill to fix that," she said in a mocking tone.

"Then why are you leaving him?"

"Because I finally I woke up. I realized I shouldn't have married a doctor. It always pissed Roger off that I sunk so low, got my teaching degree and then chose to be an art teacher. He said it made him look like a poor provider, not to mention that it added more taxable income. But he didn't like a lot of things I did. Every time he saw a bag from 'The Hippie Dippie Health Food Store' he'd make nasty comments. Wanted to know if I picked up an eye of newt and a caldron to boil my problems away. Roger thought that comment was so original and clever. He loved to mock whatever

I enjoyed. He's polished his condescending tone over the years, with the precision of the surgeon he wasn't good enough to become. I don't know how his patients stand him anymore. If he doesn't give a shit about my pain, you think he's going to give a shit about theirs?" She stared off into the distance. "I shouldn't have married a doctor. I needed to fall in love with an artist and live with him in a two-bedroom bungalow on the beach in San Diego, with wood floors that always had a gritty layer of sand scattered across them. I needed to learn to play the ukulele and astonish my eccentric neighbors with wild stories of hitchhiking around Mexico, and late night campfires spent with gunrunners and guerilla fighters. But I decided my quest for adventure was a young girl's impetuous fantasy. So I played it safe and tried to pretend I didn't crave the life of a Bohemian. I had the first kid, the second one, third one...fourth one. And when I realized what was causing it," she said with a smile, "I put an end to that." A cloud of sadness came over her. "One day, I realized I never wanted to be a mother. I love them but I don't really like them. But you can't admit that, can you? You have to pretend they're the reason you get up in the morning and they weren't. But you have to bury that so deeply, until you convince yourself it really is what you want."

Betty rested her hand on Judi's arm. "You could have told me."

"Could I? I'm not so sure of that." She tapped Betty's hand. "Just like you couldn't tell me about Jeff. But you know what? I knew you were seeing someone. I didn't know who he was. But I could tell. That day I saw you in your driveway when I told you how different you looked? You had the blush of love that is envied by those of us who forgot it existed or never had it. But when we see it in others, we don't celebrate it. We're jealous. We want the same thing, but we're not brave enough to seek it out so we hate it. And we hate you for finding that jewel, because we want to wear it too. I find it so fucking insane that happiness is the most sought after desire, but isn't it strange how the sight of it in someone else breeds such disdain?"

"I haven't cornered the market on finding happiness, Judi. There's an infinite supply out there if you want it. You could change your life in a heartbeat. Buy the bungalow on the beach. Find the artist. I'll send you the ukulele. It's never too late to become the Bohemian you've always been."

Judi considered her comment. "Can anyone show up at the *Cottonmouth Café* to see your demonstration, or is it invitation only?"

"It's invitation only. And I just invited you." She directed her to get in her car.

"I never found out how you met Jeff. Was it at his store?"

"No. He was checking out my Biedermeier..."

~~~

One week later, Betty received her red card in the mail. It was finally official. The state of Colorado allowed her to look at the world "through cannabis eyes," as Peyton once told her. Like Robert Frost, Betty chose the road less taken and, by God, it *did* make all the difference. Because of that, the "hour of lead" Emily Dickinson wrote about finally lifted. And with that, so did the mystique of a little plant called cannabis. She realized when the air of mystery is removed, the falsehoods, the rumors, the gossip and the propaganda also fall away. One is left with a seed that grows prolifically, as it's fed by water and nutrients, warmed by a light or the sun and allowed to develop into a beautiful plant.

And then from the use of that plant, the unexplained can begin to happen. Beliefs can shatter, but so be it, Betty mused. Beliefs, she discovered, are like sealed boxes that don't allow further examination. You walk into the house of your belief and suspend rational thought or debate, only associating with others who recite back to you what you think you understand. It is only knowledge, born from true-life experience, that matters. Experience pulls away the curtain of presumption that lies between what you think you know and what the truth really is. Those who have never come close to suicide cannot understand the depth of that darkness. Those who have never made love cannot advise those who have. Those who have never seen God in the eyes of an addict, cannot presume to teach faith.

As she sat in the comfortable Adirondack chair next to Jeff, on his property with the flowing stream and thermal spring, she rested her feet on the log from her old elm tree that Jeff had cut and varnished to protect it from the elements. Before he painted the first layer on it though, he rubbed coal dust into the carved letters so they would always stand out.

She took his hand in hers as they listened to the sound of the water against the rustling of the burnt orange and yellow panorama. The chill of fall would soon begin, and then the winter would come. As she eyed the corner plot of land, her thoughts turned to the next summer and all the new possibilities that could grow and thrive in that pristine dirt. But that was the future and this was now. And so she returned to the moment and found solace.

"I never told you the end of Stuart Love's story," Jeff quietly said.

"Ah, the ghost who haunted the family on the river...how does the story end?"

"I told you how they realized the edges around them softened and they stopped hurting each other."

"Yes."

"Well, one day, Stuart left and never came back. The mother of the family told me that after a few weeks, she'd figured out why Stuart chose them. He was trying to save them, just like he saved that little girl from drowning."

"Save them from what?" Betty asked.

"Themselves."

Betty nodded. A warm breeze moved across her, signaling a storm heading in. Soon the ground would turn to mud and the air would cool. The seat on the motorcycle would be wet and her hair would be a mess. Everything would be perfect in its beautiful imperfection.